Prin Daniella

Steve J Bradbury

Princess Daniella

Author: Steve J Bradbury

Copyright © Steve J Bradbury (2024)

The right of Steve J Bradbury to be identified as author of this work has been asserted by the author in accordance with section 77 and 78 of the Copyright, Designs and Patents Act 1988.

First Published in 2024

ISBN: 978-1-915996-14-5 (Paperback)
978-1-915996-15-2 (eBook)

Book layout by:

White Magic Studios
www.whitemagicstudios.co.uk

Published by:

Maple Publishers
Fairbourne Drive,
Atterbury,
Milton Keynes,
MK10 9RG, UK
www.maplepublishers.com

A CIP catalogue record for this title is available from the British Library.

All rights reserved. No part of this book may be reproduced or translated by any form or by any means, electronic or mechanical, including photocopying, recording or by any information storage and retrieval system without written permission from the author.

The book is a work of fiction. Unless otherwise indicated, all the names, characters, places and incidents are either the product of the author's imagination or used in a fictitious manner. Any resemblance to actual people living or dead, events or locales is entirely coincidental, and the Publisher hereby disclaims any responsibility for them.

Contents

Chapter 1
An Invitation

The day was miserable but, being as it was the beginning of summer, one would have expected the weather to be beautiful and the sun shining. That was not the case at all as for the past two weeks we had endured freak weather and torrential rainfall bringing excessive flooding right across the UK. Several people had drowned with many others injured having had houses or buildings collapsing on them. Whether or not it was caused by climatic change could be anyone's guess although the meteorologists always knew right or so they told us.

"Darling," my wife Rebecca said. "Remember you've got your granddaughter coming to stay with us for two weeks. Why don't you make up one of your fairy stories and write her in as the main character?"

"Why not indeed!" I, sixty-three-year-old Paul Riverton, replied excitedly to my wife Rebecca who was four years my junior. "She'd like that, I'm sure. When does the girl arrive?"

"You're absolutely useless, Paul! I don't know quite how you can think up these amazing stories and then forget about your granddaughter coming to visit! It makes no sense at all! She comes the day after tomorrow but where can we take her?" Rebecca asked me as the heavy raindrops continued to drum a beat against our window panes.

The weather was awful and she had not expected the summer to begin like this.

"I'm sure we'll think of something," I replied as I went to mop up the rainwater that had somehow slipped in from under the door of our garden. "How old is she now? You know how forgetful I am!"

"Daniella is a young lady now. She's now thirteen and has become a stunning teenager but in my eyes I still think of her as a little girl who still loves fairy stories!"

"I know but look at the weather outside! It's the 17th of July and meant to be scorching hot and what's it doing right now? It's pouring with rain all across the fields!"

We had lived in the countryside for nigh on thirty years. I had met Rebecca at a local barn dance held by Trevor Thetford, a music teacher from a village close by called Lows Ford, Warwickshire. Trevor and I had grown up together. He had become a musician while I chose science to master and finally became a scientist. After a few lonely years as a musician, Trevor went to university and became a teacher and finally a headmaster at a London private boarding school so it was inevitable we eventually lost touch.

Rebecca looked over at me through her gold-rimmed spectacles before saying, "I want to know when this blasted weather is going to change! Daniella won't enjoy being stuck inside for several days because of the rain."

My wife was right so I suggested that we might take the girl to some castle or another.

"Why don't we take the mobile home to Cornwall and take her to see Tintagel Castle, unless she's been there already," I suggested.

The thought made my wife smile, as we had not been on any form of holiday for probably two years or more.

"That's the most beautiful place in the sunshine but in this rain it becomes all mucky and muddy and I hate it! Remember, you have to take a Land Rover ride to get to the castle and if the track is too muddy then we can forget all about visiting that place."

Rebecca was right with her assumption that it was going to be raining cats and dogs in Cornwall as the Atlantic Ocean always tended to attract some of the worst weather ever but this was summer so we could at least drive down there and give it a try.

"Oh, boulder dash!" I replied. It was best I said this rather than something unorthodox and rude. "We'll go and take the girl. I'm sure she'd prefer that rather than staying around the house moping."

It was decided that when Daniella came the day after tomorrow we would have everything packed and ready to go the moment that she arrived.

I suddenly felt the urge to write so I turned to my wife and said, "I must go and put down a few ideas before Daniella arrives. Do you mind darling?"

Rebecca smiled as she watched me disappear into my study and writing room. She wondered what I would come up with this time as I had written three good novels that had sold well and had given us the lifestyle we now enjoyed as we came into our twilight years.

Sitting down at my computer, I began my story that I decided to set in the deep Oxfordshire countryside in 1974 when a young girl, also called Daniella, aged just seventeen, was forced to go and live with her real mother, Mrs June Albertson, because her own father was fed up with her clowning around and tomfoolery.

However, it was set to be a hard life living with a mother who was stuck in the past and who did not possess any modern household appliances such as a vacuum cleaner, washing machine, dishwasher or television.

Mrs Albertson had left her husband, Daniella's father, when the girl was only a year old, so she had never really got to know her mum. Daniella's dad normally did not even bother speaking to his former wife but after a brief phone conversation with her, it was agreed that the girl would go and live with her mother and he would pay the woman five thousand pounds a year towards her upkeep. Not even kissing or saying a single goodbye to Daniella, her father just dumped the girl on her mother's doorstep and drove away never to be seen again.

Thus, it was on a bitterly-cold, frosty evening when a shy and uneasy girl shivering in her open toed sandals and bare feet was seen knocking at a dingy, paint-worn door that had seen better days, carrying just a small suitcase with only a few items of clothing inside as her father had given the girl no time at all to gather anything together to take with her.

One of Daniella's stepsisters opened the door and pulled the poor girl inside so hard that her left shoulder was almost dislocated. Her mother had remarried a number of years back but had become a widow after only five years of marriage and two more daughters. While one of them still lived with their mother, the other one, Rose, was living with her stepfather in Manchester.

Daniella was forced to call her mum, Madam, and was given the worst jobs possible; she had to clean, cook, make up the dirty coal fire, make the beds and do the washing and hang it out on the line. Her hours of work, if you could call them that, were from eight in the morning to eight at night.

The girl was never given a chance to wash herself so she was always grubby and smelly and her hair messy and unkempt. She would try to clean herself every now and then with a soiled facecloth she had found in the attic but without much success.

Her chubby stepsister Anna was always bossing her around and demanding to have her hair brushed, her shoes cleaned, her bath filled with hot water that she had to boil over the open fire first, or having her filthy skin that was quite often caked with mud scrubbed.

Even when poor Daniella began to smell so badly that one would think there was a dead rat lying around, she was never allowed to wash herself since everyone would moan about her using up the cold water let alone the hot.

After slaving around for three months, enough was enough. That morning, the sky was a dark shade of grey, the wind was howling through the chimney and the snow was falling so quickly that it covered the roads and footpaths up to the knees in next to no time and was drifting in the wind as if in some arctic blizzard.

Daniella stood outside on the doorstep shivering in the thinnest of cotton clothing trying to hang the clothes, including several brassieres and large panty-type knickers belonging to her mother, that soon blew off the line to God knows where. Despite all her heroic efforts, the rest of the line of washing followed suit and was sent all over the garden and even into the woodlands that backed onto her mother's property.

The moment her father's estranged wife saw what was happening outside, she screamed at the top of her voice at the poor girl. "Daniella, you stupid girl, go and find everything and don't come back until you do!"

Anna meanwhile put her tuppence in crying, "And make sure you bring every single piece of clothing back with you!"

After a quick glancing stare at her stepsister the poor girl went in search of the clothing but with the wind gusting and heavy snow falling, this was an impossible task. The innocent young girl knew that if she did not find every single item of clothing that had blown away, her mother would beat her black and blue until she would collapse half dead onto the cold concrete flooring. Daniella was certain that either way she wouldn't be missed whether be it by her uncaring mother or her delightful stepsister Anna.

Too terrified at returning to her mother's wrath, Daniella found what seemed like a large rabbit hole beneath a thick prickly gorse bush, crawled inside and fell asleep before being woken up suddenly by someone speaking to her and prodding her in the side.

"Who are you? And why are you lying down in my home?" a strange voice asked indignantly.

Daniella looked up and realised that a large hare was speaking to her. She shivered, not because of the cold this time, and thought that she was going totally mad.

The hare continued, "Answer me, girl. Otherwise, I'll have you removed by the King!"

The girl looked in astonishment at the hare, before stammering, "You're not real! You can't talk! No animals can, except for parrots!"

"Who are you calling an animal? I'm Sir Reginald! Can't you see the elegant clothing I'm wearing!" the hare replied with a huff. "And you, what are you? Your clothes are ripped and filthy and your hair's not brushed. Now, scram before I have to make you do so myself!"

"Do what you want of me. I'm fed up with being ordered around and left in rags and never allowed to wash so if you want to move me then go ahead and do it," the girl replied.

The hare looked at Daniella and wondered what this creature was since she was far bigger than he was and he had a title unlike this wretch of a girl who he thought was being extremely impolite too.

Hopping away, he left the girl who was soon fast asleep again as she thought that was the last she would ever see of that hare. That was wrongful thinking from her side, as she was about to find out to her utmost dismay.

"Come on, girl!" a voice boomed out some time later and something pinched Daniella's skin extremely hard making her open her eyes and scream.

"Ouch!" she cried in pain as she felt blood seeping from a wound on her leg.

On seeing a large fanged creature of some kind right in front of her, the poor girl began trembling with fear.

"Now, girl, I've warned you, move! You're in someone's home!" the creature bellowed.

"I'm not bothered," Daniella replied meekly. "I don't have anywhere to go so this is now my home and no one else's!"

"My dear, it's you who's got things wrong as all areas within this forest have people's names on them and this shrub here belongs to the hare!" the sabre-toothed animal roared. "Now, do you have a receipt to show to me that you've paid for this bush? If not, you'd better hop it right now or else I'm going to have to move you with force," the creature added, snarling like the vicious tiger it was.

"Go away and let me sleep, you stupid animal!" the poor girl cried out while the tiger scratched her again in a different place on her leg. "Ouch, ouch, ouch!" the girl screamed once again as more blood trickled out from new fresh wounds. "Why can't you leave me in peace?"

"That's it!" the tiger snarled at the poor girl as it grabbed hold of the skin on the back of her neck and carried her off in its teeth, just as it would do to his young.

The creature dragged the snivelling girl away to a nearby tree, which opened up and swallowed them whole before they found themselves in a dark and dismal passageway.

Plonking the girl onto the ground as if she were a sack of potatoes, it continued, "You're coming with me! You can explain who you are and why you refused my request to budge to the King. Now, girl, get moving as I have no time to waste and I'll have to bite you even harder next time!"

Daniella slowly got to her feet, finding that she had to stoop because the tunnel was so low in height.

After shuffling forward a few paces, the tiger screamed, "Hurry up, girl, we haven't got all day! The King's busy and woolly rhinoceros are known to have a really bad temper so you'd better get a move on, do you hear me? Or are you hard of hearing?"

This was like some nightmare to the poor girl. She tried telling the tiger that she was too tall for this narrow passageway and that she had to crawl on her knees since she was unable to stand up and walk as she normally would. The creature was having none of it so it bit poor Daniella on her ass several times, sinking its teeth deeply into her skin and tearing a big hole from the girl's bottom while blood oozed out of the gaping wound.

The young female soon collapsed in a heap from the loss of body fluids. She was scared and tired from overwork and had no idea where she was being taken to, so the tiger took hold of her long straggly blond hair and dragged her along the tunnel until it finally came to a wooden door. The creature knocked twice with its paw before the door swung open magically allowing them to carry on. At that moment, the tiger released her from its grip and waited for the girl to get to her feet as they were now in a large rosebud-covered garden.

Daniella could now at least stand up properly. She could feel sensation coming back to her legs but her ass felt extremely painful from the tiger's bite. She stared at the creature and noticed that it was unlike any tiger she had ever seen before. It was purple with a yellow face, orange lips, green fluorescent eyes and a pair of long, sharp fangs coming out from the side of its mouth. It resembled no animal she knew and looked like a creature from some prehistoric era.

"Come on, girl, stop staring, we haven't got all day!" the tiger snarled, following which it dashed off with the poor girl trying her hardest to keep up.

Daniella tried to run but after a couple of minutes, the poor girl was exhausted. She tripped over some roots and came crashing to the ground banging her head against a stone, before passing out.

On hearing a loud thud behind it, the tiger ground to a halt, looked back and saw the girl's body slumped to the ground and a pool of blood quickly forming beneath her head.

"Oh, no, the King's going to be furious with me," the creature whispered harshly to itself. "I was asked to bring her to the palace but I've messed it up completely and probably killed the female!"

The tiger sat down on a nearby boulder and scratched its chin with its elongated claws when out of nowhere a bright red ambulance shrieked by with its sirens blaring. On seeing the body on the ground, the ambulance screeched to a halt and reversed quickly. Two blue camels emerged from the back pulling a sleigh-like stretcher while two tall green gorillas jumped out from the front.

Picking Daniella up in their strong muscular arms, they plonked her down rather unceremoniously onto the stretcher before putting a blanket over her. The camels then dragged the stretcher back into the ambulance while the gorillas shoved their big fat arses back in front and they were off again. The tiger followed meekly behind as he knew what lay in store for him.

The journey seemed never ending and sweat was building up on the tiger's face until at last they arrived at the entrance to the palace. The gorillas drove the ambulance through two golden gates that led up to the magnificent Palace of Yarn, Rhinestone, where King Midas resided, before stopping at some stone steps.

"Pleck, you go in first," one of the gorillas said as he saw the tiger in the rear-view mirror bent over double and panting for breath.

The tiger dragged itself sheepishly up the stone steps before disappearing into the palace. The two gorillas soon joined it as they made their way to the throne room of the palace followed by the two camels carrying the stretcher with the still unconscious girl on it.

The camels, who were still trainee nurses, were not doing a very good job of it as the stretcher was swaying dangerously from side to side and on more than one occasion, the girl was almost dumped out onto the hardwood floor.

After walking down one hallway, and joining another, it seemed like an eternity, as they came to two large doors where one of the gorillas banged on the door and waited for a reply.

It swung open as if like magic and a voice boomed, "Who is that?"

"It's Marvin and Elka," one of the gorillas replied. "You sent us to go and fetch the girl as she was unconscious after a fall."

"Yes, indeed I did," the mysterious voice rumbled. "Bring the girl to me and then leave." The voice then lowered by two octaves. "As for you, Pleck, you are to stay as I need a quiet word with you."

The two gorillas went into the room, bowed to His Majesty the King, before leaving, followed by the camels that put down the stretcher and did likewise. Pleck, the tiger, was shaking so much that one could hear his teeth chattering, also went inside the room and bowed to his Master.

Daniella was still unconscious and unable to speak or move. The king, a woolly black rhinoceros, was wearing a beautiful golden crown. He had a bright yellow tongue that kept flicking out of his mouth every now and then and large orange eyes that seemed to glare at Pleck without moving away from him.

The King pondered what to do with the tiger and wondered whether he should remove him permanently as this was not the first time the tiger had caused trouble. The King hoped that the girl would make a full recovery, both for her sake as well as his, as hurting a human was a big no no and could lead to a whole string of problems.

The girl would be taken to the Glass Palace at the bottom of the Venturian Mountains some one thousand miles away in the Kingdom of Blackstone, a magical kingdom where King Rudolf had reigned for the past five hundred years. It was he who had granted the animals permission to live in their own kingdom, Rhinestone, and it was he who had given them their bright colours and the power of speech. Equally, it was King Rudolf who could take everything back from them at the wave of his hand.

The King stared at the grief-stricken tiger before screaming out at the top of his voice, "Pleck, may I know what game you're playing at? I told you to go and bring the girl to me and instead I got to watch you drag the poor wretch by her hair and hold her in your teeth! You also didn't let go of her until she was in the tunnel. Did I tell you to treat the girl in this way?"

The tiger shook like a leaf and went down on its front legs begging for clemency. However, the King was in no mood for any mercy as he grabbed at a long curved blade that suddenly appeared and flew across the room like magic. He sliced at the tiger's head and decapitated it from its body. Before the head could hit the floor, the King caught it with his horn and tossed it onto his desk.

"I don't take malice or failure from anyone and you, my friend, did both so you had to die!" the King screamed at the head on his desk as one of the King's courtiers entered the room.

"Did you ring, Your Majesty?" he asked, rather taken aback on seeing Pleck's head sitting on the King's desk.

The courtier was a dodo, bright yellow in colour and with an even brighter orange head. It felt its legs quivering from fright as it had never seen the King remove anyone's head before and

Pleck had been one of his friends or so he thought, but now he was no more.

"Take the head away, dodo, and have it burnt! And tell those raptors who work at the rubbish dump to come for the body!" the King commanded. "Do you understand? I can't stand looking at it!"

"Yes, Your Majesty," the dodo replied meekly to the King.

He held the severed head in his beak by the hair and took it away with him before closing the door behind him. At that same moment, the King got to his four legs and galloped out at a terrific speed, smashing the door in front of him and sliding on the polished floor of the hallway.

"Theodore, where are you?" the King shouted. "I need you in the throne room right now and bring your bag with you."

Theodore, the royal physician, was a florescent green and pink walrus who had never lived in water so he never really missed the ocean. He appeared in the hallway and entered the throne room together with the King.

"Pleck hurt this girl but he's no longer," the King began. "I beheaded him but now you must make this girl better as I have to take her to the Glass Palace where she will be loved by other humans. The girl should never have been brought here but now that she is, you must make her well again so that she's ready to travel with me."

"Yes, Your Majesty," Theodore replied. "Let me see, the girl's very beautiful but she's so dirty and is wearing cheap clothing. Do you know where she comes from?"

"How do I know things like that, Theodore?" the King snapped. "I'm not a magician, am I?"

Theodore thought it best to keep his mouth shut and stay quiet. He had seen what had happened to the King's guard, Pleck, who had been with him for five years or longer. He had only been the King's physician for one year and he had always wondered where his predecessor had disappeared to, and now he knew exactly what had happened to him.

The King's personal physician Theodore opened his bag, took out his stethoscope and unbuttoned the girl's blouse. Her flesh was bleeding from several parts of her body and the physician noticed deep bite marks on her stomach and around her buttocks and neck. He was filled with remorse as Pleck had really hurt this girl badly. King Rudolf of the Kingdom of Blackstone would want answers or otherwise they could be facing a long-lasting war and that would be the last thing they wanted to happen.

"Pleck behaved like a wild animal and the girl had many deep puncture wounds all over her body," the royal physician said to the King. "I don't know, Sire, if she'll recover or not. Besides, she's so filthy and urgently needs a wash and new clothes to wear."

"Yes, bring Oswald the raptor dinosaur," the King replied with a worried look on his face. "He'll measure the girl and go away and make her a new dress and shoes to match. In addition, fetch Amanda; she'll bathe the girl and make her clean again by wrapping her coils around the girl and rubbing her all over with bath oils and making her smell wonderful. The girl should feel much better after she smells beautiful fragrances rising from her own body."

Theodore first went away to get Oswald and ten minutes later the quietest of footsteps were heard and a turquoise blue and yellow raptor appeared. He had the most beautiful red frill around his neck but it seemed to get in his way as he took the girl's measurements.

When he was finished, he turned to the King and said, "I'll bring you a beautiful golden dress to match this girl's hair, gorgeous matching golden shoes, a pair of knickers and a bodice with a brassiere. She'll look just like a Princess! I hope and pray that the girl makes a full recovery for our sake as well as hers as we don't want King Rudolf taking away our freedom again, do we, after more than two hundred years?"

"No, we don't," King Midas said to his tailor. "Now, Amanda the python is coming, I can hear her in the hallway, so shoo!"

A bright red python at least twenty feet in length and six inches thick slivered into the throne room and hissed at Oswald as he zoomed out of the room. He did not see eye to eye with the python and on several occasions, she had coiled around him and squeezed him tightly as if she wanted to eat him. Once, the King had to rescue him as she had partly swallowed him too. His Highness had appeared and stopped her squeezing the life out of him, and had managed to pull him out from her stomach. He had suffered from shock but otherwise had made a full recovery.

Chapter 2
An Idea for Amanda

"Ss, Ss, Your Highnessssssssss, what can Amanda do for you?" the giant serpent hissed to the King as she slithered across the room.

"I want you to take this young girl, bathe her in the royal bathroom and make her smell lovely and sweet," the King stammered since he too was rather fearful of the python as she was very unpredictable.

"And afterwards ssss ssss sss, I can eat her, Your Majesty?"

"Definitely not as otherwise you'll suffer the same fate as Pleck and have your head chopped off," the King replied in a grave tone of voice.

"Aw shucks, Your Highness Sssssssss. Anyway, let me gather her up in my coils sssss sssss and I'll bring her back later after I've bathed and made her nice sss ssss and clean. I just can't understand why I can't eat the girl as ss sssshe has lovely ss sss ssssoft skin that would go down just right in my sss ssstomach!."

"You touch the girl and you'll be searching for your head, do you understand me, Amanda," the King replied sternly. "You must not think like a wild reptile anymore as she has to be taken well care of and made to look beautiful to present to King Rudolf in the Glass Palace. Otherwise, we'll be searching for a new home and you'll be looking for a new head!"

Amanda slinked away with the poor girl in her coils making sure that she did not hurt the female in any way or form since she did not want to suffer the same fate as Pleck. The serpent made her way up the marble stairway to the second landing and glided into the bathroom, and as the water magically ran, filling the bath before releasing her coils and lowering the girl gently into the water. Taking her tongue and wrapping it around the sponge, she poured some bath oil onto it and began massaging the girl's body all over. The poor thing was still out for the count. The serpent felt deep sorrow on seeing so many bite marks all over her body and rebuked herself at wanting to eat the girl.

"How could I have wanted to eat this delicate and gorgeous girl?" she remarked to herself.

After bathing the young girl, washing her hair and making her smell sweet and gorgeous, while the bath emptied on its own accord the python slipped back down the stairway before entering the throne room where she found King Midas holding a set of beautiful new clothes. The King had not noticed the serpent's arrival as she had moved so silently so releasing the girl and lowering her onto a lovely comfortable bed, she hissed to the King.

"Sssss, Your Majesty, I've brought the girl back. Ssss she's lovely and clean but her clothessss sss were all sss ss sssoiled and torn so I disposed of them. She's lying on your bed. I hope you don't mind," the serpent said as she flicked her tongue in and out and slipped off to where she had come from.

The King stared at the fine-looking naked girl for a while but when he came back to his senses, he grabbed at a blanket and hid her innocence until the girl woke up from her injuries.

Daniella lay there for several hours until she finally opened her eyes and looked around her. She noticed a giant woolly rhinoceros seated in an engraved chair wearing a golden crown on his head and a chain with a big gemstone around his neck.

Her body was extremely sore and her bones were aching as though she had no strength left in them and she had a blinding headache. She touched a wound on her forehead and cried out in pain. This made King Midas jump up to his four legs as he had not realised that the young female had woken up. He went over to her and they stayed staring at each other for a couple of minutes before Daniella plucked up enough courage to speak.

"Who are you, kind Sir?" the girl stuttered. "And where are my clothes? I need to go home although I no longer know where that is anymore!"

The King put one of his large feet into the girl's hand. "I'm King Midas and welcome to my kingdom Rhinestone. You've been brought to the Palace of Yarn as you, my girl, have suffered the worst possible injuries. I was so ashamed of Pleck, one of my personal bodyguards, treating you in such a manner that I beheaded him! Now, girl, what's your name? And where did you come from?"

This had become too much for the young girl and she found herself weak and passed out. The King returned to his throne wondering what he should do with this young female. She seemed extremely naive and looked probably no older than seventeen.

Getting to his feet, the woolly rhinoceros trotted out and opened the now repaired door before going out into the hallway where he screamed out at the top of his voice, "Oswald, come here immediately and bring your wife Tatiana. She can help you as well."

Without making a single sound, the two raptors appeared as if by magic and stood to attention in front of the King.

"Sire, why do you need my wife's help?" Oswald asked. "She's no tailor."

"Do you think I'm an idiot?" the King bellowed.

The two raptors shook from the voice of the King and wondered what exactly he wanted.

“Tatiana is a female and this girl is also a female. I therefore want her to dress the young girl into the clothes you made for her. As males, we must go and leave the two girls on their own. We have no right to look at the nakedness of this young female so we must leave and let your wife attend to her. Do you understand, Tatiana?”

“Yes, Your Majesty,” Tatiana said graciously to the King as he and Oswald left the room.

The young female raptor moved quietly over to the girl, removed the blanket that covered her and took her hand in hers. Daniella stirred from her unconscious state, opened her eyes fully and stared into the bright green eyes of the female raptor. The girl wondered what this creature was as it was nothing like anything she had seen before. The colours of the creature were truly spectacular, bright purple and yellow for the snout-like head and bright red for the frill around its neck.

On noticing the girl waking up, Tatiana touched the girl on her shoulders and said, “I’m here to dress you on instructions from the King. As soon as you’re feeling stronger, you’ll be taken to the Glass Palace where the humans live and there you can make a new home for yourself. And what is your name, my dear?”

Daniella took a quick liking to the young raptor. “I’m Daniella, a girl who was lost and taken away from her mother’s home by a tiger who the King told me has been beheaded. Is that true and why should the King do such a thing? Is that what he’s planning to do to me too?”

The young raptor looked at Daniella and flicked her tongue in and out rapidly, rather like a lizard, before saying, “Of course not, the King is worried over you and wants you well so that you can travel to Blackstone where the Glass Palace stands; that’s where King Rudolf reigns. Now, Daniella, I’m Tatiana, the wife of the tailor who made these lovely new clothes for you. Can you try to sit up so that I can help you put them on? Oh, and by the way, how old are you?”

"Almost seventeen, Tatiana. My father sent me to live with my cruel mother who never wanted me there anyway. She sent me out in the cruellest of blizzards where I became lost and ended up wandering into the forest to awaken to all sorts of nightmares, from speaking hares to colourful tigers that bit me and forced me along a dark passageway before bringing me into a garden of beautiful rosebuds. I can't remember anything after this; it's a complete blur from there and it's as though this part has been erased from my mind."

"Poor thing," Tatiana said as she helped Daniella into her new bra to cover the girl's femininity before slipping on a pair of golden knickers and finally squeezing the female into the bodice that pushed up her small and delightful breasts; she finally put the golden dress on the girl and slipped on her new shoes.

Taking the King's body brush, she began brushing Daniella's hair with it until it glowed and shone and then stood back to admire her handy work.

"You're truly beautiful, my dear," the raptor remarked. "You'll soon have a suitor to marry you, maybe even King Rudolf himself, who has recently lost his wife through a tragedy not of his own making. However, you first need to become a royal and find a family who would take you in as the princess you truly are!"

"You're so kind, Tatiana," Daniella said. "I already feel far better than I was before thanks to your help in making me look like a real lady and bathing me and making my skin lovely and clean and smelling of sweet honeysuckle."

"You might prefer not to know who bathed you," the raptor snorted. "She wanted to eat you but the King warned her that if she touched you, he'd chop off her head. Amanda obviously didn't like that idea so she just slithered away with you and put you into the bath."

"Who's Amanda? Is she some kind of snake?" Daniella asked, astonished.

"Yes, she's a twenty-foot python," Tatiana replied immediately. "She almost ate my husband on more than one occasion since they don't quite see eye to eye and one day he even ended up partly in her stomach. The King found her eating him and pulled him out straight away before he ended up becoming Amanda's dinner! Thankfully, my husband only suffered a few scratches. Ever since, he's been absolutely terrified of that serpent and makes sure he's never in the same room as her!"

"Oh!" Daniella exclaimed. "And why do you have such beautiful colours unlike what I've seen in books? What colour is the python and how can you speak?"

"Enough questions now," the young raptor said to Daniella. "You're asking the wrong person. You need to question the King since he'll be able to tell you everything. However, let me answer one of your questions. Amanda, the python, is bright red. Now I've said more than enough as the King will wonder where I've got to. I must go now, my dear, and leave you in the hands of King Midas. You do look gorgeous, may I add!"

Before Daniella could say anything else, the door closed and the raptor had disappeared. It had left so quickly that the girl had not even seen her move while outside Tatiana was speaking to the King.

"Your Majesty, the girl is dressed and is looking just stunning. She's beautiful and clean and she's awake at long last so you can go and talk to her."

Meanwhile, I closed down my computer and went to find my wife who was browsing through a magazine.

"How are you getting on, my dear?" she asked as she lifted her head. "Did you put your granddaughter into the story in some way?"

"Of course I did, Rebecca," I replied to my wife with a big grin across my face. "She's the main character and now finds herself in a magical kingdom where animals speak and are of the most beautiful of colours. I've made Daniella somewhat older than she really is as the King will fall in love with the girl but that's all you're going to know for now!"

"Isn't the King married? Doesn't he have a wife or children? How can a mere mortal become a queen when she has no royal blood, you old fool?" Rebecca said while staring at her husband in the strangest of ways.

"I'll tell you one more thing about the story and then you'll have to wait until the book is released. Yes, the King did have a wife but she was killed tragically when one of the royal horse drawn coaches overturned and toppled into the river. She drowned and he now mourns her. They had no children as he's only a young King, however that's not exactly true as he's actually five-hundred-years-old. Now enough chatter as I'm starving! I lost track of the time and there's a hole in my stomach!"

Rebecca pulled herself up and made her way slowly to the kitchen. The poor woman was suffering from lumbago, as she had always done from the tender young age of twenty-one, and now she was fifty-nine. I knew that she was in pain most of the time and tablets these days never seemed to work. Thankfully, my health was pretty-good as I tried to remain active digging in the garden and filling the borders with beautiful plants that would bloom in every colour of the rainbow.

"Do you need any help in the kitchen, dear?" I shouted to my wife.

"No, I'm alright," she shouted back. "I just get older as each day passes. I wish you could give me a new back! Try to write it down in your next book and it might come true!"

At this, Rebecca went quietly into the kitchen so I took the evening paper and looked through it. Thirty minutes later, Rebecca appeared carrying a tray containing two plates with pork chops, mashed potatoes, peas and gravy. She handed me a plate and took one herself while we sat down at the table to eat.

"Marvellous, as usual, dear," I said. "And would you like a cold drink to go with it, darling?"

"I know I shouldn't with my medication but could I have a nice sweet port, please?"

"You can have whatever you want, my love. Let me get you your port. I think I'll have a beer."

I went away and came back with a glass of port for my wife and a can of beer for me. After pouring myself a glass, I held up my tumbler and chinked it against that of my wife.

"To the woman I love," I said. "And for putting up with a stupid old fool like me," I added with a boyish grin across my face.

"Not that stupid, my dear," she said. "After all, you've managed to make a living from something you love, your writing."

I smiled at her and began eating my dinner, which I found delicious.

"You've never told me, Paul, but where do you get your inspiration from writing so many exciting books that people want to read?" my wife queried.

"I don't know, darling; some people are born with it while others not. I don't quite know why I was chosen to write stories that people want to buy off the shelves of bookshops."

"But that last one, darling, 'Two Little Elves', sold five million copies worldwide! How's that possible? We can never spend all the money it earned us as we're now too old so why didn't you write it when you were younger and we could have enjoyed life to the full?"

"You're always moaning, dear," I replied rather unkindly. "Don't we have enough money now? One thing I will say is that at that time I was a scientist and couldn't be bothered to write. Perhaps, if I'd written it years ago I'd have tasted the good life without you and we would have never met!"

"I hadn't thought of it like that," Rebecca said with a loud hiccup. "Excuse me, it must be the wine! Fate was always written in the stars that we were meant for one another so you just accept it, Mr Riverton. And remember that if you kill me off to marry a younger woman, I'll haunt you for the rest of your days!"

"Yes, of course you will, my dear. Now, have you packed everything up yet as we're leaving the day after tomorrow?"

I think the rain had finally stopped but it was dark outside so we could not really tell what the weather was doing. However, time was passing fast so after filling my stomach, I went back into my study to write, not before leaning down to my wife and kissing her on the lips.

"What was that for darling?" she asked. "Do you still love me after all these years or are you fed up with me?"

I wasn't getting into any family discussions so without further ado I disappeared into my room and closed the door behind me, leaving my wife wondering how I really felt about her. Once in front of the computer I resumed where I had left off.

The woolly rhinoceros opened the door and walked in. Daniella saw the brightly coloured animal wearing a bright red cape draped across its back and with a golden crown on its head. She knew that he was the King everyone was talking about.

"Your Majesty, thank you for being so kind and letting me lie in your bed but why did you kill the tiger?" Daniella began.

"I watched him torment and hurt you," the King replied. "He had been with me for five years as my personal guard but since it seemed that he no longer cared about anyone except himself I was given no choice and I had to do what I did. I had given him fair warning many times and given Pleck the benefit of the doubt but he pushed too hard this time. He had the strength to snap your neck and this I felt could not be tolerated. This is a magical kingdom so when the swinging sword appeared I had no choice but to behead him. We abide by the rules laid down by King

Rudolf of the Kingdom of Blackstone. He gave us the higher intelligence, power of speech so we protect all humans like you and then return them in good health to the Glass Palace. He also wanted us to look different from all other animals so he turned our coats into the most beautiful array of colours before giving us the new home we live in now."

"Your coats are very beautiful, Your Majesty, and they make you look so regal and majestic. I've always been led to believe that prehistoric animals disappeared from the face of the Earth millions of years ago but seeing you it appears I was wrong. In our world, you died out and became extinct ages ago, apart from the python that we have plenty of, albeit not of such a radiant colour of bright red. She constricts her prey and squeezes the life out of it before eating it, as all pythons do, so why did she leave me alone?"

"It's quite simple, my dear. I told her that if she touched a single hair on your body, she would have had her head removed. When my subjects disobey, I have the right to banish or behead them depending on how terrible their crime is. Anyway, now that you're awake, are you hungry, young girl? If so, food is being served in the main dining room. If you're strong enough, you can climb on my back and we'll go right now."

The animal lay down to allow Daniella to scramble on board. The girl hung on to the King's brightly coloured horns as he trotted away, opening the door with his foot and slipping and sliding along the polished marble floor until they came to the dining room. Pushing the door with his nose, it opened, and the King slipped inside.

The table was groaning under the weight of all the food that had been placed on it. The food varied from roasted meat to fresh salad and from smoked salmon to strawberries so big that they were more like tennis balls. The girl thought that the table had been laid out for a whole army but in fact, it was just for the King and her.

The King lay down to let Daniella climb off and as she did so two brightly coloured dodos came in carrying two large jugs of orange juice. The King sat down at one end of the table while the girl was told to sit down at the other end. As they stared at each other, a number of raptors appeared as if from nowhere carrying a selection of delicious fruits and bread in their delicate hand-like feet. They jumped onto the table and nimbly went from one end to the other, passing over the fruits and delicious bread before springing off the table and disappearing as if by magic.

Daniella was famished so she took a little of everything, beginning with the fruit that were extremely succulent and juicy. The girl marvelled at their colours that ranged from yellow through to purple and from pink to bright red while some others were a florescent green. There was even a tiny hexagonal fruit that was a bright turquoise in colour.

The meat she could not recognise; it was similar to chicken but not quite and she thought that maybe it could be the meat of some unfortunate dodo who had betrayed the King! The girl thought that a woolly rhinoceros would eat green shoots but from the way the King tore at his meat, she quickly concluded that perhaps these animals were omnivores just as she was.

The King was sitting so far away from the girl that when he said something to her she could not make out what he was saying, so she contented herself with just nodding her head at him from time to time. It was only after eating and drinking their fill that once back together she told him that she did not reply to him at the table because she was unable to understand what he was telling her.

At the end of the meal, that Daniella found scrumptious and delicious, the girl shouted loudly so the King could at last hear what she was saying

"Sire, do you have a wife?" Daniella asked King Midas.

"No, my dear there's no Mrs Midas to my knowledge, however my father and mother always wanted me to marry, but we haven't spoken for ten years or more, and if I wished to take a wife I would need to firstly patch things up with my father, as well as obtain permission off King Rudolf who would grant her the power of speech, and then finally he would adorn her with the rightful colours of my kingdom! And only then we would be allowed to become husband and wife."

"That's a shame King Midas, as you have a heart of gold, and you deserve a good woman to look after you, and rule your kingdom together!" King Midas, coughed nervously as Daniella's words certainly hit home, as in some way he knew that the girl was telling him things that even his magician was unable to tell him, and this to the King was something truly unbelievable as King Midas trotted over to the girl, lay down on his stomach to enable Daniella to clamber aboard as he said to her in a friendly manner.

"Are you ready to leave Daniella, as I have pressing business I need to sort out!" King Midas said affectionately to this beautiful human girl.

Chapter 3
A Taste of Royalty

The girl sat on the King's back once again but this time they did not return to the throne room. Instead, the King galloped up to the second floor with the girl clinging on to his horns and fur for dear life. When they came out into a hallway, the King stopped outside a door and pushed it open with his foot.

"This is your room until you're well enough to travel," King Midas said. "The physician will be up to see you shortly so you lie down on your bed for now. You'll also find some interesting books here to keep you occupied. I'll be seeing you for breakfast in the morning. Can you walk or do you want me to fetch you?"

"I don't know. Can you wait to see if I can walk," the girl replied before trying to walk a single step that ended with her falling to the marble floor with a loud thump.

She cried out in pain and the King felt sorry for her as this was his fault. He should have taken her to the bed and not left her outside as he had.

"Climb aboard, dear child," the King said, lying down for her to get on.

She pulled herself onto his back and hung on to his horns before he trotted over to the bed and let her get off. The King said goodbye and closed the door behind him leaving the girl rubbing her bruised and battered body. At least, she was now in her own comfortable bed with clean sheets and blankets to keep her warm.

A knock on the door told Daniella the doctor was there so she called out, "Come in," in a feeble tone of voice.

The physician walked in, sat down on the edge of the bed and said to the girl, "Now pull back the covers so that I can examine you properly. Do you remember what happened to you?"

"No, not fully," she replied as she pulled back the sheets and blankets. "I can recall certain things when the tiger told me to run but I remember nothing afterwards. Is that normal, doctor?"

"Yes, it can be as you were in a state of shock and also unconsciousness after a bad fall," the doctor said matter-of-factly as he began examining the girl.

The doctor began sliding his hands all over her body and rolling her around, all the while prodding, jabbing and poking at her as if she were a bag of beans.

"The tiger bit you deeply in your bottom and this has become infected and requires cleaning and stitching," he added. "Also, you have several stomach wounds that must be stitched up so that they can heal properly. That means that you won't be able to walk properly for at least three months or longer."

"I can't walk anyway, doctor. I collapse straight away since my legs are not strong enough. Will they heal?"

"I would think so but first let's get you to surgery. The raptors will come to fetch you on a stretcher in around fifteen minutes or so. Before they come, you need to remove all your clothing, including your underwear. Now, do you want Tatiana the raptor who dressed you earlier to come and help you?"

"Yes, please, doctor, it would make things easier for me as I can't do much on my own," the young girl said to the enquiring physician.

"Leave it with me. I'll go and arrange everything so expect the female raptor to come to your room first."

Once he had said this, he said goodbye and closed the door behind him. A few minutes later, there was a sharp rap at the door but Daniella was too weak to reply. The young female raptor, Tatiana, opened the door and was suddenly at the side of her bed.

"Now, my dear," Tatiana began. "Try to pull yourself to the edge of the bed. I can then take over from there."

Daniella used all the strength in her arms and managed to pull herself to the edge. She was so tired just from moving that small distance and the female raptor looked at her with the deepest concern.

"My poor girl, that tiger hurt you really badly! I had no idea when I was dressing you earlier that you have such horrific injuries. Now, let me start removing your clothes. Try to sit up if you can as it makes things easier for me."

After ten minutes of moaning and groaning from the poor girl, Tatiana finished removing her dress, bodice and shoes leaving her in her bra and knickers.

The girl looked at the raptor and in a slurred tone of voice said, "Tatiana, can you come with me to surgery? I'm scared of being on my own."

"Okay, I will," Tatiana replied. "I'll wait until the raptors come to fetch you for surgery and will stay with you in the operating theatre too."

The young raptor kept to her word. When two male attendants appeared with a stretcher and put the girl carefully onto it, and began pushing her along, Tatiana followed closely behind even when the doctor shouted something at her.

Tatiana stood her ground and said, "Daniella wants me to remain with her at all times as she is afraid so I insist on staying, doctor."

The physician knew when he was beaten and most of the time it was by females who it seemed always had the final word.

The girl was then whisked away into surgery with the raptor following right behind. The doctor lay the girl down on the table and began looking at her wounds. However, she could not remember anything after this as the doctor gave her an injection that made her fall asleep.

"Nurse," the doctor said to Bella, the nurse by his side, another female dodo with bright red and green feathers. "Look at where the tiger's teeth penetrated the girl's skin, it's torn away the flesh and probably been eaten by the beast. All that's left are holes but we don't have the necessary facilities or technology to repair such wounds. We must tell the King that King Rudolf must send a surgeon to carry out such an operation. The tiger's even removed flesh off her left breast and his sharp claws have pierced her legs. I strongly believe that it requires some magic to make her strong and able to walk at least!"

"Who's going to tell the King? It's certainly not going to be me as he has a ferocious temper," Tatiana whispered.

"I'll have to face the King's wrath, I suppose, as otherwise, this girl will die and that's the last thing he'll want to happen," the doctor replied. "However, if she lies in her bed for months, I suspect Amanda will take her chances and have a go at her. I know of at least two such cases over the past twelve months where two human boys ended up in that serpent's stomach!"

"My God, the King would never accept that, would he?" the young raptor said out loudly while the doctor continued treating the young girl and putting large dressings on her wounds.

"Wish me luck!" he exclaimed when he was finished with the girl. "I hope I return in one piece!"

Theodore, the bright pink walrus and royal physician, left Bella and Tatiana waiting while he went to look for the King. He headed to the throne room where he found him sorting through some paperwork.

On seeing his physician walking into the room, the King bellowed, "Theodore, have you repaired the wounds and is the girl on the mend?"

The young walrus was shaking like a leaf so the King knew that he was hiding something.

"I won't ask you again, you stupid walrus! Is the girl going to get better?"

After a few seconds' pause to regain his composure, Theodore replied, "I don't think so, Your Majesty. She'll probably die if she doesn't have some magic performed on her by one of the physicians from Blackstone."

"That's impossible!" the King roared, making the glass in the windows shake.

Theodore shuddered and feared for his life since he had never seen the King so angry before.

"Now, walrus, explain to me why you can't repair the girl's body. Give me all the facts because otherwise, I'll be looking for yet another physician. Of course, I'd have to remove you first and I'm sure Amanda would be eager to help!"

Theodore knew exactly what the King meant. It was obvious to him now where his predecessors had gone before him.

"Your Majesty, on examination of the girl, I found large pieces of flesh torn off. Most likely, they were bitten off by Pleck who has left gaping holes in her body. If we can't close them, the girl will die. She's unable to walk as her legs have become infected due to the fact that the tiger's claws went down to the bone on the female's legs. The girl requires constant observation and I advise you not to trust Amanda if you wish to keep the girl alive as she'll eat her in due course! I know she's done so before as she bragged about it to everyone!"

"That serpent's big mouth will have to be removed!" the King snarled. "She had no right to tell everyone what she did for me.

However, I can vouch that Amanda will not touch the girl. I was thinking of letting the young female raptor Tatiana look after her as they seem to get on extremely well. Now, about those gaping wounds, let me think how we can go about this. If we place the girl in a carriage with a firm mattress, do you think she'd make the journey to Blackstone?"

"As a physician I don't think so, Your Highness. The only way she'll survive is for one of the physicians to come here. And it has to be done fast as I only give her a few days to live!"

"Right, you leave me now," the King said to his physician. "Meanwhile, place Daniella in her room and tell Tatiana to stay with her."

"Yes, Your Majesty," the walrus said before bowing and leaving the King to mull over what could be done.

When Theodore returned to the operating theatre, he found the girl back on her stretcher. He told the young raptor of the King's decision and she smiled as she really did like the girl and she could therefore protect her from all misfortunes such as being eaten alive by that devious python!

With the girl still knocked out by the sleeping drug, she was returned to her room and the tailor was sent for to arrange for some further clothing to be made. When Oswald walked in a few minutes later, he saw his wife tending to the girl and that made him furious.

"What are you doing here, Tatiana?" he shouted. "You must go home to look after the children!" Oswald insisted.

"I can't, dear," she replied gently. "I have orders from the King to remain with the girl twenty-four hours a day until she hopefully makes a full recovery.

Oswald realised that he had no say over the matter and that if the King had decided that his wife had to attend to the girl, then he would have to get his mother to look after the children.

Dear wife, The King mentioned that Daniella will require a wardrobe of clothes to wear, as she has to go on a long journey to Blackstone so now what sort of clothes do you want me to make for this young female, especially since she's going to die?" Oswald asked sarcastically.

"Don't say things like that! She might hear you!" his wife said. "Make her several knickers and bras as she can't wear a bodice since her wounds are too severe, and maybe a few nightgowns, at least five new dresses and a pair of strong black boots, together with a coat for the cold winter ahead of us."

"Why that many dresses, dear?" Oswald said to his wife, still reasoning to himself that if she were going to die there would not be any need for so many new clothes.

Tatiana looked at her husband's reluctance and screamed at him, something she had never done before. "This poor girl will become better and if it needs a little magic from the King of Blackstone so be it. And if it requires me to stay there for one month, I will, or longer if it calls for me to do so!"

Oswald beat a hasty retreat as he had never seen his wife quite so angry and it was known that raptors attacked and ate one another every so often. With his tail between his legs, he went away to begin designing the new clothes.

Tatiana took hold of the girl's hand and saw that blood was coming through the bandages around her stomach. She felt useless and knew that the girl would become weaker the more blood she lost. At that moment, Daniella opened her eyes and tried to sit up but found she was too frail to do so. Tears rolled down her face but when she noticed that she was not alone, she tried to raise a smile.

"Am I going to die, Tatiana?" she moaned. "I feel like I have had all my life squeezed out of me!"

The young raptor stared at the girl and wiped away a few tears. Daniella had become her friend and she felt really sorry for her.

Tatiana had no real friends and there was no way she would let this young beautiful innocent girl die.

Meanwhile, King Midas was on his way to the Sovereign Mountain Range, where he had access to a hidden cavern, a secret he had never shared with anyone else. The journey took a good two hours, and with the sun blazing down on him, he began feeling faint. Finally, he turned around the last corner, and there in front of him, stood the mountain range that rose magnificently from out of nowhere with clouds hanging over the peaks. The King sauntered over to a particular part of the rock face and pressed it with one of his feet. As if by magic, the huge stone slid away showing a doorway beyond. He disappeared through it and the entrance magically closed behind him.

The King then trotted through a short tunnel until he found himself in a large underground cavern. He cocked his ears to one side and heard the sound of running water, following which he went over to a concealed stream where he took one long drink of fresh mountain water before carrying on with his mission.

Watered and refreshed, the King made his way to the back of the cavern until he could go on no further. He touched another rock face and it slid away like the other, and there in front of him was another Kingdom, hidden away from prying eyes, where his ancestors lived and where he had been born.

King Midas trotted through the doorway and watched it close behind him as some grey woolly rhinoceros came up to him and sniffed at his genitals before allowing him to proceed.

From nowhere, other prehistoric creatures appeared. He recognised one diplodocus, a number of stegosauruses, a pride of sabre-toothed tigers and even some pterodactyls flying high above in the purple sky. As he passed by a deep river, he spotted several plesiosaurus and giant sturgeon-like fish, which he knew were extremely ferocious.

He sauntered forward, all the while being closely watched by the grey woolly rhinoceros that had sniffed at him earlier. He eventually came to another mountain range where hundreds of his own kind wandered freely. King Midas then went to the rock face of this new range of mountains, touched one of the stones and watched it slide away to reveal yet another doorway. He trotted inside and the stone door slid back into place. He followed another passageway that led to another dead end, and as he touched the rock face with his paw, it slid away to disclose yet another hidden kingdom beyond.

This time, the prehistoric creatures living in this hidden world were beautiful and colourful like he was. These animals had been living in secret and far away from King Rudolf's control. These prehistoric animals far outnumbered his army of men the King had at his disposal, and were just waiting for the right moment to attack.

Chapter 4
Getting Ready

Looking at my watch, I realised that it was way past midnight and my wife would be wondering what I was up to. Saving everything and closing down my computer, I locked my study door and went to the kitchen where I took a bottle of white wine hidden behind the milk from inside the fridge and poured myself a glass.

"You deserve that, Son," I murmured to myself.

I drank the last dregs of wine in my glass, put the bottle back into the fridge and went up to bed. I entered the bedroom, closed the door behind me and undressed thus leaving my underwear that consisted of a pair of underpants as well as a vest for warmth. I got into bed quietly, making sure I did not awaken Rebecca. I closed my eyes and was soon fast asleep dreaming of a magical kingdom where colourful prehistoric creatures of all kinds still lived.

"Come on, sleepy head!" I heard Rebecca saying as she prodded me in the ribs.

Rebecca had brought me a tray with a cup of tea and some slices of toast with marmalade. I sat up, yawned loudly and took the tray off her.

"What time did you come to bed last night you old fraud?" she enquired. "I stayed awake until ten but there was no sign of you so I left you writing and went up on my own. How's the story coming together?"

I took a bite of toast and drank a little tea before answering her. "Just fine, dear, I think it could be another best seller if I finish it the way that I'm doing at the moment."

"I know you're a mean old man and never tell me anything about the story but I thought you were writing it for our granddaughter and not for yourself!"

"Yes, Rebecca, one thing I can tell you is that Daniella does have a leading part in the story," I replied cautiously. "Now I don't want you asking me further questions about the book."

"You cantankerous old git!" Rebecca exclaimed, not at all lady like before slipping away quietly and going about her business.

She had learnt over the years that I was set in my ways and if I did not wish to tell her anything then she had to wait like all my readers did to find out. When the book was finished and the e-book was released only then would I give her a copy to read! Rebecca accepted that as she knew that there was no way I was going to give her an insight of the story. That was why I had locked the door to my study.

Having eaten my toast and finished drinking my tea, I dressed and went down to the lounge. However, I did not head there immediately as I normally would but went in the direction of the study to get some maps from the drawer of my desk before heading towards the back door.

"It's stopped raining and the sun is trying to shine," my wife shouted to me from inside the kitchen. "It's all for Daniella as she'll be coming at seven tomorrow morning so I thought you'll want to start out the moment she arrives in order to surprise her."

"I do and that's where I'm going right now, outside to the motor home to put in any maps that I might need for the trip."

"I thought you'd know the directions in your head by now! We've been there several times in and around the area of both Devon and Cornwall."

“I probably will know the way when we’re on the road but I'm not getting any younger and having the maps to assist me might come in handy. They’re a little old now and don’t show the newly built bypasses so it’s probably best I buy some new ones to replace them.”

I found it warm outside as I opened the door of the motor home. I climbed in and sat in the passenger seat before putting the maps safely into a plastic sleeve and inside the glove compartment. I started the engine to make sure that the battery was okay and the engine burst into life. I also noticed that the tank was over three quarters full of diesel. The vehicle was less than twelve months old, as thanks to the success of my first novel, I had the money to replace both the motor home as well as the car.

The Mercedes motorhome boasted of all the latest mod cons such as satellite TV, computer and internet, a top-of-the-range Boss stereo system, a games console, a luxurious kitchen and living area and three separate sleeping compartments, one of which had its own bathroom. On the other hand, my car was a top-of-the-line Range Rover that had every single extra you could wish for. One could say that I had spoiled myself silly by the successes of my books but my excuse was that we’re only born once so we should enjoy life to the full.

Since we lived out in the sticks, there were only one or two shops around and then miles and miles of open tranquil countryside that over the years had disappeared as new motorways sprouted up right through the farmland. This was because hungry farmers cashed in and sold the land to the highest bidders or unscrupulous councils had made compulsory purchases and got the land at give away prices.

Switching the engine off and checking under the bonnet, I found that the water and oil levels, as well as the distilled water in the battery, were full so I knew that our journey would be the least of our problems. Making sure that the distributor cap was fitted firmly on and the spark plugs were tight and secure, I shut the bonnet, locked the vehicle up and headed for the house.

The weather was rather pleasant and more like a summer's day when Rebecca came over to me and said, "We need to go to the shops to get some last minute items Paul and you also need a new waterproof jacket. If you remember you ripped the other one on some barbed wire when we were escaping out of that field of bulls!"

I had forgotten all about that and probably would have taken my old one with a big tear in the back of it so I agreed.

"Yes, dear, you're right as always," I said. "Shall we go to Stratford upon Avon? That's only twenty miles or so from us and there's a good selection of shops and supermarkets."

After a nice cup of tea and several more slices of toast, we were ready to go. I pulled the Range Rover out of the garage and my wife got in. We then drove down the lane and out onto the A34 road. The car quickly ate the miles away and we soon found ourselves driving along the banks of the River Avon and the Shakespeare Theatre before I pulled into the multi-storey car park.

We walked the short distance to the shops and strolled along gazing into the windows. After making several purchases and buying a smart waterproof jacket for myself, and another for my wife, I got the car out of the car park and we headed for the supermarket.

We must have been going round for over one hour inside the supermarket and my feet were killing me so God only knows how my wife put up with her constant backache and with a trolley full to the brim. Anyways, I paid with my card and we headed towards the exit.

We trundled out with a trolley full of assorted items, including chocolate and sweets for Daniella and pork pie for me. My now exhausted wife took her seat while I loaded everything into the car, returned the empty trolley to its bay and got into the car.

"I think we've bought enough for a whole army," I remarked to my wife as we drove out of the car park. "Why can't we get fresh bread and milk from Cornwall? They do have supermarkets as well, don't they, darling?"

"You know they do but I get used to drinking my own milk and eating our bread for the first few days, and then we'll get any extra things we need down there. We had better load everything non-perishable this afternoon since it will make it easier for us to leave the exact moment our granddaughter arrives. Our son will drop her off at the end of the drive because he'll be heading off to work and he won't have any time to come and see his own parents."

"Dick isn't that bad," I put in. "He'll stay for a few minutes, I'm sure."

"I bet you I'm right and you're wrong as usual," my wife said with a chuckle. "I told you before that you must say something to him as last time he left poor Daniella without a penny to her name and we ended up paying for everything!"

"And I suppose we can't afford it, my dear!" I replied with a loud snigger.

This time it was my turn to laugh as I wondered whether my wife had forgotten that we were worth several millions of pounds thanks to my writing.

"I know we have an abundance of wealth but it's the principle, dear," she replied irritably. "Our son has forgotten where his grass roots are and his rude wife Carol is even worse! Thank heavens, Daniella is not like either of them as she's kind and loves animals and her grandparents!"

"You, my dear, are getting extremely difficult. I don't need you nagging all the time!" I said to my wife with a scowl on my face as we turned into our driveway.

I let my wife get out while I put the car away into the garage and opened the boot to start unloading everything. I did not ask Rebecca to help me transfer most of the stuff to the motor home since I knew her back was troubling her. One hour later, she came out to see if I needed any help.

"Don't worry, dear, I've finished. I just have a few items I need to put into the fridge. You can go back into the house since you need to rest your back. That's what the doctor ordered."

"What are you going to do now? Lock yourself away in your study?" she enquired.

"Not at the moment as I need to rest my legs. They're aching like hell! I must be getting old or something. I think I'll go and put my feet up in the lounge."

"Let me fry some eggs and chips. How does that sound?" my wife asked. "I'll also make some nice crusty bread and butter."

I nodded at my wife. She always seemed to know how to change my bad mood into a good one. I always wondered how she quite did that but that was why we had been together for so many years, mainly happy ones, even when we did not have much money in the early days of marriage as we did now.

I sat down with my feet resting on a pouffe. I heard the sizzling of chips in the fryer as my wife put them into the oil. I waited patiently and ten minutes later, Rebecca came out carrying a tray with a plate of eggs and chips and three slices of buttered crusty bread that she handed to me.

"How does this look, darling? And would you like a beer to go with it too?"

My wife was a darling and I told her so. She returned to the kitchen to make her own meal and to pour me a cold beer that she brought to me before heading in the direction of where she had come from.

I found the eggs and chips perfect with a lovely dippy yoke that I dipped my chips in just as I used to do when I was a young boy. I found the food delicious, especially with fresh crusty bread, which could not have tasted better. I took a swig of my ale and my day was complete! I had also completely forgotten about my legs aching.

My wife then came in with some scrambled eggs on toast. She preferred that as we both had false teeth to contend with and that was one reason why Rebecca always made my chips lovely and soft.

"Thanks darling," I remarked to my wife. "This is just what the doctor ordered!"

"Don't you go on about doctors! That's all we need for one of us to go down with some illness or other! Anyway, if you're feeling better, why don't you go and write some more of your story, now what's its name?"

Rebecca thought that maybe I had forgotten that I had said that I would not tell her any of my stories but I did not blame her for trying.

"Rebecca, I'm not quite senile yet and you know my answer. I'll tell you when the publisher goes ahead and prints it."

"Meany!" Rebecca said laughing.

She did not really need to know but she loved winding me up so I turned the tables on her.

"Now, before I go to my study do you want me to carry any heavy bags for you?" I asked.

I looked into her eyes; she had a lovely shade of hazel brown eyes although you could not see them any longer as she wore glasses most of the time. I could still imagine her as the young and slim twenty-one-year-old with long blond hair that I had fallen in love with so many years ago.

"No, I'm okay," Rebecca replied. "I loaded most of the clothes when you were in your study writing so we only have the odd few things we might wish to take along with us and the fresh and frozen food that we won't put in the motor home until we leave."

"You're something else, darling," I said to Rebecca as I got to my feet and went into my study.

I sat down at my desk, switched on the computer and waited for it to boot up. A single name came up on the front of the screen; it read 'Daniella' so I selected that file and carried on writing from where I had left off.

"If I remember correctly I was in Chapter 4, oh yes, where the King meets his family," I whispered to myself in case my wife heard me, and carried on writing.

King Midas headed for the green luscious valley that had a river flowing right through it. All the colourful prehistoric beasts were drinking from it when one of the leaders of the herd of woolly rhinoceros saw the King in all his splendour.

"Look, it's our brother, Experian," he shouted using King Midas' middle name that he was known by when he was still a child. "Are you thirsty, brother, or have you come to see father?"

"I've already drank some water but yes, I need to speak to father urgently."

"Come with us brother," Dracorus said to the King as he and his family made their way through the valley until they came to a settlement. With all the noise of King Midas' return, his father came out to the open doorway.

"Quiet! What's all this noise?" he shouted. Then, noticing his son Experian standing in the middle of his brothers, sisters, aunts and uncles, he added, "Welcome, Son, what brings you here? You've not bothered to visit for seven years at least! I thought you'd forgotten where your family lives!"

"I'm sorry, father, and how's mother? She had a cold last time I saw her. Is she better?"

The woolly rhinoceros bellowed. "Amelia, our son has come to visit. Wait there and I'll bring him to you."

King Midas's father, King Theodore Rasmus, led his son towards a clearing amongst the trees. As King Midas came out of the shadows, his mother stepped out. She was old like her husband was and tired but she looked good for her age.

"Experian, I've missed you so much," she exclaimed as she nuzzled her son. "How's your kingdom and your people? Why have you taken so long to visit us again? One day you'll come and either your father or I won't be around anymore!"

"I know, mother, but I'm the only one who knows our secret and there are thousands of us waiting to make our next move when it's time for us to do so. The humans treat us well so to declare war against them is hard for me to accept as King Rudolf and his courtiers are kind and pleasant, and remember it was them who gave us the power of speech and such beautiful colours rather than our drab coats of old."

Father Theodore Rasmus appeared and roared loudly, "Are you going soft on me, Son. What's this I hear that you don't want war with the humans?"

"I'm not here to argue, father, as I need some help to make a young female human better. She was badly wounded by my own personal guard so I feel responsible."

"You should let the human die! They're nothing to us and have hunted us down for millions of years. We owe them nothing and with you asking for assistance to make this human live again, I must ask you where your values lie?"

King Midas stared at his father as tears ran down his face.

Thankfully, his mother felt differently and said in a soft voice. "Son, you care for this human. I understand if you feel like this as you've grown up with humans around you but you must realise how your father feels about everything. He wonders why he can't live in a beautiful palace and have all the luxuries of life as you do. Now explain to me what you want and I'll make the decision, with your father's help or without, and then you must leave as your father is upset with you and wants you gone!"

"This girl is only seventeen but she's been through the worst possible childhood and found herself upsetting one of my tenants on the outer world where she lived. He demanded that, as a paying hare, he should have the rights to kick her out but she refused to budge from under a bush in the forest. Unknown to me, the hare complained to my personal guard, who took it upon himself to arrest the girl and bring her to me. He also decided to hurt her badly and bit into her body with his razor sharp teeth. He was a sabre-toothed tiger so he tore the flesh as well. Now, without some magic, she'll die as we have no way of stopping the bleeding and loss of body fluids."

"Okay, my son, this seems reasonable enough. I also feel for this girl so tell me, what is it you want?" she replied.

"The girl urgently needs replacement blood and body fluids to save her life but she hasn't the time to travel the thousand miles by road to King Rudolf of the kingdom of Blackstone. I know from when I was a child that there is a hidden trail through to the Virgonian Mountains from your valley. All I'm asking of you is to allow me to pass with this girl through your kingdom and give her some hope at least. I will travel with the girl, or you can send someone with us if father doesn't trust me anymore."

"It's not that, Son, the passageway is dangerous with falling rocks and the only people who know of this alternative route are your father and me. You wanting to bring a human into our valley is unheard of and very dangerous for our people. Is the girl so important to you, Son? You're an animal so how can you feel love towards this complete stranger?"

"I don't know, mother, but as a King I have a sixth sense and believe her to be kind and gentle and everything that I could ever want in a human friend."

"Alright, you've told me everything but now I have to explain to your father and what he says will be his final decision and won't be changed for anyone. Now, while you wait with your brothers and sisters and get to know them once again, let me talk to him."

King Midas left his mother and joined his siblings sitting under a mature baobab tree to shade themselves as the sun was blazing hot. Meanwhile, his mother called her husband.

"Theodore Rasmus, I need a word with you!" she shouted. "It's important!"

The King appeared in front of his wife and said with a growl, "If it's about our son, Experian, then it had better be good as he's really peed me off. I'm seriously thinking that his brother should take his place as he no longer thinks like a ruler and has become my lost son."

This outburst was not what Amelia expected to hear from her husband but she knew that if anyone could calm him down and change his mind, then she was her son's only hope. She began to explain to her husband about this young human female but his first reaction made him stand up and foam at the mouth before launching a scathing verbal attack on his wife.

"Are you crazy, woman?" he screamed. "Why should I give him permission to enter our valley with a human of all things and who could bring down on us the worst possible atrocities?"

He realised that his temper was scaring his wife so he calmed himself down and continued in his normal voice. "Now, tell me, dear wife, why should I agree to this human passing through our valley?"

Amelia changed tactics and told her husband of the girl's troubled childhood and that she believed the girl deserved a second chance and that without their help, she would certainly die.

She then charged in like a bull and said, "At one time, you had love in your body. You were young and took awful risks but your parents didn't abandon you as you want to do to our son, and when your mighty temper drove me away, did I not come back and give you a second chance? Now, don't you think this girl deserves saving? She's terribly ill and will probably not even be aware of where she's passing through anyway, so what's the harm, darling?" Amelia added while playing the loving wife all of a sudden.

King Rasmus stamped one of his front hooves on the ground. That was a good sign as it meant that he was actually mulling over what she had said to him.

"I need to speak to my son in private. Do you mind fetching him, my dear?" King Rasmus said to his wife, sounding like someone she had not known in so many years.

Chapter 5
An Important Decision

King Midas appeared in front of his father who was seated on his throne. He wondered what his father's decision would be as the longer he took to decide the less likely it was the girl would survive.

"Son," King Rasmus said to King Midas who had not been called that for many years. "Your mother believes I should give this female a chance. I don't know if I'm going mad or something but if you feel so strongly towards this human then I can't step in your way and I'm allowing you to bring her here. Now, before you go, we must eat as you've not enjoyed a meal with us for far too long and this must change mainly for your mother's sake. I've been jealous of your lifestyle for a long time but I was being very narrow-minded. For that, I must apologise. However, I'll be coming with you as the decision is down to me and I need to see for myself that the girl is a good-natured human as you tell me she is."

"Oh, father, I'll never forget this moment. From now on, you, mother and my siblings can come and visit me whenever you want to. We were always a close-knit family but over the years that disappeared and I need it to come back as, apart from my employees, I have no one I can call a real friend."

"Now," his father said to him. "While you remain here, your mother and your sisters will prepare a banquet. We also have plenty of wine that we make ourselves and which you can taste and see for yourself if we're good wine makers. We also have a nice piece of raptor. Have you tried cooking over an open fire before?"

I shook my head so on this note, the King disappeared and went to find his wife who returned wearing a big smile.

"I can't believe this day has arrived," she said. "Father has agreed and wants to come with you to fetch this young girl. Now, your sisters and I are going to prepare a tasty stew of raptor meat. Of course, we didn't kill it as we have certain boundaries we can't cross but it had its jugular vein severed as they're forever at each other's throats. We bought it off one of your uncle's."

King Midas' mother left to go and tell her daughters to prepare a meal for their brother's homecoming while her sons were busy building a fire to cook the raptor over.

Theodore came back and said to his son, "I have a big favour to ask you, Son."

"Of course, father, tell me. What is it you want?"

"If this goes right, Son, your mother and I, and maybe your brothers and sisters too, will come and visit you at your palace on a regular basis as we've never seen it before and we're all curious to know what it's like and why you feel that's your home now."

"That's amazing, father. I've always dreamt of you and mother coming to visit and now you actually want to! It's my honour to welcome you to my home and from now on you're invited whenever you want to come."

Amelia shouted that the food was ready so Theodore and Experian went over. Experian tasted the raptor meat and realised just how delicious it was, and wondered if his chef had ever served them raptor before. Theodore poured some wine into his son's mug and then for himself and the rest of his family.

He held up his mug and said, "To my long lost son who'll always be welcome under my roof."

They all drank the wine until the two jugs were finished and everyone was feeling merry to say the least. After the raptor meat and fresh vegetables were devoured, it was time for King Midas to make a move.

"We must go now, father," he said as he got to his feet. "Otherwise, it will be too dark and we need to go through the other valley and from there we have a good one-hour journey."

At this point, Experian said goodbye to his mother, aunts, uncles and siblings before both his father and he trotted away side by side into the sunset.

With the sun having finally gone down and the air much cooler, they knew that this would make the ideal time to travel with the girl, especially if she was as ill as they believed her to be.

As King Midas and his father sauntered into the Rhinestone Kingdom, Amanda the python, who was sunning herself on the front lawn outside the palace, welcomed them.

"Ssssss, who'ssssss this Your Majesty?" she hissed to King Midas with the utmost of curiosity.

"This is my father, King Rasmus," King Midas said to the nosy snake wondering what business it was of hers.

Amanda the python kept her mouth shut as she saw how annoyed the King was becoming by her question. He was nervous about something but there was no way that she was going to ask him what it was so she slithered away hissing quietly to herself and hid under a bush as the King led his father into the courtyard, through the entrance and along a hallway until they came to a closed door. King Midas touched it twice with one of his front hooves and the door swung open. They went inside and the door shut behind them.

"Sit down, father," King Midas said while showing his father a seat. "In the meantime, I'll go and arrange for something to drink. Perhaps, you might care for some of my vintage wine or some water as we have a long journey ahead of us."

"Some wine will do nicely, Son, and your palace looks magnificent, if I may say so. Anyway, where is the girl?"

"Let me find the doctor who will arrange to bring her down on a stretcher. She's unable to walk and is extremely frail. The girl needs urgent blood and fluids pumped into her body. I'll tell the female raptor Tatiana to help get her dressed and prepare her for a long and arduous journey."

"Yes, Son, you had better go as we don't have much time if the girl's as bad as you're saying."

King Midas smiled at his father and left him on his own in the room. Five minutes later, the King returned and handed his father a glass of wine and a selection of colourful fruits.

"Right, father, Daniella will be down shortly. She's being dressed and loaded onto a stretcher so she'll be ready to leave when we are. What do you think about taking the raptor with us or is it too dangerous?"

"That's your call, Experian," his father said to King Midas. "Maybe it might be for the best as she'll have some female company. How are we going to carry her?"

"I was thinking about that," Experian said to his father. "Perhaps, we could pull her along in a carriage as she mustn't suffer any severe jolts as that'll probably kill her."

Both Kings looked at each other, thinking how they could transport this young female to the kingdom of Blackstone. At that instant, the stretcher-bearers appeared and brought the girl into the throne room. Experian's father, Theodore, looked at her worriedly as she did look extremely poorly. He felt bad since it was he who had delayed the process by insisting on his son eating with his family while this poor girl lay there dying!

Theodore looked down at the unconscious girl and realised that she was truly beautiful and he now understood why his son felt so strongly in helping her become well again.

Staring at his son, Theodore says, "We must hurry as the girl looks almost beyond recovery. Send for the female raptor and tell her to get ready to go on a long journey. Then, get one of the royal carriages prepared because if she sits on one of our backs she'll die for sure."

The two male raptor stretcher-bearers who were still in the room looked on so King Midas snapped an order at them to load the girl carefully into one of the royal carriages. The raptors did as they were told and then the female raptor Tatiana appeared and bowed before the two Kings. She wondered who the elderly one was since she had never seen him before but since he too was a woolly rhinoceros, Tatiana assumed that they might be related in some way or another. However, unlike Amanda, she remained silent on the subject and waited for King Midas to speak.

"Tatiana, you are to come with us to Blackstone as someone needs to look after the girl while we are pulling the royal carriage," King Midas said. "Can you go and inform your husband? And did he make new clothes for the girl?"

"Yes, Your Majesty, Oswald did, Sir," the young female raptor said to the King while bowing to the other royal member who acknowledged the raptor with a stern stare. "My husband made everything that I told him to do, so now she has quite a wardrobe of new clothes of many colours and looks like a real princess. She is so beautiful, Your Majesty and I don't want her to die!"

"I know, Tatiana, she hopefully won't but gather her new clothes together and you'll be accompanying her tonight. You had better go and tell Oswald as he will have to look after your children."

The female raptor bowed to both Kings and left.

King Midas' father said to his son, "She has such a kind heart for a female raptor. I thought they only wanted to kill each other for supremacy but she is something else and like you, Son, feels for this human. Your life's special and you've become a King with purpose and vision but it's time you took a wife to help you rule your kingdom!"

King Midas mulled over what his father was saying and replied in a most unorthodox way. "Who were you thinking of? I've been ruling this kingdom for ten years or more now and I could never see myself sharing my life with another rhino. I'm different from you, father, and I don't know how to behave in front of a female like you did with mother!"

Theodore roared with laughter. "Experian, you may not have the experience of women but you learn quickly enough! Anyway, a female that comes to mind is your cousin, Lara. She's irresistible even if a little naïve and she's almost eight. Lara has been with no male as far as I know and she's not courting either, so she could become your ideal mate and bear you plenty of strong sons."

King Midas thought over what his father had just said. Putting his head up into the air, he replied, "Yes, father, I know that Lara's very beautiful and would be my number one but I don't know her very well and find it difficult to speak to females of our kind. I'm ready to give it a try and see where it ends but what will her father think about her moving away?"

"He'll be delighted as eight is the ideal age for matrimony and males prefer young females of five to ten years old. However, Lara has always stuck by her principles and when males have come courting she sends them away packing with their tails between their legs!"

At that moment, Tatiana returned. "Your Majesty, all the clothes are loaded into the carriage with Daniella but she's getting weaker and I'm afraid for her life," she said worriedly. "Can we go now, sire?"

"Yes, we'll leave now," Theodore, King Midas' father, answered. "Come with us, raptor, and we'll hitch ourselves to the carriage."

Tatiana shot out of the door and got into the carriage while the two woolly rhinoceros hitched themselves to the royal coach and started their journey along the dusty roads, taking care not to drive over the bumps and potholes.

The female raptor Tatiana held the girl's hand throughout most of the journey. After some time, the roads became bumpy and uneven, but she was still able to comfort the girl who remained in an unconscious state. With it being so dark outside, she wondered how the royals managed to find their way with only a pale moon to guide them by. After several more hours of driving and with night turning to day, the carriage came to a sudden halt.

The female raptor caught sight of several large dinosaurs and winged bird-like creatures that were not as colourful as she was and wondered where they were. She quickly shut the blind down and just sat there terrified. She heard several scrapes and scratches as a number of raptors climbed on top of the roof. They knew that food was close by and they uttered a series of blood curdling shrieks.

"We must hurry, Experian, as those raptors are smelling food and want to snatch our young girl and the female raptor. They're hungry and are looking for a free meal. Let us move on and hope we can shake them off. We still have a further thirty minutes before we reach the next mountain range but this might make things rather unpleasant for our passengers now," Theodore snorted to his son.

They drove on zigzagging this way and that along the roadway. However, as several of the raptors were thrown off, others appeared and climbed back on. This was becoming like a living nightmare as the evil raptors were using their hand-like feet to reach into the carriage to try to steal away the girl and her companion. Then, something remarkable happened as a huge roar was heard and two huge Tyrannosaurus Rex dinosaurs appeared. They began grabbing at the raptors and swallowing them whole one after the other.

"Your Majesty," one of the T Rex's said. "You should have told us you were travelling."

"And who is this, Sire?" the other T Rex added to Theodore.

"My son, King Midas, he rules over Rhinestone, another kingdom on the other side of the mountains," he said proudly as he introduced his son to the two dinosaurs. "This is Trappa and his wife Gurka," he said to his son. "They are my eyes and ears and will accompany us all the way to the rock face. They know about our secret world since we've been friends for over twenty years. I've met their children and played with them on numerous occasions. They usually feed on vegetation but when our lives are in jeopardy, they return to the old days and eat meat. Now, we must leave as we have a female human on board who needs immediate surgery!"

Tatiana heard all the speaking outside but knew that she was now safe and that the other raptors had suffered the same fate as they had wished for her and the young girl. The female raptor was not bothered so much that the dinosaurs had eaten them even though they were raptors just as she was.

The carriage then got underway as King Midas and King Rasmus drove forward with the two dinosaurs following closely along. Coming to a stop soon after, Theodore touched the rock face and a door in the rock slid aside to reveal a cavern beyond. They said goodbye to the two dinosaurs and the carriage disappeared inside.

Their journey took a further hour in almost complete darkness but eventually they came to a halt. King Rasmus pressed his left front hoof against the rock face and another doorway appeared, and the two woolly rhinoceros pulled the carriage out again into daylight.

Tatiana risked putting her head out of the window and this time she saw many colourful raptors just like her mingling about with various species of dinosaur. These colourful creatures were not bothered about the carriage or its occupants and kept on feeding on the grass and other vegetarian delights of this beautiful kingdom. King Rasmus and King Midas came to a stop outside what looked like some sort of primitive settlement and unhitched themselves from the carriage.

"We stop here for refreshments but we can stay for no more than one hour," King Rasmas said to Tatiana. "We need to press on but I've stopped because we had one awful scare with those heathen raptors who only wanted to feed on you and the girl unlike the raptors in our kingdom. Now one thing, Tatiana, you must realise that you can't say a single word to anyone, not even to your husband where we came to. This place is a secret and has to remain so and the punishment of speaking about our kingdom is death!"

The female raptor swallowed hard and found a lump in her throat as she began to imagine being next in line for beheading and that was something that she did not want to happen to her.

"I won't breathe a word to anyone, Your Majesty, I promise," she said meekly.

"Good girl," Theodore said as he knocked at the door and his family appeared, saw the carriage and greeted everyone. On seeing the young colourful raptor and the young girl who looked so sick, Amelia waited for her husband to say something.

"This, my dear, is Tatiana," he said pointing at the raptor. "She's looking after our patient who lies in a critical condition from loss of blood and body fluids. We met some unscrupulous raptors on the way but my two dinosaur friends helped us. We need some refreshments as this has been one horrific journey but we can't spend long here as this girl is terribly ill and we don't know if she'll survive another night."

While Amelia went to arrange for food and drink, the two Kings sat down and Tatiana walked around and stretched her legs. It was at this point that a young male raptor came over to her.

"You're beautiful," he remarked. "Where have you come from?"

Tatiana blushed as she had never had any male advances before and this young male was obviously quite keen on her. However, she said to herself that even if she did look young and beautiful, she had a husband and children to care for back home.

"Thank you for the compliment but I'm too old for you," Tatiana said as the two King rhinos headed off to speak to their family. "Anyway, I have a husband and children. We have no future together even though I find you rather cute and interesting."

Amelia appeared and said to the young female raptor, "Is he trying to come on to you? He's quite a handsome chap, isn't he? However, one thing I know about him is that he is a womaniser and tries his luck with all the girls. Now, Tatiana, food is served. Do you eat vegetarian or do you prefer meat?"

"I'm not bothered as we have meat at the palace but I mainly eat fruit and vegetables," Tatiana replied as the young male raptor slinked away.

"Follow me over to the fire that my son has prepared," Amelia said. "You'll find my daughters and relatives sitting there but you'll be the only ones eating as I know that you have to make haste to try to save this girl's life. She's very beautiful, isn't she? She has the loveliest of blue eyes right now!"

The two females made their way towards the fire where Tatiana found the two Kings chatting away with their family. Amelia and Tatiana joined them. The family watched as the female raptor began eating in a true well-mannered and dignified way, very unlike the usual fast way raptors were known to devour their prey.

She declined to eat the meat as she had heard the raptors whispering amongst themselves if she was going to eat her own kind. She knew that the meat was that of a raptor and that made her feel rather sick inside so she continued eating the freshly picked fruit and vegetables, and taking a sip of water every now and then. After ten minutes, she began to feel refreshed.

Chapter 6
Blackstone

It was soon time to leave so the two woolly rhinoceros hitched themselves to the carriage and they were off, trotting in the direction of a fast flowing river. They crossed it with caution but despite this, the flow of the water almost sent the carriage toppling over. Thankfully, some dinosaurs showed up and put some brute strength into holding the carriage firm while the two rhinos eased slowly across to the other side.

They then trundled away into the distance until they were once again out of the valley and heading into open countryside. The weather was hot and humid and the sky was a wonderful turquoise blue. The journey took a good four hours until they found themselves at the foot of the mountains.

Tatiana poked her head out of the window and stared up at the beautiful mountains. She had never seen anything quite like them before and wondered where they were. The two Kings came to a stop and Theodore tapped one of his hooves against the rock face that slid away to reveal an open doorway through which they pulled the carriage inside into the darkness.

A river ran along the track although Tatiana could not see anything in the darkness but she did hear the sound of water flowing. The two woolly rhinoceros pulled the carriage through the cavern until they came to a dead end. Theodore tapped his hoof three times against the rock face and a secret door slid open to reveal a passageway that led to the other side of the mountain.

The rhinos unhitched themselves from the carriage and King Rasmus went to the open window and said to Tatiana, "It's too dangerous for me to proceed. I'll be going back while my son remains with you and the girl, so good luck!"

"Where are we, Your Majesty?" Tatiana found herself saying to the King.

"The Kingdom of Blackstone," he replied. "That's where we are and we need to carry on to the Glass Palace. That's a further one day's travelling. I'll be going now, young raptor. It was a pleasure meeting you but such a shame that I can't share a word with our patient but let's hope she makes a full recovery. I must now help my son hitch himself back onto the carriage and we'll say our goodbyes."

"Goodbye, Your Majesty," the young female raptor said to Theodore. "I hope to see you again one day."

King Midas said goodbye to his father as they rubbed noses affectionately and went their separate ways. Experian trotted forward pulling the heavy carriage behind him; it was a much tougher task now that he was doing this on his own.

After a while, they came to several humans working in the fields, who looked on curiously and wondered what such a colourful animal was doing in their kingdom and where he was heading for. Of course, they had no idea that the rhino was in fact a king and that he was going in the direction of the Glass Palace.

After three hours of travelling, they finally arrived at the palace and King Midas pulled the carriage up to the golden gates. An armed officer opened the gates and King Midas passed through and stopped at the bottom of some beautiful marble steps. He waited for someone to come out to find out who had come to visit and was surprised when King Rudolf himself came down to the carriage, opened the door and saw who was inside. The colourful raptor got out and bowed down low to the human King.

"We need your help, Your Majesty," she said graciously. "This young girl's severely sick and requires some magic to patch her up as a tiger attacked her and tore some pieces of flesh off her. She is still bleeding and will die unless she receives some replacement blood and fluids to make her well again."

"Yes, of course," King Rudolf said. "Now, King Midas come in with your female raptor and explain how this girl became so injured. As you know from our agreement, no human can be harmed so follow me for some food and drink as I think you've been travelling for many days."

King Rudolf entered his palace with King Midas and Tatiana following closely behind him as two royal physicians appeared and went to the carriage to check over the condition of the young girl.

King Rudolf led the party to the main dining room. He opened the door and there in front of them was the most beautiful garden they had ever seen and which put King Midas' own garden to shame. They all took a seat at the long table and several servants appeared with plates of meat, fruit and vegetables and jugs of wine and fruit juice. King Rudolf tore a piece of meat off with his fingers, chewed and swallowed it while King Midas and Tatiana took a fancy to the fruit.

"Where is Daniella?" King Midas asked his fellow King and the ruler of Blackstone. "We're very worried about the girl and pray that she lives."

"Animals that actually care for others and even more so, humans, shocks me and is something I've never seen before. The girl's in the best possible hands but she will need plenty of tender love and care. Perhaps, your raptor will remain with her as she seems to have become a good friend to the girl," King Midas said in rapid response.

"Tatiana will be honoured to remain with Daniella as they've truly forged a good friendship," King Midas said. "Like me, she's concerned over the girl's health and only wants what's best for her. If it means her staying with the girl until she recovers, then so be it. I'll travel back on my own, that's not a problem at all."

"Now," King Rudolf said while looking at King Midas in an unscrupulous fashion. "Tell me exactly what happened to the girl and then I'll decide whether or not I'm going to give you permission to leave."

King Midas explained how Daniella had suffered such atrocious injuries but when he added that he had had the perpetrator beheaded for his actions, King Rudolf smiled.

"I understand, King Midas," he replied. "You can leave with my blessing. I'll return your faithful raptor back to you when she's finished her work here so you may go now."

King Midas smiled at the King, as well as at the young female raptor, before leaving the room. Once outside, he was assisted by King Rudolf's footmen to couple himself to the carriage. He then trotted away into the distance with a little hope in his heart as, although the girl was so weak and feeble, he at least had given her a chance to live.

After King Midas had left the room, King Rudolf smiled at the young raptor and said, "How you've treated this young girl's just amazing, especially as you have your own family to think of! You've definitely won over my total admiration. Now, if you would like to follow me, we'll go and see the patient."

Tatiana followed King Rudolf up several flights of stairs and then along a long hallway until they came to a large wooden door. The King opened it and walked in, with the raptor following behind. They saw Daniella lying in bed fast asleep, looking exceedingly pale.

"She's going to be fine," the King said. "The surgeons have grafted new skin and flesh onto her; these will magically grow until she's left without scars or injuries."

"Is she going to make a full recovery, Your Highness?" Tatiana asked the King, barely able to believe that the girl was still alive and kicking, even if just barely so!

"The girl will be waking up soon," the King replied. "Would you like to remain with her? Perhaps, we can make up the other bed next to her and you can stay with her. Would you like that, Tatiana?"

"Yes, I'd love to remain with her until she's strong and doesn't need me anymore," the vividly coloured raptor responded.

"I think you may be wrong thinking she won't need you anymore as when she was delirious before her operation, the girl kept repeating your name and wanted to know where you were. The doctor told her that you were here and would remain with her until she awoke. Now, would you care for something to eat? I can get one of the servants to bring it up to you."

"You're so kind King Rudolf and so different to how I thought you would be!" Tatiana said.

"That's good to hear, my young raptor. Now just wait here and see what my servant brings up for you. I'll be leaving you now as I can see that the girl is awakening."

King Rudolf got up and left Tatiana sitting on a chair by the young girl's bed. She heard a knock at the door ten minutes later and a servant walked in holding a tray of delicious food for the young female raptor. The servant smiled and put the tray down on a table, following which she left and closed the door behind her.

Tatiana went to check out the food and was delighted to see such a variety, from fresh fruit to beef. There were also several kinds of vegetables and some green shoots as well as freshly squeezed orange juice and wine. Tatiana began to nibble away at the assortment of fruit in front of her and took a few sips of orange juice, which she found delightful. She also took a few bites out of a large piece of beef and found it to be extremely tasty.

Meanwhile, my fingers were becoming sore from all the typing and my eyes were growing tired so I decided to take a break. I looked at the time and was shocked to realise I had missed lunch completely as it was almost four o'clock in the afternoon. I felt a little guilty as I shut down my computer before getting up, locking the door behind me and going into the lounge where I found my wife asleep in the rocking chair.

"Hi, darling, I was wondering if there's anything to eat. I'm starving!"

My wife opened her eyes and stumbled to her feet. "I was going to knock at the door to ask you if you wanted anything to eat but I ended up sitting down in this chair and falling to sleep. Now, how about if I give you some pork pie, cheese sandwiches with crusty buttered bread and some homemade pickled onions, and then, while you're eating that and drinking a beer, I'll be making a Shepherd's pie for dinner tonight. How does that sound?"

I nodded at my wife and she toddled off back to the kitchen to start making me something to eat. She returned within a minute with a glass of icy cold beer before going back to the kitchen to make the sandwiches. Five minutes later, my wife came in with a plate full of crusty bread, with cheese, pork pie and pickled onions on it. I crunched my way through my first onion and took a bite of pork pie and another of delicious crusty bread. After I had almost finished the meal, I took a swig of cold beer and burped loudly.

"Are you going back to do more work, darling?" my wife shouted from the kitchen.

Instead of shouting back, I got up and went to find her. Seeing her making dinner, I said, "No, Rebecca, I've written enough for today. My eyes and fingers need a rest as I'm not as young as I used to be and I have a chronic backache."

"You go and sit down, my dear," my wife said to me. "You deserve a rest."

I did not need telling twice so I headed in the direction of my armchair. I called it my armchair because nobody else dared sit in it! They had learnt the hard way since I would shout at them to remove their fat bums from my chair!

Anyway, sitting down and making myself comfortable, I continued eating the remains of my late lunch. I soon finished everything on my plate and drank the rest of my beer, so switching on the TV, I flicked through the channels to see if there was anything of interest.

"Repeats, repeats, repeats," I screamed out loudly, following which my wife came rushing in.

"What's wrong now, Paul? Why are you moaning so loudly? I thought you were having an aneurysm or something like that!"

"Don't fret yourself over me, Rebecca. I was talking to myself and complaining that everything on the television is all repeats from last week. What do we pay the licence fee for?"

"If that's all you're moaning about, darling, perhaps you should write to Sky and tell them how you're feeling but whether they'll do anything about it is another matter! I believe you'll just be wasting your time!"

I always let my wife have her say as she was probably right after all and I just had to accept it or cancel my subscription. Occasionally, they showed the odd good film but overall it was a waste of money and Sky just got wealthier every day by showing repeats. I began reading through the newspaper and one hour seemed to fly by when my wife appeared from the kitchen.

"Dinner's ready, darling. We're eating in the dining room today. No more trays while we have our granddaughter visiting so come in and join me."

My wife went into the dining room and I followed her and sat down at the large oval table that was neatly laid out. She had even placed silk napkins and a nice bottle of German Niersteiner medium sweet white wine on the table. Rebecca poured some wine into a glass for me and went to fetch the food. She came back soon afterwards, wheeling a trolley with several dishes on it.

"I hope you like it, sweetheart. I've made it especially for you!" she exclaimed.

"Yum, yum, yum!" I enthused while my wife served the food onto our plates and handed out several pieces of crusty bread to dip into the gravy.

Rebecca then sat down at the table and I held up my glass of wine.

"To the love of my life!" I exclaimed as I clinked my glass with that of my wife.

Her smile said it all and we began to munch through the Shepherd's pie until we had both cleaned our plates. My wife watched me having finished my meal before putting before me a dish of apple pie and custard.

"This is because I love you, my darling," she said. "I thought I'd make you your favourite dessert."

I took a spoonful and found it cooked to perfection with just the right amount of sugar and just the way I liked it. We soon finished our dessert and my wife took away the dirty dishes and went to wash up.

I got up immediately after her and in a firm voice, said, "Your job was to cook the meal and my job's to load the dirty dishes and pans into the dishwasher and turn it on. Now, you go and sit down while I go and make us a nice pot of tea. No arguments, dear," I insisted as my wife was just about to open her mouth. "You just go into the lounge and put your feet up."

Rebecca came over and gave me a wet soggy kiss just as she used to do when we were younger, before going into the lounge and leaving me with the dirty dishes and cutlery that I put on the trolley before wheeling it away into the kitchen. She did not try to argue this time as she was probably feeling somewhat tired on her feet and her back was also hurting while mine had suddenly repaired itself to new again.

I loaded everything into the dishwasher, switched on the kettle and waited for the water to boil. I then put three teabags into the teapot and poured the hot water into it, and let it stand a little before taking two mugs off the hook and pouring the tea into them and adding a little milk and sugar. After that, I put them onto a tray, which I carried into the lounge and set down on a table by Rebecca's side.

"Thanks, darling, I needed a rest but I'm too proud to admit it," she said as she gave me a warm smile. "I know you work your socks off writing and I love you from my heart." I handed her a mug of tea and she took a sip before adding, "That tastes lovely, Paul, I'll give you the job again some other time!"

I took a drink of tea myself and had to agree that it did taste extremely good with just enough sugar and milk. I sat down to join my wife and realised that it was half past seven. We finished drinking the tea and refilled the mugs once or twice before my wife looked up at the antique grandfather clock in the corner of the room.

"I'm going up to read in bed, dear," she said. "I have a good story I was reading and, no, it's not one of yours before you ask me!"

I did not know my wife read books and I was curious to see what her choice was. She kissed me goodnight and sat there for another hour or so before going up myself. Entering our bedroom, I found my wife fast asleep with the book she was reading by her side. I cast a quick glance at the title of the book and was rather taken aback when I read 'Fifty Shades of Grey'.

"Good heavens!" I muttered to myself. "My wife too! What's the world coming to?"

We awoke the next morning to the chirping of the birds and with the sun shining through the cracks in the curtains. Something had awoken me and I then heard someone outside knocking at the front door.

On looking at the time, I realised that it was seven o'clock. We had planned to get up at six to welcome our granddaughter. Looking over at my wife, I saw that she was just stirring so I poked her perhaps a tad too hard in the ribs and she opened her eyes wide.

"Whaaat!" she exclaimed in a sleepy tone of voice.

"We've overslept dear and there's someone knocking at the door. I'd better go and see who it is. I suspect it's our granddaughter," I said as I yawned and went downstairs to see who was at the door.

Chapter 7
Daniella Comes to Visit

On opening the door, I looked outside only to find no one there. I then stared over at the low wall that surrounded our garden and there, sitting on it reading a book, was our granddaughter.

"Did you forget all about me, granddad?" she said with a nervous laugh. "I've been sitting here for fifteen minutes now but thank heavens, the rain's gone and the sun's beautiful and warm."

I blushed and told the girl to come straight in. I grabbed hold of one of her suitcases and took it in with me. Daniella followed me inside carrying her other suitcase as my wife came down with dishevelled hair and still in her nightdress. My wife hugged Daniella affectionately and told us that she was going up to have a quick shower and to get dressed.

"What have you planned for me, granddad?" Daniella asked curiously. "I'd love to go to the sea and paddle my feet in the water but I can only dream about things like that! Perhaps, we can visit the zoo."

I realised I was still in my pyjamas so I apologised to the girl and told her that it had been our fault that we had not been there to greet her.

"We have a surprise for you, granddaughter, and we should have been on the road by now but we overslept so our apologies. We had originally thought of going to Cornwall although we're not sure about the weather but if you haven't already been there, we were thinking of taking you to Tintagel Castle. How does that sound?"

Daniella's face lit up. "That's just fantastic, granddad! Are we going in the motor home? I have always asked Daddy to go to Tintagel but he always changed his mind at the last moment. What time are we leaving?" the girl asked enthusiastically.

"Let me go and change out of my pyjamas and take a quick shower and put some clothes on. In the meantime, your grandmother is making us some toast and marmalade and a nice pot of tea. And when do you turn thirteen?"

"Granddad, I'm already thirteen and that was five months ago! You bought me some makeup as well as sending me some money. You're so forgetful! By the way, are you writing a new book?"

"I had forgotten that we had sent you a gift for your birthday. As for the answers to your questions, we're going by motorhome and I am writing a new book; it's very different from all my others. Now, while you wait here I'll go and freshen myself up."

"Granny," my granddaughter said to my wife as she suddenly appeared fully dressed. "How long are we staying for?"

"The whole two weeks, darling, and on the way back we'll be dropping you home. Now, let me begin making breakfast so that we can get under way. Otherwise, we'll be meeting all the traffic and that was something that granddad didn't want to happen. However, it's our fault not being ready to leave the moment you arrived."

Daniella took her book and continued reading from where she had left off. As I returned downstairs, my wife appeared carrying a tray with buttered toast, a jar of marmalade and a pot of tea with empty mugs, milk and sugar before setting them down on the table in the lounge. I took over and poured us all a nice hot mug of tea.

"Two sugars, please, granddad, I'm a bit of a sweet tooth!" Daniella said. "That's what Daddy keeps calling me!"

"I'm just as bad at the ripe old age of sixty-two," I replied. "I've always taken two spoonfuls of sugar whether it is on my cereal or in my tea, coffee or cocoa. Now, how many pieces of toast do you want?"

"Two please, granddad, and with plenty of marmalade too!" Daniella replied as I spread marmalade on the six pieces of toast, two of which I handed two to Daniella.

"None for me, darling," my wife said. "I made them for you and Daniella, but the tea will go down just nicely."

"It's already made, sweetie," I said to Rebecca as I handed her her mug while she sat down in her rocking chair.

"You've been married for so long now and you still call each other lovely names like darling and sweetie," Daniella chipped in. "That's so romantic and something I never hear my mother and father do. That makes me so sad and sometimes I think that maybe they don't love each other anymore."

Rebecca took the reins here, before saying, "I think they do, my darling, but in these modern days, husbands and wives are so busy that they don't have time to be lovey dovey with each other. It's a shame, really, but we live in the modern world and we have to accept it."

"Beautifully said, darling," I said to Rebecca while eating a piece of toast and chewing it, before swallowing it down with some tea.

We had soon finished all the toast and drunk the remainder of the tea. My wife took everything to the dishwasher, loaded it and switched it on. Luckily, Daniella and I had followed her into the kitchen.

"Have you forgotten that when we close up the house we turn off the electricity?" I remarked to my wife.

By the look on Rebecca's face, she had completely forgotten so she turned the dishwasher off and left the dirty plates and dishes inside for when they returned home.

"It's ten o'clock and you're always moaning about other drivers so we had better lock up and go," Rebecca said to me before turning towards Daniella. "Are you ready, granddaughter?"

Daniella nodded her head enthusiastically so my wife gathered the food and drinks together while I picked up the girl's two bags. We then locked up and put the stuff into the motor home. I started the engine, and pulled out of our driveway while my wife locked the wooden gate with a padlock and handed me the key, which I put into the glove compartment.

My wife got into the car and we made our way down our country lane and onto the main road before joining the heavy traffic travelling on the M5 motorway. Daniella was sitting at the back in a nice comfortable captain's chair that she had reclined and was watching a DVD and listening to her favourite music through headphones.

It was the 19th of July and our journey took several hours since we had to stop a number of times for toilet breaks or refreshments. When we finally arrived at the campsite in Cornwall, the first thing I noticed was the cleanliness of the place even though the park was almost full with motor homes, tents and caravans.

I parked the vehicle under a lovely shady old oak tree and looked at the clock in the motor home. It was a quarter to six and we had been on the road for eight hours. No wonder I was feeling hungry again.

My tummy rumbled and my wife smiled at me before turning towards our granddaughter and saying, "Now, darling, while you go with granddad to stretch your legs a little, grandma will be making us something to eat. Do you want it hot or cold? The choice is down to you, my dear, as you're the guest."

"I don't mind," Daniella said looking a bit confused. "Shall we have something hot now and perhaps cheese and biscuits for supper?"

"That sounds good to me," Rebecca replied to her granddaughter. "So you two disappear for an hour or so and see what the shop is like on site. They normally have one but they can be a little expensive. Did Daddy give you any money? If not, granddad will buy you something."

I thought to myself that it was put very diplomatically indeed and was shocked when my granddaughter turned round and said, "Daddy gave me two hundred pounds! I hope that's enough as he told me to contribute towards the food."

"Nothing of the sort, darling," my wife Rebecca said to the girl. "We've bought all the food we need so you keep your money as you'll be needing it when we go into the town centre in the next few days and there you can buy some new clothes or anything else you fancy."

I went off with Daniella and, after looking around for some time, we asked one of the holidaymakers where the shop was. He pointed in the direction of the country lane and across into another field. After thirty minutes further walking, we came to a large supermarket selling pretty much everything.

We went in and mooched around, looking for nothing in particular, but Daniella decided to buy some chocolate limes, which I loved. We had forgotten to put those in our shopping trolley originally. I bought an evening newspaper, a magazine for my wife and a book for my granddaughter to read. She kept telling me that she would pay for the lot but I refused to listen, paid the bill myself and we headed back to the motor home.

We must have been walking for a good hour or so and seemed to be going around in circles. It was when we arrived at the check-in office that I noticed a small but adequate shop selling most of everything next door to where I had paid the parking fee. It was only a short five minutes' walk from our motorhome, yet we had been sent miles to the supermarket instead.

"Granddad, didn't you know there was a shop right under our noses by where we parked?" the girl remarked as she burst out laughing. "What a nasty man he was sending us miles away to somewhere else!" she added in a much more serious tone of voice.

I nodded to my granddaughter to say that I fully agreed, opened the door of our motorhome and a heavenly smell of roast pork and potatoes wafted out and greeted us.

As we walked in, my wife looked up. "Where have you been and what took you so long? Did you know it's almost eight o'clock! I tried calling you on your phone but could not get through. Anyway, I decided to start making the roast just the same."

"We were given directions to the shop and after going across a country lane and through a field and then along another country lane, we found a fair-sized supermarket," I replied to my wife. "It was only when we came back and walked past the reception office that we noticed a small shop right next door to it. Someone played a nasty game on us and now my legs are killing me!"

Our granddaughter could not take the grin off her face. Whereas I found the occasion frustrating and too much to handle, she was able to look at the funnier side of things.

My wife served the food out onto plates and brought them over together with knives and forks. She placed them down in front of us, following which she joined us at the table.

Before I could open my mouth, my wife said, "Unfortunately, I did not have the time, Paul, to make stuffing and crackling but it needs to be in the oven for a good three or four hours so it would have been pointless."

We did not mind as the pork tasted beautiful and was so delicious with the gravy and roasted potatoes to go with it.

"Do you like your dinner, Daniella?" my wife said to the young girl after a while.

"Yes," my granddaughter replied with her mouth half full. "It's delicious. I wasn't expecting such awesome food on holiday unless we were sitting in a restaurant. Perhaps, that's what we can do one of these days and I'll pay the bill so that you, granny, can take a rest from the kitchen as you deserve to."

"That's so kind of you, darling, but whether you'll be paying the bill or not, that's something we can talk about," my wife said to the girl as we continued with the rest of the meal.

Following our meal, I gave my wife her magazine and Daniella her book, while I picked up the local newspaper I had bought from the supermarket.

"Granddad, I didn't ask you to buy this. What's it about?" my granddaughter asked inquisitively.

Daniella read the title of the book, 'Tintagel Castle, the Mystery Behind it' and started reading it as she was curious to learn more about the castle and King Arthur, perhaps wondering if he was a real King, or created out of someone's imagination.

We were all locked inside our own little worlds for a time until I got up for a glass of water and saw Daniella completely engrossed in her book.

"So do you like my choice of book, Daniella?" I asked her.

"It's exciting and I can't wait to see if what I've read so far is true," she replied.

"Now, I don't know about you two but I'm going to bed," my wife muttered while stifling a yawn. "Are you doing any writing tonight, darling, or are you taking a rest since you've been driving for most of the day?"

"I should rest but you go to bed. I'll be along shortly," I replied curtly.

My wife knew that by the time I joined her she would probably be fast asleep. Daniella went over to her granny and kissed her goodnight before coming over to me and doing the same.

"Granddad, this holiday is looking like great fun, and for you and granny to bring me along, that's really cool of you! Mom and Dad never have the time for me anymore. They seem to forget that I'm just a teenager and need the occasional holiday from boring school work! Anyway, I'm going to bed and taking this book with me as it's really fascinating and I intend to put some of the writer's ideas into practice."

I hoped our trip to the castle the following day did not include clambering up some large rocks as I knew how dangerous that would be since the castle stood right on the edge of the cliff face. After a few minutes, I went to bed as well and, as expected, found my wife in the land of nod.

We awoke the following morning to the screech of seagulls and to the divine smell of fried bacon. Our granddaughter had decided to surprise us with a full English breakfast and a lovely mug of steaming hot tea and buttered toast in bed.

"That's so kind of you, darling," I said to Daniella who gave me that charming sweet smile of hers.

"Can we go to the castle today?" she asked. "I want to see if the author's right with her gut feelings, as I think she calls it."

I could see that my granddaughter was infused by a surge of energy and would not accept 'no' for an answer so I sipped on my tea and dug into my breakfast, as did my wife.

I remember the day well; it was the 20th of July 2017, with the sky a lovely shade of blue.

"Yes, perhaps if we leave immediately after breakfast, there would not be that many people queuing for the Land Rover ride," I replied to my granddaughter with my mouth stuffed with baked beans and egg. "The walk is too far for me and granny to make now that we're older. Anyway, how's the weather today, granddaughter?"

Having seen the blue sky, I thought that maybe she had already been outside and I was right.

"Absolutely tranquil," Daniella replied with a gorgeous smile. "It's the perfect day to go visiting the castle as it's so dry. I don't think they've had much rain down here like we had in Warwickshire."

I was happy to learn that and should have realised so after we had walked through the fields the day before. It seems that the weather had been good to the Cornish people and our feet had not got wet at all from the long grass.

"You go and get changed and we'll do the same," I said to Daniella. "Oh, and can you take the dirty plates into the kitchen with you as we don't have much room in here?"

Daniella gathered all the empty plates and mugs together before going into the kitchen. I heard her filling the sink and washing the few items there were, following which she went back to her room. My wife and I got up, washed and dressed, and went into the lounge where we found our granddaughter reading her new book. I stared at her only to find her attention was glued to the pages. My wife made some sandwiches and a flask of coffee and took three cans of coca cola from the fridge.

"Right, granddaughter, we'll be off," she said as I got to my feet and grabbed our jackets before telling Daniella to do the same as it was cold on the cliffs with the cool breeze and the Atlantic Ocean.

We left our mobile home and locked the door behind us. It was lucky that the campsite was fairly near to the castle so we decided to walk the short distance to where the Land Rovers operated. When we arrived, we saw that they were already busily transporting people to the end of the track. It was not muddy so the short trip took less than fifteen minutes.

The driver dropped us and we followed the other people to the steps leading upwards. We found the steps carved out in the rock thankfully dry, as if it had been raining and wet, then they would have become treacherous and slippery. Still, the climb for us old folk was painful on the leg muscles.

When we finally reached the top and walked across the bridge that led to the castle, my wife and I were rather out of breath. On the other hand, Daniella was frisking around like a newborn lamb as she had become excited for some unknown reason. She got out the book that she had brought along and followed a pathway printed on one of the pages. We lost sight of the girl for five minutes and it was only after calling her several times did the girl's head pop out from under a bush, of all places.

"The book's right!" she announced. "The pathway does lead to another set of steps. They appear to lead over the cliff but to where they go from there that's only possible to find out if we were experienced cavers. The author believes that this pathway leads down to another part of the cave and this apparently was where the dragon lived and where Merlin practised his spells, rather than the other cave where people usually visit when it's low tide. That was just a story created to make people curious to buy the author's book. It probably is someone who works at the local council and who rakes in extra revenue off gullible people like us."

I had not really thought about it previously but maybe the girl was right and the local council had conjured up such rumours to fill their pockets. Walking through the ruins, one had to agree that it was in good condition despite the number of years the castle had stood there, being continually battered by the hostile weather from the Atlantic Ocean.

On looking at Rebecca, I could see that she was cold despite the fact that she was wearing her jacket. I was feeling a bit nippy too, so I put on mine as well. Although the sun was shining brightly where we were, there was a stiff breeze blowing along the coastline as we walked through the ruins on top of the cliffs. We were glad that we had brought along our jackets for extra warmth.

Daniella was skipping along some way ahead of us so I called her back. "Granny's feeling cold," I told the girl ruefully. "Do you mind if we go now? I promise before we leave that we'll come back, maybe without Granny as she does feel the cold more than I do."

Daniella surprised me by her reply. "Are you really cold because of me, Granny? I don't mind going now as this wind feels bitterly cold. Thank heavens you told me to wear my jacket even though I thought Granddad was being stupid at the time! I really appreciate you bringing me here so if you're ready to go then I am too and then you'll feel warmer back in the motor home."

"You're such a kind young girl," my wife said to her granddaughter as we made our way back across the bridge and down the steps to catch the next Land Rover heading to the top of the track. It was funny really, because as soon as we were walking on level ground again, we could feel the warm sun beating down on us and we had to remove our jackets.

We headed through the caravan park entrance and made our way to our motorhome, where we collapsed onto the comfy black leather sofa inside. We were tired after our trek and it had certainly been an experience, especially for Daniella. However, after a couple of minutes, the girl just bounced back up like a young spring chicken and went to put the kettle on and made us all a lovely pot of tea before bringing it over.

"Granny's right; you do have a heart of gold. One day, the right man will find it and love you forever, just like Granny and me!" I observed with a crafty grin.

My granddaughter turned a shade red before looking at me and saying, "You always seem to find the right words to make me cry or get embarrassed, Granddad. I don't quite know how you do it but I'll always love both of you. Now, would you like the sandwiches that we never ate as we were too cold?"

I had forgotten all about the sandwiches, the flask of coffee and the cold cans of coke. All the while, they had been in a bag that I had carried across my shoulder. However, I had completely forgotten all about them.

"The bag's on the side over there," I said to Daniela while pointing my finger at it.

She went to fetch it and handed us each a sandwich that we gobbled up hungrily. I looked at my watch; it was almost two o'clock and we had been in that biting cold for five hours. We could not understand where the time had gone to but as we ate the sandwiches and bit into the delicious pork pie, and sipped our lovely hot mugs of tea, we soon began to feel much stronger. However, Rebecca did not say much and I was worried about her as she was normally chatty and friendly.

"I'm still cold, darling and I'm sorry I'm ruining the holiday," she said. "Perhaps, if I go to bed now I'll feel better by the morning. Can you make our granddaughter something to eat tonight? Leave me out since I'm not hungry after eating those sandwiches. Goodnight, Daniella," my wife added as she bent over and kissed the girl before coming over to me and kissing me goodnight too.

I had never seen my wife like this before and it worried me to bits, as it did to our granddaughter.

"I feel so guilty taking Granny to that cold place," Daniella said. "I hope she feels better tomorrow as I don't wish her to become ill and we have to return home."

She then wished me goodnight and I turned to her and said, "Shall I bring some cheese and pickles on crusty buttered bread in around one hour?"

"That would be nice, Grandad, as I need to eat something. I don't wish to become ill as well. Anyway, what are you going to do after I go to bed?"

"I have my laptop with me so I'll carry on with my story but I'll put my alarm on for one hour's time to remind me to make us some sandwiches," I said to her with a smile as she made her way to her bedroom blowing me a kiss before she left.

"She's a credit to her mother and father," I mumbled to myself as I unpacked my laptop and turned it on. I waited for it to boot up before selecting the right document and carried on with my writing.

"Grandad, is there any chance of you telling me what you're writing about!"

"Granddaughter, you know how I feel about giving away such things, ask Granny and she'll tell you what I say to her when she asks me, that's seldom these days as she knows what my answer will be, no, no, no!"

Daniella threw a cushion gently at me, giving me one big smile before she returned to the pages of the book she was reading.

Chapter 8
Reopen Your Eyes

Having finished eating her dinner, Tatiana was waiting for Daniella to wake up from the anaesthetic that she had been given. The hours raced by but at last, the girl began to stir. On opening her eyes, she saw Tatiana looking at her with tears in her eyes, rather unusual for a raptor to do. On seeing the girl trying to sit up, Tatiana helped her and propped her up on some pillows.

"My stomach burns like hell!" the girl cried. "What's wrong with me? And my legs feel strange. Where are we Tatiana? Are we still at the palace?"

The female raptor stared at the young girl and took hold of her hand, before saying, "You were about to die so King Midas pulled a royal carriage all the way to Blackstone. You're now under the care of King Rudolf and we are in his Glass Palace. I've been so worried over you and thought I had lost a friend. I had never had one before and now seeing you with your eyes wide open and smiling again, that's so special to me!"

"What about your children, Tatiana? Who's looking after them?" Daniella enquired worriedly.

The raptor smiled before saying, "My husband and his mother are looking after the children as I was ordered by the King of Blackstone to remain here until you want me to leave. King Midas agreed and he left last night while I stayed on watching over you."

"You're my favourite raptor!" Daniella remarked. "However, I'm rather hungry. Is there anything to eat and can I speak to a doctor?"

"Leave it to me, young lady, and I'll go to see what I can find for you. It might be a while because I don't know this place at all and it's huge!"

After the young female raptor left and closed the door behind her, she began to think about how to satisfy the girl's wish list. She cautiously knocked on a closed door and it opened to reveal a young handsome blue-eyed human. They looked each other in the eye for a few seconds before he stepped forward and said, "You're looking after the young female, aren't you? Is she awake now? My uncle King Rudolf told me she was seriously ill!"

"That's right, Sir, but excuse me, I don't know your name. I'm Tatiana," the female raptor said. "And you are?"

"Oh, sorry, that's my fault," the young human said to the raptor. "I'm Prince Leonardo Rudolf. Now that we've introduced ourselves, tell me about the girl. Is she as beautiful as my uncle told me?"

"Yes, Leonardo. Daniella is very beautiful," the raptor replied. "I thought she was going to die but your physicians managed to save her and now she is awake and asking for something to eat and drink, and also a doctor she can speak to."

"Of course, my dear," he said. "You go and tell her that I'll arrange for everything she asked for. Perhaps, I may come alone and see just how attractive she really is!"

The young raptor returned to the girl who was now sitting up properly in bed rather than propped up on pillows. The moment Tatiana appeared and walked over to the girl's bed and sat down, Daniella began bombarding her with questions.

"Did you find anybody? Are they bringing me some food and drink and the doctor?"

"Yes, Daniella, I found a nice young boy, probably about your age, and very handsome who knew all about you and your injuries as he's the King's nephew. He wishes to see you himself and promised to bring you food and something to drink and find you a doctor to speak to."

The girl took hold of the raptor's frills and pulled at them gently, before saying, "You're such a good friend, Tatiana. I won't ever want you to leave ever even though one day you'll have to go back to your family as it's not fair keeping you here."

There was a loud knock on the door. Tatiana went to open it and in walked the young man. On seeing the handsome looking male, Daniella hid under the sheets.

"This is Leonardo," the raptor whispered to the girl. "His uncle's King Rudolf. Come on, show yourself and don't be shy."

The young girl pulled the sheets off her head as the young man said, "Good morning, you're truly gorgeous just as my uncle said! Anyway, take this food that I've brought you as I believe you're hungry and thirsty. I also found the physician who operated on you and he'll be along shortly. Do you mind if I come and see you again later. I'd like to get to know you a little better. Would you like that?"

"I don't know as it depends on Tatiana as she'll be looking after me mainly," Daniella replied as she tucked into her roasted pork, potatoes and gravy.

"Would you mind, Tatiana, if I came to visit occasionally?" Leonardo asked the raptor bravely.

"Of course not, I don't bite!" she replied. "If Daniella wishes you to, then who am I to stop you from coming to see her?"

The young man smiled at both Daniella and Tatiana before leaving and closing the door behind him.

The young raptor looked at the girl. “He’s besotted over you and would do anything you ask him to do! Can’t you see that the boy has fallen in love with you?”

“Don’t be ridiculous, Tatiana. I don’t even know the boy so how could he have fallen in love with me and anyway what’s love? I’ve never experienced such a thing as love before.”

“You naïve young girl! How old did you say you are?” Tatiana asked the young female.

“Seventeen and I’ve never had a boyfriend. Many boys wanted to court me but my father never let me go outside. So what is this they call love?”

“Well,” the young raptor said to the girl, “It’s when two people enjoy one another's company as my husband and I do. You then have a courtship that may last for several years and become engaged to one another before finally getting married and living with each other and having children.”

“I’m far too young to become engaged, married and to have a baby at seventeen! That’s ridiculous! I’m not going courting until I’m at least twenty-three.”

The girl’s mind was made up. She was determined she would enjoy life to the full. If she had suitors who wanted her as their wife then they would have to wait as she felt that she was far too young for courtship or marriage.

Tatiana smiled at the girl. She knew that this girl was determined so whether Leonardo won her love or not was something she had to find out. Soon afterwards, the doctor appeared without even knocking.

“You, young lady, are very lucky,” he said as he came over to the girl. “We kept you alive by the skin of our teeth. If King Midas had got you to us any later, we’d have been attending your funeral! Now let me explain what we did. You had gaping holes from that animal’s attack in part of your breast, stomach and legs. These we had to replace with new flesh and skin. We sealed the wounds but we must now let nature take its course. You'll need to remain in bed for three months as the tissue and skin has to begin to grow again. Until it does, you're prone to infection and if you get that, then you probably won't survive. However, it's not all doom and gloom, young lady, as with the weather being so beautiful at the moment, your young nurse here can take you out in a wheelchair every now and then, although it will have to be fitted with a glass dome. You'll be able to see the beautiful garden at least even though you're not allowed to touch or smell the flowers."

Daniella looked at the doctor before saying, "I'm not used to staying in bed all the time. All I can say is that I'll try to abide by your rules but this is going to be very difficult for me as I love being outside with all the animals."

"Well, young lady, that's all I have to say," the doctor said. "King Rudolf will be visiting you later and then you can tell him of your misfortunes. Here's a book to help while away the time. However, I must leave now as I have other patients to visit."

The doctor smiled and left Daniella and Tatiana thinking hard over what he had said. Tatiana stared at the young girl; it was obvious to her that she was exceedingly sad by the thought of having to remain bedridden for so long.

At that moment, there was a sharp rap at the door and the young raptor went to open the door. The King walked in and took a seat by Daniella's side.

"The doctor told me that you have to remain in bed for three months," the King began. "I've been wracking my brains for a solution where you can convalesce somewhere else instead of here in your bedroom where you'll become exceedingly bored. I was thinking of sending you and Tatiana to my uncle's house since I believe that you don't have any real family. I suggested to my uncle that he could adopt you as his daughter and then you would become a princess and be able to marry any royal like myself or one of my nephews!"

"I don't want to get married until I'm at least twenty-three," the girl said to the King in desperation. "I'm not looking for love, engagements or babies at my age! I'm far too young!"

"Not in our kingdom, young lady," the King said, looking extremely annoyed by the girl's outburst. "Seventeen is the ideal age to start courting. Whether you like it or not those are the rules that I put down as the King. If I want to marry you then I'd court you for a number of years and would expect you to sleep in the royal chambers with me. Now I must go and start arrangements for you to go and live with my Uncle Silas and for you to learn how to become a princess."

Daniella did not even look at the King as he left, let alone bow to him.

Once he had closed the door behind him, she screamed out, "There's no way I'm going to get married to him, and for him to think I'd sleep with him before we marry, that's terrible! What do you think of him coming onto me and telling me that seventeen is a fine age to get married, Tatiana?"

Poor Tatiana thought having the King interested in her as his next wife was something wonderful as he was rich, handsome and lived in a wonderful glass palace. If she had the choice, she knew exactly what she would do and if that was to marry him, then she would agree straightaway.

"In this kingdom, you don't have much choice as women are secondary to men here," Tatiana said. "You'll have to give it a lot of consideration as the King can order you to marry him if he so wishes. And anyone who defies the King risks having their head chopped off!"

"He'd never do such a thing, would he, Tatiana?" Daniella asked hysterically as tears flowed down her rosy cheeks. "I'm little me, a seventeen-year-old virgin, untouched by any boy or man. I have no experience of life and what is expected of me in this kingdom. So far, I don't like it one bit and I want to leave as soon as I'm well again."

Tatiana stared at the girl. She understood that she was afraid and did not know where her values lay in the kingdom of Blackstone. If this King had fallen in love with her there was nothing she could do as he was one mighty ruler and she was just a girl who at this moment of time did not even have a home or friends, except for a young female raptor called Tatiana! Would she have the nerve to lead the girl away from this place? King Rudolf may decide to take it out on her family and that would be the last thing that she would want to happen.

The raptor said to Daniella, "You have to be careful if you're thinking of running away. Maybe Prince Leonardo will help you escape since he's your age. If you deserve anyone, then he's your man as he's gorgeous. However, if the King had thought about taking you himself, then why did he tell the boy about you?"

"I must make myself well again and pray I'm allowed to go outside. Then, when I'm out in the fresh air I can think more clearly and hatch out a plan," Daniella said to no one in particular.

"You're right, my dear," Tatiana said to her friend. "Until you're on the mend again, you can't do anything. Whatever they are deciding for your future, you're going to have to go along with it for the time being at least. Maybe you'll find Leonardo will support you as I know he loves you but whether he'd wish to upset his uncle, the King, we'll just have to find out."

"But how can you be so sure that Leonardo loves me?" Daniella sniffed.

"Now, let's see how we can start to take you outside," the raptor replied, completely ignoring Daniella's question. First, we need a wheelchair or buggy of some kind but it's this bubble or dome that they're on about that confuses me. Let me go and find someone who can assist us further and tell me how I can start to take you outside for walks every day."

"You're so caring and kind, Tatiana," the girl said as the raptor emitted a high-pitched shrill of joy. "If I'm ever forced to stay here, then you can join me with your husband and children and even the rest of your family."

The young female raptor smiled at the girl and left the room in order to find a doctor who could help her further. Meanwhile, Daniella started reading the book that the doctor had left for her. It was full of colourful pages and showed pictures of the world's oceans.

The girl did not quite understand why these humans in the Blackstone Kingdom were dressed in clothes from bygone ages somewhere in the twelfth century, but then had the most modern technological equipment to work with. This made her extremely curious and although she understood that this was a magical kingdom, she wondered why they could not spread a little magic, wave their wand around and she would be repaired like new again and not have to wait for three months while her body rejuvenated.

A knock at the door told her that someone was outside. "Come in!" she shouted out to the person outside. "I can't get out of bed!"

The door opened and in walked Leonardo. He was a fine-looking lad and probably no older than she was.

"Hello, Daniella, a little bird just told me that you would like to go outside. If you like, I can take you for a walk myself and give your nurse a little break. I promise not to bite!" he added mockingly.

Daniella surprised Leonardo by saying, "Aren't you afraid of your uncle, the King? He told me that he wants me as his wife and even wants me to sleep with him. I'm not used to such things and I told him that I'm only seventeen and don't wish to be married or have children at my age. That's the last thing I want from anyone, to be honest. Is that what you expect of me as well?"

"Of course I don't," Leonardo said. "I consider it shameful that my uncle wants you for himself at his age! What's he thinking of, taking a young naïve girl like you as his mistress, especially as you're without royal blood or title?"

"That's what I thought but he's planning to get his Uncle Silas to take me in for adoption and that way he can marry me as I would have become a princess and have a title," Daniella snivelled.

"There's no way he's going to marry you. He was the one who told me about you and that you'd make the perfect wife for me. However, when I found out that you were so young I told him that I'd have to court you for a few years first and besides, you held no title. Now he's thinking of having you adopted so he can marry you himself. What utter crap!" the young man snapped angrily. "I'll have to go and speak to him."

The young man left Daniella all in a tizzy as the last thing she wanted was to cause trouble in the family. When Tatiana came back, she saw that the girl looked worried over something so Daniella explained to the young dinosaur that Prince Leonardo was going to speak to the King about them both.

At this point of the story, I looked at my watch and realised that I had been writing for well over an hour. I had promised my granddaughter something to eat and drink so I popped into the kitchen and made some pieces of crusty buttered bread for both of us. I put several slices of cheddar cheese on top of them and added a piece of pork pie on each plate as I had become somewhat hungry. I then boiled some milk in a saucepan and made us both a nice mug of hot chocolate, which I was sure we would both enjoy.

I headed to Daniella's room and opened the door, expecting to find the girl asleep. However, she was engrossed watching a film and had her headphones on to listen.

When she saw me, Daniella removed her headphones before exclaiming, "That's exactly what I wanted, something to eat! I'm famished!"

I realised that I had been somewhat late with her supper so I apologised to her and said, "The problem is that I get carried away with my story and can't find a way to step away from the computer. This time, I forced myself away from the screen. Whether or not I go back and continue writing that depends, since I need to check on Granny to see how she is. Anyway, I'll be going now so I hope you enjoy your supper and hot chocolate."

"I think so and thanks a lot, Granddad," Daniella said to her grandfather. "Now, can you give me a little hint about what your story's about this time?"

"You know I never say as I think it's unlucky telling people in advance," I replied.

"Come on. Granddad, be a sport! I'm not just any person!" Daniella whined. "I happen to be your granddaughter who's interested in knowing what you're writing about."

I thought about what the girl had just said so after a few seconds, I said, "It's about you in a magical kingdom but that's all you're getting out of me, so goodnight."

"You're horrible, Granddad," the girl blurted out. "Why would you want to write about me? It makes no sense so I think you're telling me one big fib!"

I smiled at her and returned to my laptop. However, on the way, I checked on my wife. She looked very peaceful with her eyes closed so I left her there sleeping before continuing my book.

Chapter 9
The Confrontation

The young prince knocked at the door of the King's throne room and waited outside for an answer. It came in the form of his secretary who appeared at the door.

"Yes, Prince, what do you want of the King?" he asked as he let the young man inside.

"That's something between my uncle and me so please go and tell him I'm here and that I wish to speak to him in private," the Prince replied rather brusquely.

Prince Leonardo waited outside and heard the King raise his voice. "How dare he not tell you what his business is? However, I suppose you'd better send him in as this boy's just like his father, obstinate and is here just to cause me trouble," the King said as the secretary went back to the Prince and invited him in.

Since the secretary had also followed him inside, the Prince cried out, "I don't want him around to hear what I have to say to you, Uncle, as it's private."

The King looked at his nephew disappointed that he would not be speaking to him in front of his secretary. However, he dismissed his aid who left the room and closed the door behind him none too gently as King Rudolf glared at his nephew.

"Now, this had better be good as I never send my secretary out from any personal meetings," the King said in a more dulcet tone of voice. "However, for you, I'm prepared to make an exception on this occasion."

"Sire," the young prince said, not calling him Uncle, as he normally would have done. This made the King suspicious straight away and wondered why his nephew was looking so annoyed. "You told me to go and visit the young girl as you believed she was good for me and would make me a good wife. I now learn that you're not thinking like that at all and that you want her to become your mistress and then your wife, despite the fact that the girl's only seventeen!"

King Rudolf stroked his beard before glowering at his nephew and screaming, "How dare you demand this girl for yourself? When I set eyes on the girl, I immediately fell in love with her. The people are also expecting me to take a new bride after I've been grieving for five years. She's young and will bear me many strong sons. You're so upset as you believed I'd remain unmarried so that you could become the next in line to the throne but I'm still young and need a good young wife who's still pure and untouched and Daniella's the perfect choice."

The Prince found himself shaking as he too raised his voice. "Your Majesty, she has no title or royal blood so how can you think of marrying the girl?"

"That's up to me so mind your own business!" the King replied angrily. "I can make any rules I want as I'm the King so unless you wish to fight for her on the battlefield, it's best you shut up! I've arranged for my uncle to take her in and make her part of his family. She'll then have a royal title so what's the problem? I'll just be following the normal procedures that my ancestors laid down five hundred years ago but the girl will have to agree to come to my bed before we're married."

"How can you do such a thing to a young girl like that," the Prince snapped back. "If fighting you on the battlefield's the only option you give me, then pick the day and time and I'll be right there!"

On this last note, the young hot head of a prince stormed out of his uncle's room, almost knocking over the old secretary who had been eavesdropping outside the door. He headed back in the direction of Daniella's bedroom and burst in without so much as a rap at the door. He immediately apologised to the young girl and the raptor and poured out his story to them while they listened intently.

Daniella began to sob. "How can you fight him because of me, Leonardo? That's crazy and I don't want any part of it. I insist on being taken back to King Midas who'll return me back to my own world."

"It's far too late to do that now, my dear," the prince said calmly to the girl. "The King insists on you becoming his next wife so that you can bear him many strong sons. I can't let that happen as you're only a young girl of seventeen and don't know anything about life really."

"True but I can't bear seeing you killed in battle," Daniella sniffed. "If the King kills you, I'll simply refuse his hand in marriage and would rather die than sleep with him!"

"If the King wants to marry you, that's what will happen," Leonardo said slowly. "He's the king so he can do whatever he likes whenever he likes and however he likes and no one can stop him! He also believes that any female would die at the chance to become his lover and that it would be an honour to go to his bed at night before you become husband and wife."

"That's right, I will die!" Daniella replied sarcastically. "You must take me back to King Midas immediately as he understands me and will accept me. I'm sure he'll send me back to where I came from as he knows full well how to get there. I'm still very weak and it will take months for me to become my old self, strong and happy, but in the time it takes me to fully recover, the King will have killed you with his sword and made me a complete woman!"

"That's ridiculous, Daniella," the young prince said to the girl. "I don't know who I can trust anymore as the King insists on knowing everything. Even just having a conversation with him, he wanted his personal secretary in the room so that he could offer his ideas to the King. When I insisted I wanted to speak to him in private, he just went berserk and started screaming at me, saying that he had fallen in love with you and that he intends on marrying you. However, I've made up my mind to fight him the honourable way on the battlefield and thrust my sword into his chest as I'm not afraid of him like everyone else is!" the Prince boasted before taking one of the girl's tender hands and kissing it and then leaving the room.

All the while, Tatiana, the young raptor, had remained silent but now that the Prince was out of earshot, she said to the girl, "If we can find some transport, I'm ready to lay down my life for you and take you back to your world. I think I can remember the way through those secret passageways and, rather than the journey taking weeks, we can do it in just over a day. It's perilous, though, and there are dinosaurs who consider all creatures fair play!"

"Would you really lay down your life for me?" the girl asked the raptor incredulously. "What about your children?"

"My husband and his mother would bring them up," the raptor promptly replied. "However, I don't think we'll die. Of course, we'd need the help of the Prince before he goes into battle. One concern that comes to mind is what happens if we run into King Rasmus. It's him who controls the other kingdom of colourful dinosaurs like me and there are millions there just biding their time. King Rudolf of Blackstone has no idea of the numbers of gaudy dinosaurs left and he'd not be expecting a mass attack against his army. That may prove to be dangerous and you have to be ready to accept the fact that you may die from your wounds as they've not healed properly."

"I'll do whatever it takes to escape from this place," Daniella said. "I prefer living out the rest of my life with my evil mother despite knowing she'll make my life hell! However, there's nothing I can do about it and if I can persuade Leonardo not to seek revenge against his uncle then perhaps he could come with us as he would know how to defeat the King and his army."

"What you're saying, Daniella, is dangerous and crazy," Tatiana replied irritably. "If you reveal this plan to other humans, how do you know you can trust them?"

"I believe I can but I have to find a way of escaping, with or without your help, Tatiana," the girl replied candidly. "The problem is that my body is still very weak so I need someone's assistance."

At that moment, there was a sharp knock at the door. Tatiana went to see who it was and found a young dark-haired girl of around Daniella's age on the outside.

"May I come in?" she politely asked the raptor. "I'm Princess Lena."

"Yes, of course you may," was the curt reply.

Lena walked in and went over to the girl. "You're as beautiful as they say you are," she remarked. "I'm Lena, Leonardo's sister. He told me all about you and how he's fallen in love with you and is ready to fight for your honour on the battlefield. He's young and contemptuous and I know he'll be killed! I want you to stop him from doing such a foolish thing if you really love him!"

"Look, I'm young and don't wish to love anybody yet," Daniella put in. "I know your brother is handsome and strong but I'm far too young to even consider marriage. I want to remain unmarried until I am at least twenty-three. I've tried changing Leonardo's mind as I still care for him as a friend but your brother's too hard-headed so the only thing I can do is leave this kingdom. Then, hopefully, there will be no reason to fight over me if I'm not around anymore. Besides, I'm extremely weak and feeble and my wounds will not heal for another three months at least, so if I do leave then you'd have to help me escape. Would you be ready to risk your life to help me?"

Princess Lena looked at the girl and realised that she was kind and gentle. "If it means my brother will not have to fight, then I'm all for it and will assist you. However, your injuries are life threatening and I don't want to move you if you're going to collapse on me and die. Can't you try loving Leonardo instead? We're in a different kingdom and girls of seventeen do get married and have children here. My brother would never forgive me if he thought I helped bring about your death!"

"Look, I don't know what love is," Daniella said. "I'm seventeen and have led a very sheltered and difficult life. I don't belong here and I want to return to my time in the twenty-first century."

The Princess stared at the girl in surprise. "So how did you end up here in the twelfth century? You're also in a magical kingdom where spells are practised, where dragons breathe fire and where witches and warlocks abound."

"I don't know all about this stuff but what I do know is that I don't belong here in Blackstone and that the King is planning to force his uncle to adopt me as his daughter so that I can sleep in his chambers before marrying me! There's no way that I'll agree to such things, would you, Lena?"

"I'll have to if a rich prince comes and asks for my hand in marriage," Lena replied truthfully. "He'd court me for one or two years and then we'd get engaged, marry and have children. That's what's expected of girls our age but to sleep with him before you even become engaged is not something I'd agree with. However, if the King insists on you sleeping with him, then you'll have to do this without question as otherwise you'll face instant death by the hand of his sword."

"How can he do such a thing?" Daniella asked the Princess. "He's got no right to force me to do anything! I must find a way to make my escape."

"I know," Princess Lena said to the girl. "Leave this in my hands. I need some time to think as the journey to the other world will take a week or more and we'd have to travel slowly because of your injuries. I just might be able to bring my brother into this since I'm sure he'll be more than willing to help. However, you'll be breaking his heart if you leave. Why won't you love him like he does you?"

"I'm not ready for love yet," was Daniella's terse reply. "If I were, your brother would make one serious contender to win my heart!"

Princess Lena was talking to Daniella a great deal, so she said to her, "If you decide to stay, I'd be honoured if we could become friends. Anyways, I was forgetting all about food so let me go and fetch you something as I imagine you're starving!"

"Yes, I am in fact. That's very kind of you to offer to bring me some food and drink, that is, if you've got the time," Daniella said with a radiant smile.

"I was meant to ask you but we got delayed discussing everything else. Of course, I have the time as us girls only have lessons once or twice a week. And as royals, we never cook anything anyway even though that's what I've always wanted to do. Can you cook, Daniella?"

"Yes," the girl replied much to the Princess' surprise. "I can make almost anything but in our day and age we have many recipes and ingredients to choose from so cooking here would be extremely difficult for me although I'd be willing to give it a try."

"Would you teach me how to cook?" the Princess pleaded. "I could take you down to the kitchen in your wheelchair and then you wouldn't need to use a bubble like the doctors say you need."

"If only I could escape from my room for a few hours each day, then I'd be very willing to teach you how to cook but what about the kitchen staff? Wouldn't they get in our way?"

"My dear girl, the kitchen's enormous and we have three chefs and eighteen kitchen assistants. Anyhow, since I'm a princess they'll not stand in our way and will even offer to help us, I'm sure."

"Well, if Tatiana thinks I could be safe in the kitchen then I agree. What are your thoughts, Tatiana and would you also like to learn how to cook?"

"Let me go and find you something to eat as I've been rambling on and on and you need food and drink, as do you, Tatiana," the Princess said following which she rushed out of the room.

"Yes, I'd like to learn how to cook the human way but what will the cooks and assistants think of a raptor in their kitchen?" Tatiana said wistfully to her new friend.

"Well, if they don't like it, I'll simply refuse to go into their kitchen! I'm sure the Princess won't like it if I refuse to teach her."

"You're so kind, Daniella but why would you treat an animal as your equal? It makes no sense to me at all as you have your own life to think about."

The girl looked at Tatiana and smiled at her, before saying, "I love you as my sister since you've been there for me when no one else was, so whether you're an animal or not makes no difference to me. We can still be good friends."

Tatiana went over to the girl and kissed her on her nose with her long wet tongue before taking hold of one of the girl's hands in hers.

"And I too will treat you as my sister and will always be there for you," the raptor said as a tear trickled out of her right eye.

At this, Princess Lena appeared with a plate full of cooked meat, vegetables, biscuits, salad and fruit and a jug full of fruit juice.

"Now this should keep you going," she said. "I also thought I might eat with you if you don't mind."

"Of course not, Princess, sit down and enjoy yourself. It will make a nice change to have someone different to speak to," Daniella said while joining hands with both the Princess and Tatiana. "Now we're united as true friends and we will stick by each other through good and bad and will help one another at all times and love each other until the day we die!"

They drank a toast of fruit juice and after setting down their glasses, they began to eat the food that Princess Lena had brought with her.

"This meat's amazing!" the female raptor remarked after she had tasted the roasted boar. "I've never tasted meat cooked in this way before. I have eaten only vegetation, green leaves and shoots ever since our kingdom stopped eating meat after the prehistoric era ended."

Of course, Tatiana knew differently that her family was still strong in numbers and ready to fight, but she did not say anything.

After the three girls had eaten everything on their plates and had drunk all the fruit juice, the Princess said, "I can see why my brother's in love with you, Daniella. Although I have many friends throughout this land, you guys have become very special to me. Now I must leave as I have a boring mathematics lesson to attend. English is bad enough but I consider mathematics to be useless unless you intend to become a witch!"

Daniella and Tatiana laughed out loudly as Lena began gathering the dirty plates and glasses and placing them back onto the tray and leaving the room.

Daniella and Tatiana were left on their own once again so Daniella took hold of the book the doctor had given her and began to read while Tatiana closed her eyes and dozed off soon afterwards.

Chapter 10
Rebecca

That was it for tonight so I shut down the computer and went to bed. I looked at my wife; she was fast asleep and appeared peaceful and serene so I got into bed as quietly as possible and soon fell fast asleep.

It was the 21st of July 2017, a day that will haunt me for the rest of my life. I got up and pulled open the curtains and the sun's rays blinded me. On seeing my wife lying there, I went to kiss her only to find her body icy cold. With horror, I realised that Rebecca had passed away during the night without me noticing anything untoward. I had no idea what to say to young Daniella; she would be devastated and blame herself for what happened as she loved her granny to bits and this would be one unkind blow to her self-esteem.

I dressed quickly and went to find my granddaughter who was in her bedroom with her headphones on and a DVD playing.

"Granddad, what's wrong?" she remarked on seeing my distraught face. "You look so sad! Is it Granny? Is she ill?"

I sat down on the edge of the bed and felt tears rolling down my face. Daniella tried to hug me as best as she could in order to raise my spirits but I was beyond that.

"Granny died in her sleep during the night," I finally stammered between deep sobs of grief. "I don't know what to do as she meant everything to me and now she's gone!"

Daniella was flabbergasted and started to weep too. "Don't worry, Granddad," she said bravely. "I'm here to look after us both but what are we meant to do with Granny?"

The girl was being extremely heroic even though she was visibly upset. She was taking this in the most grownup way; perhaps, it would affect her on some other occasion but I was glad that she was being strong right now. I knew that this would hit her hard some time or other but was relieved by her support at this time of grief.

I phoned the local police to let them know what had happened and the female officer at the other end of the phone was extremely sympathetic and said that a police officer would come out and make a report. Fifteen minutes later, a police car pulled up to our motorhome with its siren blaring and two police officers got out and knocked on our door. I opened it and they came inside.

On seeing Daniella, one of them remarked, "And who is this lovely young lady?"

Daniella replied before I could. "I'm Daniella, my Granny and Grandpa brought me to Tintagel on holiday for two weeks but I doubt if we're staying now that Granny has chosen to move on."

The officers had to hold back the tears as Daniella's words had really hit home. The other officer decided it was best to change the subject.

"And where is your wife, Sir?" he asked me. I took both officers to our bedroom where they briefly checked the body. "We'll be going now and your wife's body will be collected a little later by the paramedics. However, it's essential that you don't go anywhere," he added.

"Yes, Officer, we're not going anywhere as I feel as though my world has fallen apart," I mumbled very much down in the dumps.

"Thanks a lot, Sir," the officer said. "We'll be going now but you needn't bother seeing us out."

I tried to raise some kind of smile but almost burst out crying instead. It was only the bravery of my granddaughter that held me back from breaking down. After the officers had left, I sat down at the table with my head in my hands.

"Would you like a nice cup of tea and a piece of toast, Granddad?" Daniella asked softly. "I don't really feel much like eating but I must force myself as that's what Granny would want me to do, I know she would!"

"That would be nice, darling," I murmured to my granddaughter with a weak smile.

Daniella went to the kettle and filled it up with water before switching it on. She put a teabag into both our mugs and waited for the water to boil. She then added the hot water, dipped the teabags around for a few seconds before removing them and adding a little milk and sugar.

"I hope it's how you like it, Granddad," the girl said as she handed me my mug of tea.

The girl had also put four slices of toast in the toaster. After they popped up, she buttered them and spread some marmalade onto them before putting two pieces onto a plate and giving it to me. She grinned awkwardly before trying to eat what was on her plate, but since there was a knock at the door, I left my plate on the table and went to see who it was. A medical team walked in with a stretcher and after a thorough examination of my wife's body, they walked out with the corpse on a stretcher covered over with a sheet.

"We'll keep her in storage until you tell us what you want to do, Sir," one of the team said extremely diplomatically, especially in front of a young girl who had just lost her grandmother.

I watched helplessly as Rebecca's lifeless body was placed gently into the ambulance before it was driven away to the morgue. Daniella sat down next to me and took hold of my hands to show me that she cared and wanted to comfort me in her own way. So far, the girl was taking it extremely well and this made it that little bit easier for me to accept my wife's sudden parting.

"What do you want to do now, darling? Do you want to go home or stay here for a bit and try to forget the horrible things that have happened over the past twenty-four hours?" I asked the girl while trying to keep a brave face.

"Would you mind if we stayed, Granddad? However, I thought you'd want to get back to bury Grandma?" she remarked.

"Grandma can wait, I'm sure she won't mind, especially if that's what will make you happy," I replied. "Now, let's go into town and buy a few things. We can take the mobile home or catch a bus, whichever you prefer, darling."

"Can we go by bus? I think I'd like that and then since you'd not be driving you can tell me all about your latest book," Daniella said before giving me the cutest of smiles.

"Okay, little one," I said to her. "We'll go by bus and I'll tell you about my book but you must promise me not to say a single word to a living soul as this will be the first time that I'd have ever released the details to anyone before the publisher gets hold of it."

As we waited for the bus, I began to tell her about my story. She could not quite comprehend that I had been telling her the truth after all when I had previously hinted to her that it was all about her. The bus trundled along and stopped to let us get on. The short trip took well over one hour as the bus wound through one country lane to another until we finally arrived at the market place where the bus terminus was located.

"It was Granny's idea to bring you into the story so you can thank her for doing that," I said to my granddaughter as we got off the bus.

We headed into the town centre where there were at least fifty shops selling all kinds of things. Every now and then, something would catch Daniella's eye, and she would stop at some shop window or other to peer in.

In one particular shop window, Daniella spotted a beautifully engraved wooden cross so she grasped hold of my hand and marched into the shop while pulling me along.

"My granny died today," she stressed to the woman behind the counter. "Can I have that beautiful cross in the window? I'd love to leave it on her grave when she's buried."

The shopkeeper had to stop herself from shedding a few tears while she saw me nodding at her to indicate that my granddaughter was speaking the truth and that her granny did die during the night. The woman took hold of Daniella's hand and together they walked to the shop window, from where she removed the large cross and handed it to the girl.

"I love you, Granny," she commented as she kissed the cross and placed it onto the counter.

After she had put it down, I read the price tag; it was thirty-three pounds. I thought this rather expensive but the woman had an ace up her sleeve.

"I can see you loved your granny dearly. She's now watching you from above so I'm going to give you the cross without charge. You're such a darling and I love to see such polite children, and there's far too few of them these days in society or the lack of society we have in this world," she said as she packed the cross into a box.

I tried to make her accept some kind of payment but the woman refused point-blank. She then handed the cross to Daniella before going over to her, giving her a grandmotherly cuddle and planting a big kiss on her forehead. We headed back out into the street and strolled around the other shops. The girl said nothing further about the present she had received, which I thought was a little odd at first, but then understood her reluctance to speak about it as maybe that was her way of grieving.

We were now feeling a bit peckish so since it was almost lunchtime anyway, we sat down in a Chinese restaurant and ordered some basic Chinese food. We ate practically in silence although we did finish everything on our plates and drank the cold coke that we had ordered with the meal. I stared into Daniella's eyes at that moment and could see that the girl was about to burst into tears but was probably holding back for my sake until she was alone in her room.

On the way out of the restaurant, I said, "When we get back we must ring your daddy and your aunts and uncles and tell them about Granny. They'll be very sad but we have to say something, I suppose."

"I know, Granddad," my granddaughter said in a really grownup voice. "Do you want me to tell Mommy and Daddy? I'm a big girl now and don't mind doing it."

"Of course you may, darling. Now, shall we go for a brisk stroll along the beach?"

Daniella's face lit up and she nodded her head vigorously as she had always loved the sea. We walked along the rocky shoreline until we reached the sandy beach. Daniella took off her sandals and I did likewise as we walked barefoot on the warm golden sand. At the far end of the beach, we came to a few stalls and an amusement arcade.

After putting on our sandals, I turned to Daniella and said, "I feel in the mood of a little dabble on these slot machines but I don't expect you to feel like wanting to play, do you?"

"Do you actually mean it, Granddad? I love those machines but Daddy always says no to me. He goes about moaning that they're all rigged and that no one wins, or at least that's what he says," she said with a little chuckle.

We headed into the amusement arcade where I changed a few pound coins to get two pence pieces. I handed the girl two piles while I took the same and started feeding them into different machines as we walked around. Daniella was happy for a while as it made her forget about our misfortunes. Her little face said it all as she was thrilled at being allowed to play at the machines. We lost more than we won but I was not bothered at losing a few pounds as, after all, my granddaughter had thoroughly enjoyed herself. When it was time for us to leave, the girl surprised me by jumping up and kissing me smartly on the lips.

"That's what Granny would have wanted you to do for me," she said. "I love you so much, Granddad. So where are we going tomorrow?"

"Before we even think about tomorrow, let's have an ice-cream," I suggested. "I'm taking a raspberry ripple. What about you?"

"I'll take a rum and raisin one, Granddad, if that's okay with you!" the girl replied.

We stopped at the nearest ice-cream parlour where we placed our orders. The ice-cream vendor placed two scoops each in two large cones, added some raspberry sauce, a Cadbury flake and some sprinkles and handed them to us. I paid the girl and we walked off to the bus stop while licking at our ice creams, which we were forced to eat quickly because of the heat.

The bus dropped us outside the holiday camp and we walked back to our mobile home. We found a big bouquet of flowers on the steps; they were from the owners of the campsite.

"Isn't that nice of them, Granddad?" my granddaughter said. "We'll have to go and thank them later. We also need some fresh milk and bread and then I'll make us some nice sandwiches for supper because that Chinese meal has filled me up completely. Now, let me put these flowers in a vase and add some water, and place it in your bedroom."

Daniella was being extremely brave, and even more she was showing to me under such a sad occasion, an extremely grown up side that made me feel so proud of her.

"That's what Granny would have wanted, darling," I mused. "She loved flowers and to see us enjoying them would have made her so happy!"

Daniella found a vase under the sink, filled it with water and unwrapped the lovely carnations, roses and daffodils before arranging them carefully in the vase and putting it down on the side table in our bedroom.

"Now, Granny can sleep in peace," she said to me after she came out of the bedroom.

The girl stared into my eyes and tears began rolling down her cheeks. I held out my arms and she came running to me and burst into tears.

"I'll miss Granny," she blubbered. "She doesn't deserve to be taken away from you. And Granny was younger than you, Granddad, wasn't she?'

"Yes, she was," I replied. "My wife would have been fifty-nine in three months' time and now I'll only have memories of her. However, I recall her telling me that we have to stay here for two weeks. What do you think about that, Daniella?"

"Thank you, Grandma," Daniella shouted at the sky. "We'll be home to bury you, we promise!" Turning to me, she continued, "Wouldn't Grandma have wanted you to carry on with your book tonight, Granddad? When it's finished you can put some nice words in memory of her from you and me. In addition, can I watch you writing? I promise I won't breathe a word!"

"It would be my pleasure to do so," I said without hesitation. "No one apart from you will ever be in the book, not even Granny, and that's the truth. And if you like, I'll begin to teach you how to write and whenever you come to visit I'll always take you inside my office and tell you what I'm writing about."

"Would you do that for me, Granddad? I've always wanted to become an accomplished author someday like you are and now that Granny's not around anymore, I'll come and visit you more often," my granddaughter said.

I decided there and then to make the necessary phone calls. One by one, I told each of the children of Rebecca's death. Of course, there were tears on the phone, which was to be expected but when it came down to ringing Daniella's father she turned to me with puppy's eyes.

"This is my turn, Granddad," she pleaded. "Although he's your son, he's also my Daddy so let me tell him.

It was pretty obvious that Daniella wanted the job so I handed over my mobile to her and she took it and rang her Daddy's number.

"Daddy, it's me," she began as soon as my son answered the phone. "Unfortunately, we have some bad news for you and Mommy. Granny died in her sleep last night here in Cornwall!"

"What are you doing there, Daniella?" my son replied in tears. "Come home right now and give me Granddad to speak to. What's he playing at giving you the task of telling me my mother's dead?"

"Granddad did nothing of the sort, Daddy," the girl replied rather taken aback. "He rang everyone himself and told them the sad news but I insisted that I wanted to tell you and Mommy myself. We're in Cornwall because Granny and Grandpa wanted to surprise me but we don't want to come home yet. Anyway, I'll hand you over to Granddad."

My granddaughter handed over the phone and I received a barrage of comments off my son that went in one ear and out the other.

When it got round to coming home immediately, I answered him in the most diplomatic way. "I suggested to your daughter that we could go home or stay so she can enjoy herself as I hear she's not been on a holiday for a while. Daniella has taken this in an extremely grownup manner and she wants to stay because she feels that's what your mother would have wanted."

"Dad, how can you think that a young girl would know what to do? Why don't you come back now? After all, you need to arrange for the funeral and to tell the relatives."

I knew that my son was speaking from his heart and that this had really affected him but there was only one possible reply.

"Look, son, Daniella and I have done our grieving and she was my rock as I was to her. Please don't force us to come home as we both need to stay at least for one week of the two weeks we had originally planned. Don't you think that this has become one big shock to us? We can bury your mother when we come home. She's lying somewhere safe now as we had to report this to the local police who took the body away. Please, son, don't be mad with me or your daughter," I added, as my son finally seemed to accept that we wished to remain in Cornwall.

"We haven't taken Daniella on holiday because we thought that she wouldn't enjoy going with her parents so she deserves a little break," my son said. "Our daughter has enough money to help you with the food bills. Just let us know when you decide to come home. I'm so sorry for your loss, Dad, and hand me over to my daughter to say goodbye."

Daniella snatched the phone out of my hands and chatted to her dad for well over half an hour before saying goodbye and handing me back the phone.

"Granddad, Daddy's told me that he'll start taking me on holiday every year from now on until I reach sixteen. Then he expects me to have my own friends and I probably won't want to go with them anymore. He was so different today, not the Daddy I've grown used to. He also said that when he takes me on holiday you're invited too!" Daniella exclaimed while hopping about from one foot to the other in excitement.

"If that's what you want, darling, of course I'll come but now that Granny has left me I'm going to start taking holidays abroad more often," I said to the thrilled girl. "That will give me the most amazing ideas for my stories. I've always stayed in the UK and my stories always travelled no further than southern Ireland because Granny never wanted to travel to faraway places. However, she'd now expect me to follow my dreams and write more stories about distant lands."

"That's great!" Daniella said. "So shall we eat the last of the pork pie, crusty bread, and pickled onions? I'm sure we still have enough cheese, and then I can also make us a nice milky hot chocolate!"

I nodded at my granddaughter and she went to prepare everything while I went to my laptop, powered it up, selected the relevant file and resumed writing.

Chapter 11
A New Beginning

"What sort of world do you come from, Daniella?" the young female raptor asked the girl. "You say that it's in the twenty-first century but how's that possible?"

The girl stared at her young friend and answered her in a way that she might just understand. "Look, you live in the twelfth century but this is a magical kingdom where spells and potions are made so sorcerers, witches and warlocks can make you believe that you're anywhere in the universe. Where I come from there is no witchcraft, well, none that I know of at least, and some of our ideas are different to yours. None of our animals speak and they don't have such beautiful colours as you have," she added before going quiet at this point.

"So do you miss being there?" Tatiana asked curiously, wondering why the girl would wish to end up in a magical kingdom.

"In some ways, I do miss home but in other ways, I'm happy to be taken away from my cruel life. I didn't deserve to be treated so badly; my family were strict and never really wanted a child but when I came along they were forced to look after me. Father divorced his first wife when I was still young. She was horrible and always pinched my skin to make me cry. He then remarried another woman who was extremely kind to me but unfortunately, she died of breast cancer. My dad didn't wish to be burdened with me so he ended up sending me to his former wife, my mother, who now has a second daughter by another man. I had to do everything in the house from the washing, ironing, cooking, cleaning and boiling pots of water over the open fire to making baths that I was not allowed to use so I seldom washed and began to smell."

Tatiana realised that this was making the girl sad, so she said to her, "Daniella, you don't need to tell me more. Life hasn't treated you fairly and that's obvious. Whether or not I'd want to return to such a life would be debatable. If you left here, would you go back to your evil mother?"

"I don't know, Tatiana, I really don't. My father wouldn't want to see me anyway and if he's still alive, I'll be the last person to be told as there would be a queue of relatives one mile long hoping to have been named in his will and inheritance!"

"Well, then, if that's the case, you must try to stick it out here and learn to accept who you are. At least, here you have two friends, Princess Lena and I. She seems pleasant enough and I know she'll look after you, as will I."

"I think she only wishes for me to marry her brother. I suspect that's the only reason why she wants to be my friend. I know that if anything happens to Leonardo, she'll no longer wish to be associated with me."

"I'm sure you're wrong," the raptor replied. "However, if you tell me that's how you feel about her then I believe you and will stand by any decision you make."

At that moment, I stopped writing since my granddaughter appeared with our late tea.

"Grab a chair from the kitchen and sit down next to me, Daniella," I said to the girl who did not need telling twice as she went to bring a chair and put it close to mine. "Now you'll just have to read it as I type but when we're back home you can start reading from the beginning on my laptop if you want to," I added before taking a mouthful of nice crusty bread with cheese on it.

"You're amazing, Granddad," she remarked after having read the first few paragraphs. "It feels as though I'm inside the story but where exactly am I?"

"Oh, yes," I said to her. "You're in the glass palace of King Rudolf in the Kingdom of Blackstone during the twelfth century. It's a kingdom of sorcery and witchcraft so everyone has to be cautious on how they speak to the King. You had several pieces of flesh and skin torn away from your stomach and legs by a sabre-toothed tiger and you almost died of your injuries. King Midas, a woolly rhinoceros, took you to the kingdom of Blackstone because he knew their magical potions could repair your body. At first, King Rudolf offered you to his nephew but after having seen you for himself, he decided he wanted you as his wife."

"Ghastly!" Daniella exclaimed with her mouth full of crusty bread and cheese.

The girl could not wait for me to continue with my story. This was obvious to me as she kept looking at my plate and staring into my mug to see if I had finished. Eventually, we both ate our last piece of sandwich and drained the last few drops of hot chocolate. As I flexed my fingers and continued to write, my granddaughter peered over my back.

There was a sudden knock at the door and the King entered. He stared at the young girl with his eyes searching for all her curves since all she was wearing was a negligee.

"Don't worry," the King remarked as the girl tried to cover herself up. "I've seen many girls before but not one as attractive as you. Your breasts are delicate and beautiful but now we must talk business."

The poor girl blushed with embarrassment since she had never been spoken to in this way before and wondered exactly what the King wanted from her.

"It's arranged," the King said in a lecherous way. "You leave this afternoon with me and your servant," he added while looking at the terrified young raptor. "Both of you will be taken to my uncle's home where you, Daniela, will be turned into a lady and be taught how to be a princess. Then, I'll be able to marry you as I truly love you!"

The King bowed to Daniella before leaving both the girl and the young raptor confused by what he had just said.

"How can you refuse him?" Tatiana, the raptor, asked incredulously after the King had closed the door. "He's very powerful and handsome and will expect you to follow his commands. What can you do but accept his terms?"

"Over my dead body! I'll refuse him and keep my legs tightly closed, you just watch me!" Daniella replied tersely. "I'm not bothered whether he's the King or the court jester! If I wish to remain pure until I get married then so be it. He'll have to have me beheaded before I agree to sleep with him."

"He'll probably do that himself and slice your slender little neck from your body with his own sword," Tatiana remarked rather unkindly. "This kind of man always gets what he demands. To him you're just another female like we all are!"

"Well, he's going to have one big surprise for starters as I'll refuse to go to his bedchamber, until he does the right thing and marries me. I'm not a bicycle that he can try out before he buys it!" Daniella screamed.

"Granddad, I've heard many girls at school saying such things but I never thought you'd be putting things like this into your book. I think it's brilliant and makes it more lifelike. Would readers expect me to put love scenes into my books?"

"I haven't put love scenes in any of my books except for the occasional flirtation or sexual innuendo," I replied. "Anyway, let me carry on with my writing as the time is creeping on."

My granddaughter smiled and remained tight-lipped while I carried on with my story.

Tatiana laughed so much so, that she almost swallowed her tongue. She had the utmost respect for Daniella but she thought that she was being rather silly by refusing the King's advances.

"If the King insists we go with him to his uncle's and I to become your maid, we'll have to comply with his orders as otherwise he'll probably have me beheaded and eat me for dinner!" the raptor replied terrified.

"He'd never do that, would he?" Daniella gasped in horror at the thought of poor Tatiana refusing to serve her and the King losing his temper and murdering the raptor.

"I think he would, my future princess," Tatiana grunted ironically.

Daniella did not like the idea of becoming a princess but she did like the sound of the title. She knew that it was every little girl's dream to become a princess some day and she was about to be given that opportunity. A knock at the door told her that someone was outside. Tatiana went to open the door and Princess Lena walked in.

"Is it true, Daniella, that you leave today and that the King's taking you to live with his uncle?" Princess Lena queried with tears in her eyes. "My brother's utterly devastated and ate hardly anything and our father has become so angry with him that his son and heir to the throne wishes to fight the King on the battlefield over you. Our father has told him that if dies by the King's sword and dishonours the family name, he'll not be buried in the family vaults but in an unmarked grave. Tell me, why is the King acting in this way? Can't you stop him as it's you that my brother wishes to marry?"

"I don't know, Lena, and I don't want to marry anyone," Daniella insisted. "What I cannot understand is why your brother has stepped in the middle and is ready to lay down his life for me. That's the last thing I expected him to do. I don't wish to go and live with the King's uncle but I'm fast running out of time and ideas. Bring your brother to me and we can decide together what's to be done."

Princess Lena smiled at Daniella and Tatiana before rushing out of the room and slamming the door behind her. Five minutes later, she was back, this time with her brother, who sat down in a chair next to Daniella.

"Don't think of me as stupid," he began. "I love you from the bottom of my heart and can't bear the thought of you being with that pompous King and being forced into his bed. Now, I have a plan but we need you to follow it to a tee. It's going to be tricky but you'll be safe and the King won't know where you've gone."

"What do you mean?" Princess Lena asked her brother. How do we move Daniella? She's bedridden and unless you think we can make her disappear then there's no hope for her or you."

"That's where you're wrong, sister," Prince Leonardo said as he pulled on his long hair. "One of the chefs owes me a big favour and he happens to be a master magician. I've spoken to him and he agrees that he can come here in the next five minutes, cast a spell over the girl and she will remain invisible for twenty-four hours. That will give us enough time before the King sends out a search party to look for her."

"The King will go ballistic and seek revenge on the whole royal court," Princess Lena moaned to her brother. "He'll question everyone and your chef will eventually break down and tell him all he knows."

"No, he won't do anything of the sort as the chef will do everything I order him to do," the Prince responded. "It was me who helped him when he desperately needed money. I also didn't charge him any interest and told him to pay me whenever he had it. He still owes me to this day but I'm not bothered as he's a good man and if he helps me hide Daniella and arranges for her disappearance then I won't be asking him to pay up."

There was a sharp knock at the door and the Prince moved quickly and opened it. The chef walked in and solemnly greeted everyone in the room.

"Now, my dear," the chef said to Daniella enthusiastically as he took out a small bottle from his pocket and tipped some of it into a silver thimble until it was full. "You won't feel a thing. You just have to drink this and it will appear you've vanished. In reality, you'll still be here of course but no one will be able to see you. Come on; now, drink up like a good girl."

"I won't take anything unless you give the same to my nurse," Daniella promptly replied while pointing at the raptor, Tatiana. "I can never leave her behind because the King will take it on her and probably eat her for supper!"

This had taken the chef by surprise as it did to the Prince and Princess but thankfully, the chef saw sense and agreed that the King might probably take his anger out onto the young female raptor. The chef filled a second thimble with potion and handed it to the young dinosaur.

Daniella counted, "One, two, three," and they both drank the liquid at the same time.

The potion took effect immediately and they instantly disappeared or so it seemed to the untrained eye. Of course, they had only been made invisible and someone could easily knock into them by mistake, so that was why they had to be moved at once. The chef then bowed low to the Prince and Princess and left the room in a hurry.

"I can't see you," Princess Lena remarked to the empty space on the bed where Daniella had been a few seconds previously. "I know you're still here so say something and my brother and I will hide you somewhere in the palace where the King will not bother looking."

"We're sitting down on the bed as before," Daniella said to her young friend. "Have we really vanished?"

"Yes, Daniella," Prince Leonardo replied. "Now, give me your hand while Tatiana gives my sister hers and then we'll know exactly where you are!"

Daniella took hold of Prince Leonardo's hand while Tatiana took hold of Princess Lena's. The Prince stepped forward and swept Daniella into his arms while the Princess led the startled raptor. The Prince touched a stone pillar in one of the walls and a door opened as if by magic to reveal a secret room, not so big however not so small.

"How did you know this was here?" Princess Lena asked her brother worriedly. "And what if Uncle Rudolf knows about it?"

"He doesn't as the plans have been lost for four hundred years. He knows nothing about this secret room or how to find it so Daniella and Tatiana will be safe in here until we're ready for them to leave. However, we can expect the King's wrath to be thrown on everyone throughout the palace when he discovers the girl and her nurse gone. He'll search the gardens high and low, and the forest too. He'll be livid when his men find no sign of the girl or the raptor. Now, Daniella, and Tatiana, follow me into this secret cavity as the King will be coming shortly to take you to his Uncle's."

While the young girl and the female raptor followed the Prince inside. Princess Lena did a quick spring clean, removing dust, several old spider webs, and nervously some newer ones as well in which she found some live specimens that she stowed safely in a jar. There were two comfortable chairs and a table inside the hidden room with the only form of light coming from the outer room.

"We're going now," the Prince said after the pair had seated themselves on the two chairs. "You'll hear the King ranting and raving when he can't find you. He'll be like a bear without his honey pot! Anyway, when he calls off the search, we'll bring some candles so that you can see around and some food and drink. And, remember, make no noise!"

Prince Leonardo closed the door to the secret room and Daniella and Tatiana were left in complete darkness. Some time later, they heard some muffled noises, the sound of furniture being moved around and the crash of cupboard doors being slammed shut apparently by one frustrated King.

"Where are you, my dear?" the King's barely audible voice came through to them. "It's time for us to go. We're not playing hide and seek! Come out and stop this silly game!"

Of course, the King received no answer and he became more and more agitated by the second.

"Now, girl, and you too, raptor, show yourselves as otherwise you'll be very sorry!" the King roared as he banged hard on the side of the wall, making the secret room shake from his anger.

He then screamed for his servants to come and search the room. Two of them appeared right away and started searching the whole room, even going as far as tearing the wallpaper down!

"Your Majesty, there is no one in here," one of the servants finally said. "They must have gone outside."

The King thought that maybe the girl had been taken out for a walk by the raptor so he told the servants to search the garden and report back to him. Meanwhile, he reluctantly returned to his throne room and sat waiting anxiously for his servants to come back with the girl and her nurse.

Thirty nail biting minutes later, the two servants were standing in front of the King trembling from head to foot.

"Your Majesty," they mumbled together. "We can't find either of them. What do you want us to do?"

King Rudolf was becoming more and more distraught by this situation. He had never felt this way before over a young girl so without warning, he withdrew his sword and struck out at the two servants across the base of their necks and watched their heads roll across the throne room of the palace floor.

"Come here, Maximas," the King bellowed to his head guard. "You stupid fool, I need you now!"

The King's head guard came in, saw the beheaded servants and decided not to say a word until spoken to; he did not want his head removed.

"I want you to gather an army and search the palace, the garden, the forest and everywhere and bring this girl and her raptor nurse to me," the King ordered his head guard. "You are to leave no stone unturned in your search but do no harm to the girl. Of course you can slay the raptor since she means nothing to me and then take her body to the head chef so that we can feast on her tonight! And I'll force the girl to gorge on her friend as well for her disobedience towards me!"

The head guard left the King stewing in his own temper.

"This doesn't look good," he grumbled to himself.

His uncle would be hugely disappointed by this and would want to know who was responsible. His immediate thoughts were that it might have something to do with his nephew but until the soldiers returned with the girl alive, he could not say anything.

Meanwhile, while the King was fuming on his throne, Daniella, and Tatiana were sitting in the pitch-black darkness of the secret chamber. They had heard the King's selection of colourful language, following which he left the outer room screaming at his staff. Daniella was certain that she wanted nothing to do with this man because he would be nothing but trouble for her and even more so he would make her life so miserable.

Some ten minutes later, the hidden door slid open and the hidden pair saw a burning candle and the silhouette of the Prince standing there. He came into the room, touched the stone on the other side of the wall and the door slid back.

"I've brought you a candle," the Prince began. "Unfortunately, it will only give you light for a few hours but it's better than nothing. My sister has also sent you some food and this jug of juice to drink. The King's furious and has beheaded two of his servants and is threatening all kinds of things to his soldiers if they don't find you. He's also prepared to behead your friend and plans on feeding her to you and forcing you to eat her flesh as a punishment for hiding from him!"

At this point, Daniella blew her top. "The beast!" she exclaimed. "There's no way I ever want to become close to him now even if I had wanted to before!"

The raptor remained silent while tears rolled down her cheeks. "What can I do?" she sobbed uncontrollably. "The soldiers will be searching for me and I'll never get to see my children and husband again!"

The Prince took hold of the young dinosaur's arm and said, "I promise that you'll be returned safely to your kingdom and family. The soldiers are searching the palace room by room so I must be going now as otherwise I'll be putting your lives in danger. I hope you enjoy the food my sister sent. You can expect me to come along with my sister after midnight in around twelve hours from now. To make sure it's me and not one of the soldiers, I'll knock five times before opening the secret door," he concluded as he left the two females on their own once again, but this time at least with a burning candle.

"Don't be scared, Tatiana," the girl said as she hugged her friend tightly. "I won't let anyone harm you and we'll be safe on our journey outside of Blackstone early tomorrow morning."

The girl prayed that the Prince would come through and get them away safely but she had huge concerns that the King would be expecting him to be involved in some way or other over her disappearance.

"Daniella, you're a very special person who thinks of others, as does the Prince, and I think you two are meant for each other, " the young raptor said as she and the girl began tucking into the food they had been given. "He's a good man and is very kind-hearted. I'm happy to be here with you and will remain your friend for the rest of your life. If the Prince wishes to make you his wife don't refuse him as he loves you dearly. However, where would you live? The King would be seeking revenge on all three of you as well as me!"

"If I'm going to be marrying anyone then Prince Leonardo is certainly worth a second look," the girl said giggling.

From there onwards, they kept on eating in silence leaving half the food and the two thirds of the jug of juice for later when they might be hungry and thirsty again.

I stared at my granddaughter so I was still fixed on my writing.

"It's past eleven o'clock," I said to her gently. "This day has been sad for both of us in many ways so I'm stopping here and we'll carry on tomorrow. So what do you think of the story so far?"

Daniella stared at me and I could see that she had been crying but turning to me and taking hold of my hands, she surprised me by saying, "This story's just amazing, Granddad. It's so happy, yet so sad that it makes you cry. I know it's written for me and that makes me even more tearful. When we take Grandma home, can I stay with you for the second week? I want to read more of your lovely story and will take good care of you, make you dinner every day and do the cleaning and washing."

I shut the computer down and the girl kissed me goodnight after which she took the empty plates and mugs to the kitchen and washed them in the sink. I joined her soon afterwards and helped her dry them on a tea towel before putting them back in the cupboard.

"I'm going to miss seeing Granny again but I'll still be visiting you Granddad," Daniella remarked as she kissed me a second time before going to her room and closing the door behind her.

She had not noticed the tears in my eyes. Her words had really hit home; my wife was gone forever!

Chapter 12
Moving on

One week had flown by and my wife had been buried in the small cemetery of our local village parish where we had originally met so many years ago. Daniella had not stayed since my son had insisted that I needed time to myself without my granddaughter around me. She was livid with her father and mother and they had to drag her to the car. I desperately tried to change her parents' minds but they were adamant that she was going home with them as in their eyes we had stepped over the mark staying in Cornwall for a week longer than we should have done.

It was ten o'clock on one hot blistering morning in August as I was outside busying myself in the garden when the phone rang. I wondered who it was as most people called me on my mobile. I dropped my trowel and rake, and went inside the house to answer the phone.

"Hello, how can I help you?" I said using my standard opening phone phrase.

A girl's voice came on the line. "It's Daniella, your favourite granddaughter! I miss you so much, Granddad. I was livid that my parents didn't let me stay for another week. Anyway, how's Daniella doing? Has she escaped from the palace yet?'

"I've not continued the story," I replied rather crestfallen. "I've jangled the keys to my office around in my pocket several times thinking that it might give me the excuse to begin writing again but my mind remained blank. However, your call may just be the trigger to give me some inspiration. I'll ring you to let you know."

"Why would you suddenly stop writing, Granddad?" Daniella said feeling rather let down. "I'm worried about you there all on your own without Granny around. I wish we didn't live so far away but Daddy said it's because of his job in Portsmouth. Why don't you come and live with us? We have plenty of room and live deep in the countryside just how you like it but we also have the sea and a beach to walk on just a few miles away. I know it would give you plenty of ideas for your stories."

"I'll have to think of it as this house is special to me. I've lived here with Granny for almost thirty years and I feel it's become part of me. However, the sea does have its appeal but there's no way your father would agree to me living with you!"

"You're wrong, Granddad. It was actually his idea, not mine and Mommy agrees with him as well. She thinks that having you around would be a good influence over me and I would behave better."

"Okay, darling, let me give it some thought. However, what would I do with everything in the house? It's way too small to take me as well as my belongings!"

"Granddad, we moved into the countryside around two years ago and you've never visited our new house. It has its own self-contained annex on the side with two ensuite bedrooms, a combined living and dining room and it comes with its own office. Please think about it as you'll also be able to help me become a truly brilliant writer just like you are."

"Don't flatter me, please! I'm going to try to do some more writing although a new house in a completely different area might make me start writing properly again as this house holds too many memories of Granny that I find hard to let go. Now, darling, I'm putting the phone down and will try to write."

"That's good to hear, Granddad," Daniella said but I had already ended the call and gone to my office to try to continue my story.

"With the candle half-burned through, the two friends were whispering merrily away to each other. However, on hearing the sound of heavy boots of soldiers on the floor coming into the room, they went quiet. The armed men had made a thorough search of the palace but had found no sign of the missing girl or the female dinosaur.

After the soldiers had made another meticulous search of the room, Maxmas turned to his men and said, "That's the whole of the palace searched. I just can't imagine where this girl could have gone! We now have to concentrate on the garden and then the forest."

"Maybe the girl's disappeared into thin air!" one of the soldiers suggested.

"You might have something there," Maxmas said as he and his soldiers headed to the throne room. "Perhaps that young headstrong prince has hidden her in his room with a magic spell. I'll mention it to the King and he may call off the search," he added as he knocked at the door.

"State your business, Captain," the secretary said bluntly after opening the door. "The King's upset today and wants no interruptions!"

The Captain demanded to see the King so the secretary popped in to ask him and appeared a short while later.

"Come in," the secretary said tersely. "The King wishes to speak to you."

For some unknown reason the secretary left the King alone with his Captain. However, he watched through the keyhole on the other side of the door to see what was going to happen.

"You've found the girl and have removed the head of the raptor! Is that why you've come to disturb me?" the King spluttered as the Captain's legs began shaking.

"No, your Majesty," he stammered to the King. "We've not found the girl but we think she may have been hidden by magic."

"I beg your pardon, Captain! Have you gone raving mad or something? The longer you leave it, the further the girl will be out of my kingdom and I'll be able to do nothing about it! If that's what happens then you know the consequences, don't you?"

"Yes, your Majesty, we'll go into the gardens and start looking," the Captain responded hesitantly. "You don't need to worry. I'm sure we'll find her there."

"Yes, you will, Captain," the King snapped. "If you find nothing then don't bother reporting back to me; just start searching the forest."

"That is not a safe place to be after darkness falls," the Captain mumbled. "There are magical beasts in there and the men will refuse to step inside."

"Well, it's your call, Captain. If you return without the girl, you know exactly what will be waiting for you," the King said while absent-mindedly stroking the sword he was wearing at his side. "And how many men do you have at your disposal?"

"Around one hundred, your Majesty," the Captain replied as he bowed low to the King. "I'll be going now."

"One hundred!" the King shrieked. "I want one thousand men searching that forest! Do you understand what I'm saying, you snivelling worm?"

Yes, your Majesty, of course, your Highness," the Captain whimpered as he bowed once again and backed out of the room to be greeted by his men who were standing in the hallway.

"Can we finish now, Sir?" one of them piped up. "The men are hungry and their wives will wonder where they are."

The Captain looked his men up and down before screaming at them at the top of his voice. "You bundling fools! There's no food or drink for anyone! The King's insisting on bringing a further nine hundred men to join the search through the enchanted forest. If anyone doesn't wish to set foot inside, they're to report to the King and will probably receive the same punishment his servants got earlier this morning! Now, men, move it and make it sharp!"

The men shuffled forwards feeling grievously sick inside their stomachs as the Corporal led the way towards the garden holding a magical lamp. Darkness began to fall and the sun began to set as the army of men trod cautiously into the semi darkness not knowing exactly where they were. However, once they got close to the forest practically all of the soldiers began trembling from head to foot.

One by one, the men disappeared inside the forest, crying out in pain as prickly overhanging bushes pierced deeply into their legs and arms, and even through their uniforms. The men felt blood trickling from deep wounds made by the bushes as they searched in the darkness on their hands and knees. They were unable to see anything and found it impossible to walk as the undergrowth grew thicker the further they went inside the forest. The creepers tangled around the men and held them in a vice like grip as they struggled to push on.

The Corporal did his utmost to illuminate the forest with his magical lamp but it was useless. He heard his men cry out as the undergrowth swallowed them up like some fiendish creature that needed constant feeding. The air was full of terrified screams and shrieks as the carnivorous plants ate their way through the soldiers.

Suddenly, the yelling and howling subsided and all was quiet in the forest. Concerned by the sudden silence from his men, the Corporal took some other soldiers with him to see if they could locate any of the missing men. After shining his magic lantern into the darkness, all the Corporal found of the men were several dozen pairs of boots strewn across the forest floor. He was filled by sudden fright and wondered where his men had vanished. He became frantic, as did his fellow compatriots, who refused to go anywhere further and sat down in protest over the situation.

"Look, we don't have much choice," the Corporal said to his men as he tried to calm down the situation. "We either go forward or face being beheaded on our return for cowardice!" he screamed as the men grumbled to each other before getting to their feet and trundling forwards with the Corporal.

Suddenly, they heard shouting from behind. It was the Captain who was also carrying a magical lantern that shone brightly in front of him. He was leading another nine hundred soldiers, all armed and ready for action. He caught up with the Corporal leaving the soldiers following in his wake.

"Corporal Carlos, what are you playing at?" the Captain shouted rather out of breath. "You should have been well into the forest by now. What have you been doing?"

"We heard our men screaming as though something had got hold of them," the Corporal replied hesitantly. "There were at least thirty or forty of them as the others were still with me. On going to their aid, all we found of them were their boots. There was absolutely no trace of the men at all! Where would they have gone to, Sir?"

"How the hell would I know, you snivelling little worm!" the Captain replied, repeating the words said to him by the King. "Men don't just vanish into thin air! Did you find any blood or anything?"

"No, Sir, we couldn't really check as it was too dark and the men I had with me began to get distressed. I told them that if we failed to find the girl, we'd be facing certain death for sure."

"That's right, men, you heard the Corporal. I don't want any of you moaning about not liking the dark and wanting to go home. There's no option as the King will just behead any of you if you chicken out and run. Now, march!" the Captain screamed at the top of his voice.

Reluctantly, the soldiers moved on in trepidation dragging their feet as they did so. Gradually, the procession slowed down to a crawl and finally to a complete halt when they came across a cottage with its lights on and smoke coming out of the chimney.

"Now, men, I'll go and ask the owner if they've seen a young girl and a dinosaur," the Captain said as he told ten of his men to accompany him.

He knocked at the door of the lodge but there was no reply. He kept on banging until finally the door creaked open and an old and wrinkled bespectacled woman peered out.

"Yes, what's all this fuss about?" she asked, as she calmly looked the Captain up and down. "I wasn't expecting any visitors today. Do you have an appointment that I've forgotten?"

"Old woman, how dare you speak to the King's Captain in this way? Your Majesty will have you beheaded for your insolence!" the Captain shouted.

The old woman pulled on the hairs that were growing from her long and pointed chin, before saying, "So the King will cut off my head! Are you sure of that, young man? Perhaps, you'd better leave before I turn you all into little green frogs or worse!"

"Are you threatening me, you old hag?" the Captain screamed. "Men, take her prisoner! We'll drag her before the King and see what he says about this woman's cheek!"

Those were the wrong words to say, and the wrong decision to make as flames flew out of the chimney like a volcano, snaking its way until burning the Captain and his ten men to a crisp. The old woman then calmly shut the door and went back to stirring her old cauldron. Her night's work was finished or so she thought.

The Corporal had watched on in horror as his Captain and ten soldiers had been burnt to a cinder. He decided to take matters into his own hands so he ordered one hundred men to accompany him and arrest the woman. He went to the door and banged on it several times.

"Come out, you devil of a woman!" the Corporal screamed. "Show yourself and let me put you in shackles."

The door squeaked open and the old woman stood there waving her walking stick and chanting some strange words. She then held her wrinkled hand up and fire shot out from her stick burning the soldiers who collapsed to the ground right in front of her. The old hag scratched her nose with her long dirty fingernails and began chanting one of her more popular spells:

Fly from here and test my wit
I've not asked you here to sit
You will find I'm not so kind
In this darkness you'll walk blind
Turn these soldiers into brine
Let them feed just like wild swine
You'll never see the time of day
Your time is up and now you pay

A trail of sparks shot out from her fingertips and cascaded over the rest of the soldiers who were standing in line waiting for the return of the Corporal. Instantaneously, the men were all turned into grunting wild swine that fought and killed each other for supremacy before what remained of them ran away into the forest. As though nothing in particular had happened, the smug old witch went back into her house and sat down on a rickety rocking chair rocking back and forth.

"That will show you, my dear King," she purred to herself as she stroked the black cat that had hopped onto her lap. "How dare you threaten to chop off my head? If you try that again you'll be next!"

It was midnight at the palace and there was no sign of the Captain or of any of the King's soldiers. The King was desperate for answers so he stormed into the hallway and demanded that his second-in-command, Captain Aria, report to him immediately. It was his day off so he was none too happy to be called by the King. However, he had no choice but to rush to the throne room where he stood before his Majesty and bowed down to him.

"Where were you, you snivelling toad?" the King ranted.

The Captain had never been insulted in such a way by the King before and he wondered what this was all about.

"Today's my day off, your Majesty," he objected.

That was totally the wrong thing to say as the King glowered at the second-in-command while fiddling with the handle of his sword and making the Captain extremely nervous.

"How dare you answer me back?" the King screamed. "If I say you're on duty then you'd better be or do you want to upset me even further and end up losing your head?"

"Where's the first-in-command and how many soldiers are with him, your Majesty?" Captain Aria asked nervously as he began feeling his head to make sure it was still securely fastened to his neck.

"They took a thousand men into the forest and haven't reported back to me yet," the King barked. "In fact, I haven't even heard a single word from either one of them for the past six hours or more. You're to gather another one thousand soldiers and search the forest in order to find out where they've gone. They were on foot so in your case take horses with you. I'll expect an answer from you later on tonight! Do you hear me, Captain?"

"Yes, your Majesty," the Captain promptly replied. "I'll begin to assemble the men together and leave within the next hour."

Before the King could answer, the Captain had saluted and had quickly left the room. He headed in the direction of the stables since he first had to arrange for a thousand saddled horses to be made ready within the next half an hour. He looked at the time and noticed it was one o'clock in the morning so he banged on the stable hands' door and waited impatiently for someone to appear.

"What time do you think this is?" the eldest hand cried out after he had opened the door. "I've been shoeing horses all day so you'd better have a good reason to wake everyone up in the middle of the night!"

"Don't talk to me like that, you old fool," the Captain shouted back as he drew his sword menacingly. "The King's demanding you make one thousand horses available and ready to ride within the next half an hour!"

"How dare you speak to me like that, Captain," the charge hand screamed. "I'm in charge of the royal stables just in case you've forgotten!"

"I'm not bothered what you're in charge of," the Captain snarled as he whacked the old man over his head with the flat of his sword. "You'll be losing this if you don't get those horses ready and that's an order from the King."

The Captain then stormed off in the direction of the barracks where all the men were sleeping, leaving the stable manager in a panic to get everyone up in the house.

Once he reached the men's quarters, the Captain began screaming at the top of his voice. "Get ready you bunch of lazy bastards! We have a mission to carry out and we're leaving in the next half an hour!"

The men began moaning at each other while hastily putting on their uniforms. They slipped their boots on and tied up the laces, and reported to the Captain who was waiting for them outside.

One of the soldiers queried to his friend the orders they had just received, "Bloody cheek, we've been squarebashing all day, and now we had settled down to sleep, we have this bastard moaning at us Peter!" Peter stared at his friend crying out in a whisper as he was being pretty loud and pretentious.

"Bartholomew, careful with your words, the Captain's pretty mean today, so let's report to him outside!" Bartholomew never had the chance to answer his friend, as a heavy sword struck out from nowhere, removing his head as Peter watched it fall to the floor in horror.

"Do you feel the same soldier, as I'm sure I can repeat my actions on you!"

"No Sir, I'm just getting a few belongings together and then I'll join the others." Peter found himself talking to no one as the Captain had gone back outside to cause further mayhem with his men.

Chapter 13
A Ghostly Figure

"Where do we have to go, Sir?" Corporal Risk asked his Commanding Officer with bleary eyes.

The Captain shone his lantern into the Corporal's eyes making him blink. "Into the forest as we have to search for a missing army of soldiers that have disappeared!" he promptly replied.

Risk knew the dangers they would be facing venturing into that place after midnight. There were rumours that evil spirits roamed through that place turning themselves into wild beasts and monsters that devoured any living creature they came across.

"Now, men, listen carefully," the Captain said. "We're going into the forest to search for another platoon of soldiers like you. You're lucky as they went in on foot but I've arranged for us to be on horseback so follow me."

The Captain and his men headed in the direction of the royal stables where the stable hands were already saddling the horses. The Captain stared at the horses and counted less than two hundred so he marched towards the stable manager.

"Where are the other horses, man?" he screamed at him. "We need one thousand of those ruddy animals! Don't you understand plain English?"

"That's the total number we can give you at the moment," the stable manager calmly replied. "The other horses are running wild across the moors and we can't look for them in the dark as someone might break a leg or something!"

The Captain drew his sword and wielded it in front of the old man's nose. "This is what you deserve, you snivelling worm!" he yelled as he severed the poor man's head with a single blow across the neck. "Now you've seen what happens with subordination!" he snarled while addressing the stable hands. "If you don't want the same treatment, you'd better go and find me some more horses?"

The stable hands hurried away from the bloody scene that lay before them. They certainly did not want the same thing to happen to them so they grabbed several lassos and head collars, and went to search for more horses.

The Captain then turned to his men and said, "Now, men, two hundred of you are to mount up while the others are to keep up a fast pace in the rear. And I don't want anyone lagging behind as you'll be facing the edge of my sword!"

There was a great scramble as the men fought each other for the horses. None of them wished to walk through the forest at that unearthly hour.

"Stop squabbling, you idiots!" the Captain screamed from atop his horse. "Those on horseback follow me and Corporal, you lead the others on foot."

Corporal Risk was rather taken aback and did not like the sound of that at all. However, he knew he had no say in the matter so he resigned himself to the situation.

"Right, men, follow me. I don't want any broken legs or dead horses so be careful," the Captain ordered his mounted men as he trotted out of the stable yard into the garden before galloping across the open moorland towards the forest.

I yawned hard and decided to take a short break as it was two o'clock and I was getting hungry. I shut down my computer and strode off into the kitchen to prepare some lunch feeling somewhat satisfied as I had finally managed to continue my story.

When I reached the kitchen, I felt a cold chill. I had no idea where it had come from as the windows were closed and anyway it was a nice warm summer's day outside. Suddenly, an apparition materialised in front of me out of nowhere making the hairs at the back of my neck stand on end. I did not believe in ghosts or any kind of phenomenon, but there was no mistaking what I was seeing. The spirit glided across the room and sat down at the kitchen table.

"Hello, darling," the spirit said; it was my wife, Rebecca! She had returned from the grave. "I had to come back to you as I've not seen you writing lately and you seem to have lost your enthusiasm. I'm worried about you and thought you were not well. I heard your conversation with our granddaughter; she blames herself for me dying but my body was old and had already suffered greatly when I was diagnosed with severe back pain. I never told you about it but the doctor had only given me one year at most to live. I had some form of cancerous growth growing inside me but the day we went to the castle, I became cold and never recovered. It was for the best as now my pain has gone away forever. Now, darling, you must sell the house, and go and live with our granddaughter since she needs you desperately. Promise me that you'll start packing right now and ring Daniella and our son to tell them of your decision. I'll always be watching over you!"

At this, Rebecca faded away to nothing, leaving me sitting there shocked that my wife had come back to tell me that it was not anyone's fault that she had died. I dialled Daniella's number there and then since I knew she had a mobile of her own.

"I've just spoken to Granny!" I said in a feeble voice when my granddaughter came on the line. "She came to visit me, darling!"

Now, if I had said this to my son, he would have had me committed for sure to some asylum or other but my granddaughter was open-minded and was very much like me in many ways.

"What did she tell you, Granddad?" she asked casually. "Is she okay?"

I told my granddaughter all that my wife had told me and that she had insisted that I should go and live with them.

The moment I said this, Daniella shouted over to her father. "Daddy, Granddad wants to speak to you."

The line went silent for a few seconds until my son came on the line.

"Daniella told me you wanted me to sell up and stay with you," I began. "If the offer's still on the table, I'd love to come as it would give me a fresh start. I just want you to promise me one thing though. When I die will you bring me home to mother?"

My son went quiet for a moment, before saying, "Of course, Dad, don't worry about that. Now, do you want me to come over with a couple of my friends to help you pack?"

"That would be nice, Son, as I'm not so young anymore. Perhaps, you could also bring Daniella so that she can say her final goodbye to her granny. I need to visit her grave before I leave and she can come with me."

"I would think so as she's still on her summer break from school. I just hope you know what you're letting yourself in for as Daniella's an unruly child."

I said a quick goodbye to Daniella who I could tell was not happy at what her father had said about her. My son came back on the line to tell me that he would ring me after speaking to his friends to see when they were free. I then ended the call before he could say anything more as he had annoyed me greatly. I now understood what my wife was going on about when she had said that Daniella needed me.

I was now starving so I opened the freezer and found some frozen lamb chops, put them into the frying pan with some oil and added three sausages. I then peeled some spuds and tossed them into a saucepan of water on the stove before doing the same with half a tin of peas.

While I waited for the food to cook, I thought about my wife's spirit coming to visit me. The thought of going to live somewhere else scared me even though I knew I was doing the right thing going to live with my granddaughter and presumingly with my wife still looking over us.

The end result was good with the potatoes lovely and soft and the peas cooked just right. I removed the lamb chops and sausages from the frying pan, put everything on a plate and added a little butter to the meal as I had forgotten to make gravy. I then poured myself a lovely cold beer, sat down at the table and began to eat.

I soon cleared my plate but my stomach was telling me that it was still hungry. I ignored its demands and sat down in the lounge to read a three-day-old paper. I knew that I had to go shopping for some fresh milk, bread, butter and some meat and cheese as we had eaten almost everything on our vacation in Cornwall. I grabbed a lightweight jacket, shut the door behind me, got into the Range Rover and drove away.

It was four o'clock by the time I arrived at the supermarket. I parked the car and walked in taking a trolley with me. It felt strange as this was the first time I had been shopping for food without Rebecca.

A young lady helped me load the trolley with the bill coming to fifty-three pounds. I told myself that this was far too much for a single man but I had bought many edible extras like chocolate biscuits, Jaffa cakes, crisps, and cashew nuts that I had a great weakness for and of course not forgetting the Pork Farms pork pie, a jar of pickled onions and a chunk of cheddar cheese. I loaded everything into the Range Rover, returned the empty trolley and headed back.

On my arrival home, it was almost six o'clock. I opened the front door of the house taking several bags in with me. I then returned to fetch more bags until I had finally unloaded everything. I locked the car and went back inside the house to put everything away neatly into cupboards, fridge or freezer. Going back into my room and closing the door behind me, I sat down at my computer and continued my story.

The forest was dark and unwelcome despite the Captain flashing his lantern around. After some time, he caught sight of a huge pile of boots. This was all that was left of the soldiers so he dismounted and looked for clues. He found several scuffmarks and blood on the ground so it was pretty obvious that something or someone had taken the men. Several soldiers on horseback then joined the Captain. They tethered their horses around the base of the surrounding trees when they heard a sudden rustling sound and creepers began to descend from above, grabbed hold of several of the horses and began to pull them into the bushes nearby.

A loud slurping noise echoed through the forest like some blood curdling scream as the horses were eaten alive by the carnivorous plants. The soldiers looked on and petrified that they were going to be next on the plants' carte du jour while the Captain was lost for words.

"Ride, men, now, or run for it if you've got no horses," he finally spluttered. "This is not good and it's probably what's killed the others since these plants are flesh eaters. Let's get out of here!" the Captain shrieked as he cracked his whip and sent his horse forward.

The men followed their Commanding Officer into the darkness, not having a clue where they were heading. After some time, they came upon an old dilapidated cottage with its lights on inside and smoke drifting out of the chimney.

The Captain dismounted and rapped on the door several times only to receive no reply. He banged repeatedly on the wooden door, making the old house shake from the roof down to its foundations, but the door remained firmly shut.

"Who lives here?" he screamed in exasperation as his voice echoed throughout the forest. "Show yourself or you'll be sorry!"

The door finally creaked open a little and he could smell some kind of broth boiling. He walked in and his eyes focused on an elderly woman sitting in her chair. He realised at once that he had made a huge mistake since this was the notorious witch of the enchanted forest.

"I think you soldiers should learn some manners," the old hag said softly. "Your predecessor thought like you and you'll be joining him and his men. There's no need to worry as the process is quick and simple. You'll no longer be a captain but the swine you deserve to be but perhaps we'll wait for your men to appear first. Now, what is my stew missing? Oh, yes, a nice fat juicy duck!" the evil woman cackled.

"You can't touch a captain of the royal palace!" was all the Captain managed to blurt out before sparks flew out of the fireplace and landed on the Captain scorching his skin.

"Ouch, ouch, ouch, you filthy cow!" the Captain screamed.

Sparks continued to rain out of the fire engulfing the Captain who cried out with pain as his skin began melting in the heat. Meanwhile, the witch hooted and whooped to herself before casting another spell:

Now my captain bright as light
You come to me in the darkest night
No invite and with such rude remarks
I'm not turning you into a dog that barks
But into a duck that quacks big and fat
Whose flesh will feed my big black cat
Despite me being so small and frail

I'll change the weather to snow and hail

The Captain was instantly turned into a fat white duck that tried to fly. On seeing the duck, the witch's cat pounced on it and waited for the witch to take it from her. She did and cut the head off with a razor sharp knife before beginning to pluck out the feathers. Once cleaned, the witch cut the duck up, removed the insides and tossed it into the cauldron.

"Will you soldiers ever learn?" the old woman squealed. "I'm giving the others a little chance to escape the severe winter that has blown in," she hooted to herself.

Smoke and sparks of all the colours of the rainbow flew out of the chimney into the warm summery skies. The soldiers approached the house and saw the Captain's horse tethered outside. They were about to dismount when large black clouds appeared from nowhere and hailstones the size of tennis balls began pelting the men and their horses, sending most of them crashing to the ground and knocking them unconscious.

The soldiers who were still standing did their utmost to run away but a strong northerly wind began blowing across the forest, making them shiver with cold, and heavy snow began falling across the forest. Soon, the soldiers were unable to walk as the snow reached up to their waists and began to drift in the wind making it impossible to see more than a yard in front of them in those blizzard whiteout conditions.

Meanwhile, the Corporal had arrived at the edge of the forest with his foot soldiers. He shone his lantern into the darkness and he and fifty of his men attempted to enter the forest. However, the snow lay too deep, even in the lee of the trees, and the men were soon stuck, unable to move forwards or backwards in that freak summer storm.

Somehow, by sheer will power alone, the Corporal managed to plough on ahead of his men despite the ever-deepening snow. However, behind him, his men were being picked off one by one by the flesh eating plants that shot out their long tentacle-like creepers that held the men in a vice-like grip before dragging them into the bushes. The air was soon filled with the sound of crunching bones and screams as the plants ate the soldiers alive.

On hearing the screams, the Corporal stopped to listen. However, after a couple of minutes, all was quiet again so he trudged back through the blizzard-like conditions to see what had happened to his men. All he found were empty boots scattered all over the place in the snow. He called out to his men but there was no reply. His entire platoon of soldiers had vanished into thin air. He looked first one way and then the other but did not know which direction to take. He was scared but knew that if he returned empty-handed, he would face certain death for failing his King.

Meanwhile, I was hungry so, leaving my computer on standby, I went to the kitchen to make myself some buttered bread with thick slices of cheddar cheese and a piece of pork pie and put them onto a plate. I also made myself a hot chocolate to go with the snack since coffee at that time of night was not good for me. Returning to my office, I suddenly realised that I had forgotten the pickled onions so I went back to fetch some and came back and sat down to eat. I was enjoying the snack when unexpectedly Rebecca appeared once again and sat down on an adjacent chair. This time I had not felt the cold chill before she became visible.

"I overheard the conversation with our son, Dick" she began. "I was disappointed to learn that he thinks Daniella is a problematic child! She's nothing of the sort and has a heart of gold."

"Very true, my dear, she does," I replied truthfully.

"I want you to promise me you'll look after your granddaughter at all costs," Rebecca said as her apparition began glowing a shade of green. "Our son wishes to send her to boarding school to become a lady. That's fine with me but you must go and visit the girl as often as you can. It could be a long distance away so if it is, I don't want you driving the whole length of England.

Just catch a train or a taxi as we, or rather you, have plenty of money!"

"Alright, dear, I will. Anyway, I was going to carry on with my writing," I replied to Rebecca as I leant over and kissed where her lips would have been.

"I know, darling as I've been reading it from your mind. It's a beautiful story and I'm so glad you opened the door for our granddaughter to learn from you. You never change even when I'm dead so make sure mine are the only lips you kiss! Otherwise, I'll have to haunt you for the rest of your life!" my wife chortled following which she began to fade away slowly until she had left me completely.

"This can never come out into the open as people will begin to think of me as mad!" I murmured to myself as I continued my fairytale.

Chapter 14
King Rudolf

It was gone one o'clock before the Prince and his sister felt it was safe to go and see the girl. They tiptoed along the hallway, crept up the stairs and entered Daniella's room.

"Lena, we must be quiet as I don't know where the King is," the Prince whispered as he closed the door behind them. "All I know is that he's furious as he dispatched two separate groups of soldiers, each one thousand strong, and neither has returned. He sent them into the enchanted forest and ever since he did that, there have been horrific blizzards bringing snow and hail the size of tennis balls. The King believes this bad weather has been sent by sorcerers who wish to throw him off the throne."

"What do you think, Leonardo?" Princess Lena asked. "Could he be right that the magicians have taken the soldiers away?"

"I don't know," the Prince replied. "One person who could be behind the disappearance of the soldiers is the evil witch. She lives in the middle of the forest and if the men come across her, then who knows what she may have done to them!"

In these last few words, the Prince knocked on the wall five times and pressed his finger on the pillar. After the door slid open, he shone his lantern inside the room to reveal the two frightened females still sitting quietly in their chairs.

"What time is it?" Daniella immediately asked. "We seem to have been waiting here for ages!"

"I'm sorry but the King is frantically searching for you," the Prince promptly replied. "He's now lost two thousand soldiers after sending them into the enchanted forest. They went in but did not return and seem to have vanished off the face of the Earth. We have an even worse situation as they may have upset one of the evil spirits that roam the forest or even the wicked witch herself. It's also teeming with snow outside and the snowdrifts are getting higher by the minute, making it nigh on impossible to get you out safely!"

Daniella stared gravely at the Prince and his sister, and after a long pause, said, "Leonardo, how long will this weather last? We can't stay here forever!"

"Of course not, Daniella, but we weren't expecting such awful weather," the Prince replied anxiously. "I suspect it's the evil witch's fault."

"How could a witch change the beautiful sunshine to heavy snow? It makes no sense at all!" Daniella cried.

"The only way she could have carried out such a spell is by using the dead souls of the soldiers," the Prince sighed with resignation. "They must all be dead to bring about such a change in the weather!"

"How terrible if she's killed them all but why would she have carried out such a dreadful deed?" the girl whimpered.

"They must have done something so bad to upset the witch," the young raptor put in.

"You may have something there, Tatiana," the Prince said. "That may be the reason behind such a weather change but if this was caused by using the lost souls of the dead soldiers then this weather could be with us for many years to come unless we find a way of breaking the spell! Someone has to defeat the wicked witch and that's going to be one heck of a problem!"

Meanwhile, outside, the weather had become worse and every tree or plant was either dead or buried deep in the snow. The immediate future of Daniella and Tatiana stood in the balance.

"Leonardo, what do you think the King will do about this?" Daniella asked the Prince. "Does he know about the weather outside or is he just waiting for his soldiers to return?"

"I don't know Daniella but he's been in his room just staring at the wall saying nothing, not even to his secretary. He just seems to be locked up in his world of fantasy," Prince Leonardo said. "I can't go to the King but maybe my sister can and find out what he's thinking?"

"I can't go in there!" Princess Lena exclaimed. "The King's madly in love with Daniella and he might lash out at me in rage!"

"You have to, Lena," her brother said. "We need to know if it's safe to try to take Daniella and Tatiana out of this secret room. Otherwise, we'll be forced to leave them here and that's ridiculous, especially with the girl's injuries."

"Okay I'll go," Lena conceded. "However, if I don't come back then you'll know that the King has chopped off my head!"

"He'd never do that to his niece and if he did, father would kill him for sure, even though it's his brother!" the Prince said.

Princess Lena got ready to leave and her brother opened the secret door for her to slip out. The Princess then tiptoed across the landing and walked down the stairs until she stood outside the throne room.

She knocked at the door and a voice bellowed, "That had better be my Captain or one of the soldiers!"

Princess Lena opened the door nervously and walked inside where she found the King sitting down on his throne with his head in his hands. Looking up, he noticed that it was the Princess and he mellowed slightly.

"This is your entire brother's fault by not minding his own business!" the King snapped.

"In a way, your Majesty, but you should not have taken him on by agreeing to fight for the girl on the battlefield. We're family and meant to be united and not one against the other," the Princess said hesitantly.

"You're right, my dear," the King said to his niece as he stroked his beard thoughtfully. "However, I need a wife and Daniella's young enough to bear me many sons who will one day take over from me and be next in line to the throne."

"I know, your Majesty, but it was you who started this feud with my brother and it's you who needs to stop it. If this girl doesn't wish to be found then leave her and move on. She'll be the one who'll miss out since there are many young girls out there who would die for such an offer from their King. Remember, she's not from our world and she needs time to adjust herself."

"Princess, you speak wisely and perhaps I should behead my present secretary and appoint you in his place. Would you consider taking up the position if it becomes available?"

"Of course, Sire, I could never refuse such an offer but there's no need to behead him, is there? By the way, have you looked outside recently?"

"What do you mean, Princess? It's dark outside and tomorrow will be another beautiful day."

"Your Majesty, we're experiencing the worst ever snowstorms in living memory. The snow lies deep all over the kingdom and has killed or buried all the grass, trees and plants. If the men are trapped in this snow, they'll surely freeze to death!"

"Why has no one bothered to tell me this? And why this sudden change in the weather? We're supposed to be in the height of summer!"

"I know, Sire, but rumours abound that the wicked witch of the enchanted forest has used the souls of the soldiers to cast a spell of devastation against you. She's probably turned the men into hideous monsters or killed them in some evil way. The only way to stop this severe weather is to stab the witch in the heart with a sword made from solid gold."

"I've always thought that she lived in peoples' imagination! You could be right that she does exist and perhaps, my Captain has upset her in some way. I'll have to gather a new army of my own and search the place in daylight. Go and tell the stable manager to prepare one thousand horses for the King."

This gave the Princess the chance she was hoping for so she bowed to the King and left for the stables. The stable manager was missing and the stable hands looked scared when the Princess appeared.

"I have an order from the King to saddle his horse together with a further one thousand horses," the Princess told the stable hands. "He's going to search the forest for his men. Now, where's the manager?"

"Princess, the manager's dead," one of the young stable hands meekly replied as he stepped forwards a couple of paces and bowed graciously. "The Captain beheaded him for disobedience and for not following his orders. However, this weather makes it too dangerous for us to find the horses as we let them run wild across the moors and they'll be looking for shelter."

The Princess understood the stable hands' position since they had no one to guide them. She also realised that the weather made their situation precarious but knew that if they refused to obey the King, they'd be facing his wrath. After fifteen minutes of gentle persuasion, the stable hands mounted up and moved off slowly in search of horses. The Princess then returned to the other three who were still waiting patiently behind the wall.

"I've been to see the King," Princess Lena began. "He hadn't even looked at the weather and had sent out an order that I took personally to the royal stables for one thousand horses to be saddled and ready to leave. I got him into believing that the witch of the enchanted forest may have turned his two thousand men into the vilest of creatures and may have used their souls to change the weather!"

"You may be right, Lena," her brother said. "I remember sorcerers teaching us at school that the evil in the forest can use dead souls to bring on the worst ever elements and if that happens to be weather then this could be here for years until she's killed by her own magic. The problem is that the weak and elderly will suffer first and more souls are lost making the curse even stronger. Anyway, the moment the King departs, we'll be moving Daniella and Tatiana to somewhere safer. Do you know what time he'll be leaving, Lena?"

"That's the problem," Lena replied. "One of the missing Captains decided to behead the stable manager and the other stable hands are just kids. They're scared stiff of having to go searching in this weather for horses that don't wish to be found. Until they return with at least fifty horses, it's too dangerous to leave this room. While I go and fetch some food for Daniella and Tatiana, go and speak to your friend, the Chef, and see what he thinks we can do."

"Good idea, Sis," the Prince said to his sister as she handed a fresh candle and a box of matches to Daniella.

The two siblings left the secret chamber together and made their separate ways through the palace.

"Don't worry, Tatiana," Daniella said to the raptor. "The Prince and his sister will find a way to help us escape. I'm sure of that and they won't let us down."

The young female raptor held Daniella's hand in hers and stared into the girl's eyes. She knew her only friend was right but wondered if she would ever see her family again. If the weather was as bad as they were saying, there was no way of getting away from the palace.

Prince Leonardo headed down to the kitchen where he found his friend Abel busy mixing something or other in a large bowl. Abel looked up when he noticed the Prince standing in front of him.

"Hello, Prince Leonardo, what can I do for you?" the Chef asked as several kitchen assistants were milling around him.

"I wish to speak to you in private, Chef Abel," the Prince said.

"I'll be available in one hour's time," the Chef replied. "Will that do? And do you want me to come to the same place as before?"

"That's fine, I'll see you a little later then," the Prince replied as he left the Chef showing his assistants a new way of mixing food.

The Prince and the Princess entered the room at the same time. She had brought along a hot stew with chicken and roasted boar, some lovely crusty bread and a jug of fruit juice. The Prince knocked five times before opening the secret wall that slid away and they walked inside.

"That smells wonderful, Lena!" Daniella commented to the Princess who handed her and the raptor a bowl of stew each and several pieces of crusty bread. "It tastes even better than it smells as it's full of tender meat and vegetables," Daniella added before tearing off a piece of bread, dipping it in the stew and popping it into her mouth.

Tatiana hoped the meat was not raptor but she was exceedingly hungry so she still took a few spoonfuls.

"It's not raptor meat," the Prince said after noticing Tatiana's reluctance. "It's wild boar and chicken which we breed for food."

Tatiana dipped into her stew with more enthusiasm and soon finished everything that was in her dish. The Princess poured some fruit juice into two cups and handed them to Daniella and Tatiana. They almost spilled their drink when they heard five loud raps at the door to their secret chamber. The Prince touched the pillar and the wall slid away to reveal the Chef.

"The weather's really bad outside but I think we can use it to our advantage," Chef Abel said to the group as the door slid back into place. "It's the perfect opportunity to take the girl and raptor out of the kingdom and for both the Prince and Princess to go with them. What do you think?"

"Why do we have this weather and when will it come to an end?" Prince Leonardo asked the Chef. "What's more, why do you suggest that my sister and I should go with Daniella and Tatiana? And where do you think of sending us?"

"This blizzard and frozen land will remain because the spell was cast by the wicked witch of the enchanted forest and will become stronger as more and more souls are lost through the weather. And if the King succeeds in putting together another army, then he too will be lost forever. The kingdom will then have no ruler and will remain under a blanket of snow and ice for all eternity until someone kills the witch with her own magic to restore the kingdom to its former glory," Chef Abel said as he scratched the end of his nose and poured himself a drink of fruit juice.

"Hmm, interesting," the Prince remarked to no one in particular.

"Prince, you're next in line to the throne and if something happens to you, your sister would become queen," the Chef continued. "That's why you two must leave this kingdom with Daniella and Tatiana and not tell anybody where you've gone. Only the four of you and I will know but it means you'll be starting a new life in the delightful kingdom of Zandar. While you're away, I promise to find ways and means of destroying the evil witch. You mustn't trust anyone as the King of Zandar will consider you a threat if he finds out who you are. In the meanwhile, you must find a way of putting together an army without the knowledge of King Rysis of Zandar."

"Can we say anything to our mother and father?" the Princess butted in apprehensively even though she knew what the answer would be.

"I'm sorry, Princess but no one, not even your own parents, can know about this," the Chef replied. "They may suffer serious consequences as, if the King dies, the witch will start wondering who is next in line to the throne. She'll do all she can to kill you two as well so that the kingdom will remain under a never-ending winter. You must remain here until the King has managed to leave with his men. The stable hands may need a little extra help in catching the horses; leave that to me as I have ways and means of persuading the animals to come rather than run wild. The sooner the King has his men together he'll leave the kingdom and will never be seen again. Then, we'll make our move! Can you wait for a few more days, Daniella and Tatiana?"

The two females nodded and smiled so the Chef bowed to the two royals and left the secret chamber. The Prince and Princess both had tears in their eyes as they realised that they would never see their mother and father again.

"This is my fault after all," Daniella whined. "I should never have come here in the first place and things would have remained the way they always were. I feel it should be me who should try to defeat the witch since I'm sure she won't be expecting a lone girl to visit her and to discover her weaknesses. I can pretend I have no one in the world and need a guardian to look after me. She probably has no heart and will want to feed me to her cat or to some horrific monster that she has conjured up but perhaps, she'll feel sorry for me. I can always offer to clean her house and cook for her and do the washing, and make her garden look tidy and beautiful."

"It's not your fault at all. It's the King's as it was he who threatened everyone with beheading. However, if you're not scared I'll come with you as your protector, even though I'll have to be invisible. Nothing will change my mind," the Prince insisted as Daniella was about to object. "There's no way I'll allow you to risk your life for this kingdom. Remember, you still have another three months before your leg mends so if we're to travel to a new kingdom in the meantime then so be it. We'll bide our time while you become stronger each day. I'll also get Chef Abel to teach you some basic spells in order to protect yourself against evil. We'll tell him of our decision when he returns."

It was Princess Lena's turn to take over. "You're such a brave young girl and if you succeed, then my brother must take you as his wife. Otherwise, I'll never speak to him again even if he becomes King! In any case, I'll always be there for you, Daniella and wish you all the luck in the world. With this weather, though, you must be strong so you can't go anywhere until you're well again. Hopefully, the Chef can make your injuries repair themselves quicker."

"You might have something there, Sis," Prince Leonardo said to his sister. "Perhaps, the Chef can speed up the healing process. Are you up to taking on the witch now rather than in three months' time, Daniella?" he asked the rather surprised girl.

"That's the least I can do for you and your sister but to win over the witch's friendship might take me a good few months!" she replied.

"You have a point, Daniella, and we'll have to draw her into a web of deceit," the Prince said. "If we leave it too long many people will suffer and die!"

"I realise that, Leonardo, so if Chef Abel can repair my body I'll agree to leave immediately," was the girl's honest reply.

"Thanks, Daniella, you're a dear," Prince Leonardo said. "If I become King the least I can do is make you a queen and my wife!"

"I could wish for no one better for my brother," Princess Lena remarked. "You're already like a sister to me and to become my future sister-in-law would be great!"

"I need to go down to the kitchen to speak to the Chef. I'll bring him back with me if it's good news," the Prince put in as he left the secret chamber.

The Prince made his way down to the kitchen only to find the Chef was not there. On looking at the time, he realised that he was probably in his apartment with his family so Leonardo made his way to the Chef's abode and knocked at the door. On seeing the Prince, the Chef stepped outside and closed the door behind him so that his wife could not hear their conversation.

"Yes, Prince, how can I be of service?" the Chef asked Leonardo diplomatically just in case someone was listening.

"We may have a change of plans," the Prince said in a low tone of voice. "Tell me, is it possible to make the girl's injuries repair themselves with a spell and make her strong again so she can walk and run?"

"I don't know; it may be possible but I've never tried such a spell before," the Chef replied frankly. "Why are you in such a hurry?"

"Daniella's willing to go and work for the witch and gain her trust while we find a spell to defeat and kill her," the Prince replied. "Since I'm next in line to the throne I insist on accompanying the girl in order to protect her. I also want you to teach her some basic magic that she could use against the witch if she begins to become suspicious in any way."

"Of course I'll teach her some spells but she must promise not to say a word to anyone as my power will be taken away from me if the Dark Lord finds out," the Chef said.

Chapter 15
Pulling Up Roots

It was the 7th of August of 2017. I had been busy over the past week or so getting ready to move. This was an historic day for me but one of sadness as I was moving from Warwickshire where I had grown up as a boy and lived all my life. I waited for my granddaughter and my son to arrive, together with his friends, who were driving down in a high-bodied Ford Transit van so that I could move some of the bulkier items to take with me. I had selected a fair few items and had already put them into cardboard boxes before sealing them and putting labels on the front listing the contents inside.

I had left the gate unlocked so my son could make his own way down the drive. A honk on the horn told me that they had arrived so I went outside to greet them. The moment my son parked, Daniella raced out of the car, rushed over to me and kissed me on the lips.

"I've missed you so much Granddad!" she exclaimed. "I've not been able to sleep much for the last two nights as I've been so excited to come to see you and Granny."

"Don't be silly, girl, now you'll upset Granddad talking about Granny in that way," my son said, scolding his young daughter who looked ready to burst into tears.

"Daniella doesn't mean anything by that, Son," I intervened as I hugged the girl. "I know she wants to come and show her respects to Granny in the churchyard."

"Yes, sorry, daughter, Daddy didn't mean to moan at you!" he said, ruffling the girl's hair with his fingers.

Another blow on the horn told us that my son's friends had arrived. They came down the driveway slowly and pulled up right by where we were standing.

"This is Dave Watson and Chris Burchfield, Dad," my son said as he introduced them to me. "They've offered to come and help you move. What time's the removal company coming and what have you arranged with them?"

I looked at my wristwatch and said to him, "In one hour's time, Son. That's what they said and I need to show you exactly what they have to take."

My son and his two friends, Dave and Chris, followed me inside while Daniella sat outside on the wall playing games on her mobile.

"These are all the boxes that I want going with me," I said after we had gone inside the house. "They're all labelled with a list of the contents inside. I've left all the furniture and ornaments for the removal company while I've packed Rebecca's clothes into so many boxes that I've lost count of the number! I never realised she had so many clothes as most of them she seldom wore!"

"You're amazing, Dad," my son Richard said as he grinned at me. "You've done so much on your own I'm really impressed. We've put some nice furniture in the apartment so you don't need to bring any at the moment. Dave, Chris, everything in Dad's bedroom and his office packed in boxes with the contents on the front are to go in the van. The rest all over the house either unpacked or boxed are to remain here for the removal company to put into storage. They'll pack anything loose as Dad's paid them extra to store everything else or bring it down to Portsmouth depending on what he decides to do with them. Anyway, what's going to happen to the house, Dad?"

I'm not sure," I replied truthfully. "I've left it in the hands of my close friend Bert. He was a good pal over the years and I've told him that if he manages to sell it, I'm ready to give him one percent of the selling price even if he goes and puts it with an estate agent. I know he and his wife Ellie will look after it and make sure that it doesn't become vandalised as they live next door and can keep a close eye on it."

"That's clever thinking, Dad," my son said. "Now you go and visit Mom's grave with Daniella while the boys and I carry on packing. We'll remember that everything you've put in your study and your bedroom goes in the Transit van."

I nodded at my son and went to look for Daniella who was still absorbed with her mobile phone. I called her and she jumped off the wall with great enthusiasm.

"Come on, darling, we're leaving your Dad and his friends to finish off while we go and visit Granny's grave," I said to the girl. "I hope you still want to!"

"Of course I do, Granddad. I want to see if Granny appears for me like she does for you!" she said in a low voice.

I smiled and opened the door of the Range Rover. We got in and I drove away while the two of us chatted merrily with each other.

"Granny's told me that she overheard your Dad saying that you're one big pain in the bum at home," I remarked to my granddaughter at one point. "Why does he feel like that?"

"Daddy can be such a beast sometimes. He picks on me for no particular reason and it makes me so upset," the girl complained. "I just couldn't believe it when he asked me to try to persuade you to come and live with us. I never dreamt he would as he thinks you're really obstinate at times!"

"Does he?" I retorted rather irritably. "I only wanted to stay here because my love and memories are in Warwickshire but Granny told me not to be stupid and go and look after you as you needed some support."

I could feel my granddaughter's eyes burning into me as I parked the car in the parking area by the church. We then took the shortcut through the broken wall and into the churchyard. Our plot was right under an old Chestnut tree and we were soon standing in front of Rebecca's grave. Looking around, I saw that we were on our own and I immediately felt my wife's spirit rise from her resting place until she materialised right in front of our eyes. I could tell by the look on Daniella's face that she either could see Granny or feel her presence. I was not sure which it was at first until my wife spoke to me and Daniella heard her voice too.

"I knew you were telling me the truth when you said Granny came back to you," my granddaughter whispered to me. "Now, I can see her for myself and can hear everything she says! Will she be coming home with us, Granddad?"

"Yes, darling," my wife Rebecca said to her granddaughter. "I'll stay until you want me to leave. I'll be there looking after the two people who need me the most, you and Granddad."

"That's fantastic if you can come with us but what happens if Daddy and Mommy see you? Will they send you away?" the girl asked worriedly.

"Let them try, darling," my wife said to the girl. "Granny and Grandpa will be looking after you from now on and if anyone gets in our way we'll have to do something about it."

"Like what, Granny?" our granddaughter said to the ghostly figure. "You wouldn't hurt Mommy and Daddy, would you?"

"Of course not," my wife immediately replied. "Maybe, I could scare them a little! That should be alright for me to do, wouldn't it, darling?"

"That's a brilliant idea, Granny," Daniella replied with a chuckle. "That would be exactly what they both deserve, a little fright!"

"She's got a heart of gold, doesn't she, Paul?" Rebecca remarked before fading away and returning from where she had come from.

"Now that we've seen Granny, we'd better go back to help your father and his friends," I said to my granddaughter.

"Why can't we go and do some shopping first? I'd much prefer doing that and it's still early," Daniella suggested while showing me her watch. "It's only eleven o'clock and we could go into town for one hour, can't we, Granddad?" she pleaded.

I stared at the girl; she always had the knack of tying me around her little finger just as Rebecca was able to do so I turned to her and said, "Alright, you win!" I declared. "We'll let the men carry on without us while we go shopping."

We jumped into the car and I started the engine and drove in the direction of Stratford-upon-Avon. We crossed the bridge, parked in the multi-storey car park and walked into the town centre.

It was funny going around the Charity Shops and buying several small items including a lovely gold ring set with a large single diamond. I put it on Daniella's finger and found it fitted perfectly so I paid three hundred and forty pounds for it.

"That's from Granny and me," I told the girl. "You deserve it, don't you think?"

"It's gorgeous, Granddad and you too, Granny," she whispered as there were many people milling around the shop and she did not want them to think that she was a raving lunatic.

We ended up in McDonald's and for a change found the fast food restaurant relatively empty. That was unusual especially since the town where Shakespeare lived was normally full of tourists. Today, it was quiet, just like the shops were. Although it made me happy the owners were probably a little disappointed with so fewer people turning out and buying stuff.

"Wait here and save our table while I go and order the food," I told my granddaughter. "What do you want to eat and drink?"

"I don't mind, Granddad," she replied. "Perhaps, we can share a box of chicken nuggets. I just love them with the sweet and sour sauce! A large bag of fries and a cold coke with plenty of ice will go down nicely too."

I smiled and left her sitting at the table while I joined the relatively small queue. I returned inside fifteen minutes, put the laden tray onto the table and sat down. When Daniella took her first chicken nugget and dipped it into the sweet and sour sauce, she smacked her lips and smiled at me before chewing and swallowing it down with a drink of coke.

"This is great, Granddad!" she exclaimed. "Mom and Dad never take me to McDonald's and I only go on the odd occasion with my pals. However, I don't have many friends as they sleep over at each other's and Mom and Dad don't think that's good for me. I end up falling out with them and staying on my own quite often. As you see, I don't receive that many phone calls."

"That's ridiculous, Daniella," I put in. "I always let your father have friends over to sleep; it's part of the growing up process so what's the harm in letting you do the same? I think I'll have a quiet word with your Dad when Carols not around and maybe Granny can find a chink in your mums armour of bringing her around to think differently."

"Would you really do so, Granddad? I have several new friends but the moment I tell them they're not allowed to sleep over they drop me like a hot potato and move onto some other girl!" she moaned.

"Life's hard, young lass," I said. "Let me see if being down in Portsmouth I can change your parents' minds and allow you a little freedom to have some friends staying over."

"Anyway, when are you going to continue with my adventure story, Granddad? I can't wait to read more. I have four more weeks without school and then Mommy and Daddy might be sending me miles away to some horrible boarding school!" the girl grumbled.

"I know, darling, but wherever you go, Granddad will come and visit you, I promise," I said as I could see tears welling in the girl's eyes.

I took hold of one of her hands and we headed in the direction of the car park. We got into the car and drove away as I had already paid and had the sticker on the windscreen to prove it.

By the time we got back we realised that we had been away for four hours, much longer than I had anticipated, but it was nice to see my son working with the removal company. His friends had already left in the van on their way to my new home. I walked in while Daniella sat outside on the wall once again.

"Sorry for taking so long," I said rather sheepishly to my son. "I decided to take Daniella into the town centre and we lost track of time. How's the removal company doing?"

"They've already left with one truck full and the other is almost half full," he replied. "And taking my daughter shopping was a good idea. Did you visit Mom?"

"Of course we did," I replied. "I bought a ring for Daniella and it really suits her so why don't you go outside and take a look?"

At first, I thought my son was not going but he surprised me when he went outside and walked over to the girl.

"Granddad said he bought you a ring," he began. "Let me have a look at it."

My granddaughter showed my son her ring on her finger with the stone dazzling in the sun.

"It's just beautiful, darling, and looks really expensive!" he exclaimed."

"It was a gift and it's gorgeous, isn't it?" the girl said, following which my son left his daughter's side and came back into the house.

"That ring's beautiful," he said to me. "God only knows how much it cost you! She'll only lose it, just you watch! Most of the things we buy her just disappear or she sells them."

At that moment, the manager of the removal company came over and said to us, "Right, we're finished so we'll be on our way. Are you leaving behind the carpets, curtains and light fittings and shades as most people do?"

"Of course we are. Why do you have people who take those things with them?" I asked curiously.

"Not only that but also the electrical fittings, plugs, bulbs, and in some cases, they've even stripped the house and taken the copper wiring with them!" the manager replied.

"Well, I'm not like that and I won't be charging extra for the carpets and curtains. Thanks for your help and here's twenty quid for you and the lads to have a drink with an old man," I said as I winked at him.

"Not so old, Sir, you look good for your age, so goodbye," he said as he left with the other men and got into the removal truck and drove away leaving my son and I staring at an empty house.

"Now, Son, don't be annoyed with me," I began as I finally managed to pluck up the courage to speak to him about his daughter. "I've got to know Daniella very well and I wish to throw something at you as she tells me that you're losing her friends because you won't let them sleep over. I always let your friends stay and Mom used to make them supper and breakfast. Do you remember fatty Gordon breaking into the fridge one night and eating Mom's trifle that she had made for the vicar?"

"Yes, I remember that," my son chortled. "But do you think I'm being too strict with her?" he asked bashfully, turning a shade of deep crimson. "I find her so difficult sometimes and lay the law down to her. You've made me understand how she feels and losing friends over our decision is the worst ever thing I could have done. With you being there for her, I'll have no problem if she wants the whole classroom to visit! Now I know why the girl's somewhat awkward to control and she'll find her Mom and Dad acting differently from now on. Anyway, while you take the keys around to the neighbour, I'll get to know my daughter a bit as she's now a young woman and I should have realised that."

My son went outside and sat on the wall with his daughter. As I went next door to take the keys, I left my son chatting away merrily to Daniella who seemed to be happy for once.

When I returned, my son was still talking away to his daughter and when he saw me, he got up and said, "Right we'll be going as it will take us a good few hours to get home. Daniella and I have become good pals and I've told her that she can have two or maybe three friends staying over from now on. And she can also remain at her present school, if I can persuade my wife, that is."

I felt my face glow and I knew that I had forced some sense into my son. He opened the Jaguar XK 200 and let me get into the front while Daniella climbed into the back and closed the door behind her. Strangely enough, I found her exceedingly quiet on the journey home.

When we stopped at a motorway service station, my son turned to the girl and said, "Right, Daniella, what food would you like? It's your choice for a change."

The young girl headed for the KFC fast-food restaurant as fast as her legs would carry her and my son ordered a family bucket.

"Is this enough for you?" he asked his daughter as he handed her a large Pepsi.

"Yes, thanks Dad, it's my favourite food," she replied as she bit into a piece of tender chicken.

We sat down and thoroughly enjoyed ourselves. My granddaughter was lost for words since she had never known her dad to be like this before. We made small talk as we ate the chicken pieces with chips and drank our drinks. My son and I had chosen to have a hot coffee rather than a cold soft drink.

"That was fantastic, Dad!" the girl exclaimed when we had reached the end of our meal. "Did you mean it when you said that I don't have to go to boarding school?"

"Yes, of course, love, if I can win your Mom over," he replied. "As long as you show your mother and me respect we'll treat you like a young lady. And if you don't feel that boarding school is for you, then you may continue at your present school as long as you get good grades so that you can continue at university when you're eighteen. That's all we ever expected of you, darling."

"Oh, Dad, you've made a sad girl so happy," she said, almost jumping up and down with joy. "But why the sudden change of heart? How can you persuade Mom? All her family went to a private boarding school up in the north of England and miles from anywhere!"

"If your mother insists on you attending boarding school then it's up to you to persuade her that you want to go to a local private school," I butted in. "I'm sure she'll agree. What do you think, Son?"

"I don't know, Dad," he replied. "My wife can be awkward at times and when it comes down to our daughter's education, she feels that the school she was sent to as a girl is perfect for Daniella. It will teach her all the rights and wrongs in life and make her become a young lady as well as an excellent scholar. Don't hold your breath, darling but we know how Mom can be when she's got a bee in her bonnet."

"Yes, I know that Dad, but perhaps Mom needs a little guidance," Daniella replied.

"True but how can you change a leopard into a pussy cat? That's how difficult it is to change Mom's decision! You're going to find it really tricky with or without my help," my son said to the girl.

"Maybe, but I'm sure I can change her mind," I said a bit too enthusiastically.

Daniella knew exactly what I meant and grinned at me. Perhaps, it also needed the gentle persuasion of her grandmother.

"I don't know, Dad. Anyway, it's time we hit the road as it's gone five and darkness will soon be upon us. I hope the boys have put everything neatly into your new place by the time we arrive home. They would have had daylight when they got back. We now have two more hours before we're home so I suggest you close your eyes and take a few hours' rest."

Chapter 16
My New Daughter-in-Law

We all jumped into the car and we were off. I took up my son's suggestion and decided to take a nap.

As I was about to doze off, I heard Rebecca whispering in my ear, "I'm here with you, darling. There's not much room in our son's car and I'm lying on the parcel shelf with my head pressed against the window! I'm glad our son has finally seen some sense and has grown closer to his daughter."

Thankfully, Rebecca remained perched where she was as otherwise, there would have been one big commotion if she climbed over everyone.

A couple of minutes later, Daniella leant over to me and whispered, "Granny's here isn't she?"

"How do you know, darling? She's visited my mind and is not here physically," I replied while my son was busy driving. "Can you actually feel her presence?"

"Yes, Granddad, I heard everything she said," the girl replied. "I can also see her lying on the parcel shelf. She tried to come across to you and trod on my leg but I felt nothing. It was as though I had been touched by a feather!"

"You, my dear, are getting too big for your boots," we both heard Rebecca remark. "With you not being afraid of spirits, we'll be the best of friends, I'm sure. Tell me, have your parents ever promised you a pet?"

"They promised me a dog if I passed all my exams," Daniella replied. "I did, and with flying colours too, but they went out and bought me a cat! I didn't want the creature at all as it would disappear early in the morning and return at around midnight bringing back either a bird, a rat or a mouse and drop it onto my carpet half-chewed. I hated the animal as I wanted a dog that I could train and take for walks on the beach."

"Poor child," Rebecca said to Daniella, blowing strongly into our son's ear.

"Who's got the window open?" my son shouted. "The car's air conditioned so whoever has it down needs to put it back up. Then, I'll feel much better."

"Son, are you going bonkers? Neither of us have the window down so what are you going on about?" I said intrepidly to my son.

"It went cold in here and it was blowing a gale in my ear," he remarked looking flustered as he drove.

"Oh, Dad, that must have been Gran!" Daniella piped up. "She was annoyed with you!"

"Don't be ridiculous, girl, Granny's dead so don't go on about her like that as otherwise, you'll wake up Granddad. We'll be home in half an hour or so as we're just joining the motorway to Portsmouth and then we come off at the next junction."

I pretended to be sleeping and Daniella squeezed my arm telling me as we came through deep countryside. When suddenly we turned into a private driveway and I opened my eyes as my son parked the car and turned off the engine.

"We're at your new home Dad?" my son said as I looked up and saw a lovely country house all lit up inside with an outside lamp to welcome us. As we got out of the car, my daughter-in-law, Carol, came to greet us.

"Hi, Dad, how was the journey?" she asked pleasantly. "I imagine you're starving so I've made a special meal to welcome you. Now, come in and see your new home. In the dark, it doesn't really look so elegant but wait until you see it tomorrow morning!"

I think Carol forgot that I too had lived deep in the countryside in a rather pleasant area and in a beautiful cottage but this at least was not far away from the sea and that was something completely new to me.

"It looks lovely from the outside, Carol, so I imagine it looks really beautiful in the daylight," I said. "What's my apartment like?"

I followed her into the house, finding it full of expensive antiques so it was obvious to me that they had spent a vast amount of money on lavish furnishings and antiquities, maybe even more than they spent on their daughter. I had only just arrived and certainly did not wish to spoil the occasion so I did not share any comments.

"Now, Dad, come and put your feet up," Carol said. "It's gone cold tonight and there's a roaring fire in the lounge so come inside and feel at home. You'll love it here."

Dick, my son, and Daniella joined me while his wife went to put the kettle on to make a cup of tea.

"There would be no mugs when she was around, only the best china!" I chuckled to myself.

"What's wrong with you, Granddad? Why are you laughing to yourself?" my granddaughter asked inquisitively.

"Nothing, darling," I quickly replied in case my son smelt a rat. "Now, where's that cat of yours?" I asked mysteriously since my son had not told me anything about the Persian cat. "I can smell something dead in here!"

"You can't, can you?" my son remarked anxiously. "Daniella, has that cat been in the lounge? Your mother will kill us if it has!"

"Granddad's only pulling your leg, Dad," Daniella said. "Don't take things so seriously all the time. You promised me that you were going to change so the first thing is not to be scared over Mom!"

"Who's scared over whom?" my daughter-in-law queried as she wheeled in a trolley laden with homemade scones, a jar of strawberry jam, a carton of fresh cream, a pot of tea, cups and saucers, a jug of milk and a bowl of sugar.

"We all are, dear!" my son said bravely to his wife who sent him daggers with her sparkling blue eyes as Carol poured the tea into the cups and handed them to each of us.

"Now who's for milk?" she asked, seemingly having forgotten her husband's remark.

She went round to everyone, pouring a little milk and adding sugar to whoever wanted it, and giving us each a spoon and a plate before serving us the scones, jam and clotted cream.

"Bon appétit!" she said to us all.

I smiled at her as she went to sit down with her cup of tea and a scone with a little cream. Carol did not have jam as the woman made up some excuse that she was on a diet of all things.

I bit into my scone and remarked to Carol, "This is truly delicious! Did you make them?"

"No, Dad, my friend, Cynthia made them and brought them round especially for you! You'll meet her in the next few days," Carol replied.

Daniella looked like she was about to be sick. "You must be joking, Mom, she's a silly old cow!"

"Daniella, I've told you before to mind your language," Carol snapped back. "It's Granddad's first night so make sure that he enjoys it as otherwise, you'll be in trouble, my girl!"

"Leave her alone, Carol," my son intervened. "I promised the girl that we'll no longer pressure her, and honestly that woman's exactly what Daniella called her! Cynthia is a meddling old fool in a young body. She's thirty but dresses more like some grumpy sixty-year-old! Her hair is always unkempt and I don't like her! Where you found her from God only knows! No one else encourages the woman throughout the whole village as she's a real busybody!"

"Richard!" his wife said tersely. "That's very unfair saying such things about my friends. I don't say anything about yours being drunk and out of work; that's why they had the day off to help Dad move. If you want to be nasty to my friends, then I can give as much as I can take!"

The two glared at each other across the room. I knew that their marriage was definitely suspect as Carol was a difficult woman to read and Rebecca had many words with her in the past. That's why I never went to visit except on odd occasions. I had always thought it was my son but it was now obvious to me that I had got things completely wrong. It was Carol who was to blame all this time. I hoped that my wife would get her good and proper but I was not sure if she would agree to what I wanted her to do.

"It's seven o'clock," my son said to us as he tried to calm things down. "Come, Dad, and I'll show you your new apartment. I hope you'll like it."

I got up and left Daniella watching a documentary. My son led me to the other side of the house and opened a door.

"This, here, is your new home from now on so follow me," he said as he switched on the lights showing a good-sized lounge with contemporary furniture and a rocking chair. Halfway into the room was another door that led into my new office. My son opened the door and inside was my computer, my boxes of files and my desk with a comfortable armed office chair placed in front of the window. Next to it, I noticed a bookcase filled with my encyclopaedias and other books.

"This is your new study, Dad," my son said. "I hope it's big enough for you."

"It's fantastic, Son! I never thought my apartment would be so grand and luxurious. You've furnished it pretty well and I think I'll be very happy here. And Mom will be for sure too!"

"You really miss Mom, don't you?" my son Dick remarked. "Will there be a time when you forget her and move on with your life?"

"I doubt it, Son, as she's watching us right now; you just have to believe me," I said.

"Don't get saying things like that when my wife's around as she'll send you to the funny farm!" my son said as he grinned at me.

"Yes, Son, I know she will but don't worry about me as your Mom will look after me," I said.

"We'd better go as I still need to show you the rest of the apartment," my son said as he led me upstairs where there were two fully furnished bedrooms, one of which was ensuite. "Dad, don't make things awkward with my wife by mentioning Mom. You know she's gone and you just have to accept that."

"I know, Son," I said, surrendering in case he thought of me as mad. Losing her just like that was one big shock to the system. I'm always talking to her as if she's still there; it's what keeps me sane!"

"I think we should book you into our local doctor," my son said worriedly. "He's very good and has been a friend of ours since Daniella was a baby. I'm sure he'll give you something to relax your mind."

"That's all I need, Son. I'm a writer so this experience is perfect for me as it stimulates my mind," I replied with a laugh.

"Okay, Dad, I'm not arguing with you. I'm just trying to help," he said as the sound of a gong told us that dinner was ready. "Come on, Dad, that's dinner being served. We can't be late as Carol has made something special for us."

I followed him to the dining room that was beautifully lit with candles and had a nice roaring fire going. Our food was already on plates and presented in a professional way.

"I thought I'd make 'Duck à l'Orange' with roasted vegetables to go with it," my daughter-in-law said as we entered the room.

"It looks beautiful, Carol," I said to her as I cut a piece of duck, added a forkful of roasted potato and greens and put it into my mouth. "This tastes delicious!" I added.

My daughter-in-law smiled at me but I noticed that she was hardly speaking to Daniella or to my son over the incident that had happened a good hour before.

"Can you open the wine, darling?" Carol finally asked her husband mischievously.

"Yes, of course, dear, something white I presume. How about a nice German medium sweet wine? Will that suit everyone?"

Carol and I nodded and my son, Richard, left the room to fetch a bottle.

"Where's Dick gone?" I asked Carol after I heard him going down some steps. "Do you have your own cellar?"

"Yes, we do, Dad, and Richard keeps all our wine down there because it stays lovely and cool without having to put it into a fridge," she replied with a smile as my son reappeared with a bottle of German white wine.

"This is a 1999 one and should have matured nicely by now," he said. "I've had it for ten years or so now."

I smiled at my son who had already opened the bottle downstairs. He poured some into a glass and handed it to me to taste. I took a sip, swished it around my mouth and swallowed the wine.

"This is excellent," I remarked. "And it's so cold too! Do you have your own walk-in refrigerator down there?"

We all laughed and it was nice to see even Carol trying to make an effort. Her husband went round filling all our glasses before pausing when he came to Daniella who wondered whether she would be given any to try.

As he walked past the girl, Carol turned to him and said, "Give her half a glass to see if she likes it."

I was shocked but my son coolly poured some wine into his daughter's glass. She sipped it carefully as this was the first time that her mother had given her permission to drink wine with them.

"I could get used to drinking this, Mom?" the girl said with a giggle.

"Maybe when you're somewhat older you'll be more responsible but it doesn't do any harm if you drink a little when we have guests," my son remarked.

We ate the rest of the meal chatting merrily to each other with all the animosity lifted. It was nice to see and maybe there was hope after all for my daughter-in-law and I would not be needing the assistance of my wife Rebecca.

"Are you working on a new book, Dad? Carol said inquiringly. "I know you lost Gran but do you think that here you'll have good vibes?"

"I think that's beautifully put," I promptly replied. "I started a new book just before we went on holiday with Daniella, and when Rebecca died I lost motivation. However, she's now guiding me to write so I'll soon finish it."

"That's nice, Dad, that you still have Mom in your heart," she replied as my son glared at me. "Sometimes, I talk to my mother who died when I was only eighteen so if I hear you speaking to yours I'll treat it as normal."

"What changed you, Mom?" Daniella interrupted. "Why have you suddenly become caring and loving? You're so different from before! What would you do if Granny paid us a visit? Would you be scared and run away or could you face it?"

"Perhaps, I'd be somewhat shocked," my daughter-in-law answered. "I now believe in the paranormal where the dead reach out to the living so we shouldn't be afraid of life after death."

"I can't believe you're saying that, darling," my son put in. "I had no idea you felt that way. It's as though Mom's already been talking to you!"

"Mom visited me while I was cooking," Carol said tentatively while we looked at her mesmerizingly. "She guided me how to prepare the duck so that's why it's so tender and delicious. I'm sorry about the way I was before and it needed Mom to tell me that so let's start afresh and become one big happy family. Daniella, I'm so tired so would you be an angel and load the dishwasher and switch it on before going to bed, please?"

"Yes, Mom, of course I will," her daughter replied before giving her mother an unusual smile.

"Now, everyone, I'm going up. I'll see you later Richard. Goodnight to you all," Carol said before going up to bed.

"What on earth has happened to her?" my son asked anxiously after his wife had gone upstairs.

He had never known his wife to support the paranormal before and to be okay with spirits and ghosts.

"Dad, if you tell me Mom is watching over you, then from now I'll believe you because to change my wife into the woman I've just seen is as though I'm married to a completely different woman!" he added.

"I told you Mom would look after everything," I replied candidly. "And to know she visited Carol and helped her cook the duck, then maybe she deserves a second chance. What do you think, granddaughter?"

"I'm stunned, Granddad! I can't believe she's the same mother as before. It's as though she's been turned into someone new! If Granny has done this, I'm impressed. Anyway, I must go and take these dirty plates to the kitchen and load the dishwasher as I promised Mom I would do," Daniella said following which she got up and cleared away the table.

"Now we're on an even keel," I remarked to my son after Daniella had left the room. "Let's see where we go from now on."

"I'm shocked, Dad, I really am," my son said to me. "I won't know how to handle it if Mom comes to visit. However, since she managed to change my wife I'm ready to believe in anything! Now, I'm off to bed as I need to speak to Carol before she goes to sleep," he added before heading to the kitchen to say goodnight to his daughter and going to bed.

I was left on my own so it was of no great surprise that my wife soon materialised in front of me and sat on the opposite side of the table.

"You're amazing, dear," I said to her. "I never believed that woman could change into what she is now. Is that permanent or will she go back to her old ways?"

"No, she won't," Rebecca replied as Daniella joined us after having finished her work in the kitchen. "This is the new Carol; she'll always remain like this until the day she dies."

"Granny, how I love you!" my granddaughter piped up. "You've made me realise that if you love someone like you did Granddad and me, then your spirit remains alive and free. Mommy has some of the worst ever friends who are all nosey and difficult and I know they'll persuade her to send me away to boarding school."

"That won't happen, dear," Rebecca said. "Your mother has not only changed but she's a much stronger person. From now on, she'll only want what you desire rather than the other way round as her selfish streak is gone. Now, I must go but I'll be keeping watch over you. Goodnight, my darlings," Rebecca finished off before fading away to nothing.

Chapter 17
A Surprise Vacation

That first night, I slept peacefully in my new bed and apartment. Daniella had told me that she would wake me up at seven so that I could carry on writing my story. However, I did not need a wakeup call as I was wearing my Rolex watch that had a built-in alarm set for half past six.

When I opened my eyes, I saw through the cracks in the curtains that it was lashing down with rain outside. It did not really matter to me with the weather being so dreadful since it gave me the perfect excuse to write.

I rose out of bed and went to the bathroom where I took a shower and dried myself all over before dressing into casual clothes. No one had shown me the rest of the house so I had no idea where my granddaughter's bedroom was. I went into my new study where I began piecing together my computer and leads, and switched it on. I was waiting for it to power up when there was a knock at the front door. I went to open it and to my surprise, I saw my daughter-in-law, Carol, standing there with a silly grin on her face.

"Good morning, Dad. Did you have a good night?" she enquired. "I've been thinking that we don't spoil our only child that often. Now, she has five weeks to go before she returns to school. I'm breaking with tradition and won't be sending her to boarding school unless she herself wants to go. I've also been speaking to Richard who agrees that we should book up and take you and her on holiday to Thailand. Do you think she would like that?"

"Absolutely, Carol, as I've never been further than southern Ireland," I replied enthusiastically. "Going to Thailand sounds fantastic but when would we be going?"

"One week from today," she said. "Do you want to be the one who tells our daughter? I think that's what Rebecca would want. We'll go business class so we can have some comfort during our flight."

Carol went to head out just as Daniella knocked at the door. Her mother opened it and let her in while beaming at her.

"Good morning," she told her daughter. "Granddad has some exciting news to tell you! By the way, may I see your new ring?"

Daniella held out her hand and showed her mother the glittering diamond and gold ring she was wearing on one of her fingers.

"Granny and Grandad chose it," she remarked. "Isn't it beautiful?"

"It is, darling and Granny told me all about it so don't look so worried. I'm not going to bite your head off or anything! Breakfast will be on the table in fifteen minutes so I'll see you two later," she said with a smile before closing the door behind her.

"I'll never get used to Mommy changing from a leopard to a pussy cat," Daniella said. "I couldn't have dreamt of anything better!"

"I think you'd better sit down then, my girl, as I have some even better news to tell you," I told the girl as we went into the lounge and she sat down in my comfortable rocking chair. "We're going on a twenty-one-day holiday next week to Thailand!"

You should have seen my granddaughter's jaw drop as she gazed into my eyes. "Are we going alone and are you treating me?" she asked, stunned.

"No, it's your parents' idea and they'll be taking us," I replied with a glint of overall triumph in my eyes. "Your mother said that they don't take you anywhere and with you being off school then this is the ideal opportunity. And also unless you want to go to boarding school she is ready to change family traditions and allow you to stay at your present school."

I looked into the girl's eyes and noticed that they were moist with emotion.

"Oh, Granddad, this is the most wonderful news I could ever have hoped for!" the girl enthused. "And to be going to Thailand is absolutely brilliant!"

It was my turn to exclaim. "Indeed! However, wait one minute while I switch the computer and power supply off as if there's a storm, it could damage the motherboard and hard drive." I went to my study and turned off everything before coming back and saying, "Now, darling, we have to go for breakfast as we don't want your mother moaning at us when she's just turned over a new leaf."

My granddaughter and I went into the main house, heading in the direction of the dining room where my son was waiting for us while his wife was busy in the kitchen.

"Daddy, do you really mean it that you and Mommy are taking Granddad and me to Thailand?" Daniella asked excitedly as she hugged my son.

"It was your Mom's idea. She thought you'd both like it and we feel that you both deserve something like that. It's been far too long since we went on any form of holiday together and this will hopefully make it up to you," my son said as Carol walked in wheeling the trolley with our breakfasts on it.

"Oh, Mom, this is fantastic news," Daniella said to her mother. "And Dad said it was all your idea. I love you so much and I'm so sorry I've been such an awkward cow!"

"No, you're not, darling," her mother said to the girl. "It needed Granny to come and visit me from her grave to make me realise how important you are to me! I hope she stays around as she brightens up the place. Do you think she'll be coming to Thailand with us, Dad?"

We all laughed as my daughter-in-law served out the food. It was a full English breakfast and included bacon, sausages, eggs, baked beans, fried bread, black pudding, crusty homemade bread, ketchup and brown sauce. Carol then went back to the kitchen and brought some mugs of tea, a jug of milk and a bowl of sugar.

"Rebecca told me you prefer your tea in a mug so I thought from now on we should all enjoy it that way and get used to it," Carol said. "One other thing, the weather isn't brilliant today so do you fancy going into Portsmouth to do a spot of shopping?"

"No, I'm fine as I need to work on my story," I said to her with a grin.

Daniella was about to say that she would also be staying when my son said, "You both have to come as we're buying you some new clothes for the trip. And Dad, don't you need some nice shorts and some short-sleeved shirts or perhaps a pair of sandals?"

This would be the first time that my son insisted on me going anywhere with him so I reluctantly agreed.

"Okay, you win," I said, "but I'll have to continue writing when I get home and perhaps have dinner in my room."

"Of course, Dad, we don't run a prison here, you know," my daughter-in-law chuckled.

Once finished, we went our separate ways to get ready. I had all my clothes in boxes that I still had to start putting away so I picked a warm long-sleeved shirt, a pullover and a pair of corduroy jeans out of one box and put them on before unpacking my new jacket and carrying it over my arm. I went downstairs and found everyone back in the lounge wearing comfortable casual clothing and waterproof jackets to keep dry.

We went outside and my son opened the car. We all got in and closed our doors behind us. He started the engine and pulled out of the driveway and we soon found ourselves in a lovely country lane that was already becoming flooded by the rainfall. With me sitting in the front and Carol and her daughter in the back, I wondered if my wife was still lying on the parcel shelf but said nothing as my son headed into Portsmouth city centre and parked the car.

Walking through a glass tunnel leading from the car park into one of the main department stores, we found ourselves standing in the middle of a shop selling coats of all things. Daniella turned up her nose at some of the designs although her mother found them quite delightful but she knew that from now on she would be expected to listen more to what her daughter wanted than what she did.

We walked down the stairs to the second floor where we found bras and knickers as well as swimsuits and sexy bikinis. Daniella took one look at the bikinis and stared longingly at them.

“Can I have this bikini in blue or black, Mom? I need a size 34, I think,” the girl said hopefully.

“What’s wrong with a swimsuit, girl? Aren’t they stunning enough for you?” her mother snapped as she temporarily returned to her old self. “We’re going to a foreign country and all the men will be ogling all over you!”

“Mom, you promised to let me do the things I wanted to and my breasts are large enough now for a bikini!” Daniella complained.

My son and I made a hasty retreat to the men’s underwear section on the same floor since we did not wish to get involved in an argument over swimsuits and breast sizes!

“Go on then, Daniella,” Carol said to her daughter as she calmed down. “If you have too many men staring at you on the beach then it’s your fault and you‘ll have to put up with it!”

"Okay, Mom, that's fine," the girl replied with a huff. "And which colours do you like, navy blue or black?"

"Why not brighter colours like red or yellow? Or take one black and one colourful bikini," her Mom suggested.

"Okay, Mom, that's a good idea," Daniella replied. "I'll take one in black and the other in red. Why don't you buy one so that we look like sisters?"

"Don't be silly, Daniella," was the curt reply. "Don't make me buy one for myself as I'll look stupid!"

"Come on, Mom, be young for once and make me happy!" Daniella pleaded.

Carol relented for probably the first time in her life and took the red and black bikini in size 34 for her daughter and in size 36 for herself. She then took them up to the counter nervously.

"Can I have these, please? And we need some underwear as well," she told the girl behind the counter.

Carol and Daniella went over to the underwear section where they selected three black sports bras, in white, black and red, with a dozen assorted coloured briefs and six pairs of tights, three black and three flesh-coloured. They went back to the counter and Carol paid for everything with her credit card.

Mother and daughter then went to find the men. They found us buying several pairs of underwear, some lightweight socks and swimming trunks. My son was paying for all of it and he smiled at his wife and daughter when he saw them weighed down with an assortment of bags.

"Is that all?" he asked mockingly.

"No, stupid!" Carol said to Richard with a grin. "We also need to buy Daniella some jeans, tops, summer dresses, skirts and shorts as we'll be going out to eat and maybe do some dancing too. We'll find them one floor down or on the ground floor or even in the basement. I don't know this store that well but this is our daughter's day."

Daniella smiled at her mother as she had just persuaded her to step out and show her flesh to the men in Thailand. We headed in the direction of the basement as my wife saw a sign saying 'Ladies Dress Wear'. We went down two escalators and found ourselves in the basement where there was every kind of fashionable clothing for men as well as for women. Making some excuse or other, I followed my son to find some shorts and short-sleeved shirts.

After mooching around for over an hour, we met up with the girls who were carrying at least five big bags between them while we had one bag each containing two shirts and two pairs of shorts each.

"Is that it, darling?" my son asked his wife.

"We need to buy some sandals," was her prompt reply.

Richard had forgotten that they needed some footwear for the beach so we headed back to the third floor. Splitting up, the girls headed one way while we went the other. Another hour passed by before we met in the middle carrying even more bags.

"I don't know about you but it's two o'clock," Carol remarked. "I had no idea we've been walking around the shops for over five hours! Daniella and I are hungry so where can we go for a bite, Richard?"

My son knew that Carol was not keen on fast food outlets so he suggested a Chinese meal.

However, Daniella had other ideas and said, "Why not Pizza Hut? You're always saying no to me but now it's my day!"

"That's a good idea," her Mom put in. "I've never been there before so let's give it a try," she added to her husband who was bowled over by his wife's sudden change of heart.

"Okay," he conceded. "The restaurants are on the top floor so shall we head in that direction?"

Everyone followed him up the escalators to the top floor. They walked into Pizza Hut and asked for a table for four so the girl took them over to an empty table at the back.

"The menu is on the table," the waitress began. "Now, what cold drink would you like? It's free refills while you're eating so sit down and I'll bring your drinks over and then you can tell me which pizza you'd like?"

After we ordered four large cokes, three original and one zero for Carol the girl went away to fill up the glasses.

Carol turned to her daughter and said, "It's your day so which pizza would you like?"

"Chicken with pineapple is the best thing on the menu," she replied. "Shall we have two large ones?"

"And can you eat one whole one by yourself?" her Dad asked curiously.

"Yes, Daddy, I'm so hungry I could eat a horse!" she replied.

"Well, in that case, let's take two different ones. Perhaps, we could also order a pepperoni with cheese topping."

"You win, Dad, that's my second choice so I'm okay with that. The girl's coming back with the drinks so you know what to order."

My son smiled at his daughter and gave the waitress our order. After she went away, we took a drink of coke; it was icy cold and tasted wonderful. We also noticed from the window that the rain had stopped and the sun was shining.

"I'm taking the bags to the car as we're only five minutes' walk away through the glass tunnel," my son said as he went to take several bags in his hands.

"You can't manage all those," Daniella said. "Here, let me help you while Mom and Granddad have a rest."

"That's nice of you, darling," Carol said to her daughter as she and her father grabbed the bags and headed in the direction of the car.

The pizzas were already on the table ten minutes later when Daniella and my son returned.

"That was quick," my son said. "I wasn't expecting the food to have arrived so quickly."

"Don't worry dear, it's piping hot as the girl has only just bought it," Carol said to her husband with a lovely smile, something that I had never seen before.

Like Carol, I had never tried Pizza Hut before, but to be honest, I found my pizza extremely delicious and Daniella's choice of chicken and pineapple was definitely to my liking. The pepperoni one, I did find a little spicy but I ate a couple of slices since my granddaughter loved it as well. Daniella had the job of refilling our glasses but she did not seem to mind at all.

We finally came to the end and my son went up and paid the bill, leaving a five-pound tip for the girl that would be shared between all the waiters and waitresses but that was the policy of the restaurant.

Getting up to leave, her mother turned to Daniella and said, "So did you enjoy your day out, darling?"

"Yes, of course I did but can we finish it with a night at the cinema?" my granddaughter enquired.

I looked at my son who looked at his wife who smiled and nodded her head.

"I'll agree if there's something decent on," Carol said. "Let's go and have a look."

I could not believe my ears! With everyone tired from trudging around the shops all day, we had agreed to take my granddaughter to the cinema. Carol led the way to the cinema to search for something suitable for us to watch.

"I don't know any of these films," Daniella remarked. "Let's go home as Granddad deserves a rest. Thanks so much for my day out. As a further treat, I'll be staying with Granddad tonight. Is that okay with you, Mom and Dad?"

My daughter-in-law and my son smiled and nodded their heads in unison. I grinned since I knew exactly what her little plan was; to watch me start writing again. She was my granddaughter so how could I say no to her when she was the main star of the story.

We walked the short journey to the car park and got into the car before closing the doors. My son made haste to the exit as he had already paid in advance so the barrier lifted and he drove away. The journey home took less than fifteen minutes because the roads were empty of traffic by this time.

When we arrived, we all carried a few bags each from the boot of the car, took them in and laid them down onto the two couches in the lounge. Everyone gathered his or her own bags together and took them into our rooms.

"What did you buy, dear?" Richard asked his wife Carol when they entered their bedroom.

He went to dig into one of her bags but she grabbed it off him and turned bright red in the process.

"No, I'm embarrassed as our daughter made us buy matching swimwear. She wants me to look like her big sister," Carol murmured.

"Come on, Dad and I bought trunks so why are you embarrassed over such a thing?" Richard replied.

"I'll put it on and you can see for yourself. Promise me that if I look stupid you tell me as I've never owned such a thing before," Carol replied as she took hold of the bag and disappeared into the ensuite bathroom.

Five minutes later, she came out wearing her red bikini. My son was gobsmacked to say the least since she looked truly stunning with her long slim legs, flat stomach and prominent breasts.

"Darling, all the men are going to be drooling over you on the beach," my son said with a hearty laugh. "I think you're truly gorgeous!"

"Do you honestly like it, darling?" his wife asked, no longer embarrassed. "But don't I look like a tart?"

"Of course you don't and if Daniella has the same one you'll look fantastic together and people will think you're definitely sisters!"

Meanwhile, I put my new clothes away in a suitcase since I knew they would be coming with me when we went to Thailand the following week. Daniella was trying on some of her new underwear and dresses; she did not bother so much with the jeans and t-shirts as she already had plenty of those. She put on a lovely black mid-length dress that showed ample cleavage and slipped on a pair of new black matching sling back sandals.

"You look gorgeous!" she said to herself as she stared at her own reflection in the mirror. "Wait until the boys see you!"

She took off the clothes and put on her original jeans and t-shirt and her Nike trainers. She threw a few bits of underwear, a new bra, a fresh pair of jeans and a new t-shirt into a bag, slung it over her shoulder and headed in the direction of my apartment.

Chapter 18
A Princess is Reborn

A knock on the door told me my granddaughter had arrived. I went to welcome her and she walked in.

"Have you started writing yet?" she asked. "I haven't missed anything, Granddad, have I?"

"No, my dear, I haven't begun yet as I've been putting some of my clothes into a suitcase. In fact, I'm ready to begin right now. I've even put a spare chair in my study especially for you. One thing I must get is a lock put on the door as you know how secretive I normally am!"

With my granddaughter following, I went into the study and switched on the desktop. I always used the main computer but had everything backed up on my laptop, plus a further copy on a memory stick. I had never trusted electronic equipment, only my own handwriting, which over the years had become exceedingly shaky probably from a touch of arthritis.

The invention of the computer had removed one major hurdle for me as I got older and I was grateful for such technology. I took the mouse, ran it over the relevant file and watched my story come to life.

The stable hands had returned with around five hundred horses. They were happy as the snow was deep and treacherous but at least they were still alive. I knew Chef Abel had something to do with their safe return and capture of so many horses.

Peter, one of the older boys and almost eighteen, said, "Whoever was planning to go out in that driving blizzard must be one crazy son of a bitch. You won't get me going back out there!"

Unluckily for him, Oscar, the head of the Kings' Guard overheard his outspoken tone and went over to the boy. "Did I hear you mention something about the King? Perhaps, you should come and explain yourself to his Majesty himself," he said.

Peter shook like a leaf and in his defence said, "I meant nothing and would certainly not insult the King. I was cold and freezing my nuts off and we've managed to capture five hundred horses. Isn't that enough for you?"

"Forget all about that. Follow me and you can explain your words to his Majesty. I'm sure he'll enjoy you squirming for your life," Oscar chortled away as he led Peter like a lamb to his prospective slaughter.

They went to the King's throne room and Oscar knocked at the door once.

"Come in," the King bellowed. "It had better be good news!"

Oscar grabbed Peter by the collar, opened the door and pulled him inside while the King stared at his officer.

"Why are you giving him such rough treatment," the King growled. "Has he found me enough horses?"

"We have five hundred horses, your Majesty," Peter stammered.

"That's good," the King said. "Captain, get the men ready. We're going into the forest."

"Out in this atrocious weather, Sire?" Captain Oscar exclaimed. "We'll all be frozen to death for sure!"

"You pathetic little toad!" the King snapped. "Are you refusing my orders?"

"No, Sire, I'll go and get the other men ready," Oscar mumbled. "They're resting at the moment so let me go and wake them up."

King Rudolf glared at his Captain who hurried away without another word. Peter had got off lightly and bowing to the King, he made a quick exit for the door. The incident was quickly forgotten but he knew that he had better watch his mouth from now on as it was certain to get him into big trouble one day.

Captain Oscar went to the barracks and screamed loudly, "You horrible pile of shit, get dressed and mount your horses. They're already saddled and ready out in the courtyard. We're going on an exercise with the King."

Some of the men moaned since they knew what the weather was doing outside. They would probably die of hypothermia or become lost and end up buried in the snow in such unpredictable and treacherous conditions. No one had the guts to say anything to their Captain who they knew was under orders from the King so they reluctantly dressed into battle uniform and took extra overcoats and blankets with them. Finally, they strapped their swords to their legs and headed out into the blizzard.

The Captain took one look at his sorry bunch of men and shouted at them above the howling icy cold wind. "Men, mount your horses and wait until I return."

Captain Oscar went directly to his King and said, "Sire, the men are ready to leave. I have them mounted on their horses and yours, your Majesty, is ready with your royal saddle."

"Good work, Captain," the King said in a quieter tone of voice. "I'll get my aid to help me dress and I'll join you shortly. Now, you go and make sure none of the men crawl away. One thing I won't tolerate is cowardice!"

Oscar went back outside to his men who looked very much the worse for wear despite being wrapped up tightly in their overcoats. Thirty minutes later, with the men almost frozen solid, the King appeared wearing thick leather gloves, a hat, boots and bearskin coat. He mounted his horse with the aid of a groom.

"Now, men," the King shouted. "We have a job to do so let's get moving."

The King cantered away on his horse with his men following in his tracks. The horses almost stumbled because of the deep snow but he expected everyone to stay with him so he kicked his horse to move faster and managed to get it to gallop. The men increased their speed but several of the horses tripped and fell heavily into the frozen snow underfoot, throwing the men off.

The broken horses had no further energy to get up and they lay in the snow dying of exhaustion and cold with their battered and bruised riders suffering the same fate. The blizzard conditions soon hid the bodies with a fresh covering of snow.

Meanwhile, the King disappeared with the rest of his army and headed in the direction of the forest. The men had heard all kinds of rumours about this place of evil but had no idea that the King wanted to take his soldiers and himself inside. The Captain had told them that this was an exercise but now they found out that the King wanted them to search the forest for this girl and her companion.

"Dismount, men," the King cried over the howling wind. "We're going on foot into the forest so get your swords at the ready."

The King led half the regiment into the forest while the Captain took the remaining soldiers, splitting the men into squads of fifty.

"Now, men, follow me and make sure none of you fall," the King shouted. "I don't trust this witch and her magic. We've already lost in the region of two thousand men and officers as well, so we need to find out where they've been taken to."

"Or been turned into!" one of the soldiers shouted bravely to his King.

"Did I hear someone say something? If I did, you'll be very sorry! Was it you, boy?" the King screamed into the darkness while pointing at one of the young soldiers.

In reality, he had no idea who it was so he decided to give them the benefit of the doubt since they were at least being loyal to the Kingdom of Blackstone.

"Sire, what are we looking for exactly? You haven't told us yet," the same boy who had opened his mouth earlier said.

"Lad," the King answered. "If you see anything suspicious, you know, something out of the ordinary just let me know."

Both groups went their own way and began to search the forest that was intent on harming anything that walked within it. The enchanted forest seemed to be able to watch everything that moved, whether it was animal or human. It was not bothered what it could eat so long as there was flesh and blood for it to gorge on.

All around the forest, the carnivorous plants got to work. They were able to smell any animal or human flesh and passed on their vibrated thoughts to the overhanging branches and creepers to take hold of the unsuspecting enemy, in this case, the soldiers as they made their way through the forest.

One by one, the branches and the creepers grabbed hold of their victims and pulled them through the blanket of snow and right into the open mouths of the living plants enclosed in the centre of the prickly bushes. A loud crunching of bones could just about be heard above the sound of the howling wind but no one was able to hear their cries of pain as they were eaten alive by the carnivorous plants.

However, the witch, who was meanwhile watching the whole affair in her crystal ball, had purposely kept the King and his men alive because she had other plans for them.

My granddaughter interrupted me at this part of the story and said, "It's horrible, Granddad, what makes you write such things?

I won't be able to walk through a forest on my own again after reading those last two paragraphs you've written!"

I thought she was joking but after studying the expression on the girl's face, I realised that my words had made her think.

"Daniella, in a story there are good things and bad," I said to the girl. "It makes the story more interesting and the reader more vigilant."

"Sorry, Granddad, carry on; it's becoming really gripping and exciting!" Daniella quipped as I pressed a key and the text came back onto the screen.

King Rudolf and his men finally found themselves in the middle of the forest when they came upon the same stone cottage that had become the downfall of the previous regiment. As before there was smoke coming out of the chimney. The King wondered if this was the dwelling of the dreaded witch of the enchanted forest. He took ten of his trusted soldiers with him and told the others to remain under cover until he returned.

He rapped heavily on the door with the butt of his sword but no one came to open it. He became more and more frustrated by the second and he banged so hard the second time that the foundations of the building shook violently. The door finally creaked open and he forced his way into the house with his soldiers only to find an old woman with a pointed chin, a long crooked nose and a mouthful of rotten teeth sitting on a rickety rocking chair with a big fat black cat sitting on her lap purring.

"Your Majesty, you've finally come to visit me," the wicked witch croaked. "The last time, you sent your Captain and soldiers but they were extremely rude to me and said something about chopping my head off!"

"Yes, old woman," the King replied impatiently. "And what would you have done about that and where are my men? And I suppose you sent this weather to frighten me too!"

"This weather will remain in your kingdom forever," the old hag cackled. "And you, my dear King, will stay here with me forever! Your men are no longer; they've either been eaten alive by the trees and bushes or they've been turned into wild swine or perhaps rats for my cat to chase and eat!"

"How dare you, woman!" the King snapped as he struck out with his sword to chop the woman's head off.

In a split second, flames shot out from the open fire, encircling the King's head and curling themselves around his legs before dragging him towards the fire. Two of his men tried to douse the flames with water that they found in a bucket in the kitchen but as soon as they tried to throw the water on the King, the heat drove them back. More flames shot out from the fire and curled around the men, suspending them in midair as they felt the heat of the fire burning their skin. The men writhed and screamed as they watched their flesh melt in front of their eyes.

"I'm the supreme ruler of this forest and you, your Majesty, are a trespasser so you have to pay a forfeit to leave," the wicked witch hooted sarcastically as the flames still held the King tightly in a grip that he was unable to escape from.

"Woman, what are you and where are my men?" the King cried. "Change them back from swine to soldiers and come with me quietly so that I can behead you in private. You won't have to go through the humiliation of being laughed at by the people of my Kingdom so let me go and you'll die peacefully."

"I don't think so, King Rudolf," the witch screeched. "It will be you who will be facing death but perhaps I'll give you a second chance and turn you into something my cat can enjoy playing with!"

"You wouldn't dare touch a hair on my head, old woman," the King moaned. "Release me right now and let me take you to the Palace. My men are outside waiting for my return and if they don't see me going back to them they'll come to search for me and then you'll be very sorry."

"I've had enough of your big mouth!" the depraved woman shrieked as she began chanting her royal spell.

King Rudolf, you're not for my pot
I won't turn you into a forget-me-not
Instead, I'll let you live your life
Of evil, pain and utter strife
You dare to come and threaten me
Are you blind or something, can't you see?
Your life is over, stupid King
Feel the heat and start to sing
There's only me for you to fear
You'll soon be gone and sup no beer
A yellow canary will appear
The minute you shed your final tear

The moment the sinister hag had finished chanting her spell, sparks flew into the air and smoke rose to the ceiling before billowing out of the chimney into the frozen night. The wind blew the smoke over to the waiting soldiers who found themselves unable to move. They knew that the end was nigh as the smoke enveloped them and smothered them to death.

Meanwhile, inside the old cottage, the King was released from the flames only to find himself turned into a yellow canary. The cat watched it flying around the room while the old witch cackled away. However, she caught the bird nimbly before the cat could pounce on the bird.

"This is not for you, my little one," she cried out. "You're becoming enormous so let me put it in this cage," she added before opening a golden cage and putting the bird inside. "You can sing as much as you like, little bird, but I won't have to hear that moaning voice of yours ever again! Your men have been dealt with severely and none of the five hundred soldiers that came with you will be leaving as they'll form a part of this forest for all eternity!"

"That, my darling, is all for tonight," I said to my granddaughter. "It's almost ten o'clock so I imagine everyone's gone to bed. I don't know about you but I'm feeling peckish after all that writing. Can we find anything to eat in the kitchen?"

"Leave that to me, Granddad," my granddaughter said, all businesslike. "Come into the dining room as that's far away from the bedrooms. If Mom and Dad are in bed, they won't hear us," she added before shooting away to the kitchen and leaving me to turn off the lights and close the door after me.

Chapter 19
My New Home

I went into the dining room and sat down in a rocking chair. Daniella was making something or other and I smelt a lovely aroma coming from the kitchen. The embers of the fire were still glowing and the room was nice and warm. My son and his wife had gone to bed just as Daniella had said they would.

The girl soon came in with a tray on which there were two plates of cheese on toast. I now knew that the smell coming from the kitchen had been melting cheese.

"Yummy!" I exclaimed to my granddaughter as she handed me one of the plates and a mug of hot chocolate.

"Will this do, Grandad? You said it was your favourite when we were on holiday," she said as I smiled at her and began biting into a piece of cheese on toast.

"This will go down nicely, Granddaughter," I said as I took a sip of my hot chocolate. "After this, we must go to bed but you can join me again in my study at eight in the morning. Perhaps, if it's a nice day like it turned out to be this afternoon, we might go for a walk along the beach. Do you have any idea where the nearest one is?

"It's at a place called Whitehaven," she replied. "Portsmouth is really just one big dock with many ships coming and going from all corners of the world. The nearest beach for us is Sandy Cove in Whitehaven where there are several hotels and holiday camps. In the height of summer, it's packed with people and as I said before in Cornwall, people and I don't get on so well."

"Well, in that case we'll be carrying on with the story unless you want to go somewhere in particular. Now, I'll be wishing you goodnight, Granddaughter, so sweet dreams!" I said with a big grin as I took my last mouthful of cheese on toast and the final dregs of hot chocolate at the bottom of my mug.

Daniella came over and kissed me goodnight before collecting all the dirty dishes and taking them to the kitchen. On looking at the clock on the wall, I saw that it was close to midnight and my bed was calling. Daniella stayed behind, and washed and dried the mugs and plates before she went up to her bedroom. She did not want her mother to know that there had been two hungry mice down in the dining room eating the cheese.

I undressed and got into bed but after I turned the lights off, I became aware of a presence sitting on the edge of my bed; it was Rebecca.

"I'll be coming along to Thailand!" she said none to my surprise. "I've never been anywhere further than the UK. Anyway, my darling, what do you think of the new Carol? Is she more to your liking?"

"I can't quite believe how she accepted you without being scared and then said that she asked me whether or not you'll be coming with us to Thailand. I wasn't sure at the time so I didn't give her an answer but now I know that you will. Perhaps, I'll say something in the morning."

"She's a new person, darling," Rebecca said to me. "I might also awaken her mother and bring her along too. I think she'd like that."

"I don't know," I said to my wife. "It might scare her completely. Why would you do such a thing when you two get on so well?"

"I won't do it unless I ask her beforehand so don't worry. By the way, you need not write today as the Range Rover is being delivered first thing in the morning so we can go for a stroll along the beach with our granddaughter and paddle in the water," my wife said following which she blew me a kiss and her apparition faded away to nothing.

I got into bed, closed my eyes and was soon fast asleep. It seemed as though I had only been sleeping for a couple of hours when I was awoken by the sound of my mobile ringing. On looking at my watch, I realised that it was half past seven so I got out of bed to answer the call. It was the delivery driver, so I put on my dressing gown and headed towards the kitchen. I found my son and asked him to speak to the driver since he was lost. After my son had given him directions, I quickly went to my room to get dressed.

A few minutes later, I heard the sound of a single peep on the horn as a Land Rover with trailer appeared down the driveway and parked outside. I went out to meet the driver who was already unloading the Range Rover and winching it off the trailer.

“I believe this is yours, Sir,” he began. “The invoice is to be settled within a month if that’s okay with you.”

“I’ll be paying you cash right now as I don’t like having any debts.” I replied as I looked at the total and gave the driver two hundred and fifty pounds with a further twenty for himself.

“That’s very good of you, Sir,” he replied as he handed me the keys. “The owner likes customers paying cash. Have a pleasant day,” he added as he jumped back into his Land Rover, turned around in the spacious driveway and drove away slowly.

“With the Range Rover looking so handsome and with my Jaguar on the driveway, people will think we’ve hit the jackpot!” my son said with a chuckle.

“Son, it’s beautiful out here. Do you have five minutes? I need to tell you something,” I said.

“Yes, of course I have. I always have some spare time for my Dad,” he said. “Now, tell me what you’re thinking.”

"You're a quantity surveyor, aren't you son? Do you work for someone in Portsmouth?" I asked curiously.

"I did, Dad, but I never say much to anyone about my work," he replied. "However, when my own father wants to know, then that's different so here goes. I left the company of Jarvis & Sons three years ago now. They were the only company I worked for as I had trained with them as an apprentice right after I had left school in Warwickshire. Something then told me to go out and try it on my own. It was difficult for the first two years but then, like a bubble, it burst giving me the trappings of life that we now enjoy. As my reputation grew, I started to get work from outside Portsmouth, became friends with other surveyors throughout England and passed over work to them with a thirty percent take for myself while giving them seventy percent for doing nothing. I gradually accumulated a pot of gold that turned me from rags to riches. I lived on my own personal recommendations and banked the rest. I had no idea that my account had reached well over the million- pound mark and my accountant suggested I should invest in some offshore activities. I had no interest in this so I bought a bankrupt company with assets instead. I refurbished the offices and sold off the ten luxurious cars that came with the buyout until the building was completed looking truly magnificent. One by one, the surveyors I had worked with in the past from all around England moved to Portsmouth to work for me. Of course, with me being the sole owner without any partners, I now enjoyed paying them the thirty percent salary while I took seventy percent profit for myself. I took this a stage further and employed five architects and did exactly the same with them before employing five secretaries that I hired out to each of the quantity surveyors and the architects, thereby covering their wages without digging into my own pocket. Riverton Richard and Company plc is now known throughout the world and we have enjoyed several contracts in the USA, Australia and China and right across Europe.

"I had no idea that your company was so big," I remarked. "I'm truly impressed but why didn't you say anything when I offered you money from my book sales?"

"I don't know, Dad. I became too big for my boots and it didn't end there as we're now in even newer and bigger offices in the city centre of Portsmouth because the building is sitting in twelve acres of brown land. I thought land was land until I had the lawyer representing Tesco turn up at my office one day with an offer for the land of one hundred million pounds. I took it of course under the understanding that the company found me an alternative office for my workers. Now, as you can see, I don't need to work anymore and my employees do everything for me so taking a three-week holiday is no big deal for me and I don't need to inform anyone. I just bring in one of my architects or trusted surveyors to run the office together with a secretary and if they need me urgently, I'm always available on my mobile. I'm sorry, Dad, that I sent Daniella without any money and expected you and Mom to buy her everything. I have no excuse for doing that and one day our daughter will inherit one major company. However, I've never taken the girl into the office and that was unfair of me but from now on things are going to change around here. Anyway, I'm hungry," my son said to me. "We've been chatting for almost an hour but I've enjoyed telling you about my company so whenever you want just come along and I'll be more than happy to show you around."

"That would be nice," I said as we headed into the house.

"Where have you two been?" Carol asked, visibly irritated as we entered the house. "I've called you three times for breakfast and received no answer."

"It was my fault, dear," my son said to his wife. "Dad and I were out the front talking since his car has just been delivered."

"That's fine, darling," Carol said calmly, unlike her normal self. "Sit down at the table and I'll go and fetch breakfast."

We made our way to the dining room just as Daniella appeared, washed and dressed.

"I'm ravenous this morning and the sun's shining," she remarked cheerily as Carol entered the room with our breakfasts. "Granddad and I are off to Whitehaven for a walk along the beach. I saw your car being delivered from my bedroom window, Granddad, so I assume we'll be keeping to our original plans."

"Yes, dear, we'll go straight after breakfast," I said. "Does anyone wish to join us?"

Daniella looked at me in despair since she wanted us to go alone. However, thankfully, my son said he was going into the office to do some work while my daughter-in-law said that she had things to do.

After enjoying a lovely breakfast that went down well with two mugs of tea, Daniella and I grabbed a lightweight jacket each, said goodbye and made our way to the car. She got in and buckled her belt before I did the same and started the engine, selected drive and drove off. We did not bother joining the motorway as I thought it would be a much more picturesque drive along the secondary roads that took us through all sorts of small villages.

"That was fun," Daniella said when we arrived in Whitehaven. "I hate motorways and Dad always joins them wherever he's going. I've no idea what Dad does for a job or who he works for but he's usually gone all day so I seldom see him. However, since you've been here he's spent more time at home than he's ever done before."

"I know how you feel, darling, but your Dad's only trying to protect you," I said. "Up until this morning, I too had no idea what work your Dad does and that he's so wealthy. He also told me that he plans to begin taking you into the office as one day you'll be inheriting his company."

"The girls at school are always saying to me that I'm a little rich bitch but I don't feel like one and have always wondered what they meant. By the way, Granddad, take the next turn as it will bring you into a narrow country lane that winds all the way to the beach at Sandy Cove."

I followed the girl's directions and turned down a narrow country lane. Thankfully, the lane was wide enough to take the car but a truck of any description would have had a nightmare to get down it. Once the lane widened out, we came across sand dunes and rows upon rows of beach huts. I followed the lane to the end where I found a car park with several motorhomes parked overnight with the curtains still drawn. This scene made me think of the holidays that Rebecca and I had enjoyed together.

We parked the Range Rover and Daniella and I got out. We found the sun lovely and hot so we discarded our jackets and left them in the car. I followed the girl as she led me through the sand dunes and out onto the sandy beach where the sea looked calm and inviting.

"Did you know Granny's come with us? She's a little way behind us looking at the shells," the girl whispered.

I wondered whether my granddaughter was playing me up but looking behind me, I saw Rebecca kneeling down in the sand searching for shells so we went over and joined her.

"Help me collect the shells, darling," she said. "They keep falling through my hands every time I try to pick them up!"

We laughed as our granddaughter knelt down and began putting the shells into a bag that she had brought along with her.

"How many do you want, Granny?" the girl asked after a while. "My bag's getting rather heavy."

Rebecca smiled at her granddaughter and said, "That's enough, my dear. And how is Granddad's story coming along?"

"I can't tell you Granny until the book is published and on the bookshelves," Daniella replied unpredictably. "You know how Granddad feels about releasing the story before he's finished!"

Rebecca smiled at her granddaughter before scowling at me. Her apparition faded away and I knew that she was disappointed but as a ghostly phenomenon, she could always come into the study and see for herself. However, the woman knew my rules and always abided by them even when she was dead.

Removing our shoes and socks, we walked around a quarter of a mile along the sandy beach, before coming to the town of Whitehaven where we found a nice cafeteria overlooking the beach. We sat down and ordered two toasted sandwiches and a milkshake each; I chose banana while Daniella took strawberry. The walk had made us hungry so we wolfed down the sandwiches and gulped down the milkshakes after the girl had brought them over to us. I looked at my watch and realised that it was midday and time for lunch so I ordered a bowl of chips between us and another milkshake each.

Once we had finished eating the chips and drunk our last few drops of milkshake, I paid the bill and we left. We joined the beach once again and walked along chatting merrily away. Well, I walked as Daniella skipped along like a frisky gazelle!

"I'm so happy that you and Granny have joined the family," Daniella said at one point. "Mom and Dad are so different and they have so much time for me now. Mom has even asked me if I want to join the fitness centre she always goes to with her friends."

"Darling, your Mom was always a good person but she was locked into a time warp," I said tentatively. "She had forgotten that we are living in a different world nowadays and that children are more demanding than when she was a child. I was surprised that my wife chose to visit her and make her realise that you're no longer a little girl. Anyway, Granny wants to surprise her by bringing your Mom's own mother to Thailand with us. This is because she said that she tried to make contact with her but without any success. What do you think of this?"

My granddaughter went cold at the thought since she did not know whether she would like or dislike the woman.

"Darling, what are you thinking of? You've turned completely white!" I commented anxiously.

My granddaughter moved nearer to me and I held her tightly before she explained her grievances about having her other granny return.

"In that case, if you're so worried, I'll tell my wife to forget about the whole affair," I said. "I hope she hasn't done it already though as otherwise, we'll have no say in the matter."

Walking back to the car, Daniella was very quiet as the thought of having her other granny around demanding everything and reverting her mother to the way she was before terrified her. I should have guessed that she would take it like this and somehow I would have to find a way to send her back unless my wife had carried out her plan already.

Once back at the house, my granddaughter went up to her room and sobbed into her pillow, unknown to us all, except to my wife, Rebecca materialised, and sat down on the girl's bed to try to comfort her.

"Darling, why are you crying and looking so sad?" she asked worriedly. "I could hear you from out in the meadow where I've been searching for four-leaf clovers."

"Grandpa told me you were going to speak to my mother to get my other granny to come on holiday with us," she whimpered. "It scares me as I know it will change Mom into how she was before and if that happens, I'll run away for good!"

"No, you won't because I've not mentioned anything to her yet and if you feel that emotional then I don't wish to bring her back. Are we still friends?"

"Yes, of course, Granny. Even if she had returned I'd still love you to bits but could you imagine her seeing Mom and me jiggling our boobies in bikinis along the beach? She'd have died a second time!" the girl said giggling out loudly.

"Don't laugh so loudly as otherwise your mother will come in here. She's downstairs in the kitchen and I don't want her to know I'm around even though we get on like a house on fire; she still makes me nervous," Rebecca said as she returned to the meadow to search for four-leaf clovers.

A knock at my door told me that someone wanted me for something so I went to open it and Daniella walked in. She had washed the tears away from her face and was smiling.

"Are you carrying on with your writing, Granddad?" she enquired cheerfully. "I want to know more about what I become!"

"Why are you so happy now all of a sudden? You didn't say a single word to me on our journey back from the beach!" I said as I winked at the girl.

"I know," Daniella said sheepishly. "I was worried that Granny was going to bring Mom's mother back and felt that my mother would become like she was before. Granny heard me crying and came to see what was wrong with me. She promised me that she would not say a word to my Mom and that I should forget all about it so now I'm one happy lark again. Could you imagine Mom's mother seeing us walking around in flimsy bikinis," she tittered.

"Ha, ha, indeed!" I cried out with glee as I began to visualise Carol and my granddaughter strolling around wearing next to nothing on the beach while Carol's mother gave them both black looks.

Even I was not sure how I would take it, let alone my wife's mother, if she came on holiday with us. I still wondered if Rebecca knew what was in store for her at the end of the day but that was something that I was about to find out.

"Now, Granddaughter, let's go and bring the Princess back to life," I suggested as I went into my study.

The girl followed me into my room and I turned on the computer and waited for it to power up before loading up the relevant file and continuing my writing.

Chapter 20
A Lonely Palace

No one had heard anything from the King or his men. The weather had grown worse by the minute and the Kingdom was covered by six feet of snow. Daniella and Tatiana waited patiently for the Prince to return with Chef Abel. Seconds turned to minutes, minutes turned to hours and hours turned to days so Princess Lana left to go and speak to her mother as no one had heard anything from the King.

Daniella and Tatiana were still hidden in the safety of the secret chamber inside the bedroom. Without his Majesty chasing after them, they were safe. They learnt the truth the moment Chef Abel arrived with Prince Leonardo who he had met on the landing outside Daniella's bedroom.

"I have some important news but I'll tell you with the others," the Chef said curtly to the Prince.

The Prince raised his eyebrows in surprise but did not say a word as the two entered the bedroom and opened the door to the secret chamber.

Once inside, the two men shut the door and the Chef continued, "My Master has told me that the King is no longer. He now resides in a golden cage that hangs over the window of the cottage of the wicked witch of the enchanted forest. His men have been devoured by the carnivorous plants and bushes and the King sings for the witch every single day as he's been turned into a yellow canary!"

"How do you know such things?" Prince Leonardo asked the Chef suspiciously.

"The Dark Lord, Lucifer, told me," the Chef replied promptly. "He's happy to see souls being sent to him for magic but has told me that if there's a goodhearted person who can replace King Rudolf, he'll undo the spell that the witch has weaved over the Kingdom. For doing this, he wants you to cut out the witch's heart and take it to him on a plate. It needs someone with guts to do this and then he'll remove the curse over the Kingdom and allow the new King to rule for all eternity."

"We don't want darkness to replace blizzards and ice," the Prince replied sardonically. "Either way, we won't see the sun again. The Dark Lord is no better than the witch so all the subjects of this kingdom will surely perish!"

"You must think outside the box, Prince Leonardo, as the Dark Lord has spoken and you have to believe in him," the Chef said. "If you want my help you need to understand that Lucifer doesn't wish for you to remain in darkness; he's ready to give you back your sun and will lift all the winds, ice and snow from the Kingdom. He's good as well as evil but you must believe in him."

"I don't know who to believe in," the Prince put in. "If it's true that my predecessor now sings as a bird in a golden cage, I prefer to forget all of this as it seems like some horrible nightmare. And if you're going to help me destroy this witch, we must leave this land and go and find strength. However, you must first teach the girl some spells to protect her against this wicked witch."

"Yes, Prince Leonardo, I'll do as you command as you're our new King," the Chef said as he bowed to his friend, before continuing to add, "Now sire, please cover your eyes as I need to complete my magic." Leonardo took the cue at this point and did as asked. Chef Abel, on turning his attention to the girl added further. "Daniella, let me begin teaching you some basic magic. However, we first need to start on healing your wounds."

Daniella hobbled over and stood before the Chef who removed the girl's gown, while he cut through the girl's bandages leaving the wounds wide open and leaking with puss. The young lass grimaced with pain and ground her teeth together to avoid screaming out. Chef Abel waved his hand over Daniella's head and then over her wounds before chanting a growing spell.

Wounds so deep and flesh so thin
Repair yourself and now begin
Skin now gone begin to grow
Remove that pain and let it show
Turn the hands of the clock
Now, young girl, release the lock
That holds you tightly in its grip
As blood starts to flow, take a sip

The Chef drew a knife from his pocket and cut deeply into the girl's wrist, catching the blood in a silver goblet that he then handed to the girl who took it in her trembling hands.

"Now drink this and see what happens," he said to her.

Nervously, Daniella put the goblet to her lips and forced herself to drink the contents. She hated the taste of her own blood but the obedient girl drank until the last drop. The moment she did this, her pain was lifted as the wounds began repairing themselves before her very eyes. Prince Leonardo and the young raptor looked on in amazement as the lesions healed themselves completely without leaving a scar or a mark.

Daniella meanwhile redressed, feeling reborn again she got to her feet and danced around the room in joy as if nothing had ever happened.

"I feel fantastic with my body like new again," Daniella squealed with delight. "My pain has been taken away and I'm ready to face anything the witch throws at me. Teach me some spells before you leave so at least I'll have a fighting chance against her if she discovers the reasons for my being there in the first place."

"Of course, I will, young girl," the Chef said eagerly. "Now, come over to me while the Prince and Tatiana go as I can't reveal these spells to anyone except you. No offence, Prince Leonardo but this is the first time I've ever taught my magic to anyone and I'm only doing this because you've helped my family so much without expecting anything in return."

The Prince left together with the raptor and they went downstairs to wait. Two hours later, Daniella went to find the Prince and her friend Tatiana and found them both sitting inside the throne room. She also saw the secretary's body lying on the floor in the corner of the room and his head on the desk.

"Who did such a thing?" the girl asked in dismay.

"We don't know, Daniella," the Prince replied, equally distraught. "We found him like this when we entered the room. It has to be the disgusting work of the King as it has all his trademarks on it. Now, we have the whole city in panic and several thousand people not knowing if they're going to remain alive through this horrific weather outside. They're becoming exceedingly desperate and have started running amok and even attacking one another!"

"We must leave today then so let's go and pack and then find the Chef and bring him back to my room together with your sister," Daniella said to the Prince who looked at the girl in admiration as he held her in great esteem for her fighting spirit.

The young girl and the Prince left the throne room with Tatiana following behind. He went one way while the two girls went the other. Once in her room, Daniella spoke to the young raptor that had remained silent for most of the day.

"Tatiana, you're being very brave but somehow I must find a way of sending you back home. I'm going to ask the Chef for a favour as you truly deserve it and if I'm successful and manage to break the witch's spell, I'll send for you and your family to live in the Glass Palace for the remainder of your days."

"Oh, Daniella, that's so kind of you," the raptor said to the girl. "If you can do that, I won't be so sad but even if you can't I'll remain with you till the end of my days as I have great respect for you. However, I still hope you defeat the witch and destroy her for good."

On this last note, there was a knock at the door. Tatiana went to see who it was and Prince Leonardo and his sister Lena shuffled into the room dragging a number of trunks containing their clothes and personal items. Princess Lena opened her trunk, took hold of Daniella's clothes and a few others belonging to Tatiana and laid them carefully on top of her own possessions. There was another knock at the door and the Chef sauntered in and closed the door behind him.

"Is everyone ready?" he asked.

He had a spell book with him that he was going to recite from when, suddenly, Daniella stopped him and said, "Chef Abel, can you do me a favour and send Tatiana back to her family? She's been a rock to me but I know her heart's sad even though she's ready to follow me till the end of her time."

The Chef scratched his well-kept beard before answering the girl, "I'm sorry, my dear, but until you bring me the witch's heart on a plate, I can only grant you one spell and that's going to be used to send you all to the magical kingdom of Zandar where King Rysis rules, so are you ready to leave?"

"Yes, my friend, we are," the Prince said. "I'm really sorry, Tatiana and realise what you must be going through but we have to stick together to enable me to return and claim this kingdom."

The Chef opened his book to a particular page and began to recite his spell.

Now my chosen children nigh

Let the heavens open high
With a flash you're gone so fast
To a new kingdom made to last
I cast this spell as the four winds blow
Zandar awaits you so now you go
Take the path to pastures new
Herein my spoken words are true.

With a flash of light and coloured sparks, the four friends disappeared and were teleported to the kingdom of Zandar. The Prince found that his clothes were that of a peasant boy while the girls found themselves wearing brightly coloured dresses that revealed quite a lot of cleavage and open toe sandals. Tatiana was terrified to find herself naked as to the people of this kingdom she was just an animal.

It was obvious that they were just commoners and no longer royals. The Princess believed they were in the middle of the deepest countryside so they decided to follow some nearby cart ruts without knowing where they would lead them.

The Prince was the first to say something, "This is weird! Why are we dressed as commoners and not the royals we've always been?"

"We're in a foreign land, dear brother, and no one knows who we are here," Princess Lena said to Leonardo.

Leonardo realised that life in this new kingdom was going to be tougher than they had previously thought it would be. There was the issue of how they were going to communicate with the King of this foreign land. Other matters of concern were how they were going to earn a living in Zandar and how they were going to get out of this kingdom eventually since they did not seem to possess any more magic.

"I'm not afraid of getting my hands dirty and fighting for my rights since I'm now as strong as an ox," Daniella spoke up.

"You're right, Daniella," the Prince said. "We shouldn't be licking our wounds as we've managed to escape our frozen kingdom. We have to fight this situation since we need to help our people that are left behind. Crying makes it that much harder for us and will not solve anything. I agree that if I need to work then I damn well will and my sister will do the same."

"We have to make this successful and escape from here," Princess Lena said, agreeing with her brother. "I'm ready to work too if necessary. Now we'd better put some clothes on Tatiana because people will think she's their next dinner and may try to kill her when they see her walking around naked!"

The Princess opened her trunk and handed the raptor some of her clothing, which she put on gratefully. She felt much better once she had done so and flicked her tongue in and out with approval.

"I thank you from the bottom of my heart, Princess Lena," the raptor said appreciatively. "It will make me feel more at home with clothes on."

They tried to laugh at the irony of the situation but their circumstances were dire and none of them could raise more than a feeble smile. They struggled along the dusty road heading to somewhere although they still had no idea where that was.

"It's best that we do not use titles but just call each other by our first names, Tatiana. Just Lena and Leonardo and Daniella although we'll call her Ella from now on just in case as we can never know who may be hanging around listening," Lena said to the raptor before giving her a friendly grin.

"Ella, I quite like that name and could get used to it," Daniella replied with a chuckle. "Queen Ella! What do you think, Leonardo?" Daniella added mischievously to the Prince as Lena and Tatiana laughed so much that they collapsed to the ground holding their sides with mirth.

Suddenly, as if from nowhere, a large-winged bird of prey with a hooked beak and razor-sharp talons that was comically wearing a colourful hat on top of its large triangular head appeared above them looking for its next meal. It spotted Tatiana, and swooped down and headed right for the raptor. The Prince picked up a broken branch from the ground, bravely stepped in front of its dive and hit the bird sharply across the head. It fell down stone dead, following which the quartet heard the sound of galloping hooves and hid quickly behind some bushes.

A well-dressed man wearing a gold and red tunic, satin trousers and a golden crown on his head riding atop a lovely white stallion trotted into sight. He got off his horse, withdrew his sword at the ready and began hunting around the bushes before spotting the dead bird.

"Who's responsible for killing my prized eagle?" he cried out as several men came forward dressed in black uniforms.

"Sire, we'll search around to see if anyone's near," one of the men replied. "If we find the perpetrator, we'll bring him back and you can hang him in the main square!"

The men rode away to start their search without realising that the eagle slayer was actually near at hand. The King cradled his prized bird in his arms and began rocking it in his arms while moaning softly to himself. He did not hear the soft footsteps approaching from behind and he certainly was not able to feel the crack across his head as the Prince brought the branch crashing down as hard as he could. The King fell to the ground and lay still without a single movement. Leonardo was not sure if the King was unconscious or worse but he was not bothered either way. However, on feeling the King's pulse, he realised that he was in fact dead.

The other three came out from behind the bushes and looked at the body of the King while Prince Leonardo removed all his clothing, together with his golden crown and bejewelled sword, and placed them carefully into his trunk.

"What have you done, Leonardo?" his sister cried out. "That was the King! I don't think you did the rightful thing by killing him!"

"I don't know, Sis, but I grabbed the bull by the horns, or the King in this case," Leonardo said with a loud chuckle. "I don't think I'd have had a better opportunity. I understand how you feel but our survival is at stake and we must stay together and take his horse with us. No one knows who killed the bird or the King so we'll move slowly into the city and start making friends. At least, I have two swords now!" the Prince said laughing out loudly as they walked quickly away from the scene leaving the naked body of the King behind.

It was two hours later when the men rode back and found the body of a deceased man lying on the ground with a dead eagle by his side. They could not make head or tails who it was since none of them had ever seen the King close up, especially looking so helpless without clothes. Laying the corpse across the saddle of one of the horses, the men returned to the palace thinking that their King would have ridden back by then since they had taken so long to return. When they arrived, they removed the body from the horse's back and put it into an empty stable. They locked the door securely to make sure that no one tampered with the evidence while they went to their barracks, stripped and washed before going home to their families.

Hours later, the King had still not shown up and the royal household were beginning to become worried. The Captain of the Royal Regiment sent for his men and they galloped away on their horses to begin their search that took them into the dark and unpleasant forest.

"Now, dismount and search the forest," the Captain ordered. "The King can't have disappeared without a single word to anyone; maybe he's lying injured somewhere."

The men stayed in the forest all night searching for someone who was not there. However, unknown to them, a mysterious female lived in the middle of the forest by herself. She watched the men from her window with beady eyes as they searched for something or other. Once they came to her house, the Captain knocked loudly at the door that swung open to reveal a beautiful young woman staring nervously at them. She was everything that a man could ever dream of, tall, blue-eyed and slim with a lovely pert body that boasted delicious boobs, pale skin and long and shining blonde hair.

"Wait here," the Captain instructed his men. "I need to speak to the young lady in private."

"Captain, Sir, you're so handsome!" the young woman said effectively. "Stay with me and send your men away! We can have fun together and enjoy each other's company."

The Captain stared at the girl and found her eyes drawing him closer to her until he felt his lips on hers and they kissed passionately for a few seconds. The Captain then went to the door and opened it a few inches.

"I need to make further enquiries with this woman as she may know something we don't. You men can go and continue with your search of the forest," the Captain shouted before slamming the door shut.

"Captain, I'm Caspian, I live with the animals as they're my friends," the gorgeous female said while undoing the buttons on her dress. "Let me go and make us a nice cup of tea."

She got up and gave the Captain an eyeful of pale flesh. He then sat down on the couch in front of the blazing fire and thought it a little odd having an open fire with such beautiful weather outside. He was far away in his thoughts when Caspian returned with a single cup of tea.

"Miss, aren't you thirsty?" he queried.

"No, Captain, my body's thirsting for love so drink this and you'll then have the strength to introduce yourself better to me upstairs in my bedroom!" she replied.

The Captain quickly finished his cup of tea and Caspian led him upstairs. They made love as any couple would do but when he turned over the next morning he did not find a beautiful girl in bed with him. He was shocked as lying next to him was the ugliest woman he had ever seen. He tried to get up but his body no longer belonged to him.

"Captain, I'm in love with you and I want you to stay here for all eternity," she crooned. "Your King's dead and no one is ruling over your kingdom. I thought that when we get to know each other better, you and I could become King and Queen. I have magic that's stronger than anyone else's but I live here on my own with the animals and I need someone to share my life with and to have many children from!"

"Never, Madam!" the Captain cried out wondering why he could not budge an inch. "Let me go as I don't wish to remain here with someone so ugly!"

"That's the problem with the men I sleep with. They see me as beautiful but when I show them the real me the next morning they're rude and hurt my feelings. You're going to be sorry for saying such insensitive words, Captain," she said as she raised her hands above her head and began chanting a spell.

Captain so brave and full of might
Made a fool of himself alright
Cast this rude man of flesh and blood
Out of my bed with a loud thud

The evil witch of the forest repeated the spell some four or five times. No one had ever realised that she lived deep inside the forest or that she had tricked at least five hundred men and turned them into her pets. All she wished for was for the man of her dreams to say how beautiful she really was the next morning but they never did so she cast a spell over them.

There were sparks and smoke everywhere and the Captain was no more. All that was left of him was a snivelling common rat. The woman shot forward and grabbed it by the tail before going down the stone steps that led deep underground into a cellar where there were hundreds of cages with other rats inside.

"Here, my beauties, you have a new friend," the old hag croaked. "He's just as ignorant as you lot and must be taught some manners."

She opened a cage containing at least twenty other rodents and placed the Captain inside. She shut the door and the other rats began sniffing at him before one of them jumped straight at his neck and began ripping through his flesh and arteries until he bled to death following which the other rats gorged themselves on his dead body.

"Now, my beauties, you're going to taste freedom," the wicked witch said as she opened all the cages and a secret door. "Go and find the soldiers; they'll keep you nice and fat for many months!"

The rats did not try to attack the woman as they swarmed through the doorway. They found themselves in a passage of darkness and followed the bodily smells and sounds of the men's footsteps until they emerged from the darkness into the forest. The rats crawled all over the soldiers and bit deeply into their necks until they crumpled to the ground and bled to death. There was not a single soldier left alive in the forest and their bodies ended up mutilated and torn apart. What the rats did not eat, other creatures of the forest and living shrubbery gorged on any leftovers.

Chapter 21
On The Run

Nobody knew the exact time, and as the sun shone brightly the four friends yawned simultaneously finding themselves with aching bones after their night of ordeal sleeping rough under a bush. One by one, they came out of their hideaway, pricking themselves on the thorns in the process until they found themselves once again sitting under the bright warm sunshine. And on taking a brush and mirror from her trunk, Princess Lena began brushing her hair before handing the brush and mirror to Daniella who smiled and ran the brush through her own hair too as Lena said.

"All this dust has made us filthy," she remarked as she noticed her dirty face. "We need to find some water to wash in."

"Yes, very true and apart from that, we're all thirsty too," Prince Leonardo put in as he looked all around him only to find dry countryside and dusty tracks that seemed to lead nowhere.

The four found themselves climbing up a steep hill that made them feel weak at the knees since they had not slept very well that night and they were also not used to such rough terrain finding it extremely hard going underfoot.

"I wonder what lies beyond this hill," the Prince remarked. "I hope it's a river where we can bathe in and fish to catch our morning breakfast."

The four did not have to wait long to find out what lay beyond as when they reached the crest of the hill they saw a gurgling brook down below. They ran down the hill and jumped into the water that was lovely and cold. They soon removed the dirt from their bodies and after a good wash of their hair and bodies, the Prince and Princess dried themselves and dressed in their entire splendour, as did Daniella and Tatiana. All they needed was a royal carriage but the Prince had a trick up his sleeve.

"Now we walk towards Zandar to be found across the other side of the water," the Prince said as he pointed to buildings in the distance. "It doesn't look too far and the roads are not as dusty from here onwards. I hope someone finds us as with the King missing we can always pretend we were robbed and that our carriage and horses were taken. They'll never discover the truth and when the people realise we're of royal blood maybe they'll show us a kind of respect."

"Not a bad idea, brother," Princess Lena said. "However, if they find out you murdered their King, then I'm sure they'll give us a very different kind of reception!"

"Oh, come on, Sis!" Leonardo said with a sigh. "If I hadn't come along and killed his bird of prey, we'd never have had the opportunity to take out the King, and for us to receive that kind of assistance couldn't have come at a better time. We can now introduce ourselves as royals from a neighbouring kingdom, who have come to pay respects to their royal monarch. They'll never discover where we've come from because if anyone tries to get to Blackstone they'll find it lies under ten feet of snow and ice!"

"He's right, Lena," the raptor cut in with her own input. "No one will go and check on us and if they do, they'll come unstuck and will probably never return!"

Daniella nodded in agreement so the four friends waded through the shallow water to the other side and continued to head in the direction of the town. After some time, they heard the sound of galloping hooves but this time they did not hide. A carriage pulled by four black horses came to a halt and the coachman jumped from the carriage, opened the door and a young man got out. He had a pleasant but mature sort of face with a fair amount of facial hair. At around six feet tall, and dressed in a smart black suit and polished boots; this aristocratic stranger had tidy shoulder-length blond locks tied at the back with a piece of red ribbon and some kind of quilted hat placed loosely on his head made it obvious that he was from a well to do family.

"Who are you, my dears? For one I see you're certainly not farmers, nor peasants!" he asked as he placed his left hand on the scabbard of his sword. "It's not safe walking along these roads these days even more so especially since my uncle, the King, has gone missing. There's a reward for his return of one hundred pieces of gold," he added out of interest.

It was obvious to Leonardo that the man wanted an explanation, so the Prince said, "Some thieves came along and stole our money, jewels, and horses and carriage! We've come from the Kingdom of Blackstone; I'm Prince Leonardo and this is my sister, Princess Lena. This, here, is Lady Daniella and her servant Miss Tatiana," he added as the girls all bowed to the young man.

"No, don't bow," he said. "It should be me bowing to you so please accept my sincere apologies. I'm Lord Jonathan Bridgestone, by the way. Now, ladies and Prince Leonardo, the least I can do is offer my carriage. Here, Jarvis load the trunks into the back," he added, addressing his footman who opened the door to allow everyone to climb inside.

And as the driver gathered speed again the conversation inside the carriage was limited since Lord Jonasthan could not keep his eyes off Daniella who just smiled back at him naively, immediately hitting at the heartstrings of the young man. The horses finally pulled into a driveway that seemed never-ending until the driver drew up outside the entrance of a magnificent mansion. The young Lord jumped out and opened the doors for everyone, dismissing the footmen whose job it normally was to open the doors. He was certain that his parents would love meeting such polite aristocracy.

"This is my humble abode, Bridgestone Manor," he said modestly. "Let me introduce you to my parents, the Duke and Duchess of Bridgestone," he continued as he rang the doorbell and a butler appeared and opened the door.

"Good to see you, Sir. I see you've brought along some guests," the butler remarked.

"Yes, I have Jenkins. This is the Prince and Princess of Blackstone and this sweet girl is Lady Daniella and her servant Miss Tatiana. Are Mother and Father free? I wish to introduce these royals to them since they're quite charming. Oh dear, I'm forgetting my manners; please come into the drawing room," Lord Bridgestone said while staring intently at Daniella who felt rather uncomfortable as it was quite obvious that the young man was besotted over the young girl.

"Of course, Sir," the butler said. "I'll tell them you're home and wish to bring some guests to meet them."

"Thank you, Jenkins," Lord Jonathan said as the butler went away in the direction of the long sweeping hallway leaving the five waiting in the drawing room. He was back some five minutes later.

"Come this way, Sir," the butler stated. "Your father's pretty miserable about the disappearance of his brother. There's been no word from him even though the soldiers have searched high and low and have even ventured into the forest but so far they've not returned and we've not heard a single word from their captain either."

Jenkins led the way to the far side veranda where they found the Duke and Duchess relaxing on a velvety couch with the Duke smoking a large cigar while both of them sipped some kind of refreshing drink.

When he caught sight of the strangers dressed elegantly in royal clothing, he got up to bow but the Prince waved him down.

"There's no need, Duke," Prince Leonardo said. "We're your humble servants in need of your assistance as several armed soldiers stole our horses and carriage and our chest of gold and precious stones that we were bringing as a gift to the King. For some unknown reason, they left us with our clothes and my sword, thankfully. I think I managed to wound a couple of them but there were far too many for me to fight off and I could not have expected the ladies to intervene now could I, dear Duke!"

"No, of course not," the Duke replied. "However, this is becoming impossible as the secretary sent out a further troop of soldiers to search for the King. The Captain and his men have also disappeared and no one seems to know their whereabouts and our kingdom is left without a ruler. I know this is a highly unusual request but perhaps, you two could assist," he added while pointing at the Prince and Princess. "I'm sure it would make the people here more relaxed knowing people of royal blood have been brought in to look after the kingdom of Zandar while the search goes on for my dear brother."

"We're humbled by such an offer but if we agree to help, several of your soldiers will have to go and inform my uncle, King Rudolf of Blackstone," the Prince said, folding his fingers backwards in a nervous disposition before continuing further. "We have pressing business matters in hand that he'll expect to receive, answers on and we don't wish to upset our King and my uncle as he has the most frightful of tempers."

"Well we don't wish to upset your uncle Prince Leonardo, so of course if you agree to my suggestion then of course I can arrange for our secretary and a small battalion of soldiers to visit him and explain the reason why you're delayed!"

Thank you Duke, that's extremely kind of you, as I wouldn't wish for any harm to come down on my family due to my disobedience!"

"Did you hear that Jonathan, this here Prince is extremely thoughtful towards his family, and that's something you have to learn from!"

Meanwhile, Lord Jonathan had taken hold of Daniella's hands; when he realised that his father was speaking to him, however he seemingly ignored his fathers comments, and addressed him saying. "This girl's so beautiful, Father! I'd love to get to know her better."

"Look, Son, the girl's probably married or engaged. Normally, one so beautiful is always taken," he replied to his son. "Isn't that right, my dear?" he added to the young girl.

"No, Sir, I'm not married but I have a boyfriend and he's fighting against an enemy of the King so I must remain loyal to him," Daniella replied openly.

"What a charming young lady!" the Duke exclaimed. "Whoever ends up with you, my dear, will be a very lucky man. Nonetheless, is there no chance for my son? He is of good aristocracy after all."

The poor girl blushed and tried to hide her face with her hands but this was becoming somewhat difficult for Prince Leonardo to endure.

"Daniella's promised to a good friend of mine," he cut in. "If he thought I was trying to break them apart, he'd fight me on the battlefield. He might even try to level matters with your own son and he has a frightful temper, I tell you, even though to me and the girl he's like one big pussy cat!"

"Anyway, I'm sure you're all hungry," the Duke said hurriedly, changing the subject. "Let me arrange something for you to eat and drink; tonight, we'll be having a banquet in your honour. There I'll introduce you to the other Lords and Ladies, Prince Leonardo. There are many single females, as well as my own daughter Melissa, who will immediately fall in love with you and will love you to dance with her. And, perhaps, Prince Sassoon might interest Princess Lena while you, Daniella, can't refuse to dance with my son, now, can you?"

The poor girl looked at the Duke who was smiling jovially; he seemed like a kind middle-aged nobleman but she did not want to be engaged to Lord Jonathan when in her heart she knew that she really loved Leonardo, as well as his sister.

In the meantime, the Duke had gone to arrange breakfast, and as he came back and announced, "We will be called the moment breakfast is ready, so meanwhile please adjourn to the sitting room, so please follow me!"

They all followed the Duke in the direction of the sitting room, where they chose a place to sit, and chatted to one another with the Duke saying to the young prince, "So I hear that some unscrupulous bounder stole everything from you yesterday."

"Yes, Duke leaving us without jewels we bought especially for your brother, and the majority of our expensive wardrobe. Amazingly they left us with a few clothes, however not what we would have worn in front of your brother!"

"Well dear boy, my brother has far too many jewels, and

"Prince Leonardo, I hope you don't mind but I sent for my daughter Melissa," the Duke continued. "She was out riding her mare and I think you'll like her very much. She's from a good aristocracy and has royal blood flowing through her veins, just like my son, Jonathan. My brother and I have not spoken for five years; he is obnoxious and even though he was King, our people did not like him any longer. Therefore, you'll make an excellent substitute for him, however the decision doesn't only lie with me as you'll see from the Lords and Ladies who'll be attending my banquet tonight."

"Where do you think the King is? He can't just have disappeared, can he?" Prince Leonardo asked off the cuff, as of course he knew exactly what had happened to the Duke's brother but having had the greatest form of luck, somehow or other he, together with his sister, Daniella and Tatiana had found themselves in an aristocratic family in Zandar.

The Duke stared at the Prince and scratched the end of his prominent nose, before saying. "Between you and me, my brother had many enemies as he raised taxes far beyond what people could afford and anyone caught behind on payments was either thrown into prison and forgotten about or faced the guillotine. He also stole personal property and land belonging to families over many years so his death doesn't surprise me one bit, to be honest!"

Daniella stepped into the conversation; the Duke was not used to being interrupted, especially by a female but he let it go this time since he was not sure how powerful the kingdom of Blackstone really was.

"Duke, I was thinking, why don't you become the next King?" she enquired. "Why do you need your daughter and Prince Leonardo to take over the kingdom when I assume you're next in line to the throne?"

Lord Jonathan stared at the girl, wondering how his father was going to react to such a statement, as there was no way he would have interrupted his father in the middle of an important conversation.

The Duke shrugged it off by saying, "Look, my dear, we are four brothers and two sisters but I'm the sole survivor, apart from the King wherever he is. The reason is that the King used to have many arguments with my other siblings and ended up beheading all of them, leaving only me," the Duke admitted. "I have no wish to take the throne and the King has no heirs so my daughter's hand with Prince Leonardo would be the perfect solution and the people would adore them, I'm sure."

A knock at the door and the majestic entrance of the Duke's daughter Melissa stopped all conversations and made everyone's head turn. She was an attractive girl with long waist length brown hair, brown eyes, a voluptuous figure and a delicate mouth. She looked around the dining room and when she saw Leonardo, she smiled immediately as she had taken an instant liking to him, however she waited patiently for her father to make the introductions.

"This, my dear, is Prince Leonardo," the Duke said when he noticed her look. "And this is his sister, Princess Lena, Lady Daniella and her valet Tatiana, a well-mannered young raptor," he added, pointing to each in turn. "I'm not sure where she came from but she's extremely exquisite."

Lady Melissa smiled at everyone in the room before taking a seat at the table but not next to the Prince as her father had hoped but next to Tatiana. The Chef walked in together with the servants who were carrying a number of silver dishes filled with sausage, bacon, all kinds of fruit including pears, apples, oranges, lemons and strawberries. And not forgetting fresh crusty bread, cheese etc. They placed the dishes down gently onto a nearby table before putting down large plates and a silver goblet in front of everyone. The breakfast was then served and the wine poured.

"To a new beginning and a fresh start to our kingdom!" the Duke announced as he raised his goblet in the air and drank a toast.

They all drank in honour of what the Duke had proclaimed, following which they all tucked into the delicious meal in front of them.

After she had finished swallowing a few mouthfuls of food, Melissa turned towards the raptor and said, "I understand you speak! None of the animals talk in our kingdom so how come you're able to do so?"

Tatiana explained as best as she could. "Lady Melissa, I'm from the kingdom of Rhinestone, a kingdom of special animals who have been given beautiful colours and the power of speech by

King Rudolf of Blackstone, the uncle of Prince Leonardo and Princess Lena, and a magician in his own right. Daniella's also part of their family and is also of royal heritage."

They continued to eat their meal before Melissa said further, "I can see why Daniella looks after you as you're a really good friend to her. She's so beautiful and delicate that I'm surprised Leonardo hasn't taken a fancy to her!"

"That's not fair asking me, Lady Melissa," Tatiana replied. "The truth is that I don't know. I just look after my lady and she takes care of me. To her, I'm not just a lady-in-waiting but more of a friend. I have a family of course but I prefer to remain with her especially through her serious illness."

"Oh, I see!" Melissa said. "Leonardo's an extremely handsome man, and if he's next in line to become King of Blackstone, I'd be one lucky woman if he chose me to rule with him. However, I feel he has eyes for one girl only and that's Lady Daniella."

"Did I hear my name being mentioned?" Daniella butted in as both Melissa and Tatiana looked at the girl sheepishly.

"I was saying that you and Leonardo are well-suited for each other," Melissa said.

"We are just distant cousins," Daniella said. "Why would he wish to marry me? You're probably better suited for him so why don't you ask him if he's interested in you?"

Melissa got up and went to join Prince Leonardo and his sister. She sat down between them and her father winked at her since this had been his plan all along.

"Prince Leonardo, can I ask you a question?" Melissa asked with an exquisite smile and a lick of the lips as any predator would have done moving in for the kill.

"Yes, of course, my dear Melissa. What do you want of me?" the Prince asked as Princess Lena looked over at Daniella and wondered what she had been saying to her.

"I think, Sire, that you'd make the perfect ruler of our kingdom," Melissa said in a meaningful way as she smiled longingly at the Prince. "And if the King doesn't return we can marry and rule over this land together. We are both young and I will bear you many strong sons and daughters!" she added as Prince Leonardo looked stunned at what she had just told him.

"Look, I promised your father we'd assist in running your country while the King's missing," he managed to say. "We never mentioned anything about me ruling over your territory, or that I was expected to marry you Melissa, although you are extremely beautiful my dear. I'm the sole heir of Blackstone, where I hail from, so how can I be King of both kingdoms at the same time?"

"Sister, you do not know this Prince so how can you throw yourself at him and say you wish to marry him?" Jonathan interjected as he had been listening in to the heated conversation. "Let's see what Father thinks about all this."

The Duke too joined in on hearing his name mentioned although he was the main instigator of their betrothal in some way or other so he surrendered saying in an aristocratic way. "Now, Son, it was me who suggested that your sister and the Prince should marry and take over this kingdom," he stated as he gave his son a stern look. "He's a true gentleman, a people's man, and my daughter would make the perfect bride for him. Of course, she'd bring a large dowry with her. I'm nothing like my brother and plan to refuse becoming the next monarch. Whether or not you can rule over both kingdoms is entirely up to you and my daughter, Prince Leonardo." The Duke suddenly brought the young Prince into his conversation between him and his son.

"I cannot believe what I'm hearing!" cried Princess Lena. "As Melissa's father, how can you suggest that my brother's a suitable heir for your kingdom? You hardly know him, and what if your brother turns up out of the blue?"

"He's been gone for twenty-four hours and no one's heard a word from him," the Duke scoffed out loudly. "The people are becoming nervous and it needs the firm hand of a royal like your brother to stabilise the ship. The King has no heirs as he's hunted them down and murdered them all, except for me. He's never been missing for so long before so it's obvious that someone managed to find him alone and killed him and probably cut up his body and fed it to the vultures in revenge for taking the life of one of their family. He was always being threatened but he just laughed off these threats because he has neither a wife nor children. I'm the only living heir so if I wish to pass our kingdom over to Prince Leonardo, that decision is mine and mine only."

Jonathan turned to his father and pleaded, "How can you do such a thing, Father? Why not let me rule over our land together with Daniella who's one gorgeous girl and will give me many heirs?"

The girl looked sullenly at Jonathan and then over at the Prince. She was terrified by the thought of becoming queen of this kingdom to a man she did not love.

"I can't marry you as I'm promised to a Captain in the King's army who'd be devastated if I turn him down," Daniella said. "Ask Prince Leonardo and he'll tell you exactly what I'm trying to say to you."

"That's right, my dear chap, and you'll need to fight for the girl's hand in marriage," Leonardo said to Jonathan. "And to do that you'd have to come back with us as I promised the King of Blackstone that I'd look after the girl and make sure she remains safe."

Lord Jonathan glared at the prince as he wanted this girl desperately and if it meant him fighting over her hand in marriage then so be it. He had nothing to live for, especially if his father refused to pass over the sovereignty of the kingdom.

"I want this girl badly," Jonathan said unsurprisingly. "She's my future queen so if I have to fight him and kill this Captain, I will!"

"Jonathan pack your things and leave this kingdom," the Duke screamed as he glowered at his son. "I don't want you under this roof anymore, do you understand, my boy? It's my decision that Prince Leonardo will be betrothed to your sister and will be named the next King and Duchess of this kingdom!" the Duke continued angrily as Prince Leonardo tried to change the Duke's mind but found it was set in concrete.

"That's not fair, Father! Why should he become the peoples' choice and not me?" Jonathan shrieked as he stormed out of the room.

"I'm sorry you had to see that," the Duke said ruefully. "And Lady Daniella, you wouldn't want my son to become your husband. He's not worthy enough even for his own family, do you agree, Melissa?"

"Yes, Papa, he's not a prince even though he has royal blood flowing through his veins," Melissa replied nonchalantly. "If the King's dead, it's your decision as you're the only remaining brother. Jonathan's unable to change his status and I love Leonardo and would welcome the opportunity of becoming his wife if he feels the same about me."

"You don't love just anyone, daughter, and one thing that you'll need to learn is that to win the heart of a man like Prince Leonardo, then you'll have to earn his total trust before there's any mention of marriage or love, as I did with your mother!" The Duchess threw a gentle smile in the direction of her husband, making sure that her daughter saw her doing it.

"My brother wishes to return to Blackstone," Princess Lena interrupted. "He's next in line to the throne and wishes to lead his people one day. The King is strong and will never abdicate so he must remain patient and wait for the right moment but if Leonardo stays here how can he become the next King of Blackstone?"

"We must think this out carefully," the Duke said to everyone seated. Before addressing his daughter and adding. "And tell your brother that he need not leave for the moment as I have an idea. Send for him, Melissa and then listen to what I have to say."

Melissa went to find her brother only to find him gone with his horse so she went back to give the Duke the news.

"Why are you so hard on the boy?" the Duchess intervened with tears running down her face. "Now, we'll probably never see him again. Send some of your officers to look for him!"

"No, woman, if he can't listen to the truth and runs away like some scared rabbit when anyone raises their voice against him. What good could he do for the people as their King? I must drive over to the Palace and see if anyone has any news of the King," the Duke said as he got up. "If not, I'll remove his title and hold it temporarily until Prince Leonardo decides whether he can take over our kingdom," he growled softly and gave Leonardo a devious smile before adding. "You'll not refuse my offer as if you do, I'll show you how I take disappointments and that's something you don't wish to see!"

Prince Leonardo felt a lump in his throat as things were going horribly wrong! Not only did he have to face the wicked witch's wrath and the Duke's anger but he also had his son and daughter demanding all kinds of things.

"Listen Prince Leonardo, let you and I go to my study, there we can get to know one another a little better?" The Duke and Leonardo did just that, and as the Duke took a cigar from the box on the table, lit it and took a puff of the cigar, leaving smoke rising up to the ceiling as he added. "I'm so sorry Prince Leonardo, please I was forgetting my manners, take one my dear boy!"

Leonardo wasn't sure if he was going to like such things, however he did take a cigar, copying exactly what the Duke did, all except that when he swallowed the smoke, he coughed and coughed making the Duke burst out laughing and saying, "It's your first time smoking, let me pour you some whisky. I'm sure you'll enjoy that!" The Duke poured two glasses from a decanter to be found on one of the shelves of his office, and as he waited for the Prince to take his glass, he had already downed his in one, Leonardo tried to do the same, only finding that the liquid burnt his entire mouth. The poor boy couldn't get his breath back until the Duke hit him twice across the back, as Leonardo stammered to give any kind of answer.

"I'm so sorry Duke. As you can see I don't smoke nor do I drink alcoholic beverages. Is this something I need to get used to if I'm going to remain here!"

"Of course not, it's not necessary for you to drink, or smoke come to think of it, however aristocrats tend to do both, but don't worry, it's not compulsory to either smoke or drink, although it was mean of me not to explain to you the simple rules of not swallowing the smoke of the cigar, or taking whole mouthfuls when it comes down to drinks like whisky!"

I was wondering as I now have to go to the palace, and see for myself if anyone can recall when they saw my brother, the King last, now perhaps this could be the most ideal occasion for me to introduce you and your sister, to the Ambassador who handles all my brothers affairs.

"Prince Leonardo, can you and your sister come to the Palace so that I can show you around?" the Duke added to the young prince.

"Yes, we can but what about Lady Daniella and her assistant?" the Prince asked worriedly.

"Just bring them along with you then," the Duke replied curtly.

The four got up and followed the Duke out of the room and into the grand hallway where they found the Captain waiting.

"Have you heard any news about the King, Captain Silas?" the Duke asked as Melissa crept out of the room and stood by the door.

"No, Duke, the five hundred men who left last night have also not returned so this is becoming extremely worrying for the people to handle without a King and an army to protect them," he replied somberly. "What can we do, Sire? We need someone to rule our kingdom!"

"Yes, Captain, now go and prepare my carriage and horses. I need to go to the Palace to get an update. These aristocrats will be coming with me," he said while pointing not only at the Prince and Princess but also at Lady Daniella and the raptor. "They may be able to assist us as they're royals from the kingdom of Blackstone."

"Yes, Sir," the Captain said as he saluted everyone in the hallway before leaving to arrange everything his master had ordered.

"You seem to get on well with each other so I want you all to live at the Palace and see how you can help us as you're all of royal descent. I'm sure you'll have no problem with that," the Duke said cheerfully. "Of course, that's unless my evil brother has magically appeared. However, having been missing for so long, I doubt if he'll ever be found alive, anyway."

"What about me, Papa?" his daughter Melissa piped up.

"Enough, girl, I don't need any more complications," the Duke said as he frowned at his daughter and pushed her away. "However, before we even think of marriage, we need stability in our kingdom as otherwise the people will lose faith and start fighting and killing each other. I hope that Prince Leonardo and his sister can bring calm to our land. Do you have any immediate plans to offer our kingdom, Son?"

"I think I do! I know exactly how to bring peace and tranquillity back to this Kingdom," the Prince replied as the Duke gave out a deep sigh of relief.

At that moment, the Captain returned. "Your carriage awaits you and your guests, Sir," he said as he saluted the Duke who promptly left to gather his belongings together.

The others followed behind with his daughter scowling at the leaving party as she had hoped that she would be joining them as well.

"Prince Leonardo, can you and your sister come to the Palace so that I can show you around?" the Duke added to the young prince.

"Yes, we can but what about Lady Daniella and her assistant?" the Prince asked worriedly.

"Just bring them along with you then," the Duke replied curtly.

The four got up and followed the Duke out of the room and into the grand hallway where they found the Captain waiting.

"Have you heard any news about the King, Captain Silas?" the Duke asked as Melissa crept out of the room and stood by the door.

"No, Duke, the five hundred men who left last night have also not returned so this is becoming extremely worrying for the people to handle without a King and an army to protect them," he replied somberly. "What can we do, Sire? We need someone to rule our kingdom!"

"Yes, Captain, now go and prepare my carriage and horses. I need to go to the Palace to get an update. These aristocrats will be coming with me," he said while pointing not only at the Prince and Princess but also at Lady Daniella and the raptor. "They may be able to assist us as they're royals from the kingdom of Blackstone."

"Yes, Sir," the Captain said as he saluted everyone in the hallway before leaving to arrange everything his master had ordered.

"You seem to get on well with each other so I want you all to live at the Palace and see how you can help us as you're all of royal descent. I'm sure you'll have no problem with that," the Duke said cheerfully. "Of course, that's unless my evil brother has magically appeared. However, having been missing for so long, I doubt if he'll be found alive, anyway."

"What about me, Papa?" his daughter Melissa piped up.

"Enough, girl, I don't need any more complications," the Duke said as he frowned at his daughter and pushed her away. "However, before we even think of marriage, we need stability in our kingdom as otherwise the people will lose faith and start fighting and killing each other. I hope that Prince Leonardo and his sister can bring calm to our land. Do you have any immediate plans to offer our kingdom, Son?"

"I think I do! I know exactly how to bring peace and tranquillity back to this Kingdom," the Prince replied as the Duke gave out a deep sigh of relief.

At that moment, the Captain returned. "Your carriage is awaiting you and your guests, Sir," he said as he saluted the Duke who promptly left to gather his belongings together.

The others followed behind with his daughter scowling at the leaving party as she had hoped that she would be joining them as well.

Chapter 22
An Inner Vision

After writing those two chapters I was now tired and my granddaughter Daniella was asleep in her chair. I prodded her gently and she woke up with a start.

"What time is it, Granddad?" she asked as I looked at my watch.

"It's way past midnight, dear, so we'd better go up to bed," I suggested. "I'll see you in the morning."

Daniella yawned and nodded her head as she made her way past me and went up to her bedroom while I shut down my computer and made a beeline for mine soon afterwards.

The following morning, I was awoken by a knock at my door. I got out of bed, slipped on my dressing gown and went to see who it was. I was surprised to see my daughter-in-law, Carol, who had a big beaming smile on her face.

"Good morning, Dad," she said. "I came to tell you that breakfast is ready so get washed and dressed and I'll see you in the dining room in fifteen minutes or so."

I nodded my head and went to have a quick shower. A quarter of an hour later, now fresh and clean, I headed to the dining room where I found Daniella and my son Dick waiting to be served.

"Did you have a good night's sleep, Dad? Our daughter found it difficult to get up today! Did you send her to bed late?" my son asked me, visibly irritated.

"That's my fault, Son," I replied awkwardly. "I was writing two chapters and forgot the time. Daniella was with me as I'm teaching her how to write as I promised Mom that I would do."

"You never showed anyone before, not even Mom, so what's my daughter's secret?" he enquired.

"There's no secret, Son. I just felt it was about time I shared my stories with someone else and thought it was a good time for Daniella to learn how to express herself," I replied as my daughter-in-law, Carol, appeared wheeling in the heated trolley.

"Do you want some help, Mom?" Daniella asked as she got up and pushed back her chair.

"That would be nice, daughter," Carol said. "Can you put plates down for everyone and start to serve the breakfasts from the covered dishes while I go and make sure the toast isn't getting burnt?"

Carol went back to the kitchen while Daniella began serving everyone around the table. It was a full English breakfast and included sausages, eggs, bacon, fried bread, mushrooms, tomatoes and thick crusty bread. As I was adding some brown sauce to my plate, Carol appeared with a rack of toast that she put down in the middle of the table before sitting down next to her husband.

"Bon appétit, I hope you like everything on your plates," she said as we all began to eat, finding the food cooked to perfection and tasting even better.

After eating her first mouthful, Carol turned to her daughter and asked, "Have you any plans for today, my dear?"

Daniella was shocked by her mother's gentleness but she did not miss a beat and asked, "No, Mom, why?"

"Well, I was wondering if you'd like to join me at the Health Club," she replied jovially. "I can make you a member and then you can go whenever you want to. As a signed up member, you're allowed to take one friend along with you for free!"

My son smiled at his wife, as I did too, because the old Carol would never have offered such a thing to her daughter.

"That would be great, Mommy, and I'd like us two to wear our matching bikinis when we go to the pool," Daniella said calmly.

My son and I burst out laughing as Carol's expression changed dramatically.

"They're used to seeing us in full bathing suits," she stuttered, shocked by what her daughter had suggested. "I'm not sure if we'd be allowed to wear such things at the club. By the way, do you have a plain tracksuit?"

"Yes, I do," Daniella replied to her mother. "Perhaps, you can ask the management if we're allowed to wear bikinis."

Carol smiled at her daughter and began clearing away the table and putting the dirty plates down on the trolley before taking them to the kitchen to put in the dishwasher. Daniella went to her bedroom, put on her jogging suit, ankle socks and trainers and then ran downstairs and into the kitchen to talk to her mother.

"Mom, who are we meeting today, any of your friends?" she asked.

Carol looked at her daughter before giving her an answer that she was not expecting. "No, darling, just you and me and perhaps Daddy if he's got the time, that is."

"Shall we ask him to join us?" the girl asked. "Would you like that, Mommy?"

"That would be nice but we've given him no notice so I imagine he won't have time to come with us. Maybe, some other time he'll fit us in," Carol replied.

Daniella was having none of this so she marched off into the dining room where my son and I were chatting.

"Daddy, what meetings do you have today?" she demanded.

"None, my dear, because Steve Lily is looking after the office," her Dad replied. "But why do you ask?"

"How about coming to the club with Mommy and me? You could do with some exercise, and you too, Granddad!" Daniella said, trying hard not to snigger in the process.

My son stroked his chin since he had never thought that his daughter and wife would ever expect him to go along. He tried to think of some excuse to escape Daniella's clutches but they were going on holiday in a week's time so lifting a few weights in the gym might do him a load of good.

"Okay, daughter, you're on," he said much to Daniella's delight. "I'll come but I can spend no more than a few hours or so."

I was almost roped in too but I told the girl that I was far too old for exercise. She did get her own way eventually but that was some months later. I watched my granddaughter Daniella and her parents get in the car and drive away leaving me all on my own. Fed and watered, I went to my room to turn on my computer and continue my story. However, when I entered the room, Rebecca was sitting on my desk with her hands over the keyboard.

"Why didn't you go and do some exercises? You're putting on far too much weight and I don't want to be going to your funeral next," she said sarcastically. The apparition laughed so much that she fell off the desk and onto the floor. "Ouch, that hurt! It wasn't supposed to as I'm dead, aren't I?" she cried out as she gradually began to fade away to nothing.

Seeing that my wife had vanished completely, I returned to writing my story.

The footmen opened the carriage doors and they all got inside, finding the carriage far more comfortable and spacious than the one Jonathan had taken them in; they had no idea that the Duke owned several such carriages. The driver whipped the four magnificent beasts and they began to move slowly out of the long and winding driveway before coming to the main roadway leading towards the Palace. Their journey took over an hour as the Duke lived far away from his brother.

When they approached the Palace, the horses trotted through the open golden gates, which the Duke thought very strange as these were normally locked for security reasons. The driver halted the carriage outside the front entrance and a welcoming party came out to greet the Duke.

"We're happy to see you, my Lord," the King's secretary announced. "The King has not yet returned, nor has the army of soldiers that left last night. The Ambassador has sent out the relief captain and more armed soldiers to search the forest and the surrounding land but they too have not come back and our people are getting desperate and want answers fast."

The Duke stroked his facial growth of hair as he was in urgent need of a shave but with all the goings on, he had pushed it down his list of priorities.

"I think I have a short-term solution that just may work," he replied cheerfully. "Can we see the Ambassador please? It's a matter of urgency"

"Yes, my Lord, follow me," the secretary said before leading the way to the Ambassador's quarters.

"Thank heavens you've arrived," the Ambassador exclaimed when he saw the Duke. "The citizens of this kingdom are getting nervous without their ruler, what with all these rumours of his death flying all over the place! So have you heard anything from your brother?"

"We hardly speak as he killed most of our family," the Duke replied grimly. "I still don't understand why he never took a wife; at least, he'd have had an heir to take his rightful place."

"Indeed but who are these people? Are they royals too?" the Ambassador asked curiously.

"Yes, Ambassador, they are. They've come from the Kingdom of Blackstone. This is Prince Leonardo, his sister, Princess Lena, Lady Daniella and her charming assistant Tatiana!"

"I have heard of this Kingdom. Their sovereign, King Rudolf, is a cruel man and his people are so scared of him that he'll have them beheaded if they speak out of line or spread malicious gossip about him! In fact, Duke I hope you don't think I'm speaking out of turn, but your brother doesn't seem a million miles away from how King Rudolf rules his kingdom!"

"You're right, Ambassador," Prince Leonardo put in. "My uncle's a nasty piece of work but he too has no children so I'm next in line to the throne. When I become king, I plan on making some drastic changes in Blackstone as I want it to be a happy place once again."

I like this young Prince," the Ambassador remarked to the Duke as he took him aside. "He speaks wisely and we need someone like him to replace your brother. You mentioned that you have a plan so what is it and does it involve this young Prince?"

"Yes, it does, Sir," Prince Leonardo said, cutting short the Ambassador. "We four are here to be of assistance, albeit on a temporary basis of course as we'll have to return to Blackstone eventually."

"If you can help us out, Prince Leonardo, then you have my blessing and that of the King's personal secretary. Let us wait until the soldiers return from their last search and then I wish you to address the people in the royal square. This has given me hope, dear boy," the Ambassador said before getting to his feet and bowing down low before the Prince.

"I knew this was a good plan of execution," the Duke said ironically to the Ambassador. "However, I still wonder where the King could have disappeared to. I suspect he suffered a dose of his own medicine and met one or several of his disillusioned taxpayers so we'll probably never find him as he will have been spliced in two, and then divided out to the wild animals that roam through the forest!"

"Well, I never!" the Ambassador exclaimed. "For his brother to think like that just shows how reviled the King has become! Anyway, can I arrange for some food and drink for you and your guests?"

"Yes, that's an excellent idea," the Duke replied, following which the Ambassador went out into the hallway and passed over the message to the King's secretary to take to the chef. A few minutes later, he was back.

"Mr Ambassador, Sir, your food is being served in the dining room," he announced.

"Everyone, follow me if you don't mind," the Ambassador said with a flourish of his hands. "I'm hungry and I suppose you all are too!" Turning to Tatiana, he asked, "Do raptors eat meat? We don't have creatures like you in our kingdom, especially ones that talk and with the highest IQ!"

"Well, they do, but in our kingdom we've stopped eating meat completely. However, I'm okay with that as I use a knife and fork just like you would!" Tatiana said as she winked at the Ambassador.

They arrived at a huge door and the Ambassador pushed it open and led them into an enormous banqueting room. There was a single table looking completely out of place in the centre of the room laid out beautifully with lace tablecloth, silk napkins, and silver cutlery and goblets. There also was an array of beautifully scented flowers in a vase in the middle of the table.

They walked over to the table and the Duke turned to his guests and said, "Please take a seat. This is your Palace for the time being so you'd better get used to it!" he added with a chuckle.

Everyone sat down as a servant emerged from a side room with a jug of wine and proceeded to fill their goblets. Once done, the Duke raised his goblet in the air.

"To our esteemed guests," he announced in a loud booming voice. "Welcome to your new abode."

Several more servants came forward and placed large silver trays of meat, vegetables and potatoes on the table following which they all began tucking into the lavish meal laid in front of them.

"I could get used to this," the Prince said cheerfully to the Duke. "This meal's truly delicious."

"You can have such meals every day if you so wish to as the kingdom is yours to do what you want of it, and if the people wish for you to remain here then you must stay and never go back to Blackstone," the Duke said unemotionally.

"I have no choice as Daniella and I have a mission to complete. Till then, the world's not a safe place!" Prince Leonardo remarked mysteriously.

"I understand, Son," the Duke said to Leonardo despite the fact that he did not quite comprehend the situation. "However, before you go you must get our people to believe in themselves again. I know you can do this. And maybe the stars say that you should be King of Blackstone as well as here!"

"I can't answer that, Sir," Leonardo said promptly. "Let us see what the soldiers say on their return. Perhaps, they'll bring his Majesty back with them."

"Don't hold your breath, my boy, as the King has many enemies and with him missing like this it's obvious to me as his brother that someone has done him in good and proper. In any case, he deserves all he's got as he's become one nasty piece of work!" the Duke said cold-heartedly. "Now, do you still want me to hold a ball in your honour? Or shall we forget about it as you may find another more suitable female to your liking?"

"If the King is not found, our priority is to get the people to believe again," the Prince said to the Duke. "Even with Melissa here, that's not the right thing to do at the moment, especially if the people demand the whereabouts of their King. Have you thought that some may think that as his brother you might have something to do with his disappearance?"

"Yes, I have," the Duke answered at once. "I'd say that I haven't seen my brother for a long time and that I have absolutely no ambitions in becoming king! Of course, I wouldn't mention that I'd gladly offer a thousand gold coins to anyone who kills him!" he added with a hearty laugh.

"I can't believe you speak like that about your own brother!" Leonardo remarked in dismay. "Was he a tyrant and that bad a king?"

"Yes, I believe he was, although I never got to know why he never took a wife. He did have several mistresses but none of them bore him a child and he had them all beheaded. He was greedy and never wished to share anything with anyone!"

"So were your parents wealthy?" Prince Leonardo asked the Duke.

"My father as King was just like my brother; he had no compassion and I was shocked when he died as the throne was promised to my younger brother. I should have reigned as I was the oldest male in the family but my father said I was weak and could never be a ruler!"

"I'm beginning to understand your family," Leonardo said. "I agree you'd have made a much more understanding monarch than your father and brother put together."

At this point of the conversation, they heard the sound of several neighs in the distance and the Duke stopped the Prince in his tracks.

"I think we're about to find out what happened to the King," he said. "Let me go and question the men while you and your friends remain here for the time being. Please help yourselves from the fruit bowl and the wine barrel; the servants are at your command."

After the Duke had left, the Prince turned to his sister and said, "This will never do, Sis! I don't love his daughter as I want to marry Daniella!"

Daniella turned a deep shade of crimson before stuttering out, "I think highly of you, Leonardo, and love your sister dearly, but why not marry Melissa? She's beautiful, rich and holds a title unlike little me! I think you're left with no other options and it may be the only way we can escape this kingdom especially if the people fall in love with you the same way I've done."

"I love the way you tell me you're in love with me, my dear. I'm in love with you too so how can I marry someone who I don't care about? You must start to realise this and not push me away. I'll make a good King and an even better husband only if you become my queen and I don't wish for anyone else," the Prince said just as the Duke strolled back in looking far too jolly.

"I was right! He's dead!" the Duke exclaimed. "They left his body in the woods and it became mutilated by animals feeding on it. Now, Prince Leonardo and Princess Lena, you have to address the people first thing in the morning. Do you have any idea what you're going to say, Prince Leonardo?"

"I do, Sir, and I believe that the people will honour me until we're ready to depart," the Prince replied to the baffled Duke.

"Fine, so let me send for the King's secretary," the Duke said to Prince Leonardo. "He'll make notes and arrange for all that you require. I'll tell him that you'll be ruling over our kingdom for the time being until we have the people's choice put forward."

"That's the right idea and if your son wishes to be on that list I don't mind as he's the rightful heir after all. Otherwise, you'll become distant like your brother and end up never speaking to one another!" Leonardo remarked.

"If he wishes to be like my father then he's no good for our kingdom, Prince Leonardo, and I won't be welcoming him back. The only way he can return is by bringing an army against us and if he happens to be killed I'll be the last man to shed a tear over him and I won't have him buried in the family vault!"

"How can you be so insensitive, Sir?" Princess Lena butted in. "Isn't it fair to give him a chance to redeem himself? I'm sure he didn't mean what he said last time!"

"This is the last time I'll be speaking about my son Jonathan," the Duke said. "Do we understand one another, Prince Leonardo? And he'll not be welcome at the wedding if you are to marry my daughter. Now, it will be your job to tell the people that someone has murdered the King and that you'll be remaining in power until someone can take your place," the Duke added, changing the subject completely. "You are to advise them that I don't wish to take up the throne after my brother's demise and that I wish for you to succeed."

"Yes, I can do that," Leonardo said. "I know the exact thing to say to them to bring them onto my side. I won't let you down, Sir, and your people will end up respecting me and my sister."

"Now we must return to my home and make plans for tomorrow," the Duke said. "Do you need any writing instruments to make notes about what to say to the people or do you have a good memory?"

"I don't need to write anything down and if I need to make notes my sister will do that for me," Leonardo replied. "I'll speak from the heart as that is what the people deserve especially since your brother was so brutal with them."

"That's exactly what I wanted to hear from the next King," the Duke said as he got to his feet and applauded the young prince. "You have the right sort of attitude to lead my people to the good life that they deserve. My brother's death won't bring any tears to my eyes and my heart won't grieve over him. Now, Princess, what do you think about your brother? Is he able to rule over this kingdom until we can find a replacement?"

"I think he can, Sir, as he's wise for his age and will think only of the people but what will your son do about it if my brother is to be made King? He's already told him that he's not afraid to take up arms and seize what's rightfully his!" Princess Lena said worriedly.

"That's what you may think, my dear, but if my son sets one single foot in this kingdom he'll be beheaded for treason," the Duke growled.

"If you do that to your own flesh and blood, then you'll be no different to your brother!" the Princess said.

"You speak wisely, Princess, just like your brother. If your brother becomes King then you must become his secretary but where does Lady Daniella fit into all of this?" the Duke asked.

"I don't mind, Sir," Daniella put it truthfully, even though she knew she would lose everything if Leonardo married Melissa.

The girl knew that she had no royal blood flowing through her veins so the rightful queen for Leonardo had to be Melissa. However, before that happened there was one huge hurdle to jump and that was to kill the wicked witch and break her evil spell.

Prince Leonardo turned round to the Duke and said, "Daniella's special to me as she was badly injured and almost died. I sat by her bedside and prayed she'd be well again. She's a distant cousin but to me she's the world. If I'm to be King, I'd expect her to be my queen as that was my original plan for Blackstone as here the poor girl's playing piggy in the middle with your daughter on one side and her on the other."

"Look, Son, I realise that the girl's special to you and deserves your love and understanding," the Duke said. "However, why are you prepared to take such great risks in defeating something evil?"

Leonardo winked at his sister, Lena and then at Daniella, who both smiled back. They knew that this was the right time to tell the Duke what they knew, except for murdering his brother, that is!

"In Blackstone, there's a dark evil forest in which many magical plants live," Leonardo began to explain to the Duke. "They're carnivorous so if people go in there they're either eaten alive by the plants or taken by the evil witch. She's dangerous and if anyone upsets her she casts a spell over them and turns them into wild pigs, rats or worse! She promised to bring the worst ever winter to Blackstone but we left before finding out if she had actually carried out her idealistic threat."

"My God, thank heavens we don't have an evil witch here!" the Duke exclaimed. "Well, at least, I don't think we have but we do have a dark forest that no one has ever set foot inside so we could quite easily have an alternative evil presence in there. Anyhow, why do you want to go back to your kingdom when I can offer you one of your own? And if it's good for our people if you marry Daniella then so be it and my daughter will have to find an alternative love in her life. Now, we must leave as it will be dark soon and you have a crowd to greet at eight o'clock tomorrow morning."

They all climbed into the carriage and the coachmen shut the doors behind them. The driver then whipped the horses gently into a steady trot until the palace was soon out of sight.

Chapter 23
A Ruler in the Making

Prince Leonardo, stared out from the carriage window, wondering if this was a good idea or not, as he knew in his heart that with his uncle somewhat missing, and the unfortunate murder of the Dukes brother, such travesties didn't seem to matter to Leonardo, as he told himself with the greatest of vengeance, "that I'm no murderer, and I was in the wrong place at the wrong time," however things were now happening in the rightful way, and the King of Zandar had stepped over the line for the very last time. His people had spoken out, and it was them who were the future of the new kingdom of Zandar, and if he could help in any way then he was there to do just that, however destiny is a strong word, more so than even Prince Leonardo could ever have imagined it to be.

Meanwhile the group chatted readily to one another as they enjoyed nature's companion, with lush green countryside all around them. Finally, they pulled into a long driveway and the horses slowed down to a walking pace until the driver brought them to a halt outside the Duke's residence. The footmen jumped off and opened the doors. After the girls had departed first and walked up the steps and entered the manor Prince Leonardo went to get up and do the same, however the Duke motioned to him to remain behind.

"Now, my boy, I know something about your mission," the Duke began with a worried look on his face. "However, I consider it foolish to go and fight this witch. Why must you place your lives on the line? It makes no sense to me at all when you've got an amazing opportunity here in Zandar!"

"I know, Sir, but Daniella could not walk as she'd been mutilated by a sabre-toothed tiger and her injuries were so bad that the surgeons believed she'd end up losing both her legs," the Prince continued while the Duke listened intently. "I stupidly agreed with our Chef, who also doubles up as a sorcerer, to cast a spell on the girl and magically make her legs repair themselves. He did so but insisted that we kill the witch and take her heart to his master Lucifer in return. This would not only satisfy the Master but would also remove any curse the witch had put down on Blackstone. As you can see, it's my destiny to destroy her but the girl's brave and insists on becoming her servant and tricking her. I refused to let the girl go by herself and felt it was my responsibility to at least offer the girl some form of protection."

"You're a man to be admired," the Duke said, cutting the Prince short. "I fully understand why you feel like this but as the ruler of our kingdom you can take your own army with you and destroy this witch. I promise I won't say a word to my daughter as Daniella deserves you lad for the rest of her life!"

"I thank you, Sir," the Prince said to the Duke. "I didn't know whether I should tell you or not but you've been the most amazing host to us. I still feel bad about your hatred towards your son but perhaps he doesn't have the courage to become king as you had hoped."

"You're damn right, my dear Prince," the Duke said, nodding his head. "He's always shying away from his responsibilities so how could I even consider him as a replacement to my brother? He always insisted he was right and never paid heed to my advice, exactly as my father was to me. That was why I insisted on you becoming our next king as you have the makings of a future ruler of Zandar, otherwise if my son had taken over then we would have had further misery within our kingdom and that was something I wasn't prepared to allow my dear Prince Leonardo!"

"Let me dwell on the matter Sir," Leonardo put in. "Tomorrow morning, I'll introduce myself to your people with my sister as my secretary. I think I know exactly what to say to them to win over their support. Anyway, I don't mean to be rude, Sir, but are we going to have something to eat as my stomach's rumbling?"

The Duke laughed out loudly. He thoroughly enjoyed Leonardo's company as well as that of his sister.

"Of course we are, Son," he replied warmly. "Our meal's being prepared right at this moment, and for the record if my daughter makes advances to you just tell her that your main criteria is to keep the people happy and that you can't even contemplate anything to do with love or marriage at the moment as you have far too much on your plate to sort out."

"All well and done, Sir, but will she believe me?" the Prince asked warily.

"Well, she'll have to but I'll be there to back you up, Prince Leonardo. Remember that Daniella's your future bride, and not even my own daughter is going to change those plans, as you deserve one another, even though I won't be saying a single word to Melissa about this evil witch!"

Prince Leonardo bowed graciously to the Duke and the two went into the house together and sat down in the drawing room where the Duke offered the Prince a glass of some type of homemade alcoholic beverage.

"To Prince Leonardo of Blackstone, our future king!" the Duke proclaimed pompously as he raised his glass to toast the occasion.

The Prince downed the potent contents of his glass with one swallow and found it burnt the inside of his mouth and stomach. He turned a shade of deep purple since he was not used to drinking.

"I'm sorry, Sir, but I don't drink so often and that tasted like fire," the Prince spluttered. "It just took my breath away at first but I feel much better."

The Duke poured himself another drink and politely raised the decanter to ask the Prince if he wanted a second drink. However, Leonardo shook his head vigorously and grinned at the Duke as he tipped his head back and downed his drink in one gulp.

"I needed that!" the Duke said as he got up. "Let's go to the women and see what they've been up to."

The young Prince got up rather shakily since he was still feeling a little groggy from the effects of just a single drink. He followed the Duke rather wobbly on his feet and into the lounge next door where they found the Duchess, Princess Lena, Daniella and Tatiana sitting on chairs chatting merrily away while watching Melissa weaving a tapestry she was working on.

When the girls saw the two men, they stopped their chitchat and the Duchess addressed the young prince. "Good afternoon to you, Sir. Has my husband been giving you some of his homemade brew?" she asked on noticing his rosy cheeks.

Leonardo stared at the Duchess and rubbed his eyes. To him she appeared all fuzzy and blurry and sounded as though she was speaking miles down some distant tunnel.

"So how was your day? I need to tell you both something extremely important but without the girls being present. Let's go into the dining room where we can speak in private," the Duchess added as she sprung to her feet.

The Duke and Prince Leonardo followed the Duchess while the girls carried on listening to the talented Melissa telling them how to make a tapestry. The three of them went into the dining room and chose to sit near the fireplace even though the fire had not been lit since the day was warm and muggy.

The Duchess turned to her husband and said, "Your cousin Rupert came over today with some bad news. He didn't know what to say or do on the matter and has left it with me to explain further. A few nights ago, the master huntsman put his horse away in the Royal Stables as usual but when he went to get it out this morning, he noticed the horse covered in blood. It was human blood so after a brief search, they found the trampled remains of a naked man with his head smashed in. Rupert was called and after examining the poor man's mouth, he alleged that the body must have been a male of major importance and stature since the man had a mouthful of 24 ct gold teeth. He thinks it may be the remains of his Majesty, however until he speaks to you about it he feels that he's not ready to cause a fracas over some malicious rumour or other as he was your brother after all."

Prince Leonardo felt the hairs stand up at the back of his neck as he realised what the Duchess was about to reveal, however the Duke responded in a feverish way after listening to his wife's story, making Prince Leonardo realise that he had the Duke's backing over the story he had told him.

"Woman, Rupert should mind his own business!" the Duke snapped angrily. "What would the King be doing sleeping naked in his own royal stables? The soldiers have already told me they found the dead body of their king in the woods so if my cousin is thinking of turning the local people against me, then Prince Leonardo's first job will be to remove his tongue, and then cut off his head for such insolence. We'll have this stranger's body burnt and then tell everyone he was a sorcerer whose fate was determined by the hooves of a horse! And tomorrow morning, Prince Leonardo will be in charge of our kingdom," he added as the Duchess forced a smile. "Anyway, enough chit-chat for now. I'm so sorry for you to hear family squabbles, my dear Prince, and now follow me down to our cellar while my wife returns, to the other women.",

The Duchess smiled, got up and left the men on their own. Prince Leonardo felt the noose loosening around his neck as he followed the Duke to a closed door. Lighting a candle, the Duke inserted a key into the lock, opened the door and went down some steep steps and into the dark and damp cellar with Leonardo following closely behind.

"It's not so pleasant down here, Son," the Duke remarked on noticing the Prince holding his nose. "There's a rumour that the spirits of three enemy soldiers roam around this cellar. They died a slow horrible death after the rats nibbled away at their starved bodies. Anyway, do you feel a sudden chill around us?"

"Yes, I do, in fact, but why has it turned so cold? Do you think it could be the spirits causing it?" Prince Leonardo asked.

As the candlelight lit up the Duke's face eerily, he answered in the strangest of ways. "If we stay down here too long, I believe the spirits will spirit us away and take us into their world forever, so I make sure I only stay in here for no more than fifteen minutes," the Duke said as he led the way through a dark and dismal passageway before arriving at his final destination.

They came to a heavily bolted door, which the Duke unbolted and swung open. Right in front of them, under the dim candlelight, were an endless line of glass bottles.

"Now, my dear prince, as you can see, we have a vast selection of wines and spirits made from many kinds of fruit and left to mature," the Duke continued. "We're also growing some kind of seedless small green fruit that was discovered in a faraway land by one of our envoys. No one had seen such fruit before but we decided to squeeze the juice out of the fruits and make this white wine," he added as he picked up a particular bottle and showed it to Leonardo. "It's become famous and we sell it to many kingdoms who can't buy enough of it so I charge a good price and it helps us live a comfortable life. Anyway, we've been down here long enough now and I don't want any spirits seizing you before you take over the reins of our kingdom. We'll take five bottles of the white and two bottles of the green; you'll find they taste delicious."

The two new friends gathered the bottles and moved out of the darkness and back into the lit hallway but not before the Duke made sure the two doors were securely shut behind them. Once upstairs he rang a bell to call one of his servants.

Leonardo had seen nothing quite like these bottles before and could not recall having seen let alone taste such a delicacy at the palace of the King of Blackstone. After having experienced that dreadful firewater he had been offered earlier, he hoped he would be able to enjoy this particular wine.

"Right, Roc, I need you to clean this bottle and to pull out the bung," the Duke ordered when the servant appeared. "Here's a tool to remove the cork. Put the sharp part of the screw into it and carefully pull it upwards making sure you don't break the bottle or spill any of its contents."

"Yes, Sir," the servant said, worried that he might make a mess of what was actually a simple procedure.

Once in the kitchen, the servant first wiped away the dust, cleaned the bottle with some soap and water and opened it without any difficulty. Luckily, the bung in the bottle had popped out neatly. He went back to his master and handed him the opened bottle of wine.

"See, Roc, that wasn't so hard, was it?" the Duke said sarcastically to his servant who bowed graciously before him. "Now, Roc, pour some of the wine into two glasses, one for my friend Prince Leonardo and the other for myself."

The servant did as he was told and put the bottle onto the table before bowing once again to his master.

"Now, Roc, do the same to the rest of these bottles and bring them back here nice and clean," the Duke ordered his servant. Turning to Leonardo, he continued, "Son, taste this and tell me what you think of it?" the Duke said following which Leonardo took a careful sip as he did not want to burn his insides as he had done the previous time with that homemade spirit.

"Sir, this is beautiful, just like the most delicious woman!" Leonardo remarked in amazement as the wine hit his taste buds. "I can see why the other royals want it so badly. I'm sure the King of Blackstone would have found it very desirable!"

"Your words fit perfectly, my son," the Duke said as he gave out one of his hearty laughs. "It's exactly like a beautiful woman as she's also very desirable. I like your style, Prince Leonardo and I think you'll make the best ever ruler. Now, drink up and this time we'll finish the bottle before dinner is served."

When the bottle was empty, the two men, now completely drunk, staggered into the grand dining room where poor Leonardo almost slipped on the polished floor. However, he managed to steady himself by putting one hand down onto the table, feeling it shudder beneath him. Luckily, apart from being laid with tablecloth, napkins, cutlery and silver goblets, it was empty and waiting for the entrance of the Duke and Duchess.

The Duke told Leonardo to sit at one end of the table while he went to fetch the women. The poor boy felt his head spinning around but in those days, there was no remedy to take away a hangover. A couple of minutes later, the women walked in and sat down, with the Princess and Melissa sitting on either side of Leonardo while the Duke took his seat at the other end of the table together with his wife, while Daniella and Tatiana sat on opposite sides of the table.

The food appeared the moment the Duke sat down. Several servants dressed for the occasion in spotless white uniforms, brought in the dishes and began serving everyone in turn, starting with the Duke and Duchess first and then moving around the table. There was a vast selection of meat which Tatiana forced herself to eat, hoping it was not raptor meat. However, to her pleasant surprise, she found the taste pleasant, as they all did.

"Tatiana, don't worry," the Duke said on noticing the raptor's reluctance at eating the meat. "We don't have raptors in this kingdom. What you're eating is called beef and comes from an animal that we call a cow; it grazes on grass and produces white liquid which we call milk. The lighter-coloured meat is chicken; this is a small feathered creature that lays eggs or is eaten for food as we're doing right now."

"Well, I never, Sir!" Tatiana exclaimed to the Duke, flicking her tongue in and out of her mouth nervously. "I've never heard of any of those creatures as the ones I know about are dinosaurs of all types, flying pterodactyls and various kinds of fish and reptiles. Many of them are far bigger than this room!" she added while the Duke looked on in astonishment, as did his wife and daughter Melissa.

The meal was thoroughly enjoyed by all seated around the table, and as the Duchess on seeing the state of the poor boy said graciously, "Prince Leonardo, I would imagine your day with my husband proved interesting for you to say the least, and did you learn anything useful from your day out!"

"Yes, Madam, and I've realised that the people of Zandar need someone who believes in what they believe in, as over the years they've grown to despise the Duke's brother, and for everyone's sake this has to change sooner rather than later to bring love, peace, and harmony throughout the kingdom!"

"Bravo," Melissa cooed affectionately, staring directly into the Prince's eyes, making him feel extremely awkward. "That's the kind of man for me," The girl continued to add, taking another mouthful of wine, made her more and more intoxicated by the minute, and something the Duke had noticed.

With several bottles of wine opened and everyone getting extremely merry, Melissa turned to the Prince and kissed him directly on the lips much to the disgust of her father, the Duke, who was seated right opposite her.

"You harlot, go to your room right now!" he screamed. "Your behaviour is a disgrace and tomorrow you have to apologise to everyone in this room."

Melissa got to her feet, spilling a number of wine bottles in the process, before running out of the dining room and heading upstairs to her bedroom where she buried her face in her pillow and cried herself to sleep.

"It's not her fault, it was the wine but she did take me completely by surprise!" Leonardo remarked, trying to calm down the situation.

"I won't hear of it, my son," the Duke retorted. "She has to learn that she can't go around kissing people on the lips without even asking! Imagine if it were your sister kissing me!"

"I definitely wouldn't enjoy that!" the Duke's wife put in before giving her husband a stony glare.

"Shut up, you stupid woman!" the Duke shouted arrogantly.

This was the second time Leonardo and the others had heard the Duke chastising his wife over nothing. However, he was happy that he was respected as an alternative ruler to his brother.

"I think we're all ready for bed now as we have a big day in front of us tomorrow and you still have to be shown your bedrooms," the Duke bellowed. "Now, wife, have you arranged enough bedrooms for our guests?"

The Duchess had not realised that they were having guests staying for the night but she did not wish to upset her husband as he did have a mean streak in him, just like his brother, even though he was always telling people that he was far more lenient than his sibling was.

"Let me go and inform the servants to make up five extra rooms," the Duchess calmly replied. "Will you be needing one for the reptile as well?"

The Duke glared at his wife before saying, "Woman, this reptile has a name, Tatiana, and she's Daniella's lady-in-waiting. She's been taking care of the poor girl who had been extremely ill and almost died. Therefore, Tatiana deserves the utmost respect, do you understand?"

"Yes, dear, and my apologies, Tatiana," the Duchess said as she went to get up, however she changed and waited to say something further.

"I'm so sorry about that disgraceful behaviour from my daughter, and it's made me realise more than ever that Melissa hasn't the wisdom to rule over Zandar with you Prince Leonardo."

"Look Duke, Melissa was hoping for something she wasn't able to control, my falling in love with her. My heart's always been with Daniella sir, as I made a promise to myself that I would journey from heaven to hell to protect this girl from anything the witch decides to throw upon us!"

"You deserve each other Leonardo," harped the Duchess, "And to be honest with you Prince Leonardo, Daniella is one lucky girl to win your affection, however now knowing a few of the facts behind the reason why you chose this gorgeous female over any other, then I realise that you'll make Zandar the most perfect of Kings, and I can't wait until you accept the crown from my husband now I must go and instruct the servants to prepare the rooms."

"Well said," The Duke cried before continuing to add, "You're dead right my dear, there is no one more suitable than both Prince Leaonardo and Princess Daniella to rule Zandar together as husband and wife."

In fact I can't wait to reveal this young Prince and his fiancee tomorrow to the people of Zandar. I'm sure they'll love this man and woman as much as I do, and that's the greatest reason to step down and hand the crown over to someone who will care for his people, so I don't need to spell it out to you my dear why I chose Prince Leonardo, and his future bride Princess Daniella!"

Chapter 24
Relaxation

One week soon flew by and it was time for us to leave for Thailand. The night before our flight, I packed my suitcase and got everything together. That evening, I hardly had much time to think about writing and I needed to sleep early anyway as our taxi was booked for half past four in the morning.

I woke up at half past three with a start and went to the bathroom for a quick wash. Feeling fresh and clean, I put on my clothes and took my luggage out into the landing and down the stairs where I met up with the others who were already having breakfast. I made myself a quick breakfast of toast and marmalade and poured myself a cup of tea. Just as I finished, we saw the lights of the taxi pull up and reverse into the driveway. The driver knocked at the door and my son went to open it.

"Good morning, Sir," the taxi driver said as he tipped his cap. "I believe you've booked a taxi for Heathrow Airport."

"Yes, that's right," my son replied. "Our luggage is in the hallway. Can you help me put it into the vehicle?"

"Of course, Sir, you do what you need to do, and Edward, that's me, Sir, will put everything into the car while you and your family can make themselves comfortable inside. You can then check to make sure I've not forgotten anything before you lock up the house."

Edward began taking the luggage out from the hallway while we all went to the taxi to get in, leaving my son to check and lock everything up. With everyone seated in the taxi and with the luggage packed securely, we drove off in the direction of the M40 motorway that led towards London and the airport. We were all jabbering away at each other during the two-hour journey as we were excited by the thought of travelling to a country so far away and so different in culture from what we were used to in the UK.

We got to the airport with plenty of time to spare and checked our luggage in. Daniella was thrilled at the thought of seeing the last wild elephants in Thailand and when we boarded the plane she sat down next to me as I had planned to do some writing on the long thirteen-hour flight and had my laptop with me.

We were flying Thai Air so were keen to taste some of the local delicacies. After going through the flight magazine, I learnt that the main food dished up on the plane was chicken, rice, noodles, peppers, and hot chillies. We were flying business class and enjoyed seats that were more comfortable and with more legroom than those offered in economy as well as a superior selection of food.

I looked behind to see if Carol and my son were sleeping and was surprised to see them chattering away to each other and also laughing and giggling like a newlywed couple. Maybe this holiday was the medicine we all needed, and taking Daniella and me along was an extra bonus.

The plane began moving and after rumbling along a myriad of taxiways took its place behind a number of other aircraft. Finally, it was our turn and the pilot revved up the engines. The plane began to accelerate down the runway and took off after it reached its threshold speed. The aircraft climbed higher and higher before levelling out; looking out of the window it seemed as though we were floating on top of the clouds. I had never seen anything looking so beautiful before.

Some ten minutes later, we were amazed to see the cabin crew already busy as they began handing out breakfast trays to the passengers. There were a number of small dishes with a selection of meat, a small bowl of fried rice and a type of pancake. There were hardly any spices at all except in one particular dish of what seemed like curried lamb that was incredibly fiery and burnt my throat from the first bite. I warned Daniella who heeded my words and ate very cautiously by taking a drink of her cold coke after every forkful to take away the burning sensation of the curry. Overall, I found the breakfast to be extremely tasty, as did Daniella.

"Thanks, Granddad, you're a saviour!" Daniella exclaimed after we had finished our breakfasts. "That lamb was very spicy and I know already how a dragon feels! Is this the kind of food we'll be eating in Thailand?"

"I don't think so, child," I replied to the young girl. "We'll be staying in some of the best hotels in the country so we'll probably find many varieties of dishes to choose from. It wouldn't surprise me if we even get served English breakfast's on most morning's in the hotel restaurant!"

"Do you think so, Granddad? That sounds great but I do want to try the occasional local food, or perhaps even delicacies from other countries as well, especially if you think that the hotels will cater to meet everyones palate."

"Of course, that's why we're going to Thailand, to experience some traditional Thai foods as well. Now, my dear, I need you to remain silent as I'm about to bring Princess Daniella back to life."

My granddaughter stared at me for a few seconds before leaning over to me and kissing me on the cheek.

"That's what I was hoping you'd say, Granddad. I can't wait to read where she goes next. Does she marry Leonardo or does Melissa get him?"

"You'll have to wait and find out, Granddaughter. Remember, you're honoured that I let you watch me as it was something I never allowed Granny to do anything like that. Looking back, I now realise it was grossly unfair of me as she was a major part of my life and I should have shared it more with her. I'm doing this for her as well as you, darling, as I now appreciate that I was mean to Granny not showing her my stories in advance."

"Oh well, Granddad, it's not as though Granny has gone forever as she's watching over us. I wonder which seat she's chosen to sit in!" Daniella remarked as she looked around. "Did you see Granny perched on the back of the seat of the taxi?"

"No, I didn't really look so if you're telling me she's with us then of course I know she is as you can see her just as well as I can."

"Granny looked so comfortable riding on the luggage train that went out to the aircraft!" Daniella added with a chuckle. "I watched her disappear into the hold together with the suitcases when I looked out of the observation window while we were going through the final checkout."

I had not noticed my wife in the taxi or being loaded into the aircraft's hold. However, I could somehow feel that Rebecca was with us in spirit and mind. I smiled at my granddaughter, brought out my laptop and turned it on to continue my story.

"Prince Leonardo, your first official task is to inform the people of the death of their King," the Duke continued once his wife had left the room. "Secondly, have your soldiers arrest my cousin and put him in prison to await trial. Inform the people that you've been brought in from Blackstone to rule until the Duke of Bridgestone decides otherwise but that it's possible you may become the next king. Finally, tell them of your plans to make this a happy kingdom once again. From tomorrow, I also expect you to take over from my dead brother and call the palace your new home, as will your sister and friends. Now, no more talking as we need to sleep. Your rooms are ready and the servants will show you the way. Breakfast will be served at six o'clock sharp as we have a one-hour journey ahead of us and need to get ready. Wear your most elegant clothes, all of you, as you'll be on official duty when presenting yourselves to the people of our kingdom. I'm not sure how they'll take it but hopefully all will be fine."

Prince Leonardo rose to his feet, as did his sister, Daniella and Tatiana, following which the Prince said, "Thank you for your kind hospitality, Sir. We'll be seeing you in the morning bright and early."

On this last note, the four left the room, leaving the Duke pondering how the people would respond at being told of the death of his brother. After spending a long time deep in thought, the Duke went up to bed since he too was tired after the past events that had unfolded throughout that day, especially his daughter's misconduct.

The next morning, Prince Leonardo awoke to the sound of a rooster crowing. It was the day of reckoning when he was about to introduce himself to the people. A sharp knock at the door told him that someone was waiting to come in. He got out of bed, opened the door and three servants walked in, two carrying a steel bath while the female held a jug of water. At first, the Prince wondered why they had come but he then realised that it was normal for the servants to wash and dress you when you're royalty.

One of the male servants undressed him while the young attractive female washed his naked body all over using a cloth and soap. When the girl rubbed his privates, he was a little shocked to say the least but the female just smiled up at him before continuing with her work. She finally asked Leonardo to stand up and she dried him lovingly all over with a soft fleece towel. She was extremely thorough, as was the male servant, who had taken the clothes that Leonardo had selected to wear, including the undergarments and a smart black and gold tailored suit and black polished lace up boots, and dressed him. It made the Prince look regal and inspiring, a fact that most certainly would be put to the test that same day.

Once dressed with his hair neatly brushed and shining, Leonardo went out into the hallway where he came across his sister, Princess Lena, and Daniella and Tatiana who were coming from another direction.

"Were you bathed and dressed by the servants as soon as you woke up?" the Prince asked the three girls.

"Yes, it was a total embarrassment," the Princess replied to her brother. "However, the servants seem used to washing people and dressing them so how could you refuse?"

"You all look so clean and beautiful, ladies!" the Prince said, offering a little encouragement. "Daniella and Tatiana, you should be extremely proud of Oswald's tailoring as he's made the most elegant of clothes and they look perfect on both of you."

"Yes, indeed, and we're very happy with our clothes," Daniella said.

"Anyway, let's not waste any more time," Leonardo put in. "We must go downstairs for breakfast as we promised the Duke that we'd arrive no later than six and it's two minutes before the hour right now."

All four of them went downstairs where Jenkins, the Duke's head housekeeper, greeted them.

"Good morning," he said. "Follow me as the table's laid and breakfast's about to be served. The Duke was telling me you're going to speak to the people today so I wish you luck, young Sir."

"Thank you, Jenkins, that's very kind of you," the Prince said as he gave the housekeeper a pleasant smile.

The four of them took a seat around the table waiting for the arrival of the Duke who came in soon afterwards arm in arm with his wife.

"You look so elegant in that black and gold suit, Prince Leonardo and all you ladies look so beautiful as well," the Duke remarked after wishing them all a good morning. "The people of our kingdom will adore you for sure." Everyone was wondering where Melissa was so he continued while the servants brought in their breakfast, "Melissa's carrying on with her tapestry. I told the girl that this business has nothing to do with her and that I'd tell her the outcome on my return. She didn't ask whether you'd be coming back with me so I left it at that. Now, eat up before the food runs away!" he concluded with a chuckle.

Their breakfast consisted of some freshly baked bread, various slices and cuts of cold meat, a selection of local fruit and a jug of freshly squeezed orange juice.

"How many members of staff are employed at the palace, Sir?" the Prince asked the Duke before helping himself to some bread and a few slices of cold pork.

"Well, up to a few days ago, there were five thousand soldiers but some three thousand of them have vanished into thin air. There are also around three hundred servants and ten supervisors; some of these work in the garden or keep the manor clean while others take care of the horses or work in the kitchen. Besides, there are also their wives and children living with them. However, what's constantly on my mind at the moment are the families of those poor soldiers who disappeared near the forest. Perhaps, we also have an evil presence there!"

"That thought did occur to me too, Sir, to be honest," the Prince said nervously. "However, things may become complicated if we also have to contend with a witch or sorcerer in this kingdom too!"

"Forget about witches and enchanted forests," the Duke replied very matter-of-factly after a servant whispered something to him. "We have a far more pressing task to complete this morning. We must leave right now as the royal coach has arrived. Your luggage is right now being loaded into the carriage as you'll be staying at the Palace from now on."

They all made their way out to the royal coach with the Duke saying goodbye to his wife and his daughter staring longingly at Leonardo from the window of her bedroom. The driver whipped the horses and they were off. They made good progress along the bumpy road and they were soon in the town centre and then passing through the open palace gates before coming to a stop outside the main entrance.

The Ambassador came down the stone steps and welcomed everyone before sending for some servants to bring in the trunks and cases off the carriage and to take them upstairs to the main bedrooms. Leading the way, he then took them to his office and invited them to sit down while he attended to some last minute touches prior to the introduction to the people of Prince Leonardo and his sister. It was now almost a quarter to eight and the palace square was already almost full of people both from the town as well as from outside.

After some time, the Ambassador came marching into the room and spoke to Prince Leonardo. "It's time for you and your sister to be introduced to the people. You'll be addressing them from the main balcony upstairs where everything's been arranged," he said before turning to the Duke. "Will you be speaking first, Sir? I think it might be better for you to introduce this fresh blood from Blackstone as you know them better than anyone else does."

"Yes, I think you could be right but it will be Prince Leonardo who will announce my brother's death," the Duke said. "By the way, what did the soldiers say on their return?"

"That's another matter to worry over, Sir," the Ambassador replied tensely. "They didn't all come back. I sent out one thousand men with their Captain and only two hundred returned. Somehow, the others got lost in the forest and now the remaining soldiers are refusing to go back to that evil place as they believe that some bad spirits wander inside!"

"What utter tosh!" the Duke cried, sending shivers down everyone's back. "If the soldiers refuse my orders, Prince Leonardo will make things extremely difficult for them. Now lead us to the balcony and I'll begin addressing the people of Zandar."

The Ambassador led the Duke, Prince and Princess along a long corridor and into a huge congress room that had several balconies on different sides of the room while Daniella and the raptor waited in the Ambassador's office.

"Good luck to you and your sister, Prince Leonardo, and I hope all goes well," the Ambassador said as he shook the Prince's hand. "Meanwhile, Lady Daniella and Miss Tatiana can remain with me until you're finished."

Chapter 25
A Royal Appointment Awaits

There was a sudden cheer from the town and country folk when they saw the Duke but they also wondered who the elegantly dressed man and woman were. The Duke waited until the people grew quiet before he went up to the podium.

"Good morning and thank you for coming," he announced. "I wish to introduce you to Prince Leonardo and his sister, Princess Lena, who are both here on my request. They've travelled from the kingdom of Blackstone where King Rudolf reigns."

The crowd below began hissing and booing since they had heard about this king's brutality.

At that moment, a young well-dressed man stepped forward and shouted loudly, "And has the worst ever temper!"

This was unexpected but the Duke hardly batted an eyelid as he motioned to the Prince to stand up and address the people.

"People of Zandar," Prince Leonardo began. "King Rudolf is everything you say he is but I'm not here to speak about the kingdom of Blackstone."

The same individual stepped forward and yelled, "Let's hear it then as we haven't got all day! We need to go back to our work as the King's taxes are so high that we're forced to work long hours just to scrape a living!"

The Duke almost swallowed his tongue on hearing this man's rude outburst and was about to have him arrested when the Prince waved him down.

"Young man, what's your name?" the Prince asked gently as the Duke reluctantly went back to his chair.

"Radmas Stutt, Sir," the young man stammered to the Prince.

"Well, Mr Radmas Stutt, I think you'll want to hear what I have to say next so please come forward," the Prince said politely. The crowd parted down the middle to allow the young man through, following which the Prince continued, "After my speech, young man, I wish to speak to you behind closed doors. Is that understood?"

"Yes, Sir," the man replied as he kept on moving forwards until he stood right under the balcony and almost within spitting distance of the Prince.

"Now, people of Zandar, my sister and I have come here in order to temporarily lead you after the sudden disappearance of your King," the Prince said as his booming voice echoed all around the square. "It's my duty to tell you that the Duke has no intention of taking over from his brother and that's why he sent me a message asking for my assistance. I'm also the harbinger of bad news as the King's remains were discovered deep inside the forest; it seems he's been torn to shreds by wild animals," he added as an uneasy murmur went through the crowd.

The same young man spoke further; it was as though he was speaking on the people's behalf. "Prince Leonardo, I represent everyone here and we're all wondering how you can help us. Do you intend to remain here?"

"Yes, that's my plan," the Prince replied, following which he turned to Rasmas Stutt and addressed the smartly dressed man. "Tell me, what taxes are you being charged at the moment?"

"Ninety percent of whatever we earn. How can we possibly earn a crust like this? We're starving to death!" the man moaned as the crowd began jeering and shouting.

The Duke wondered how the Prince was going to get out of this pickle and sincerely hoped they did not have the beginnings of a riot on their hands.

However, Prince Leonardo held up his hands and shouted above the jeers of the crowd. "From this day forward, the sovereignty will take fifty percent tax and no more. If you wish me to be appointed king, then I will seriously consider it. Now, people of Zandar, who do you want as your next ruler?"

The people began jumping up and down simultaneously, making the ground shake beneath their feet while they repeatedly roared, "Long live King Leonardo!"

Prince Leonardo put up his hands once again to try to bring some calm to the situation, before saying, "I'll be consulting with the Duke to see how I can help you. However, before I say goodbye, I give your spokesperson, Mr Rasmas Stutt, permission to sit with me in my chambers to discuss your needs. I wish you all a fruitful day and promise you that you'll never experience high taxes again if I decide to take control of your kingdom."

The people began walking out of the square with big smiles on their faces, something they had not done for years, as they chatted animatedly to each other. They could not believe their ears that this Prince was prepared to deduct their taxes by a whopping forty percent. This Prince had to be their next King, the people told themselves as they returned home or to their workplace.

Once off the balcony and inside the congress hall, the Duke turned to Leonardo to congratulate him. "You'll have the people eating out of your hand!" he exclaimed as he shook the Prince's hand vigorously. "I'm not sure I agree to the forty percent cut in taxes as that will put a big hole in the royal coffers but to be honest I've never seen the people looking so happy. I also applaud you on the way you told them about the demise of my brother. They may not even expect a funeral as the body has been torn to shreds and cannot be paraded around as we normally do when a member of the royal family passes away. Anyway, while I go and think this offer over, you can hold your meeting with that nasty young man and if he causes any more grievances then he's to be clapped in irons! I also want you to give me a report first thing in the morning. You may also be sworn in as king as early as tomorrow if I agree to your proposal. What are your ideas about this?"

"I'll do my best to rule this kingdom fairly together with my sister who will stand in for me when I'm away with Daniella in Blackstone," the Prince replied hesitantly.

"That's fine, Son, even though I wish you weren't going on such a dangerous mission to take on that evil presence in your kingdom. Of course, I hope your journey is successful and that you come back to us soon," the Duke said as a few tears rolled down his face. "Anyhow, let's go down to the Ambassador's room."

Prince Leonardo had not seen the Duke cry before but hoped this meant that he was showing more compassion towards his people. The Duke led the Prince and his sister downstairs where they met up with Daniella and Tatiana.

"Did your speech go well, Prince Leonardo?" the Ambassador asked.

"Yes," the Duke butted in. "He's gone and promised the people the world!"

"I hope that's a good thing, Sir, as the people will expect the new King to follow through with his proposals," the Ambassador remarked. "However, he'll receive great respect from me as I've always had a soft touch for the people and I hate to see them struggling as they're doing right now."

"You could be right, Ambassador," the Duke said thoughtfully. "I'm going to think about this very carefully. Perhaps, it's the right thing to do."

Meanwhile, Leonardo had moved closer to Daniella. "I've promised the people a hefty cut in their tax dues to the king," the Prince whispered to the girl. "I hope I've done the rightful thing!"

"Leonardo, I'm sure it's justified as the King sucked these poor people dry just as King Rudolf did to the people of Blackstone. I stand behind you one hundred percent and now I know you'll be the perfect king for Zandar."

The Prince bent down and kissed Daniella's hands. "Only if you'll be my wife, though!" he exclaimed. "However, before we can even discuss marriage, we have to bring Blackstone to its former glory. I wish I hadn't been so stupid selling us to the Dark Lord to make you stronger and to repair your injuries faster. I know that if we fail in our mission, he'll come for both of our souls to make up for the disappointment of not having the witch's heart. Now, follow me, as we have a meeting to attend."

The Prince led the way out of the room and asked one of the royal guards on duty in the hallway to the way to his office. The guard looked suspiciously at the Prince before realising who he was following which he escorted the Prince and his royal entourage down the hallway. After opening a heavy engraved door, he took them into a large spacious room overlooking the most wonderful of gardens. The room boasted a polished wooden floor with animal skins for rugs and hand painted tapestries and various swords and shields decorated with the King's own emblem on the walls. This was a place of grandeur and on the far side, there were a number of comfortable armchairs and a desk with a huge unlit fireplace made of natural stone.

The guard was about to salute when the Prince said, "We have a guest, a certain Mr Stutt waiting outside. Can you bring him in here? I told him I wished to speak with him."

"Yes, Sire, I'll go this minute and bring him for you," the guard replied in a rather gruff voice before bowing to everyone in the room and disappearing in order to go and find that young man.

"This room's so elegant and exquisite," Princess Lena remarked after the guard had left the room. "Do you think this is the King's private study, Leonardo?"

Before Leonardo could answer his sister, there was a knock at the door and the Prince shouted. "Come in!"

The door swung open and a young man stood there. He had never been in the King's palace before and he was scared stiff. He shuffled in slowly with his hands behind his back and his head bowed low.

"It's me, Sire, Stutt," he managed to say after a long pause. "You invited me to speak to you."

"Oh, yes, you're the outspoken young man who interrupted me on several occasions," the Prince said with a stern voice. "Do you know what King Rysis would have done about this situation?" Stutt felt his legs shaking and about to give way when the Prince continued, "Join us over here, Mr Stutt, and I'm not going to behead you, well not today anyway so don't fret, so take that worried look off your face and tell me what other grievances the people of Zandar have."

Stutt ambled his way over to the desk and bowed graciously to the ladies, before saying, "I shouldn't say this, Sire, but the people hated the King and everything about him. None of them killed him, I'm certain of that, but not one of them shed a tear when you told them he was dead. He destroyed our livelihoods with his exorbitant taxes he charged us and the people were living in poverty and had lost all will to live. Every Tuesday, the King expected the people to bring the cash to him or face his wrath even if they were one percent less of the total amount due. He'd throw them into the dungeons and we never saw them again. We still don't know to this very day where some of our family are or if they're still alive!"

"My God!" the Princess cried out while the Prince indicated to Stutt that he could sit down.

"I was forgetting myself, Mr Stutt," the Prince said. "Please sit down as I want you to feel more relaxed with me. Let me start by introducing you to my sister, Princess Lena. This young lady on my right is my distant cousin, Lady Daniella, and next to her is her lady-in-waiting, Tatiana. I promise you that if the Duke decides to appoint me as King of Zandar, I'll be fulfilling all the promises I make. I'd also like to tell you that besides lowering the tax rate by forty per cent, I'll also make sure that any unfortunate people held in the dungeons for not paying their taxes will be released unconditionally."

"I thank you from the bottom of my heart, Sire, and hope the Duke appoints you as our new king. You're a breath of fresh air for our kingdom and you seem to be a man of substance who keeps to his word. The people will respect you for sure they will Sire, for changing the harsh tax regime and for releasing stricken members of their families. Now, I've taken up too much of your time so I beg my leave, Sire," Stutt concluded as he got up and bowed low to the Prince who had one final trick up his sleeve.

"We want you to join us for lunch, young Stutt, as we need to speak to you further," the Prince said much to the young man's surprise.

Even if the young man had just eaten a full English breakfast, he was ready to die for the opportunity of dining at the Palace.

"That would be nice, Sire," he replied. "Do you want me to remain outside and wait until you're ready to eat, Sire?"

Leonardo liked this young man and wondered perhaps if he could find him a position on his team. He looked the reliable sort as well as being trustworthy to the people.

"Rasmas, stay here while I go and arrange for lunch to be prepared," the Prince said as he got to his feet and left the room.

Out in the hallway, the young Prince tried to locate the same guard who had helped him previously but since he could not spot him, he stopped an attractive young female of about twenty years or so who was hurrying on some errand or other. She had neatly brushed long brown hair tied at the back, blue eyes and a curvy delectable figure.

"I was wondering where I could order lunch for my guests," the Prince asked the girl. "Can you tell me the way to the kitchen?"

"Sire, you stay in your room and I, Jeanette, will go and arrange everything with the chef and will come back to inform you when it's ready," she replied with a warm smile.

"Thank you, Jeanette," the Prince said to the startled girl who had never had a royal calling her by her first name before.

She curtsied to Leonardo before hurrying away to tell the rest of the staff while the Prince made his way back to his office to join the others. Once back in his room, he headed straight over to the French windows overlooking the magnificent gardens, far better than the ones at Blackstone, opening them fully and feeling the gentle breeze blowing into the room.

"I've arranged for lunch and a young girl called Jeanette will be letting us know when it's ready," the Prince announced as he went over to his desk and sat down.

"Sire," Rasmas said to the young Prince. "It's not customary for a future monarch to call a servant girl by her first name. In this kingdom, the people don't accept such familiarity from a royal but that's your decision at the end of the day."

"How ridiculous!" Daniella exclaimed loudly. "Why can't you call someone by their Christian name? What's the problem with that? Why, I've always called my lady-in-waiting by her proper name. I don't call her raptor, Tatiana, and I also expect you to call me Daniella. Are you saying that if we live in this kingdom we must do what all other royals have done in the past?" Daniella asked as she glared at poor Rasmas who suddenly felt vulnerable by her wrath and cowered down in his chair.

"No, your lady," he replied as he was rescued by Jeanette knocking on the door.

"Dinner's served, Sire," she said after she came into the room. "If you follow me, I'll show you to the dining hall."

"Thank you, Jeanette," Princess Lena said to the girl, showing Daniella and the Prince that she too welcomed the idea of calling the staff by their proper names.

They all got to their feet and followed the young servant girl as she led them into the main dining hall. It was empty except for a long polished wooden table set with padded chairs and laid with a silk tablecloth, napkins, silver cutlery and crystal wine glasses.

Chapter 26
A New Regime

Following a clap from Jeanette's hands, a number of smartly dressed waiters appeared as if by magic. One or two of them wheeled in trolleys laden with all kinds of meat, vegetables and fruit while others brought in warm China plates that they set down in front of everyone. One of the male waiters also brought several bottles of wine from the Duke's private cellar and began to fill all the glasses before returning the bottles to the table.

"Sire," he said to Leonardo. "If you need any more wine, please do not hesitate to ask one of the waiters. Meanwhile, enjoy your meal as you have some interesting dessert to enjoy afterwards."

Prince Leonardo smiled at the waiter who went back to the kitchen while a couple of servers began dishing the food out onto the plates.

Before they tucked into their food, the Prince raised his glass, as did the others. "To friendship; we all need it at some time or other in our lives," he announced as they all put the glasses to their lips and drank the refreshing wine.

"Sire, this wine, as you call it, is delicious; it's nothing like I've ever tried before," Rasmas exclaimed as the others laughed heartily and began digging into the food on their plates.

"Are you enjoying the food, young Rasmas?" the Prince said to his newly acquainted friend after taking a few mouthfuls of meat and vegetables.

"Yes, Sire, the food's excellent but there's so much to eat I'll soon be as fat as a pig!" Rasmas replied.

"A what?" Prince Leonardo asked, wondering what the boy meant by pig.

"Pig, Sire, don't you have this animal in Blackstone? We call the meat from the pig pork and it's often eaten in our kingdom," the young man explained.

"I've never heard of it but have you eaten raptor meat?" the Prince said, forgetting that they had a raptor that was extremely well mannered at the table.

At that, Princess Lena snapped at her brother. "Leonardo, are you forgetting that we have Tatiana with us at the table and that she is the most enjoyable being I've ever known. And what does Daniella make of your insensitive comment?"

"I'm really sorry so please accept my sincere apologies, Tatiana," the Prince said to the raptor.

"Of course, Leonardo," Tatiana replied. "However, let me explain to Rasmas what you meant. Raptors are vicious flesh eaters that we sometimes call dinosaurs. These roamed the world many millions of years ago but they still live in certain parts of the planet. In my case, I come from a group of raptors that have been gifted with the power of speech and beautifully coloured coats to make us look important and regal. However, some of us slipped the net and these are the ones enjoyed by King Rudolf and his citizens, even though when we met he felt humbled as I was looking after Lady Daniella."

"Well put, Tatiana, and I won't slip up again, I promise," Prince Leonardo said as he smiled at the raptor who was grinning like a Cheshire cat leaving Rasmas wondering where these royals got all their endearing charm from.

At one point during their meal, Rasmas turned to the young raptor and asked her, "Do you have a family, Tatiana?"

"Yes," the raptor replied to Rasmas. "However, I had to leave them to fend for themselves. I miss them a lot but one day soon, I hope to go back to them since my children are still young. At the moment, they're being taken care of by my husband, Oswald, who's a master tailor and makes the most beautiful clothes for King Midas."

"I've never heard that name before. Where does he come from?" Rasmas asked inquisitively.

"Forget that name, Rasmas, that is, if you still wish us to be friends," the Prince snapped as he lost his temper and looked sharply at the raptor who realised she had said too much and that Leonardo was not happy with her.

"I don't wish to pry into private matters, Sire," Rasmas stammered ruefully. "That's the last thing I would do and if you think I am then I must apologise as you've shown me great courtesy inviting me today to dine with you and your family. I am left without a family as the King held them in the dungeons without ever giving them food or water. When I was finally allowed to visit them, it was too late as my mother, father, sister and younger brother had all died!" he added before burying his head in his hands and breaking down into loud sobs.

"We're really sorry for your terrible loss, Rasmas," the Princess said, speaking on everyone's behalf. "If my brother is chosen to be your next King we promise to release anyone who's still locked up in the dungeons. Now I'm going to say something out of turn and whether or not my brother agrees, you deserve so much credit for making the people proud and standing up for your rights. I'd be really honoured for you to work together with us to turn this kingdom into something extremely special."

"Rasmas, my sister beat me to it," the Prince added while nodding his head. "That's the main reason why I asked you to join us today. May I ask what payment you used to receive for being the people's spokesman?"

Rasmas looked astonished by the question that the Prince was asking but he came straight out with it. "I never received any money, Sire, as these people have lost so much and I'd be as heartless as the King if I'd asked for a single penny!"

"I thought as much, Rasmas," Prince Leonardo said. "If I'm appointed tomorrow, will you become my advisor? You'll receive a handsome salary of four hundred gold coins per annum together with your own horse and carriage and you can live at the Palace without charge and eat for free."

"That's so good of you, Sire," Rasmas said with tears in his eyes since no one had ever been so kind to him before. "I'll never forget such generosity. With that kind of salary and with my own horse and carriage, I can command any female I want! Sorry for being so impolite ladies but I've been so poor and desolate for three whole years!"

Princess Lena, Lady Daniella and Tatiana all smiled at the young man who had shown that he was worthy of a position at the Palace.

"Rasmas, when my brother and Lady Daniella leave for Blackstone, you'll become my right hand man," Princess Lena put in. "It will be your job to tell me if there is any unrest with any of the people or if any crimes are being committed within the town or in the villages. If I have to have people executed then it must be for a valid reason such as murder or something as sinister. Taxation laws will be revised and you, Rasmas, will visit the people every month with an armed escort and collect any payments owed by them. And if you do the work right, you'll get a substantial pay rise at the end of the year."

Rasmas fiddled with his shirt buttons before answering the Princess. "My Lady, it will be my pleasure to take on such an important position. Perhaps, we could have a secure metal box placed on wheels to put the money in with bars all the way around with just a single door at the back like we use for the transport of dangerous prisoners. There may be robbers along the way but if the coins are locked inside an armed coach then they'll think twice before attacking us, I hope!" he added with a guffaw.

"Good thinking, Rasmas," Prince Leonardo said once more coming into the conversation. "If I'm appointed tomorrow your job will be to visit the people, get to know them, find out what kind of business they're operating and if they have problems coughing up their dues, we can give them an extra month in which to pay up. If it does come down to holding people in prison, they'll have three daily meals and sufficient water each day. And no more life sentences will be handed down except to those who have committed murder."

"That's amazing, Sire, so when are you carrying out these reforms?" Rasmas asked.

"The moment I'm appointed ruler of this kingdom," the Prince promptly replied. "From that day onwards, your job is to go round informing the people of my new laws besides collecting their taxes. For this extra work, you'll receive an additional one hundred gold coins per annum. How does that sound, young Rasmas?"

"I've never dreamt of having so much money, Sire, and your generosity is beyond anything I could ever have hoped for," Rasmas said with tears streaming down his cheeks. "I won't let you down, Sire, and I'll remain loyal to all your family and friends."

The girls all applauded the young man who turned a deep shade of red. He was feeling extremely hot so he took a long drink of wine and felt the cool liquid hitting the back of his throat. He just could not stop smiling as this was the best day of his life.

"Now, where were you staying tonight, my dear friend?" Prince Leonardo asked.

"Where I normally stay, Sire, at my parents' home," the young man replied while wiping away his tears with a soiled handkerchief.

“The house needs urgent repair but I don’t have enough money to do anything about it.”

“Well, Rasmas, after the first taxes are received, I can make sure you have enough money to repair the house to how you want it if you still wish to live there rather than at your new home here at the Palace. Think about it, living outside in one of the villages is probably better as you can then check on your fellow villagers more easily. What do you think?”

“You’re right, Sire, that’s an excellent plan. If my home is rebuilt to its former glory, my family won’t have died in vain. Now, I beg you to allow me to leave as I promised to speak to several of the villagers and townsfolk. They’ll want to know what we were discussing, but I’ll only tell them what’s necessary for them to know.”

The Prince smiled at the young man, as did the girls, as he got to his feet but not before bowing to everyone. He toddled out feeling somewhat muzzy from the effects of the wine although he did not know at the time the reason why he felt so legless.

Once outside, Rasmas put on his hat to shield himself from the hot bright sunshine, walked out of the palace gates and headed into the town centre. Once there, He knocked on a wooden door and the barber, Maxamillious Rufus, welcomed him in. He smiled as the young man went inside and sat down.

“How did your meeting go, my boy?” the barber asked curiously. “Are we in for an even worse life than before?”

“The Prince is a good man, Max, and you should pray that the lad is given a chance by the Duke as he’ll make a first class King. Did you hear about the lower tax payment?”

“Yes, we did but who knows what he decides if he takes over?” the barber remarked sarcastically.

“Not this one, Max,” Rasmas said. “I’m also to be made Royal Advisor so I’ll always be looking after the people as I’m one of you and it will always remain like that.”

Rufus stared at Rasmas in shock. He was so stunned by the news of him being made Royal Advisor that he forgot all about the free haircut and shave he had promised him. However, he quickly came to his senses, poured some ale into two tankards and handed one to the boy.

"Let's drink to success then," Rufus said. "If this Prince is appointed our next king and is ready to reduce taxes as he said, he'll have my support for sure."

Rasmas felt the cool liquid quenching his thirst. His first meeting had gone well so excusing himself he left and went five doors further down the street before coming to the candlestick maker. Walking up to the door, he knocked loudly and waited. A middle-aged man appeared, around six foot tall, with grey hair, a bushy moustache and strong but angular facial features.

"Rasmas, I was expecting you two hours ago!" he complained. "Anyway, did your meeting go down well with the Prince?"

"So and so," the young man said to Brahm Hardy as he entered the shop and repeated all that he had said to the barber.

"So the young Prince has offered you a job as his advisor, has he? A very important position!" he scoffed enviously. "Does it pay well? And where will your loyalties lie from then on?"

"You don't even have to question me over such things, Hardy," Rasmas replied feeling offended. "You know the amount of time I've put into this work and I never charged the people a penny. Don't I deserve a well paid job after losing my family because of the King's greed?"

"You've got me all wrong, Son," the candlestick maker said, trying to wheedle his way out of an awkward situation. "Of course you deserve a good job but I'm worried we won't be as friendly as before. Do you understand what I mean?"

"I think so," Rasmas answered. "Anyhow, it's time for me to leave as I need to visit Elsa, the baker. I'll visit you again when

I know what my position entails," Rasmas added as he bid the candlestick maker goodbye.

He was still annoyed by the man's attitude as he had always treated him fairly. He kept on walking along the street until he reached the bakery where a friendly smiling face greeted him. It was Elsa; she always enjoyed flirting a little with the young man.

"Rasmas!" Elsa said as she fluttered her eyes all girly like at the young man. "Come in, my favourite man! If I were younger, we'd be courting for sure especially with my husband six feet under and you with no family. Maybe, we're made for each other!" she added as, for the first time ever, she leant over to the poor boy and drowned him in voluptuous lust with her passionate kisses, refusing to let him go.

"Elsa, what are you thinking?" Rasmas gasped as he finally managed to emerge from the woman's flesh and wipe the sweat that had suddenly built up on his brow. "I can't replace Ned, your husband, as we're very different from each other. I had no idea you thought of me in this way so perhaps I should go."

"Don't be silly, Rasmas, but I fancy you a lot and when a woman feels that way she must show her affection," Elsa said. "Let me get you some cold orange juice. I squeezed the oranges myself this morning and I'm sure you'll enjoy it."

The overenthusiastic female waddled away, her size and height making it difficult for her to walk properly. When she returned to the drawing room where she had taken Rasmas into, she smiled at the young man before handing him the drink.

Tasting the orange juice, he said to the woman, "Elsa, this is really good and I'm flattered to think that you fancy me but there are other guys out there that deserve you more than I do. Anyway, do you want to hear what went on with the Prince today?"

"Yes, my beauty," Elsa said, licking her lips like some hungry predator.

Rasmas told her what had gone on, repeating to the letter what he had said to the barber and candlestick maker. When it came down to the fact that the Prince had offered the young man a senior position at the palace, she showed no remorse.

"That's brilliant news and no more than you deserve my dear boy!" she remarked. "You've helped so many people and received nothing in return so you truly deserve it. But do you honestly believe the Prince will reduce our taxes and wipe away all debts to the realm?"

Elsa stared longingly at the young man who felt a little troubled. It seemed as though the woman was ready to dive on him so he excused himself by saying that he had further appointments. The woman, forced to give up, had to let the poor boy get up and leave.

Once outside, Rasmas walked back towards the Palace but as he drew near to the main gates, he decided to head home instead.

"That was damn lucky," he remarked to himself with a chuckle. "Elsa almost suffocated me! She's one big girl so just imagine if I were married to her; she'd kill me for sure with her over enthusiastic indulgence!"

Meanwhile, the Prince, his sister and Daniella were being given a guided tour around the palace by the young servant girl, Jeanette, who smiled at them as she led them from room to room, down this hallway and then the next. The Prince soon lost count of the number of rooms since the Palace was huge.

Jeanette then took them outside into the garden that was paved with colourful stonework. It looked beautiful with an array of unusual flowers in bloom and the grass was so green and luscious to look at.

The Princess turned to the young girl. "Jeanette, how long have you been working for the King?" she asked curiously.

"Three years, Princess," the girl replied. "My mother and father worked here as well but the King dismissed them suddenly one day after accusing my father of stealing some tapestries and silverware. He had no proof and found nothing on my papa or in our home but he had him arrested and had his head cut off in public. My mother was devastated to say the least, as was my youngest sister. I'm still only nineteen and started working for the King when just sixteen but he used to follow me around like an evil pair of eyes. I'm sure he was egging me on to take something but my parents taught me not to steal so he was unable to dismiss me. Mother committed suicide one summer day. She slit her wrists and died while my only sister, Marmie, was sent to an asylum; she died last year. I tried visiting her but they wouldn't let me see her as they said she was sick and violent but I can't remember anything about my sister hurting anyone. Why she'd suddenly change like that and become dangerous, I guess I'll never know the truth about her."

"You poor child," the Princess said to the girl. "This King was barbaric and deserved to die since he killed so many innocent people. So where do you live now?"

"With my aunt as the King didn't trust me and wouldn't let me stay at the Palace like the others because of my father," the girl replied. "If you're going to reduce the taxes, I'll stay here forever and serve you like the best ever servant should do. My aunt is poor and the reduction in tax will help her so much. I give her my wages each month and don't take anything for myself as she helped me when none of my relatives would even speak to me after my father was beheaded."

"Tell me, Jeanette, did the King use to deduct ninety percent of your wages?" Prince Leonardo asked wondering how he could possibly do such a thing against his own employees.

Jeanette stared at the Prince with tears rolling down her face. "Yes, Sire, he did, that's why the staff wants you to be appointed king!"

"That King was a monster, Jeanette," the Princess said as she hugged the girl. "It would be my pleasure employing you as my personal aide where you can dress and bathe me. In return, I'll teach you to become a lady. Do you own any clothes?"

"Not really, Princess, as the clothes I wear are old and worn," the girl replied mournfully. "I have no money to buy new ones, or sufficient enough fabric to make my own."

"Don't worry, Jeanette, I'll call for the royal tailor and the cobbler," the Princess said in earnest. "They'll measure you all over and have new clothes and shoes made especially for you. Would you mind if I do that for you?"

"No, Madame," the girl replied with a big smile as no one had treated her in this way before.

"Jeanette, do you read, write and draw?" Daniella put in. "I'm asking you because you mentioned that you'd make your own clothes if you had the fabric."

"Yes, I do," she replied. "My father taught me how to read and write with a quill. One day, he brought home some pencils and paper that one of his friends had given to him and I began drawing pictures of lovely dresses. I made up the sizes and then designed them. I would then take an old sheet off my mother, mark out the dress and cut the pieces out with a sharp knife before sewing them together with needle and thread. I love making things with my hands and if I could earn enough money, I'd open my own dressmaking shop. However, I could never afford this since the King deducted so much tax off my wages."

"My dear young girl," Prince Leonardo said to Jeanette. "If I become King, I promise to let you have a room here at the palace free of charge and large enough for you to run your own dressmaking business. I'll supply you with enough material from around the world, the most modern machinery that I've heard about on my travels and give you two servant girls to train to become seamstresses. You can also remain as an aide to my sister but I'll pay you extra to train yourself and the two females into first class dressmakers. I don't wish to tread on the toes of the royal tailor so you can specialise in making beautiful dresses for the young girls and ladies as with my tax reduction they'll have extra money to spend on new clothes. I'll also give you the necessary transportation to visit the ladies to measure them and let them see samples of your beautifully coloured fabric and drawings of the dresses you will be designing. They'll pay you a ten percent non-refundable deposit and pay the balance on delivery. How does that sound, Jeanette?"

"Sire, I'm truly flattered," the girl replied, flummoxed by what the Prince had said. "I'm no royal and don't deserve to be treated as such."

"How can I refuse such a talented individual like your good self the opportunity to turn herself into a lady?" Prince Leonardo remarked. "However, what's vitally important is that you don't say a single word to any of the other servants as they may feel jealous of such a noble gesture and we don't want to ferment any unrest between them, do we?"

"No, Sir, I promise I won't breathe a word," the girl replied as she crossed her heart. "I've never told anyone of my love for dressmaking so if I leave my job they won't think any different unless of course one of them finds out but it will not be from me and I give you my word on that."

"I know, my girl, so go back to the others and if I'm appointed King your life will begin to change immediately. However, before you go, can you take us back to the study as it's well past three o'clock in the afternoon? I doubt if any of us can remember the way there," Prince Leonardo said with a chuckle.

Jeanette nodded and led the group to the study where she curtsied and left with her head full of all sorts of wonderful ideas.

In the intervening time, Tatiana had stayed behind in the Prince's study where she had sat on an armchair staring at the fireplace and thinking whether she would ever get to see her family again. Taking a cushion from the armchair, she buried her face into it and wept silently to herself. All the female raptor knew was that if the Prince and Daniella returned from their dangerous quest, she could go back home, however what would happen to her if the Prince and Daniella failed and was defeated by the witch. She knew the answer to that and quite simply she would never see her family again.

Chapter 27
Welcome to Thailand

We walked out into the welcome sunshine; it was around half past ten in the morning. After going through customs, we walked over to the taxi rank and waited in line for the next available car. Once inside a taxi, with our luggage packed securely in the boot, we left for the domestic airport where we were going to take a second flight to Chiang Mai.

Although our ticket said first class, it was no more than business class, really, and most of the passengers chose to sit in economy but we settled down in our seats, ready for takeoff. This time I looked around for signs of Rebecca but saw and heard nothing and wondered if she had missed the flight. At that moment, my granddaughter pinched me quite hard and I was about to reprimand the girl when she pointed to an empty seat just across from us and there was her Granny lying down looking comfortable.

The flight to Chiang Mai would take a good couple of hours but if we had decided to do the trip by road, it would have taken probably over thirteen hours since the place was way in the north of Thailand and close to the border of Myanmar where it was more mountainous.

At one point, I noticed my son and wife actually smooching on the plane like young lovers! Rebecca had been the cause of this new romance so I dug Daniella in the ribs and the girl smiled back impishly; it made her feel very happy to see her Mom and Dad acting in this way. She had thought that they did not love each other anymore so she was more than pleased to see her parents looking so lovey dovey with one another.

I did not bother writing since the flight was a relatively short one so I whiled away the time chatting to my granddaughter.

"Darling, I was wondering if we'll be getting anything to eat," I said right after we were up in the air. "Or maybe this flight is too short."

"I don't know, Granddad," Daniella answered. "To be honest, I'm a little peckish as well."

I grinned at my granddaughter just as an air hostess came into view pushing a trolley with trays of food; it appeared that we would be getting food after all. The girl gave us a warm smile and handed us both a tray before moving on to hand out more food trays to the other passengers behind us.

The food was interesting to say the least as there was chicken, a little fried rice and noodles with bamboo shoots and onions. I opened my can of cold coke first as I knew that certain dishes were extremely fiery as the Thais loved spices and fresh chillies. I was proved right after the first bite so I warned Daniella by panting like a dog to indicate to the girl that it was spicy.

She took a mouthful and as soon as it hit the back of her throat she gasped, "It's burning so much, Granddad! Give me some of your coke!"

One of the air hostesses overheard the poor girl and went to fetch some lovely cold melon, and told her that she would go and get her something not so spicy. She reappeared within a minute with a dish of plain chicken and noodles.

"This should be better for you, young lady," she said. "We like our food to be hot and spicy so unless you tell the people serving you, you should always expect a big amount of chillies and peppers."

Daniella took a small forkful, put it into her mouth and smiled at the airhostess since this was nowhere near as hot as the other dish. The airhostess then surprised us both by sitting next to the girl since the seat was empty.

"Are you going to visit the elephants in Chiang Mai, young lady?" she asked. "I live in Chiang Mai and I'm off work this week so if you want I can show you around!"

I thought it was nice of the airhostess to take the time to speak to the girl and even more so to offer to show us the sights.

"My Mom and Dad are with us," Daniella said. "However, it's very kind of you to offer to help us. Perhaps, we could go out one evening for dinner. By the way, I'm Daniella and this is my Granddad, Paul," she added as she held out her hand to the airhostess who shook it warmly.

"Pleased to meet you, Daniella!" the flight attendant said. "Did anyone ever tell you that you're beautiful? Anyway, I'm Sara and have lived in Chiang Mai all my life. I think that with your long golden hair and sparkling blue eyes you're gorgeous and you'll be a real catch for the right boy one day! How old are you, my dear?"

"I'm thirteen," the girl replied. "And how old are you, Sara?"

I smiled since it was rather inappropriate to ask an older person her age and wondered if she would answer her but Sara did, much to my surprise.

"Oh, that was an unexpected question but I asked you too so I'll tell you. I'm twenty-one, unmarried and my parents are dead. They caught some awful tropical disease when I was only seven so I've stayed with my Grandma for fourteen years. I don't know what I'll do if anything happens to her but at the moment she's in good health and we live comfortably on my salary."

Daniella looked at the Asian girl, before saying to her, "You're so nice, Sara. I'll speak to my mother and father about you. I'm sure they'd be delighted if you show us around Chiang Mai."

Sara took out a pen and a piece of paper from her uniform pocket and wrote her name, address and phone number on it before handing it to Daniella.

"When you're settled in your hotel please give me a ring. It will be my pleasure as I seldom go out when I'm at home," Sara said following which she went back to her duties to look after the other passengers.

The flight only took a further forty-five minutes. When we got up to leave and approached the exit door, Sara said goodbye to Daniella and I. As we walked down the steps from the aircraft, my son stared at me and at his daughter wondering how the airhostess knew the girl's name.

After going through passport control and customs, we were shown the green door since we had nothing to declare, except for my wife Rebecca but where she had gone was anyone's guess. I tittered to myself as we went outside into the hot tropical sunshine and headed in the direction of the taxis where we found an empty one and got in. My son told the driver the name of the hotel, the Jungle Paradise; he said he knew it well so he drove off taking the road to the mountains.

On our way towards our hotel, we saw a sign saying 'Elephant Sanctuary' and another close by pointing to the 'Jungle Paradise Hotel'. My son had hit the jackpot since the main attraction we had come to visit was right on our doorstep. The driver turned into the hotel driveway, which seemed to go on for miles, until we eventually arrived at a magnificent stone built hotel.

"We've arrived, Sir," the taxi driver announced unnecessarily. "This is the most beautiful hotel in the area. The elephants sometimes get loose and roam into the hotel's gardens but nowadays they've become very tame and won't hurt you. All they're looking for is food but it's not recommended you feed them as otherwise they'll be visiting you every day! Chiang Mai has some beautiful areas to visit so if you need me just give me a call," he added as he handed my son his business card. "I won't rip you off like some of the other drivers around here!"

We got out of the taxi and were met by a blast of hot humid air. The driver smiled at us and began unloading the suitcases and bags from the boot of the car following which my son paid him the fare and an extra ten dollars tip.

"Karl," my son said after looking at the business card. "I think your price was very fair so we'll be ringing you the moment we decide where to visit. We seem to have been travelling all day so I doubt if we'll be going out tonight but you never know as we're on holiday! Also, could you tell me where we have to go to book in? Normally, a porter would have welcomed us as in most other hotels but nobody has come so far."

"Yes, you just wait here, Sir, while I go and get one of my friends who will look after you from here," Karl said as he left us by the car and headed in the direction of the entrance of the hotel and disappeared inside.

Five minutes later, he came back out together with the hotel manager and a porter pushing a trolley.

"This is Luke, the manager at this hotel, who will be attending to your needs from now on. I hope to hear from you in the next day or so," Karl said following which he got into his car and drove away.

"Welcome to the Jungle Paradise Hotel," Luke declared with great pomp as he shook our hands warmly. "If you give me your names, Jon will take your bags while I take you inside and register you."

We handed our passports over to Luke who led us into the hotel lobby and over to reception while the porter loaded the cases and bags onto the trolley. At reception, the girl behind the desk greeted us with a polite smile and handed us three key cards.

I thought this was extremely unusual for the manager to get involved in booking in guests but it seems we had come highly recommended by his friend Karl. He motioned to two female assistants who were sitting at a desk and they came over to see what the manager needed. After a short conversation with him, one of them walked over to us.

"Mr Karl told me to introduce myself. I'm Cam," she said amiably. "If you follow me, I'll show you up to your rooms which are on the top floor. This hotel only has three floors but boasts over two hundred double bedrooms and a further three hundred singles. Your luggage is already in your rooms so you can take a bath or shower to suit before you sit down for dinner. We're close to the mountains here so unfortunately the weather can be beautiful one day or with torrential downpours the next. The elephants love this kind of weather as there's plenty for them to eat and drink during the storms as everything falls out of the trees!"

Cam stopped talking and opened one of the double rooms. It was magnificent as it boasted a wooden four-poster bed and a large panoramic window from which you could see right across to the Elephant Sanctuary. The room was fully air-conditioned and was a welcome relief to the sweltering heat outside. Daniella looked at me and then at the room hoping that her room would also have the same outstanding view.

Cam noticed her concern so she turned to the girl and said. "Don't worry as your room's just as magnificent. In fact, I think you can even see the outside swimming pool! By the way, what's your name, my dear?"

"Daniella," my granddaughter squeaked.

"What a beautiful name! Your hair is the colour of gold whereas your eyes are as blue as the sea!" Cam exclaimed affectionately.

"That's so nice of you, Cam," my son said to the young female. "Now, can you show us our rooms, please? I hope they're next door to each other."

"Yes they are and Daniella's is the last room with the view of the outdoor pool," Cam answered. "We also have an indoor swimming pool, a spa and a fully-equipped gym, badminton court and tennis courts for the sporty ones."

"So how far away from the sea are we here?" Carol put in. "And is there a nice beach close by, Cam?"

"If you are referring to Thailand, then Phuket Island is the closest," Cam replied. "We're probably around ten hours drive but if you wish to go over the border into Myanmar, Yangon is no more than two or three hours away. The manager can tell you more as I don't drive at the moment. However, I thought you'd come to see the elephants and the mountains! I hadn't realised you also wanted to visit the beach. Anyway, let me open your rooms and show you where you are."

At this, Cam put one of the cards into the lock and opened the room. This one was slightly larger and boasted its own Jacuzzi.

"Has my room got its own Jacuzzi too?" Daniella asked Cam.

"No, but if you want to use the Jacuzzi you can always come to our room, Doughnut," my son said to his daughter.

"Daddy, I'm not a doughnut and never will be!" Daniella groaned, none too impressed that her father had used her much-reviled pet name. "You know how much I hate that name!"

"While I leave you here to settle in," Cam said as she stepped in to try to save the situation. "I'll take your daughter to her room. I think she'll like the views," the girl added as she left with Daniella following closely behind her.

Cam opened the third and last room and, together with Daniella, walked over to the large panoramic window. Daniella gasped when she saw the view over the outdoor swimming pool and right across to the Elephant Sanctuary.

"Cam, you were right!" a beaming Daniella exclaimed. "Who needs a Jacuzzi anyway? The view from here's breathtaking and the bed's enormous and so high I might fall off if I have any dreams!" she added as she sat down on the bed. "And the mattress is so comfortable I could close my eyes right now and go to sleep."

In fact, that is what Daniella did so Cam left her lying on the bed with her eyes tightly shut and gently closed the door behind her and went downstairs to join her colleagues.

Daniella lay there on her bed when she suddenly felt a gust of wind blow in from somewhere even though the window was closed. It was Rebecca who floated over to the bed and prodded hard at the young girl who opened her eyes and stared at the apparition.

"Granny, you're here with us!" the girl cried out. "Do you want to stay in my room or are you going to visit Granddad? I think he misses you a great deal like I do but with you around it's as though you never left us in the first place."

"I'll stop in both rooms to keep you company even though that stupid old man didn't even speak to me on the aircraft!" Rebecca remarked. "By the way, who was that strange airhostess who kept coming and going, and calling you by your first name, so unusual for a stewardess to do? This is my first trip I've taken with Granddad outside the UK and Ireland and I love elephants so why does my daughter-in-law insist on going to the beach when we're so far away from the sea? It means I'll have to perch like a bird on the back of the taxi seat where it's so uncomfortable!" Rebecca concluded before fading away to nothing.

Daniella got up and went into the bathroom to take a shower while Rebecca paid our son and his wife a visit. Carol had just finished her Jacuzzi and with her towel wrapped around her delectable body headed over to the bed where our son was taking a nap as he waited for his wife to return. She leant over and kissed him before almost jumping out of her skin as Rebecca materialised.

"Hello, you two," Rebecca said matter-of-factly.

"This was the first time my son had met his mother after she had passed away and the look of horror on the man's face said it all. However, Carol rode above it as she had already seen her mother-in-law on other occasions. She had always wondered if her husband would be able to see her but by the looks of things, he could since he was also a family member.

“How is this possible?” he stammered. “I saw you buried and laid to rest! Go away! You can’t be real! If I close my eyes you’ll be gone!” He did but on reopening his eyes, he still saw his mother. “For Pete’s sake, Mom, how’s this possible?” he cried. “If you go and visit Daniella she’ll have a nervous breakdown for sure as she loved you very much. Why aren’t you scared of her like I am, Carol?”

“Darling,” Carol cooed to her husband. “Why do you think I changed into something so soft and cuddly rather than the cruel beast I was before? Don’t you prefer me as I am now and not so bitter to everyone anymore?”

“Of course I do, darling, but are you trying to tell me that my mother made you change? And have you met Mom before?” he asked.

Carol stared at her husband, took hold of one of his hands and squeezed it gently before replying to him. “Rebecca was responsible for turning me into the woman I am now not only for your sake but for our daughter’s as well as we never showed her any love. Your Mom made me realise this was wrong so I forced myself to become the woman you married when we loved each other so much. Our lives were dictated by our work and my pigheadedness and I knew we both had to change or otherwise we’d lose the chance of seeing our daughter grow up into the beautiful young girl she is now. There’s no way Daniella will ever be going to boarding school as she needs love and understanding from her family and friends.”

“Well said, daughter-in-law,” Rebecca said wistfully. “Now, Son, do you believe that my soul has risen and is here with you in Thailand? I know it might be a shock for you but I’ve walked on the beach collecting shells with Dad and Daniella and found it so relaxing. I can't tell you why this has happened but maybe it's for us to become a family again and to give us a second chance. Don't worry, though, as only members of the family can see me. Well, that's what I believe but maybe some psychic will be able to communicate with me if they feel my presence nearby!"

"Oh, Mom!" our son cried as tears rolled down his cheeks. "I've missed you so much but if you've come back to look after us that's fine with me. I applaud you for changing Carol back into the person I married as our love has blossomed once again and is now stronger than it ever was. We both have you to thank for giving us a second chance with Daniella. We'll always take her and Granddad on regular annual holidays and if you want you can come along too."

"I think that maybe my work's almost done as you seem to have your family back," Rebecca said. "That was why I returned in the first place as you had lost your way. Let me say goodbye to your Dad and Daniella since it might be time for me to leave. However, if you ever change back to the fiends you had become then I'll haunt you for the rest of your lives!"

"Okay, Mom, you win," my son said grinning from ear to ear as the apparition faded away to nothing as she went next door.

I found Rebecca lying on my bed looking like some lady of the manor as I came out from the bathroom in just my towel after my shower and shave.

"So you are here, then, love!" I exclaimed. "But why are you crying? Tell me what's wrong with you, darling."

"I've just come back from visiting our son," she replied. "Carol and he are so much in love again, exactly how I wanted to see them. They've also promised to take you and Daniella on family holidays every year so I know my time's up and I'll be called back soon!"

"What do you mean by saying your time's up?" I shouted as I glowered at Rebecca feeling I knew exactly what she was about to tell me.

"Exactly that, darling," she replied softly. "The reason I came back was because our son and his wife were treating Daniella badly. However, on hearing them say what they did and that they love each other more than ever, I realise I'm not needed anymore. My soul can now move on and you'll only see me again if our son and his wife make Daniella's life difficult once more. Don't think I'm abandoning you, darling, as I'll always come to your beck and call and Daniella's if you're feeling lonely. I'll always be watching over you and my granddaughter to make sure you're safe," she added since it was now my turn to have tears rolling down my cheeks. "I'll always love you from the bottom of my heart!" she whispered just before she faded away to nothing.

She was gone and I went cold at the thought of not seeing her ever again. However, deep down I knew it was the rightful thing for her to do.

Unknown to me, Rebecca went to find Daniella to say goodbye. When she saw the girl staring out through the window onto the lovely gardens below, she materialised and took hold of the girl's hands.

"I must go now, Daniella," she told the grief-stricken girl who looked like she was about to burst into tears. "I only came back to change your mother and father. After seeing my son for the first time and hearing him admit to the fact that he loves his wife more than anything and will always take you and Granddad on holidays until you're old enough to go on your own, I know my time here is at an end."

"You can't go, Granny! I'll miss you so much!" Daniella sobbed. "Don't you love me anymore? Promise that you'll come and see me or at least keep watch over us."

"I knew this departure would be the hardest of them all!" Rebecca lamented. "It's even more difficult than saying goodbye to Granddad. I told him I'd only come back to change our son and daughter-in-law and to make your life happier. At first, he'd thought I'd come back for him and he was sad to learn this wasn't the case at all. Anyway, I'll always love you and promise you that occasionally I'll come to visit."

Daniella watched her Granny fade away to nothing and she began to wipe away her tears. "You're a big girl now!" she muttered to herself. "You need to look after Granddad as that's what Granny would want you to do."

Grinning to herself, the girl stared out of the window and noticed that there were many adults and children in the outdoor swimming pool. Perhaps, she might make a new friend there.

"No, Daniella, you're meant to be looking after Granddad!" she said sternly to herself in the mirror following which she headed to my room.

Chapter 28
Settling In

A knock at my door caught me by surprise and I was even more astonished when I went to open it. It was Daniella and I realised she had been crying too so I took the young girl into my arms and closed the door behind us.

"Granny said her goodbyes to you as well, didn't she, darling?" I said. "I think she'll be back one day as she promised to keep an eye on us and I know Granny won't let us down. Did you know that she also introduced herself to your Dad? He was shocked and thought he was dreaming but after she explained that she had only returned to make things better between your mother and him, he finally understood and told her that if they went on holiday with you and I, Granny could come along too. It was then that Granny realised that her work was complete and that it was time for her to move on."

"It's for the best, Granddad," the brave girl said as she smiled at me. "Although we're going to miss her, I'll always know she's watching over us," she added as I held her close to my heart. "Anyway, do you fancy going for a dip in the swimming pool, Granddad, or do you prefer going after we eat?"

"Neither," I answered as I stared at the girl, making her feel guilty. "I don't really enjoy swimming. I swim like a fish but I hate the taste of chlorine and for health reasons these pools are filled with the stuff. If we go to the sea, I promise I'll show you just how good a swimmer I am! Is that a deal?"

“I suppose so and perhaps Mommy will come swimming with me and try out her new bikini!” she replied with a mischievous grin as I almost swallowed my false teeth.

At that exact moment, someone knocked at the door. Daniella went to open it and in walked my son and his wife.

“We were looking for you, Daniella,” Carol said with a lovely smile. “I don’t know about you but it’s lunchtime and we’re starving! “And I was thinking that after lunch we could go to the pool. Do you fancy the outdoor or the inside one?”

Daniella grinned so much that her jaw began to ache! Her prayers had been answered. Even though I did not want to go swimming, it appeared that my daughter-in-law, as well as my son, did. However, I was sure that Carol did not yet realise that her daughter was expecting her to wear her bikini!

Daniella was merrily hopping from one leg to the next as we all made our way downstairs where we headed for the dining room, since this was where lunch and breakfast were served, whereas the restaurant on the top floor was where we would be eating dinner later that evening.

To help reduce the costs, we had taken a package holiday, which included three meals: breakfast, lunch and dinner. However, if we wanted something more expensive off the restaurant menu then we could add this onto our final bill at the end of our stay.

Our lunchtime meal consisted of a buffet so we went straight to a central table that was stacked with all kinds of food, from hot and cold meats to rice and noodle dishes, some spicy and others much milder in taste. A number of large trays of fresh and roasted vegetables and lovely homemade bread were at one side while there was a grand selection of cheeses and biscuits on the other. I promised to myself that I would make sure I had some of those if I still had any room at the end of our lunch.

After filling our plates full of the tasty food, we went over to a table that had our name on it. We sat down with our food in front us and promptly realised that we had nothing to drink.

My son called a girl over and amazingly, it happened to be Cal, who smiled at us all but especially at Daniella. My son immediately took out a ten-dollar note from his wallet and handed it to her.

“This I completely forgot about as you were so helpful on our arrival this morning,” my son told Cal. “I bet you told the others we were a right stingy family but as you can see it was just a slip up from my side.”

Cal smiled at us all as she had not been expecting anything at all. This had taken her completely by surprise and ten dollars was a great tip to receive.

“That’s so kind of you, Sir,” the young girl said, looking quite embarrassed. “I’ll share this with the others as we always put everything in a jar and each week we split it up fairly with each other. Now, forget about me for the time being. Can I get you something to drink?”

“Yes, that would be nice,” my son replied. “Do you have a good medium sweet house wine or is that only found in the restaurant upstairs?”

“No, Sir,” Cam replied while shaking her head. “Let me go and get you a bottle of the hotel’s special wine. I think you’ll like the taste but what shall I get for Daniella?”

My son looked at his wife and then at his daughter who was about to give her father a right scowl.

“Get Daniella a wine glass as I want her to at least tell her friends that we allowed her to taste it,” my son said. “However, please also bring along a nice cold coke just in case she doesn’t like the wine.”

"Good idea," Cal said grinning at Daniella. "Let me go and fetch it for you and then you'll have something to drink while you enjoy your meal," she added before walking away.

"Did Rebecca mean what she said?" Carol whispered to me. "Has she really left us forever?"

I actually saw tears in Carol's eyes. I knew that my wife's departure had saddened her a great deal.

"My darling's gone for the time being since she feels we're now a closely-knit family once again and that her work is done. That's all she wanted to see at the end of the day but I'll miss her and pray that one day she'll be back when we need her."

"That's wonderful to hear, Dad," my son remarked surprisingly. "I never thought Mom could come back like she did and it made me happy to see our daughter in high spirits once again. I plan on taking Daniella into the office from now on so that from an early age she can learn how to run the company that she'll one day own," he added as Daniella stared at her father wondering if he really meant what he was saying.

"Son, that's amazing," I stepped in. "Daniella's so pleased that she's gained your trust and I'm so delighted to hear you telling the girl this before I join your mother for all eternity!"

"I hope not yet, Dad," my son said in reply to my words. "I don't want you dying on me as we don't know each other as well as we should and that's my fault and not yours. I need time to show you that I really care about my family and you too, Dad."

At this, Cal returned with the bottle of wine, opened it with a corkscrew and poured some into my son's glass. He tasted the wine and rolled it around his mouth before swallowing it.

"This will do nicely, Cal," he said as the girl began filling our glasses and left us with the remainder of the bottle following which she went into the kitchen to let us enjoy our meal.

The food tasted excellent and since it was a buffet lunch, we went up for second helpings. Daniella liked the taste of the wine as it made her feel so grownup and ladylike and not a young girl as her father and mother had thought she was. After she had drunk the small amount that Cal had purposely put in her glass, my son took the bottle and filled her glass with some more wine.

"Thanks, Daddy, you've made me feel so grownup," she said as she gave him a beaming smile. "I realise that I can't drink anymore so the coke's fine for me after I've finished my wine first of course!"

We all laughed making the girl flush from embarrassment or maybe it was the after-effects of the wine but on this occasion we gave her the benefit of the doubt as we were on holiday and enjoying ourselves.

After eating our second plateful, my belly was about to burst. I looked over at Carol and then at Daniella and it was obvious they too were feeling a little stuffed to say the least. There was no way that I would be taking a dessert or some of that lovely cheese and biscuits.

Another waitress appeared and came over to take away the plates as my son had finally finished eating. We asked her for some coffee to end our meal. The girl smiled and left before coming back five minutes later with four coffees that were so dark and uninviting that the bitter taste remained lurking inside our mouths until the girl came over with after dinner mints.

We remained tight lipped about the coffee and decided that the following day we would request coffee and cream and hope it would taste better than that we had just drunk. Looking at our watches, we saw that it was past two o'clock and we had been sitting down for lunch for two solid hours.

"Darling, do you still want to go swimming or shall we leave it until tomorrow?" Carol said to her daughter as everyone began getting up from the table.

"I feel rather full and Granddad's going to be writing his book so can I stay with him?" she asked. "He's teaching me how to become the perfect writer. After all, we can always go swimming tomorrow."

I had not said anything about writing or having invited her to stay. To be honest, I was not sure whether I would since I felt extremely stuffed inside but as we made our way back to our rooms we arranged to see each other for dinner at six. Daniella took hold of my hand as I went to my room. We walked in together and she sat down in an armchair near the window while I remained standing.

"That was rather naughty of you, dear," I began. "I'm so bloated I don't know if I could write a thing but for your sake I'll at least try."

I went over to my desk as Daniella brought a chair over to sit next to me. I opened the laptop, found the file and continued writing my story.

Tatiana pulled herself together as someone was about to come into the study. The door opened and she saw Prince Leonardo, his sister and Daniella entering the room so she bounded over to them in a flash.

"I've missed you and should have come along as being left here on my own I just kept thinking about my family and whether or not I'd ever see them again!" she complained.

"Of course you will, my dear," the Princess said to the young raptor. "I'm sure my brother and Daniella will be successful in their mission," she added despite the fact that she too had reservations about this as she knew that the witch was devious and had cruelly taken the lives of so many innocent people.

The raptor tried to smile at the Princess but found it extremely difficult to do while Leonardo and Daniella remained silent since they had no idea what the evil witch had in store for them. They all sat down on the comfortable sofa with the Prince not going to his normal place behind his desk. Tatiana balanced herself on Daniella's knees and snuggled her head against the girl's neck making Daniella realise just how much this raptor loved her. The Prince and Princess smiled at the girl as they too thought that this was a genuine display of the young raptor's affection towards the female. In fact, the four of them sat silently on the sofa enjoying each other's company until they were all soon fast asleep.

A loud knock on the study door awoke everyone and Leonardo jumped to his feet and went to open the door.

Young Jeanette walked in smiling and said, "Sir, it seems you forgot about dinner! We rang the gong ten minutes ago now! Are you coming to eat?"

"Well, I never, we all fell asleep," the Prince replied. "Thank you for waking us up but don't say a word to anyone, is that understood?"

"I wouldn't dream of it, Sir. I'll go and tell the Chef that you'll be at the table in about ten minutes. That should allow you enough time to get ready," Jeanette said to the Prince going back to the kitchen.

They all got up and smoothed down any visible creases in their clothes before exiting the room and heading directly to the grand dining hall where Jeanette greeted them.

"Sir, please take a seat and my colleagues will be serving you your food soon," she said with a smile. "In the meanwhile, can I get you a bottle of wine or perhaps some beer?"

The beer the young girl was offering was something that none of them recognised.

"Jeanette, I think we'll try this beer and see what we think of it. Is it served cold?"

"Sir, we serve it in jugs that are filled from large kegs that are kept cold underground by a river that flows beneath the Palace.

The water is icy cold so we keep all our drinks there and store them in large quantities. The King likes his beer but no one knows where he gets it from!"

"I understand, young lady, and yes, please get us some and perhaps this new grape wine for the ladies too," the Prince said as the girl went away to fetch the drinks.

Three servants appeared carrying silver platters laden with all kinds of food. There were various meats, cold as well as hot, potatoes and other vegetables, and a jug of gravy-like substance. They put down hot plates in front of everyone and dished out helpings to everyone.

"Is that alright, Sir, or would you like more?" one of the servants asked the Prince.

"No, no, that's fine, my dear girl. By the way, what's your name?" the Prince asked the poor girl who was stunned that a royal would want to know her name.

"Annabelle, Sir, and these two are Gregory and Martha," she replied as she pointed in their direction.

The moment she said this, Jeanette appeared with a jug of beer, an open bottle of white wine and a number of silver goblets. She put the jug of ale down in front of the Prince and began pouring out the wine into the ladies' goblets without saying anything to anyone.

"Thank you, Jeanette," the Prince said as she curtsied to the Prince and his sister following which she left to return to the kitchen leaving Annabelle standing there in horror.

"As you can see, Annabelle, I use first names," the Prince said to the bemused young girl.

"Yes, Sir," the girl said automatically. "Enjoy your meal, Sire, and you too, Princess and ladies," she added as she curtsied and left.

"I offer this toast to change!" the Prince said as he raised his goblet.

The ladies smiled and raised their goblets before taking a sip of their wine. On the other hand, the Prince was drinking beer and he thoroughly enjoyed its taste as he felt the cold liquid hitting all the right places and quenching his thirst at the same time. One by one, they began eating and found that the food tasted delicious, with the slices of hot meat melting in their mouths and the vegetables cooked to their liking. This gravy, or whatever they called it, made the food taste even more scrumptious and inside ten minutes, everyone had cleared their plates completely.

Annabelle and Gregory soon reappeared together with a new servant. All three of them began clearing away the empty plates for washing while Jeanette emerged with a new jug of ale and another bottle of wine. The girl put the jug in front of Leonardo and poured more wine into the ladies' goblets while she motioned to the Prince if he wanted any more ale.

"Jeanette, I understand your King was always drunk and had the worst ever temper but you won't find that with me or my sister as we don't often drink," the Prince said to the girl. "Ruling a kingdom requires a level head to think right but on this occasion you can pour me another goblet. However, in the future, serve us just a single drink even if we ask for more."

"Yes, Sir, I'll remember that but what about when you have banquets? The King had to be carried to bed and undressed by one of the maidens he had chosen for the night! Are you the same, Sir?"

"Prince Leonardo only keeps one woman and certainly won't be asking any of you young servant girls to join him in bed, will you brother?" Princess Lena put in.

"No, of course not so you don't need to worry from now on, Jeanette. I realise there will be banquets held for different occasions but you won't see me getting drunk. I hope you're not too disappointed."

"Yes, Sir, completely but what about the guests?" Jeanette queried. "They often harass the women as well as the men so how will you stop them when they're full of ale and wine?"

"I had no idea such things took place but I can't change all the customs in the Palace," the Prince said. "However, from now on, if there are any unruly guests they'll be dumped in the dungeons till the following morning to cool off before being allowed to leave. I expect everyone to behave themselves properly even if they're of royal blood like me."

"I'm impressed, Sir, and my prayers will be with you and the Princess tonight," Jeanette said as she curtsied and left.

"Leonardo, is that the right thing to do?" Daniella chipped in. "If the King allowed his fellow royals to sleep with a servant for the night, won't they become upset with you if you take away this disgusting habit? Like you, I don't agree with such things but you don't want to create problems with the other royals, do you?"

"You speak wisely, my dear, and I have to agree with you but I'll be placing armed guards on all the inside doors and windows around the banqueting hall so I think that will cure them of these deviant tendencies. I want to teach them to respect the servants and not think they're there solely for their gratification," the Prince declared solemnly.

"Leonardo, behave yourself! Tatiana doesn't expect to hear such things, do you, my dear?" the Princess asked the young raptor."

"You have children, Tatiana," the Prince said with a big grin. "If your husband didn't ask you permission and just expected you to agree to his demands, how would you react? This is how other royals have been treating our servants and I plan to bring this to an end!"

"Here, here, Leonardo, that's the right thing to do," the young female raptor remarked as Princess Lena was forced to smile.

Chapter 29
A Visit

With dinner finished, the four of them returned to the study. Leonardo rang the bell and Jeanette appeared soon afterwards.

"Maxine and Martin are preparing your rooms at the moment, Sir. Now, would you like a bedtime drink before you go to sleep?" the girl asked sympathetically.

"Nothing cold, my dear," the Prince said. "I don't know about the girls, though."

They also did not want further wine or fruit juice but Jeanette surprised them by saying, "Sir, I can prepare something non-alcoholic and hot with sugar?"

"That sounds interesting, my dear," the Prince replied wondering what the girl was going to bring back.

Jeanette curtsied and left them talking. She came back fifteen minutes later with three goblets full of hot milk and honey that she had collected from the cows and bees.

"I've never served this to the King or to any royals, come to think of it," she remarked as she put the goblets down in front of them. "This recipe came from my Grandma so many years ago. I hope you like it as this is my favourite drink."

Jeanette curtsied and left them to enjoy their drink. They quite enjoyed the taste even though they had never drunk anything like this before.

"I loved that! I could drink this every single night from now on. How about you?" the Princess asked the others as she glanced across at them.

"Yes, Sis, I also liked it and could quite easily get used to drinking it. I wonder if it has a name. We'll have to ask Jeanette when we next see her," her brother said.

A knock at the door told them that someone was outside so the Prince got to his feet and opened it.

A male servant came in and said, "Sir, your chambers are ready when you are, so give a single ring on the bell and a servant will come and attend to each of you. Now, would you like me to show you to your rooms?"

"Could you come back in about an hour or so? It will then be time for bed. Are you Martin by the way?" Prince Leonardo asked in reply to the servant.

"Yes, Sir, Jeanette told me you call the servants by their first names but I didn't believe her until Annabelle appeared and told me the same. Now, I beg you permission to leave. I'll be back in an hour precisely," he added as he bowed graciously to the Prince and then to the ladies before leaving the room.

Leonardo walked over to his desk and unusually for him took a cigar from a box, lit it with a match and began to puff on it. This was new to him completely and he began coughing so much that he thought he was going to bring up all his dinner. At this, the women could not help themselves and burst out laughing.

"That stinks, brother! What on earth is it?" the Princess asked as her brother looked alarmingly at his sister, trying to gasp for air but finding it nigh on impossible.

"The Duke always smokes them but I've never seen him coughing like I did," the Prince gasped as he struggled for breath. "Perhaps, whoever invented them made them to torture the prisoners! My throat has become so dry after just one or two puffs. I'll have to put it out and ask the Duke how I should smoke it, and even more so how I'm meant to enjoy such a thing."

Princess Lena and Daniella laughed at seeing poor Leonardo admitting defeat with Daniella chipping in too. "Let's hope the witch doesn't force you to smoke such things, Leonardo, as otherwise you'll be the one eating out of her hand!"

Prince Leonardo smiled at Daniella as Princess Lena and Tatiana sniggered. The one hour soon passed and Martin returned with eight other servants, who he introduced to the royals.

"Would you, Sir, Princess Lena, Lady Daniella, and Miss Tatiana follow me to your chambers where your servants will attend to you?" Martin politely asked. "A bath of hot water has been prepared in advance for each of you and your luggage is already in your rooms."

The group got up and followed Martin and the other servants. He first took the Prince to his room and walked in while the others remained in the hallway. Two of the servants followed him and Prince Leonardo realised just how grand the bedroom was, with a four-poster bed made up with white silk sheets and some other expensive looking bed covers. Furthermore, there were dark green silk curtains, already drawn, a large walnut desk, a leather-bound chair, several wardrobes and sets of drawers, a comfortable couch, and a vase of beautiful blue and yellow flowers standing on a side table to welcome him.

Then there was the light coming from the ceiling, which of course was an invention from the twentieth century and had been picked up along the way by the King's sorcerer. It was funny as he was there to protect His Majesty but when he died, he was nowhere to be found. The Duke said that he had fled the kingdom and wondered if it had anything to do with his brother's disappearance.

Martin left the Prince alone with his two servants. Leonardo knew exactly what to expect as he had experienced the same ritual at the Duke's residence. The male servant he found out was Grim whereas the pretty, young blonde-haired woman was Gwen. Grim began to undress the Prince, taking his clothes and folding them neatly before hanging them in one of the wardrobes or putting them away into a chest of drawers. Gwen then told the naked Prince to get into the bath where she would attend to him. She took a sponge, poured some expensive oil onto it and began washing the Prince's body all over. The girl was quite a pretty young filly and when she bent down to wash the Prince, he got a right eyeful of pale breasts. She noticed him looking and just smiled and carried on washing him as though he was not even there.

Meanwhile, Martin was showing Princess Lena to her room where he left her in the hands of two other servants. He bowed low to the Princess and left to attend to the wants of the other two females who he led along the hallway to their two separate rooms.

As a male servant was undressing Daniella, leaving her standing there naked, she began giggling to herself and wondering how the servants in the next room would wash a raptor. After the servants had finished washing the royals, they bowed or curtsied, turned off the lights and left until the following morning.

Unknown to the Prince, he would be having a visitor during the night, someone who he had not expected to meet. With it being summer, the curtains were drawn and the windows left open for fresh air. The Prince was sleeping with his head resting on soft feather pillows; he felt that he was in heaven or somewhere like that but what was about to materialise in his room could only be found in his worst ever nightmare.

At some time during the night, the wicked witch of the forest, Caspian, appeared right in front of his bed and sat down naked as the day she was born. This female was truly gorgeous but not who she seemed to be. The witch pushed the young man gently and he opened his eyes and felt around in the darkness. His fingers touched soft skin and he jumped out of bed, startling Caspian, who by this time was lying down expecting the Prince to make love to her.

"Who are you?" he shouted. "You're not welcome in my chambers!" Are you the witch of the enchanted forest?"

"Yes, but how do you know that?" the witch screeched. "I'm Caspian, the witch, and I can quite easily turn you into something unpleasant as I'm the most powerful witch throughout the kingdom!"

"May I ask you why you chose my room to come to?" the Prince asked nervously.

"That's easy to answer as you're a handsome young man and I'm a gorgeous looking female. Only stupid men fall into my trap but you're very different and I wonder why this is."

"Quite simple, my dear," the Prince replied obnoxiously. "You might be the only witch here but there's another far more evil one in the Kingdom of Blackstone."

"Where's that? I've never heard of such a place," the witch shrieked. "Tell me, kind Sir, why aren't you afraid of me like all others? And don't you find me absolutely gorgeous to look at?" She added idling closer to the Prince and rubbed her body against his.

"No, I'm promised to another woman," the Prince replied as he pushed the witch away. "And I'm Prince Leonardo of Blackstone. Was it you who killed the King?"

"No, it wasn't," the witch croaked. "However, if I had had the chance I'd have changed him into something else. I'm here because the Kingdom's without a ruler. I now know who you are; I've heard you're the people's choice and now you tell me you're from Blackstone which I've never heard of?

"What do you really look like and how old are you?" the Prince said. "Are you the same as the witch in our forest? If she finds out about you, she'll want to destroy you for sure as you're one big threat to her! She's turned Blackstone into a frozen wilderness where people are dying every single day. She's also changed the King into a canary and his army of men and their horses have been eaten by carnivorous plants, or turned to wild pigs killing each other in the forest. And perhaps you can tell me what you've done with the soldiers of Zandar too!"

"You're too clever for your own good," the witch cackled with vigour. "I was thinking that if the kingdom has no ruler then perhaps I should be Queen of Zandar as the people would only see me as this gorgeous female and not my ugly self. You're the only one who knows my true identity so if I turn you into something else, no one will ever know that it's the witch of the forest who rules over their kingdom. And, anyway, why should I tell you what I've done to the armies of soldiers and their Captains? What will you give me in return? I see that you're not interested by my body but don't you find me gorgeous to look at?" the evil witch said once again trying to get closer to the Prince but as before, being pushed away much harder this time.

"No, witch, to me you're not beautiful and will never be in my eyes. Somehow, I'll expose you if you try to trick the Duke and the people. However, I have a proposal to put to you. If you're ready to work with me, I know we can defeat this other witch. There is one proviso and that is we have to cut out her heart and deliver it to Satan. Are you prepared to risk your life? Then, as King of both Zandar and Blackstone, it would be my honour to appoint you as my personal magician and let you live at the Palace with your own room where you can carry out your spells and potions to protect me and the kingdom of Zandar."

The beautiful young girl suddenly changed back into the old and ugly witch that she really was with wrinkled skin, long fingernails, black and rotten teeth and a wart on her long protrusive nose.

"I think that would be a good thing for me to do, concocting potions and spells and keeping you safe from predators that wish to bring you harm. And having a comfortable bed to lie down on too, then I agree. This is the first time a mortal and a future king, at that has offered me anything like this so let me go and I'll begin producing some new spells to defeat this witch. You, my Prince, are very stupid, and having become involved with Satan is not a good thing for you, but he doesn't scare me. I have enough magic of my own to throw against him but my dear boy, did you know that a witch or warlock has eternal life and can't be killed? Well, that's not entirely true as it needs a royal sword made of gold to cut out one of our hearts."

At this, the witch disappeared while Prince Leonardo sat there thinking what had he gone and done. However, he was not left with any choice since he could not allow the witch to become the evil queen she wanted to be. Somehow or other, the Prince fell back to sleep and was awoken by a loud rapping at the door.

"Yes, come in!" he hollered.

The door opened and in walked the same two servants from the night before. Gwen undid the sash around the Prince's nightgown and let it fall to the floor. Gazing at Leonardo's nakedness, she told him to lie down on his bed as another male servant arrived carrying a bowl of hot water. After he left, Gwen poured some oil into the water, dipped a flannel in the mixture and started washing the Prince all over. He enjoyed this female washing his body since she was so gentle and extremely attractive to look at. The Prince was mesmerised by the girl's delicate fruitful body and the lower she came to Leonardo, the more of her flesh was revealed. The girl knew by the reaction of Leonardo's body that he found her extremely interesting so she threw the flannel over the offending part just in case Grim saw his reaction over the girl.

"Are you finished with the Prince, Gwen?" Grim said to the girl since he wanted to start dressing him.

"No, I just have to dry the Prince, Grim," the girl said before taking a large bath towel and began drying the Prince from head to toe.

"Sire, stand up as Grim wishes to dress you," she instructed after she had finished towelling the Prince. "I'll be seeing you later tonight," she added before curtsying to the Prince and leaving.

Meanwhile, things were beginning to get hot next door as a young servant boy tried to remove the Princess' clothes.

"What are you doing, boy? How dare you?" she screamed. "I'm a Princess and I want a female to wash and bathe me, not a male!"

"Princess, I beg you to calm down as the King has always demanded that female servants bathe the men while the male servants bathe the women. Don't make my job difficult as otherwise I'll be dismissed by the Duke and I need the money to feed my family."

Princess Lena reluctantly got undressed and stood naked like the day she was born in front of the young boy as another boy entered carrying a bowl of hot water. He bowed graciously to the Princess as the other boy took the flannel, poured some oil onto it and began to wash the female all over. He blushed when he came to the girl's breasts but carried on as though nothing was untoward.

"You have a very gentle touch, boy, and I'm sorry for screaming at you! What's your name?" she asked.

"Edward, Princess," the young boy bleated.

He had been shouted at previously but found this royal very different to the others he had washed. The boy took a towel and dried the Princess all over before bowing graciously and leaving. The female servant walked over and started to dress the Princess beginning with her underwear and bodice until she came to put a lovely gold and green silken gown on her.

"If I may say so, you look gorgeous, Princess," she said. "Here, let me brush your hair and make it shine, and then you can go down for breakfast."

"And what is your name?" the Princess asked the girl who began brushing Lena's hair with long and gentle strokes.

"Grace, Princess, but no one calls me by my first name here at the Palace. However, the other servants said you and your brother are different and use our first names and that's so nice to hear."

"Well, Grace, if you'll be the one who'll be attending to me every time, then of course I'll call you by your proper name. One thing though is that I ranted and raved at the poor boy earlier when he wanted to undress and bathe me. This is something that will have to be changed if I have anything to do with it even though he was extremely gentle with me. He also told me that he bathes other women too! Is that true as he looks no more than sixteen?"

Grace guffawed loudly and said, "Sorry, Princess, forgive me, the boy's seventeen but looks younger. I bet when you refused him to bathe you, he was close to tears as the Duke would dismiss him for sure if he couldn't attend to you."

"That's what he told me and that he was the only one in his family earning money so I relented and got undressed and let him bathe me," the Princess said. "To be honest, I quite enjoyed it but don't tell him that, Grace."

"Of course I won't, Princess, but please excuse me as I must go since I'm on breakfast duty today," the girl said before curtsying and leaving.

The Princess got up from her chair and went next door to see if her brother was awake.

"Come in," a muffled voice said after she had tapped lightly on the door.

The Princess entered the room and saw her brother dressed smartly for the day but looking very worried as he paced up and down the room.

"You look extremely smart, brother, but something's troubling you. Tell your sister all about it and I'll see if I have any ideas on how to help you."

Prince Leonardo looked at his sister and wondered if he should say anything to her. This had become far more dangerous than before and only he and Daniella would know what to do. He realised that he had to say something to his sister since she would be in charge of the kingdom while he was away so he told her everything about the gorgeous naked young girl visiting him in the middle of the night and that she was in fact an old and haggard witch from the forest of Zandar.

"I can't believe it, yet you offered her a royal appointment," the Princess said with a look of terror in her eyes. "If she helps you kill the witch and remove her heart how do you know you can trust her, brother?"

"I don't, Lena, but having her working here at the Palace for me rather than against me means I can keep a watchful eye on her," the Prince replied. "I'm rather scared to fight the witch on my own and her having to face an alternative evil means she'll have to think again!"

"Oh, brother, but what's Daniella going to say about all this?" Princess Lena asked.

"I'll explain things to Daniella but it will mean she doesn't have to risk her life by living with the witch," the Prince said. "However, knowing Daniella, she still may decide to do that and there'll be nothing we can say to stop her from doing it."

Princess Lena stared at her brother and changing the subject completely, said, "I don't know about you but my stomach tells me I'm hungry. Shall we go for breakfast?"

The two of them forced a smile and went to breakfast. On their way down, they almost bumped into Daniella and Tatiana.

"Good morning, Lena and Leonardo," Daniella said cheerfully. "I hope you had a good night's sleep. And are you going for breakfast too?"

The two royal siblings smiled at Daniella and her lady-in-waiting and proceeded towards the dining hall where they sat down at a table at the far end of the room. A couple of minutes later, servants came from several directions carrying silver platters with all sorts of meat. This time there were no vegetables but a wide selection of gorgeous-looking fruit. Jeanette appeared with two large jugs, one of orange juice and the other of apple juice. After she had filled the goblets, the girl curtsied and left. The group drank the juice and remarked that it was lovely and cold. Leonardo told them that these had been stored in an icy cold river that flowed under the Palace.

Two new female servants came over bringing hot ceramic plates that they placed down in front of the royals before dishing out various slices of meat and a selection of colourful fruit of various strange shapes and sizes, which they found to be delicious. Within fifteen minutes, they had all polished off everything on their plates and the servants came to clear away the tables.

Chapter 30
A Future Queen

With the four of them now alone, Prince Leonardo looked at Daniella and took hold of the girl's hand. She felt her body trembling as she knew that he had something important to say.

The girl's eyes opened wide when Leonardo told her that there was a witch in this kingdom too. And when she heard that the witch could change herself into the most delectable girl and that the Prince had lain naked with her all night, she was upset despite the fact that Leonardo insisted that he had not touched her in any way.

"How can I trust you, Leonardo?" Daniella cried out to the Prince as she pulled her hand from Leonardo's.

His sister looked on in astonishment and wondered why the girl was acting in this way, but thinking about it, she realised that Daniella was right after all.

"Look, Leonardo, when I finish this quest with you I intend to travel back to my time so if you wish to proceed with the witch go ahead as it won't bother me anymore," a sullen Daniella continued as she got up from the table and went to her room where she cried herself to sleep.

The girl was in love with the Prince but he had to learn that she was not so stupid to believe that he did not touch that gorgeous female.

Back at the dining table, Leonardo looked as though he was about to burst into tears.

"Why doesn't she believe me?" he bemoaned. "I realised immediately that this gorgeous female had appeared in my room through magic and knew that she was some kind of a witch. When she tried to make advances to me, I pushed her away because I love only one girl and that's Daniella but how can I tell her when she's not even speaking to me?"

"Leave her in her room and let her think what she wants," Princess Lena said. "Whether or not that's you, Leonardo, I can't say as I'd have felt exactly how Daniella's feeling and you have no one to blame but yourself!" she added as Tatiana jumped onto the table to everyone's amazement.

"Let me go and speak to her," the raptor said. "I think I can make her see sense even though I've never seen her looking so upset. However, I'm ready to give it a try for your sake, Leonardo, as I know you love her deeply."

The raptor then jumped off the table and was gone. Once outside Daniella's bedroom, Tatiana knocked loudly at the door.

"Go away, leave me alone, Leonardo!" Daniella yelled.

"It's me, Tatiana!" the raptor announced. "Let me come in and speak to you."

The girl said nothing but someone opened the door to allow the raptor entrance to go inside as if by magic. Tatiana went into the room, closed the door behind her and saw Daniella lying on her bed.

"I'm the one who should be crying," the raptor said softly. "I've lost all my family and after hearing about this other witch I'm even more scared as I need you with me since you're my one and only friend."

"I'm being foolish, aren't I?" Daniella said as she sat up and began wiping away her tears. "Many kings have slept with gorgeous women and their queens never said a word to their husbands. Leonardo has only done it once since I've known him so perhaps I should forgive him this once."

"I think you're wrong, Daniella," Tatiana said. "After you left, Leonardo wept and told us that he pushed this beautiful female away as he knew she was evil and perhaps a witch. I believe that ever since he got to know you he's remained one hundred percent faithful to you. And as you know, without you being around, he'll refuse to rule over Blackstone as well as here as he wants you to be his queen."

"Okay, tell him I'm coming back," Daniella said a bit more willingly. "I just need to wash my face and the tears from my eyes and I'll be ready to meet the Duke."

Tatiana smiled at the girl, flicked out her long tongue, licked Daniella's face like a dog and left. Princess Lena had gone somewhere and the Prince was sitting at the table drinking a flagon of ale. When he saw the raptor, he wondered if she had been successful.

Tatiana sprung onto the now empty table and whispered in the Prince's ear. "Leonardo, Daniella has forgiven you so there's no need to drink anymore! I told her you cried after telling us you pushed that evil creature away and she believed you and said that she'll be down shortly to meet the Duke."

"Oh, Tatiana," the Prince said before leaning over to the raptor and kissing her on the lips.

She was shocked to say the least as this was the first time any man had kissed her like that. Embarrassed, the raptor jumped off the table and was gone like the wind.

Five minutes later, Daniella was ready. She appeared looking gorgeous with a brand new gown that she had put on herself. She had not bothered to ask one of the servants to do so as she had been embarrassed earlier that morning when a male servant came and undressed her before washing her all over. Walking down the stairway, she headed for the dining hall where she found no one except for Leonardo.

"I'm sorry, my darling for not believing you," Daniella announced. "I do now even though I don't trust this witch at all."

Leonardo stared into Daniella's eyes and kissed the girl passionately on the lips, something he had wanted to do for ages.

"Forgive me too, Daniella, as I love you from the bottom of my heart. My lips wanted to taste yours so much, my darling future queen!" he said as he looked at the timepiece King Rudolf had given him. "The Duke will be here within the next few minutes. Do you want a drink before he comes?"

"No, I'll wait as I'm still full of apple juice," she replied. "Darling, what do you think of the female servants washing you and the male ones dressing you? For us girls, it's terribly embarrassing being undressed and washed by a man or young boy! Who came up with this stupid idea? Can't you change it if you become King?"

"I was thinking exactly the same, dear, but was told by one of the females that this rule had been made by the Duke and not by the King," the Prince replied. "I don't know what he'd think of me changing his ideals. That's something we'll have to find out. Besides, did you know that the Duke agrees wholeheartedly to the fact that male servants as well as females are to attend to the royalty during and after a banquet held by the King?"

"That's disgusting but I realise we can't do anything about changing such customs until you become King," Daniella said sadly.

Leonardo knew by the disappointment shown on her face that the girl did not agree to this arrangement at all. As they continued talking, the Ambassador came into the room and saluted the Prince.

"Prince Leonardo, you're summoned together with your sister, Lady Daniella and Lady Tatiana for a meeting with the Duke," the Ambassador announced not realising that he had called the raptor a lady. "Follow me to the throne room where the Duke's waiting for you at this moment."

"Ambassador, my sister and Lady Tatiana are not here," the Prince said. "They're probably in their chambers. Do you want me to fetch them?"

"Of course not!" the Ambassador snapped. "You must remember that a royal does not raise a finger and a future King even less. There are servants to fetch and carry; that's what they're here for!" he added as he rang the bell.

A young girl came in and stared at the Ambassador; from the look on her face, it was obvious that she was scared of the man.

"Now, girl go and tell Princess Lena and Lady Tatiana to come to the throne room," the Ambassador ordered. "If they don't know where it is then bring them along. Go now as we've got no time to lose as the Duke's waiting."

The girl curtsied to the Ambassador and left in haste with her walk turning into a run even though running in the Palace was strictly forbidden and meant instant dismissal. The Ambassador glanced at Leonardo and Daniella and then walked away expecting them to follow him, which they did. On coming to the throne room, the Ambassador stopped and knocked at the door, waiting for someone to let them in. Unusually for him, the Duke himself opened the door.

"Come in, my dear Prince and you too, Lady Daniella," the Duke said. "I see you're together; that's good!"

Dismissing the Ambassador and telling him that he would send for him in due course, the Duke led the way into the throne room. This was the first time that either of them had been in there. Both the Prince and his sister gasped on seeing the King's throne of gold and precious stones. The Prince got butterflies in his stomach as the Duke ushered them to sit down.

"I'll wait until your sister and Lady Tatiana have arrived," the Duke said. "I hope you don't mind."

The Prince and Daniella smiled at the Duke and wondered what he had to say to them but they had no choice but to wait until the others came. A knock at the door told the Duke that they had arrived so he himself went to open the door.

“Come in, my dears, we’re just about to start,” the Duke said.

Princess Lena and Tatiana looked in amazement at the gold and jewelled throne as they had never seen anything quite like it before. The pair then sat down at the table where the Prince and Daniella were already seated.

“I’ve thought seriously over what you promised the people if you become King,” the Duke began as he turned towards Leonardo. “After sleeping on it and discussing it with my wife, we’ve agreed that you have the right mind and attitude to make a first class ruler but we’re concerned that you’ll be taking on the wicked witch of Blackstone because you may never come back. This, my boy, is something we have to discuss after the royal ceremony.”

“I have something urgent I need to tell you that could jeopardise our original plans,” the Prince cut in. “If you remember, when several thousand of your soldiers disappeared in the forest, I said to you that perhaps they’d been taken by another evil presence and you replied that you’d never heard of a witch living in the forest.”

“Yes, of course, Son, but what are you trying to tell me?” the Duke asked.

The Prince poured out his story to the Duke about the gorgeous female trying to trick him into sleeping with her and then adding that she had the intention of ruling over the kingdom herself as a beautiful young woman. The Duke turned pale on hearing this and wondered what he could do to stop her.

“I thought over this carefully and made her angry when I told her I wasn’t afraid of her and that there was an even more powerful witch living in the enchanted forest of Blackstone,” the Prince continued to explain. “It was then that she told me that since

Zandar had no ruler she thought of becoming its queen. I told her that if she kept everything as it was and came with me to fight the witch I'd invite her to live at the Palace and become my sorceress. I know this isn't what you wanted to hear, Sir, but what other choice did I have?"

The Duke pondered his thoughts and scratched his beard nervously before replying, "No, Prince Leonardo, I think you've done the rightful thing. If she can defeat this witch, she could become our future enemies' worst ever nightmare. Anyway, where is she right now, Son?"

"Caspian told me she's going to prepare something special for the witch of the enchanted forest," Leonardo replied. "When she returns to the Palace, it's time for Daniella and I to leave for Blackstone. I wonder how we'll be getting to Blackstone but I have some ideas of my own and believe Caspian can send us there without travelling by carriage."

"If you're right, Son, then your job couldn't be easier but how do you know that after killing the evil witch and giving her heart to Satan that Caspian will stand by her words or that Satan won't keep you locked away for all eternity?" the Duke asked worriedly.

"We don't, Sir, but we have to take the risk," Leonardo replied calmly. "I just have to find a way to free the people of Blackstone from those dreadful everlasting winters!"

"You, Prince and Lady Daniella, will make the ideal King and Queen. Now, Prince Leonardo, the time has come so kneel before me," the Duke instructed.

Leonardo got up from his chair and knelt down in front of the Duke who touched the Prince's shoulders with the tip of his sword.

"From this day onwards, I hereby appoint you King Leonardo, the ruler of the Kingdom of Zandar," the Duke proclaimed as he placed a golden crown on Leonardo's head.

The Duke then proceeded to bring out a beautiful silk robe and a large set diamond on a thick golden chain from a wardrobe in the corner of the room. Bending down, he then pulled out a handcrafted diamond and sapphire encrusted sword from a large chest on the floor. The Duke took the robe and placed it around Leonardo's shoulders, and subsequently put the thick gold chain around his neck. From his pocket, he then took out an impressive diamond ring that he placed onto Leonardo's finger.

"Your Majesty, welcome to the Kingdom of Zandar," the Duke announced with much pomp. "You were always the people's choice and mine as well and I'm sure you can bring joy and serenity to our kingdom."

King Leonardo strutted proudly up and down the throne room to the applause of his sister, Daniella and Tatiana. He then went to his throne and sat down, feeling that this piece of elegant furniture had been made especially for him and not for the evil King.

"Now, your Majesty, tomorrow morning you'll be welcomed by the people of Zandar," the Duke said. "However, make sure the servants do as you command them as they need to show you respect even more so now you're King."

Neither Leonardo nor Daniella said anything to the Duke as this was really his kingdom after all, especially as he had decided to abdicate the throne and hand it over to a complete stranger.

"Your Highness, I must beg you permission to leave. I'll be seeing you at seven tomorrow morning and the people are expected an hour later at eight," the Duke said as he bowed several times to the new King and walked out backwards.

King Leonardo was the first to speak. "Look, I know what the servants expect me to do but I still want to use their first names. And with the Duke wanting you to address me as your Highness or Majesty, this is something I can't accept especially as you,

Daniella, are to be my future wife and queen and you, Tatiana, my dearest and closest friend."

"Look, brother, as from now on you're King Leonardo but when we're on our own and away from prying eyes and listening ears we don't need to abide by these laws," Princess Lena suggested. "However, we'd best use your official title in front of the Duke as we don't want to upset him," the Princess said curtsying as she would to any noble since she was brought up to respect royalty from when she was a young girl.

Daniella turned to Leonardo and said, "Your Highness, like your sister said, we have to remain watchful about how we conduct ourselves in front of you from now on."

"Yes, your Majesty, Daniella and Princess Lena are right," the young raptor added, following which she left the room with just Daniella and Princess Lena remaining.

King Leonardo smiled at them both before saying, "Okay, you've made it quite obvious how you feel about conducting yourself in front of me and reluctantly I have to accept your wishes but if you forget to address me correctly then I won't be saying anything about it. Now, one last thing before you leave, find Jeanette and send her to me as I promised her something and I'm going to stand by my decision with the girl."

"Yes, your Majesty," Princess Lena said to her brother. "We'll go and find her and tell her to come straight to the throne room."

The girls curtsied and walked backwards until they got to the door, which they opened and went into the hallway to find Jeanette. King Leonardo sat there grinning to himself but not quite understanding why he could not conduct himself in the way that he was used to doing.

Chapter 31
A Dressmaker is born

There was a knock at the door and Leonardo shouted to whoever was on the other side, "Come in!"

The door swung open and young Jeanette entered the room looking worried. She closed the door quietly behind her, curtsied and shuffled forwards until she was standing directly in front of Leonardo who she knew had just been appointed King.

"You, my dear, will leave your position as from now," Leonardo said to the terrified girl who wrongly thought she was being dismissed from her job, which she needed so badly. "Don't look so sad, Jeanette, I'm not getting rid of you but I'm promoting you. I've not forgotten the promise I made to you and I wish to see your drawings of those clothes you intend to make," he added to the young girl who was stunned to hear this from the King.

"Your Majesty, why do you want to help a poor servant girl?" the shocked girl asked. "What is it you want in return from me? I've never been with a man before, let alone a King and a handsome one at that."

"Jeanette, I don't want you to sleep with me. I just wish you to fulfil your ambitions and dreams to become a master dressmaker. I'm ready to help you become what you always wanted to be, and give you that opportunity to change you and your aunts lives forever." Leonardo said with a warm smile.

"Oh, Sire," the girl bleated feeling her eyes beginning to well up. "No one, especially not a King, has ever been so kind to me like this and it takes some getting used to. And to become a dressmaker would be everything a young girl could hope for."

At these words, there was a further knock at the door and the King shouted out, "Yes, come in and show yourself."

The door swung open and the Ambassador stormed into the room. On seeing Jeanette standing in front of Leonardo and with the girl tearful, he jumped to the wrong conclusion.

"Now, girl, if the King has dismissed you, you must leave this minute as we have urgent business to attend to. Now, go immediately!" the Ambassador cried out to the poor girl.

Jeanette went to leave but the King raised his hand and said, "No, my dear, but come back in an hour as the Ambassador will be finished by then."

The girl curtsied to the King, walked backwards until she reached the door and exited the room.

The Ambassador was pulling on his beard thinking that this was so irregular, especially with the King calling the girl 'my dear!' He wondered if perhaps she would be joining the King later in his chambers as his predecessor often did. These mistresses had borne him several sons and daughters who of course were illegitimate and had to be banished from his kingdom. Only the Ambassador knew of this promiscuous behaviour and maybe the new King felt the same way about these young females.

"Sire, you can't have a soft spot for one particular girl," the Ambassador remarked. "She's still very young but for you to promise her that she can keep her job if she makes you happy tonight that I fully understand as your predecessor felt the same about these young girls. Let's face it, they are extremely pretty but only for one night and then you can change her for a new one, as let's face it Sire as our new ruler then you can choose any of these girls! It's quite normal for a King to feel like this."

"Ambassador," King Leonardo growled. "I'm not interested in taking any girl and only wish to help the child. She has a talent far exceeding her present job and I want to turn her into a master dressmaker for the Palace and the ladies of Zandar. I've told her to remain silent on this matter as otherwise the other servants may feel aggrieved over this gesture of goodwill. This is between my sister, Lady Daniella and Lady Tatiana, as they know about my arrangement with the girl, and now that I've told you, I'd appreciate it if you don't utter a word to anyone, do you understand me, Ambassador?"

"Yes, your Majesty, I'm one hundred percent trustworthy and will not breathe a word about your arrangement. However, if you want to make this girl a master dressmaker, what will the royal tailor say?"

"I'm not bothered what he thinks as a little competition won't hurt him at all," King Leonardo replied. "Anyway, to have a female attending to the women's needs is the rightful thing to do and my sister's in agreement with this as well. Now, Ambassador, do you need anything else or can I go ahead and see this young lady for myself?"

"Sir, all I wanted to do was to ask you if we'll be having a banquet to celebrate this very special occasion. I'm sure that the rulers of the other kingdoms will wish to meet you personally as the new King of Zandar."

"Ambassador, as the Duke is aware, I have pressing business over in Blackstone to attend to. My sister, Princess Lena, will be in charge of everything. Lady Tatiana and Mr Stott, who is our new royal advisor and collector of taxes, will be assisting her. Any banquet will have to take place after Lady Daniella and I return to court from Blackstone. When that will be, only the Duke has the privilege of knowing. Now, if you've got nothing further to say, I'd like to ask you to leave as I promised the young girl I'd take no longer than one hour and it is two minutes before the hour."

The Ambassador bowed graciously, backed to the door and was gone like a flash as he realised that he had outstayed his welcome.

Five minutes later, there was a knock at the door and Leonardo went to open it, stepped back a little to allow the young girl entrance. She made a curtsy but he told her not to on this occasion. Jeanette looked shocked, but Leonardo took hold of her hands and led her over to the table where she placed her work down neatly for the King to see. King Leonardo did not go back to his throne but stood with the girl side by side showing Jeanette that he thought of her as an equal.

"My dear," the King said to the girl. "These are brilliant and I was right! You do have amazing talent! Now that we understand each other, follow me and don't curtsy as I've given you permission not to address me as King and I plan for my sister to turn you into the lady you've always dreamt of being one day, and that day starts from right now!"

King Leonardo left his room with Jeanette following closely at his heels hoping that no one saw her. They climbed up the stairs until they came to a door which Leonardo opened. The pair made a quick entrance and the girl closed the door behind them. They were in an empty room, far larger than the dining hall itself.

"Now, Jeanette, this will be your new workshop," Leonardo announced. "By any chance, have you chosen the girls you wish to train? I'll arrange to have five large tables made by the royal carpenter to be put in here together with a drawing board on the wall and several comfortable chairs for you to sit on. What do you say, dear Jeanette?"

"Sire, I'm lost for words but if I'm working here how can I earn a living without being a servant? I have no money and can't rely on your charity forever," the girl said.

"No, my dear Jeanette," the King said to the girl. "I plan to give you one hundred gold coins per year as a salary for taking up this position since you told me that your family died under the King's hands. And your two assistants will be paid a higher wage than you previously earned as a servant girl."

"I cannot believe this, Sire," the girl said, flummoxed by what Leonardo had said to her. "Why are you and your family taking pity on poor little me? Of course, I can never refuse something like this as it was always a dream of mine to make dresses one day but I thought dreams never came true!"

"Well, Jeanette," Leonardo said to the young girl who was shaking at the knees. "This dream has come true because you're a very talented young girl and therefore you deserve success. I'll order you paints, colouring pens, easels, paper, pencils and new fountain pens that you put ink inside. They have this in Blackstone but it was only used by the royals to make their letters stand out more."

"Oh, Sire, you've made a young girl so happy! My Aunt Ellie will never believe me when I get home tonight!" Jeanette said joyfully while King Leonardo stroked his new beard that was now taking shape extremely nicely.

"Now, young lady, as a dressmaker you no longer have to work seven days a week," Leonardo said. "Your new hours will be from eight in the morning to six in the evening five days a week and you'll have two days off to enjoy yourself with your aunt. One last thing, Jeanette, before I introduce you to my sister, do you know what happened to the girl who received all she had ever dreamed of?"

"No, Sir," the young girl replied with deep concern wondering if this was where the King asked for something in return.

"Quite easy to answer, young lady, as she was happy for the rest of her life. Now, go home early and tell your aunt that all your money problems are a thing of the past. My sister will be doing your salary, my dear, as you're now an important part of this kingdom and I'll tell her so. From tomorrow, you'll begin your lessons in learning how to be a lady from my sister who will also arrange new clothing and shoes for you. For today, that's enough, so you may go," Leonardo said to the young girl.

"Sire, look how much I'm shaking! I'll never be able to walk home!" Jeanette exclaimed.

"Okay, Jeanette, leave it to me," Leonardo said as he rang the bell and the Head Guardsman came in.

"Yes, Sire, do you want this girl put into the dungeons?" he asked.

Poor Jeanette wondered if this was to be her fate and that the King had been lying to her but Leonardo screamed at the guard, "No, I don't want her taken anywhere! Get me my sister and bring her to me at once."

"The Head Guardsman looked shocked but he saluted the King, bowed graciously to him and exited the room while poor Jeanette was left shaking at the knees.

"My dear, don't shake as there's nothing for you to be afraid of," Leonardo said. "Here, sit down on one of these chairs."

The girl sat down sheepishly as this kind of thing had never happened to anyone she had known in her short but industrious life.

There was another knock at the door and the King got up to see who it was. Princess Lena then sauntered in and smiled at her brother when she saw Jeanette in the room since she knew that her brother had kept to his word.

"Good morning, Sire," the Princess said as she curtsied. "How can I help you, your Majesty?"

"Lena, as you know, when I met Jeanette, I promised to change her life from that of a poor lass to that of a lady of standing so I want you to take the royal carriage and take Jeanette home where I want you to meet her aunt and report back to me about the condition of her house. From tomorrow, you're to become Jeanette's mentor so you need to order her some new clothes and shoes. I also want you to teach the girl to become a lady like your good self. Can you do that for me, Lena?"

"Yes, Sire," Lena replied. "However, will Jeanette have time to become my lady-in-waiting as I did promise her this position and would prefer her to bathe and dress me rather than the male servants?"

"Well, that's entirely up to Jeanette, I suppose. For the time being, she'll only be doing some new drawings and gathering together some ideas about how the women here like their gowns made and waiting for her materials to arrive before she can begin her work. If Jeanette's alright with doing two jobs at the same time, that's fine with me," the Prince replied. "However, I promised the girl she only needs to work five days per week. It's up to her if she wishes to remain working for the full seven days until I return from Blackstone. While you're in charge, the girl will receive one hundred gold coins per year as master dressmaker. What do you intend on giving her for being your lady-in-waiting?"

"I'll give Jeanette an extra twenty-five gold coins untaxed, do you understand, Sire?" the girl said with a mischievous sort of look at her brother.

"That sounds good to me, Sister, as long as Jeanette feels the same," King Leonardo said as he looked at the girl who nodded her head vigorously as a sign of approval. "Jeannette, I hereby grant you permission to become my sister's lady-in-waiting until Daniella and I return to the Palace. However, you must remember that your main job is to be master dressmaker of the Palace. It's probably also a good idea if she leaves her current position and tells the other servants that she's been chosen to become your lady-in-waiting, Lena."

"Sire, I'm sorry to interrupt you but I think that's a brilliant idea," Jeanette cut in. "It will then look no different to telling the other servants that I've been given a promotion."

“Excellently put, my dear,” Leonardo said to the girl. “Now, let me call the guard to prepare the royal carriage. In the meantime, you, Lena, can take Jeanette up to your room. I’ll let you know when the carriage is ready. And, perhaps, Jeanette will like to design herself a new uniform over the next few days.”

In their haste to leave the room, Princess Lena and Jeanette forgot to curtsy to the King but he just smiled to himself as they closed the door behind them, leaving him sitting there on his throne feeling important.

Chapter 32
Distant Feelings

I lay there watching the family splashing around in the outdoor swimming pool. It was quite full of people so I relaxed and closed my eyes feeling very comfortable in the sun lounger that I had taken.

"Come on, Granddad, come into the water! It's great here, so lovely and warm! Can't you swim?" Daniella said to me, leaning on the edge of the pool.

"I can swim like a fish, Granddaughter, but I'm tired after all that writing and hearing my wife saying her last goodbyes. Let me just lie here and I promise to join you some other day when my mind's much clearer."

My son appeared from under the water and said to his daughter, "Leave Granddad alone and I'll race you to the end of the pool."

Daniella turned and struck out before my son had even thought about it and even with his superior athletic body strength she beat him fair and square. As they swam back to Carol, they saw a young man chatting to her in the pool, perhaps thinking that she was single. Richard growled at the young guy who immediately apologised and swam away.

"I came back just at the right time, I see, my darling. What did he want? However, you do look gorgeous in that red bikini as does our daughter!" my son remarked with a chuckle.

Daniella had come over to me and tugged at a sun lounger until she had dragged it right by my side. She then lay down and held my hand and we closed our eyes as the loungers had their own sunshade that shielded the hot sun off our faces.

Carol, meanwhile, stared at Richard and replied with a double-edged answer. "I think so as well, darling, and to be honest he was one of five men who have tried to come on to me. I can't quite believe it as I thought that I was old and finished but they think differently so you'll have to keep me under lock and key!" she said laughing at her husband and kissing him passionately on the lips to show any bystander that she was taken after all.

The two lovebirds swam over to us, grabbed hold of two more loungers and settled down next door, closing their eyes as we had done. Carol did look stunning in her revealing new bikini with her lovely flat stomach and without an ounce of fat on her. No wonder the men were ogling over her.

Richard was the first to open his eyes. Staring over at his lovely wife, he realised that he still loved this girl even more so than before and it needed his mother's touch to reawaken them from this never-ending nightmare. Looking over at his sleeping wife and then at me, he decided to give me a prod and wake me up.

"Ouch," I cried. "I'm old now and bruise easier than before," I added laughing. "What do you want, Dick?"

"The time, Dad!" he replied. "It's almost six and we said we'd be eating at this hour yet we're still out here by the pool. How's your book coming along by the way?" my son added trying to catch me off guard.

"Fine, just fine," I replied, giving him no hint at all.

"Just like Mom said, pigheaded and afraid to share your secrets with us! What's Daniella got that I haven't?" my son said, giving me a glare but smiling after doing so.

"After hearing Rebecca rebuke me by saying I was mean not showing anything to her, then I knew that if I was going to share my secrets with anyone it had to be my granddaughter as you're far too busy with your work anyway."

"Nicely put, Dad," Richard said with a grin. "Now, let me wake up Carol while you give Daniella a prod."

I pushed my granddaughter awake and she opened her eyes. I told her the time and she sat up and smiled at me. Meanwhile, Richard was tickling Carol's back and she shot up thinking it was maybe some sort of insect crawling over her.

"You horrible beast!" Carol howled with a mischievous smile. "What do you want? I was enjoying myself without a care in the world." She stared over at her daughter and me and seeing us wide-awake added, "Are you telling me it's five o'clock already? I thought we were going to eat at six."

"Wrong, darling, it's far later than that," Richard said, showing Carol his watch.

"Half past six?" Carol asked surprisingly as she rubbed her eyes. "I need to take a shower and put some decent clothes on. How can I walk into the restaurant in just my bikini?"

We all burst out laughing but got to our feet soon afterwards and grabbed our towels. My back was hurting and I ambled along slowly behind the others as we made our way to our rooms. We had arranged to meet on the landing at seven thirty.

I entered my room, got undressed and went into the ensuite shower. The water came on just like magic without me touching anything and at just the right temperature. I stayed there enjoying my shower and washing myself all over with a lovely smelling fragranced liquid soap that the hotel supplied. After I dried my body, I put my underpants on. I also chose to wear a nice pair of lightweight Levi trousers, a smart white Lacrosse t-shirt and a pair of nice white ankle socks following which I slipped into my new leather brogues. Brushing my hair that was still colourful as well as plentiful, I looked at the time. It was a quarter past seven and I realised that my backache had gone away completely.

In the meantime, Daniella had been relaxing in the bath. When she dried herself, she looked at her watch and saw that it was already seven fifteen. She only had a quarter of an hour to get ready and dry her hair but she managed it with a minute to spare. As the girl went out of her room, she saw her mother and father waiting for me to arrive. They saw my door open and me coming out and closing the door behind me. I walked over to them and noticed how elegant and gorgeous both girls were looking while Bob was also looking very handsome in a lightweight suit with an open necked shirt and black leather moccasins.

Mom and daughter were wearing something very similar. Whereas Daniella was wearing a mid-length, green silken dress with a plunge line, Carol was wearing the same dress in black. With their long and shiny hair, they looked more like sisters rather than mother and daughter. We made our way to the restaurant where my son gave his name and room number following which we were led over to a reserved table where we sat down.

"Would you care for a drink, Sir?" the girl asked.

"That would be nice," my son replied to the young girl. "Can you get us two cold glasses of lager and two medium sweet white wines for the ladies?" he added as the girl curtsied and left.

Daniella turned to her father and said, "Thanks, Dad, for making me feel grownup. It means so much to me and I'll sip it so that it lasts me the whole night!"

We all smiled when Daniella said this to her father and I was pleased how my son reacted by just ordering the girl the same drink as her mother's.

When the drinks arrived, we began sipping from them and felt them refreshing all our vital body parts.

"I suppose you could get used to this, darling," Carol told her daughter. "However, do yourself a favour and if your friends tell you to drink such things then refuse as Mom and Dad will always give you a glass on special occasions."

"Of course, Mom," the girl replied. "I know you trust me and that means so much to me and I won't let you down."

"That's good to hear, darling," her Mom said. "I know Dad and I have been mean to you over the years but we've changed now."

The waitress came over and handed us a menu before saying, "These items on the menu are included in your package holiday but if you prefer something else then we'll have to charge your room accordingly. However, I'm sure you'll find the selection of food excellent as well as scrumptious so why pay more when our meals are so exciting."

"Thank you, my dear," my son said to the young girl who gave him a beaming smile.

We had a look at the menu and saw that the girl was right as the meals even included rib eye steak, which we all plumbed for, taking a mixture of melon and prawn cocktail as starters.

The girl tapped it out on her handheld computer before saying to my son, "Do you want a bottle of house wine, Sir? This again comes free with your package deal. Would you like it brought over to you now or with your main meal?"

Richard smiled and said to the girl, "I think we'd prefer it if you can bring it with the main course, please."

"Yes, Sir, of course," the waitress said with a warm smile. "Let me go and arrange everything. Now, before I go, do you want any refills? These unfortunately have to be put on your room number."

"We've only just arrived, my dear, but can you get us two more lagers and two more glasses of wine?" my son added.

"Yes, of course, Sir," the girl said, giving Daniella a big grin which she returned.

To our right there were four feisty men sitting and they called over to the girl as she was leaving our table. "Come on, we don't have all night! And then you can come and visit us later tonight too!"

The girl, concerned by such offensiveness, made haste and quickly disappeared over to the bar to fetch our drinks. Richard was about to say something but I touched his arm to tell him that I did not think that was a good idea as these louts were American and did not give a damn about any other customers.

Then something happened that made me wish in a way that I had been younger as I would have given them a right going over. One of the four threw a piece of screwed up paper in the direction of Carol and hit her hard on the arm. She picked up the offending missile and opened it.

'My darling in the red bikini,' the message read. 'I think you're amazing! I'd like to get to know you better so come to room 215 at midnight! John xxx.'

"What's wrong, Carol?" my son asked as his wife turned a bright red.

She showed him the paper and he read the contents. He then got to his feet and walked over to the table where the four guys were sitting.

"Which one of you is John?" he growled. "You've just offended my wife in front of my daughter."

"So what, old man!" one of the men replied. "That woman needs some spice in her life and I thought the other young filly was her sister and my other friend was going to send for her as well."

This became too much for Richard and he launched himself at John. They grappled on top of the table sending drinks and food flying everywhere. With fists being thrown at each other, I saw blow after blow as their heads rocked backwards and forwards, sending customers running for cover.

After a couple of minutes of fighting, the manager sent his security men to pull them apart. They both had cut eyes, noses and mouths and it seemed that gradually my son was getting the upper hand. However, unknown to him, one of the other men passed something to John and he thrust out with a six-inch bladed knife and stabbed my son in the stomach.

We watched him crumple and fall to the ground bleeding profusely from the knife wound to his stomach. He closed his eyes and we thought he was dead. Daniella and Carol screamed to high heaven while I went over to my son and felt for his pulse.

"He's still got a strong heart beat," I stammered. "We must send for an ambulance," I shouted to the manager who had already done this. "And send for the police too."

The guys had legged it the moment they saw my son collapse to the ground as they knew he was seriously wounded. The manager came over to tell us as he realised that the four men were guests who had just arrived that morning.

"I'm so sorry," the manager said to Carol and her daughter who were in tears. "But why on earth did your husband go and fight four grown men? He stood no chance at all!"

I surrendered the piece of paper that Carol had thrown at her and the manager read it and began to understand everything. At that moment, an ambulance pulled up outside the hotel and a number of paramedics rushed in just as a couple of police cars arrived.

"We must hurry up and get him to hospital as his wound is serious," one of the paramedics said after giving my son the onceover. "Who's his next of kin? He or she has to come with us," he added as Carol got up from her chair and tried wiping away her tears.

"I'm his wife," she said solemnly. "I'll be going along with him but please don't let him die as he means everything to me!" Turning to me, she added, "And Dad please look after our daughter for me."

Daniella burst out crying as she sobbed in my arms. I did not know what to say or do as this holiday had turned out to be the worst ever nightmare.

A certain Captain Ruus then came over to me and asked me what had happened. The manager then took the officer over to reception where he handed him the screwed up note and the details of the missing offenders. Within fifteen minutes, several more police cars descended on the area around the hotel. They quickly found the perpetrators who had taken a taxi to try to get out of Chiang Mai, leaving all their possessions behind in the hotel.

Unknown to them, the taxi base had contacted the driver and spoke to him in Thai, and told him to drive to a rendezvous point where the police would then take over. When the taxi reached the requested location, the driver stopped the car and several armed officers surrounded the taxi and arrested the men.

After a brief phone conversation, Captain Ruus came over with the news. "We've managed to capture the men," he announced to me. Then turning to Daniella, he added, "I'm so sorry, my dear. Several guests have told us that these men also gave you abusive language and all kinds of innuendos. By the way, how old are you, my child?"

"Thirteen," Daniella sobbed to the Captain. "Please don't let Daddy die! We love him so much!"

This had become too difficult for the Captain to deal with as he found himself on the edge of tears so he apologised to the girl and left us on our own in order to make a written report in his car.

It was close to ten o'clock and my son had been taken to hospital some two hours earlier. I had no idea what I could do since my granddaughter was distraught at the thought of losing her father. She was still snivelling in my arms when, thankfully, Cal turned up.

"I've just heard the awful news about your father, my darling," Cal said to Daniella. "Your mother phoned the hotel a few minutes ago and said that he's in good care. She sends her love and will speak to you in the morning. My heart goes out to you, my little one! The manager has also informed me that he'll be moving you into a nice suite so that you can be with your grandfather."

"I think that's a good idea, Cal," I replied gratefully. "And please thank the manager on my behalf. Could we also have a hot chocolate with milk and sugar please? Hopefully, it will go a long way to help us sleep."

"Of course, I will. I'll do it myself," Cal said as she strode off to arrange everything.

"Granddad," Daniella said to me, wiping away the tears as she was gradually feeling a little better. "Why did this happen on our very first day? In some strange way, I feel that if Granny had not interfered with Mommy and Daddy and left them as they were, I would at least still have a Daddy to love. I feel so mixed up but I'm happy you're here with me," she added as Cal came over carrying a tray on which there were two mugs of steaming hot chocolate and a plate of cheese on toast.

"The girl told me you didn't even eat your starters so I wondered if you're still hungry. I don't mind if you want to leave it but it's here if you feel like it," Cal announced as she smiled warmly at both of us.

"You're just lovely, my dear, and to be honest at this moment I'm hungry but Daniella has to try to eat as she's extremely worried about her father."

Daniella took a sip of hot chocolate and forced herself a brief smile at Cal. My granddaughter then shocked me as she began eating a piece of cheese on toast.

"This is what Daddy would want me to do," she said with her mouth half full. "We're in Thailand and he'd want us to enjoy ourselves as best as we can. I know it's difficult, Granddad, but life has to go on as you often tell me. After all, Daddy's in the best hands and Mommy is with him."

Cal remained with us and grinned at the girl as she tried to be brave not knowing how bad her Daddy really was.

"Now," Cal said to us both. "Your new room is ready and your luggage and belongings have all been moved so follow me."

She took us to the top floor where the restaurant was and down to the end of a hallway, turned left and along yet another hallway where we saw a sign saying, 'Suites'. When Cal opened the door to the room, we gasped in astonishment as we had seen nothing quite like this before. Cal then led the way into the enormous room where there was a lovely bunch of roses and some unusual purple flowers with yellow centres standing on a table. It was also full of presents of all kinds and we were curious to know whom they were from.

Cal saw us staring at the gifts so she smiled and said, "These are a small number of gifts for Daniella. Everyone in the hotel has bought her something as they're really touched by this terrible ordeal and feel so sorry for Daniella. We've probably got another hundred or more gifts and cards for the family and Daniella in our secure room. They all insist on seeing the girl as soon as she can speak to them.

Daniella and I were stunned by the news of so many strangers becoming involved in this sordid business. It was a kind gesture and I could see that the girl was really touched.

"I'm lost for words, Cal, with all these lovely people buying so many presents for me," Daniella stated. "This is so touching and will help me overcome my concerns over Dad. Of course, when we eat breakfast tomorrow morning, I'll be making a little thank you speech and giving them an update about how Daddy's doing."

"Come along with me and I'll show you around the suite," Cal said amicably. "It costs three thousand dollars per night but the hotel owner has insisted that you move in here for as long as you need to because they're so saddened by this situation."

We followed the girl into a large bedroom with beautiful views over the sanctuary and the open-air swimming pool as well as across to the forest. There were a further two such bedrooms, all with beautiful Queen Anne beds, chairs and couch, an expensive desk, cupboards and sets of drawers, a flat screen TV and a Jacuzzi big enough to take the whole family. There was also a magnificent lounge with leather and hardwood furniture, an enormous flat screen TV with quadraphonic speakers on each of the walls and a cupboard full of the latest DVDs and music CDs. Apart from a fantastic view from all the rooms, there was even a lovely kitchen and dining room area. Our faces said it all as we were stunned to say the least.

"That's not all, come with me," Cal continued as she took us out of the room and went about five doors down the hallway until we reached the fitness centre. We entered with the place deserted and in complete darkness so Cal turned on the lights, in the process revealing all kinds of exercising machines, from walking and jogging to weight lifting and cycling. Another room was a dance hall for aerobics, a gymnasium and two indoor swimming pools, one for grownups and a smaller one for kids.

"Membership is free when you take one of the suites," the kind girl announced. "It's never crowded as there are only ten suites and a honeymoon suite for married couples. I've never known there to be more than thirty people tops so at least it will help you try to forget what happened today and try to enjoy the rest of your holiday."

"I'm so tired after crying so much," Daniella sighed. "Can we go to our room now as I still have to make some thank you cards for all those lovely people?"

Cal thought that this was such a lovely thought with the girl going through so much pain and still insisting on making those cards.

"My darling," Cal said to my granddaughter. "Let me go down to my office where I have the perfect things for you to write your name on and it will allow you to sleep, young lady, and that is what you and your granddad need so much."

Cal disappeared leaving us on our own but five minutes later, she was back carrying a big box, which she opened. She then brought out a number of elegant gold embossed 'Thank You Cards' and some expensive ink pens and fluorescent markers of all colours to decorate the cards with.

"I'll leave these with you for a few days and that will allow you to finish them gradually," Cal said before leaving the room.

Chapter 33
Carol's Dilemma

Carol sat in the waiting room with her head resting in her hands. She knew nothing about what was happening to Richard and tears quickly filled her eyes. A woman came over and handed her a new handkerchief. Carol took it and tried to raise a smile.

"I know what you're going through, my dear, since my little girl was knocked over by a car and she's in a critical condition, that's what the doctor told me," the woman said. "They won't allow me in with her until her condition becomes stable."

"I'm so sorry," Carol said to the woman. "My husband was stabbed during a fight at the hotel where we're staying. He hasn't woken up since and I'm terrified I'm going to lose him as he has a father and a thirteen-year-old daughter still at the hotel waiting for news."

At this, a doctor came over looking grave and Carol began thinking the worst. However, he ignored her and walked over to the woman and said in Thai, "I'm really sorry; we did all we could but we lost her in theatre."

The woman wept so loudly that the doctor told a nurse to take her to somewhere quiet for her to grieve. The doctor said nothing to poor Carol and returned to where he had come from while she sat there with her head in her hands for several more hours until eventually another doctor came over to speak to her.

"Mrs Riverton, your husband's been seriously hurt and is still unconscious," the doctor declared solemnly. "We've managed to stop the bleeding but we don't know until we carry out some more tests whether or not he'll pull through as the knife was driven deeply into his stomach. Luckily, it just missed his arteries and any other major organs."

"What are you saying doctor? I'm his wife so give me the full picture. Will he be able to walk and talk?" Carol asked with tears in her eyes once again.

"As I said, Madam, until he comes out of his coma we can only guess. However, would you like to be with him? He's now in the trauma ward."

"Carol nodded and the doctor began walking and beckoned to her to follow. She did not know what to expect as the doctor opened the door and the two of them entered the trauma ward where a nurse greeted them.

"Doctor Fels, have you come to see the patient, Mr Riverton?" the nurse queried. "And who is this doctor?" she added, looking Carol up and down. "Did you tell her that visitors can only stay for half an hour?"

"Sister Aals, this is the gentleman's wife. She can stay for as long as she likes as this can only help Mr Riverton's recovery," the doctor replied.

"Yes, doctor, I understand, and I apologise, Madam," the nurse said remorsefully. "Do you want me to make up a bed for Mrs Riverton? Will she be staying by her husband's side?" she added to the doctor who stared at Carol and wondered if she wanted to stay with her husband.

"Yes, doctor, I would if I'm allowed to as I'm so worried about him," Carol answered.

"Come with me, Mrs Riverton, as I bet you can't wait to see your husband," the doctor said as he led Carol over to see her husband who had all sorts of tubes coming and going from his body. Carol sat down and held Richard's hand; he looked extremely pale and had his eyes tightly shut.

"Mrs Riverton, your husband has suffered a serious stab wound to the stomach and has lost a lot of blood," the doctor continued. "He's very lucky to be alive but until he comes out of his coma we can only guess what sort of long-term damage he may have suffered."

The doctor gave Carol a wry smile since he did not wish to upset her. However, he wondered how this man would rise above such a severe injury as in his eyes and those of his professional colleagues they believed that he would not make it.

Carol sat quietly holding her husband's hand for a further three hours with that distant hope that he might open his eyes. She thought that she had fallen out of love with him but ever since Mom's intervention, she loved him more than anything and was terrified of losing him.

At that moment, a nurse came over and said, "Mrs Riverton, I'm sure you're hungry. Would you like me to get you something to eat? The last thing your husband would want is for you to become ill as well!"

Carol raised her head and nodded weakly at the nurse to show to her that she would perhaps like a little food and maybe a cold drink.

"Yes, my dear, I'll just go and arrange it for you," the nurse said.

A tearful Carol said to the nurse, "I need to give you my husband's insurance details but these are over in the hotel," a tearful Carol said to the nurse before she left. "Perhaps, I can get my husband's father to bring them over as my daughter will be so worried that she's not heard anything from anyone."

"Don't fret, Mrs Riverton, we are in constant communication with Mr Riverton's father at the hotel. By the way, you won't need your husband's insurance details as the hotel has told us they're covering all expenses from hospital care to taxi fares. Now, let me go and get you something to eat and drink," the nurse said as she left Carol wiping the tears away from her eyes with the handkerchief that the poor woman who had lost her daughter so tragically had previously given her.

Just looking at her husband, she knew that this would be an extremely long process, if he recovered at all. However, she quickly put that thought out of her mind before it even got there.

Meanwhile in the hotel, Daniella had finished all her writing. The cards looked lovely with a gorgeous teddy bear on the front and saying a big thank you for the gift. The poor girl had not even opened a single present so after putting down her smart fountain pen, she gazed longingly at the gifts given to her.

"Granddad, I think we'd better start opening some of these presents, especially since Cal said that this is just a small number of them!" she squealed.

I grinned at my granddaughter for being so brave and said, "That's such a beautiful thought, my dear. I had no idea the other guests would do such a thing for us."

We both took a present each and began unwrapping them. I opened mine and found it to be a very expensive Cartier pen set that had a small note inside saying, 'I'm so sorry, little girl. I hope these pens will help you forget your pain. Love from Patricia and Douglas.'

I was close to tears as I found this so moving. On the other hand, Daniella withdrew three beautiful embroidered Versace t-shirts. They were just the right size so it was obvious that they were from guests who had seen the girl. Like mine, there was a note inside, saying, 'We hope that you enjoy the t-shirts also with Love from Patricia and Douglas.'

This time it was Daniella who was tearful. "Granddad, these are gorgeous and from guests we don't even know. To send me such expensive gifts is just unbelievable."

I felt just as she did as we opened more and more of the gifts. Some had names whereas others did not or just stated, 'From well wishers. I hope your Daddy gets better'.

I knew that opening these gifts would make it far more difficult for the girl but at the end of it all, we were left with reams of colourful paper. Out of the thirty gifts, we managed to put ten cards to them as the others only had the guests' first names and not their last names. Amongst the gifts, there were clothes, gold chains, necklaces, bracelets, storybooks, a beautiful gold and diamond ring, several quality games, a handheld computer game and at least fifty DVDs. It was obvious that these people truly cared since these few items must be worth a small fortune. It was close to midnight with the presents all finally opened and a pile of lovely gifts sitting on the table.

"Come on, darling, let's go to bed and see what the morning brings," I said to Daniella while trying to stifle a yawn.

She had already chosen her room; it overlooked the swimming pool and the reserve.

"Come and give me another kiss before I go to sleep, promise me, Granddad?" she said as she kissed me on the cheek before going to bed.

I grinned at her as she sauntered slowly to her room leaving me staring at the wonderful everything that the people had brought for the dear girl. I got up and went to Daniella's room to say goodnight but she was already fast asleep already so I went to leave.

"Haven't you forgotten something, Granddad?" she said sleepily, making me jump.

I went back and gave my granddaughter a wet smoochy kiss on her forehead before walking to the door.

"I'll see you nice, bright and early in the morning," I added. "I love you darling! Sleep tight and don't let the bedbugs bite."

"That's a funny thing to say when we're in a five-star hotel, Granddad!" the girl exclaimed. "They wouldn't have bed bugs in here, would they?"

"Darling," I said to my granddaughter. "It's a saying we use in the UK and something you say to someone as they go to bed. Don't take it literally as this was something I always said to your Dad when he was a young boy."

Daniella gave me a big beaming smile as I left her thinking about her father and mother. It was morning when I awoke, and on looking at my watch, saw that it was seven o'clock. I was just about to go for a shower when my mobile began ringing. I answered it and the nurse from the hospital was on the line.

"Are you the father of Richard Riverton?" she asked.

"Yes," I answered. "And how's my son and daughter-in-law?"

"Mrs Riverton's fine but her husband lies in a deep coma. However, the doctors are keeping a close watch over him," the nurse said, following which she rang off before I could reply to her.

Rising to my feet, I went to take a nice cool shower. After drying myself, I got dressed into fresh pants, a white Lacrosse cotton short-sleeved shirt and a smart pair of trousers before slipping on my new leather sandals. Not bothering about socks, I went next door to find Daniella.

I knocked on the door but did not have to wait long. My granddaughter who was dressed in a bright orange pair of shorts, a yellow t-shirt and a pair of sandals as I was wearing greeted me.

"I feel so much better today," she remarked. "Let's hope Daddy's making a full recovery."

Of course, the girl had no idea that her father was actually lying in a coma and that her mother was doing a bedside vigil.

"I'm hungry. Let's go down for breakfast, shall we?" she added as we exited our suite and began walking towards the breakfast room.

I told the girl what the hospital said and surprisingly, she took it quite well. When we reached the breakfast room, we did not even have to introduce ourselves as the guests stood up and applauded us.

One of them even came over and just as we had sat down spoke to Daniella. "Hello, my dear, and you too, Sir. I sent a little something for your granddaughter, I hope she doesn't mind. I put it in sparkling purple paper. Did you see it?"

Daniella beamed at the woman and said, "All the presents are so wonderful but all I want is my Daddy back."

"What an absolute darling," the woman remarked. "She deserves her Daddy back. Do you have any news about him? We're all so worried and would never have expected such a terrible event to happen at our hotel."

"Only that he's lying in a coma," I replied to the woman as I held out my hand.

However, an elderly man came over and joined her, probably her husband, I told myself.

"This is my granddaughter, Daniella and I'm her grandfather, Paul Riverton," I announced.

The girl did a small curtsy. I had no idea she would do such a thing but she obviously knew that these people had sent her very expensive gifts. It was acknowledged by the couple who shook both our hands.

"Well, Daniella and you, Paul, I'm Countess Patricia Rees and this is my husband, Count Douglas Rees," the woman said. "We're from Virginia in the USA but originally from Zurich in Switzerland. The moment we heard about you we knew that somehow or other we had to introduce ourselves and now here we are."

"You're so kind, Countess and you too, Count, for thinking of Daniella at such a time," I said.

"Don't be so formal, Paul. I'm just Patricia and my husband is Douglas. Now, I imagine you've come down for breakfast and I'm holding you up, aren't I?" the Countess asked.

"If you don't mind Countess Patricia, I am a little hungry as last night I didn't eat much," Daniella replied with a wry smile.

"Oh, darling, she's not only gorgeous but with excellent manners too! And where are you from, young lady?" the Count asked, brimming over with excitement.

"Granddad and I live with Mommy and Daddy," the girl replied. "Yesterday was our first day here in Chiang Mai. Mommy remains at the hospital but she has not rung us so we're desperate to see Daddy for ourselves. However, we did hear from a nurse who said that he's in a coma."

"Now, my dear," the Count said as he and his wife got to their feet. "We'd be really honoured if you join us for dinner tonight at around eight. Just tell the waiter that you're dining with the Count and Countess and they'll bring you over to our table. We must go now as we've kept you far too long. Enjoy your breakfast, young lady, and you Paul."

We smiled and watched the couple, leave and go out into the hallway, where they disappeared completely as we wondered where they had gone to but said nothing as we thought that we had just missed seeing them, although that was not the case at all, but we did not find that out until a little later that night.

Cal appeared from nowhere, and said to us, "Now you sit here while I go and fetch you some breakfast. How does an English fry up sound to you, and a nice mug of hot chocolate, like I made last night?"

"Yes, please," Daniella croaked. "That sounds really good."

"I hope you're not going down with something or other. Do you have a sore throat?" Cam asked Daniella.

"No, Cam, I've just been crying most of the night as I'm worried over Daddy and if you don't mind I'm starving," the girl complained.

"Sorry, my dear, I talk too much," Cam said ruefully. "Let me go and arrange everything."

The girl left us talking and Daniella said to me, "What did you think about the Countess and her husband? They seem very different to anyone I've spoken to. They were also dressed so elegantly and smartly but their clothes are like those from centuries ago!"

I pondered over what my granddaughter was saying and realised that there was a ring of truth in what she was telling me.

"I see where you're coming from, darling, but maybe they're just a little eccentric and prefer to be dressed in clothes from that era. Anyway, did you see that diamond necklace she was wearing? No one in their right mind walks around with something as expensive around their neck as someone could easily pull it off!"

"Yes, Granddad, I did but who would want to steal it and risk damaging it in the process?" my granddaughter asked.

At that moment, Cam came over and Daniella decided to say something further to the girl who had just put down two coffees and two full plates of fried breakfast in front of us. The plates were full of everything English you could wish for and included several slices of warm crusty bread and butter. On seeing us almost finishing our breakfast, Cam returned to tell us something but Daniella opened the conversation first.

"Cam," Daniella began in a mysterious tone of voice. "What do you know about the Countess and her husband, the Count? They seem so unusual!"

Cam, who was the assistant manager as we eventually found out, turned to us both and said, "Daniella, I wish you hadn't asked me that question but let me try and explain. The Countess and her husband turned up here almost five years ago now, always paying cash for everything and leaving considerable tips when they left. They never book in but just turn up. Even if we're full, they take the most expensive suite so we've never had to let them down. However, they always sit on their own and to this day, I've never seen them with anyone, not even family, come to think of it. Stay well clear of them and that's a friendly warning as they truly send shivers down my spine. Now, you best eat and when you're finished I'll come over and tell you something more about them."

Cal left us thinking as we made quick work of eating our almost cold breakfast and drinking our still hot chocolate to go with it. We were so hungry that when my mobile rang, I did not bother looking at the number since I was not wearing my glasses.

"Paul Riverton speaking, who's on the line," I said as Daniella continued to eat.

I waited for someone to say something when I suddenly heard Carol's voice at the other end of the line.

"How's my daughter doing, Dad? I miss her so much and poor Richard hasn't opened his eyes yet and remains on a life support machine. I sit there holding his hand but he says nothing to me and just lies there so still and motionless. I have to stay here, Dad, as if he wakes up suddenly and I'm not around, I'll never forgive myself. The hospital has given me a bed next to him but I just cry and can't stop. Anyway, how's my baby taking it? I bet she's devastated from not having either of us around? I want to talk to her but maybe it's the wrong thing to do. What do you think I should do, Dad?"

I did not have to say another word as Daniella had almost finished eating. "Is that Mommy, Granddad? And how's my Daddy?" she asked.

Carol overheard her daughter and asked me to pass her over, which I promptly did.

Mommy, I miss you so much," the girl said. "I've received so many presents from probably all three hundred guests staying here at the hotel! But how's Daddy?"

The line went silent for a minute as Carol drew on all her inner strength and managed to say to her daughter, "Isn't that kind, darling, that all the guests have bought you a little something? Daddy is sleeping and lies in a coma. Do you know what that is, little one?"

"Grandpa told me this morning when one of the nurses rang him to give us an update," she said with tears in her eyes as she began sobbing her heart out to her mother. "I know what a coma is, Mommy, as we learnt all about how the brain shuts down suddenly after a trauma or illness. He might come out of it or he could die! Can I come and see him, Mommy?"

It was obvious that both mother and daughter were sobbing to each other on the phone but Carol tried her best to pull herself together.

"My darling, can you pass me over to Granddad as I need to speak to him before I go," Carol managed to say.

Daniella said a quick goodbye to her mother and handed the phone over to me. I saw the girl crying her heart out but somehow I held out and managed to speak to Carol.

"This is worse than I thought it would be. Daniella's far too clever for her age and knows exactly the state of play with Dick, darling," I said, feeling myself welling up with tears.

"Dad, I don't know how to deal with this as the poor girl wants to see her Daddy desperately but will I be doing the right thing?" Carol asked tearfully.

"Look, Carol, if something happens to her father and she doesn't go to see him then she might hold it against you for the rest of her life," I replied. "Perhaps, I can bring her in the morning and you can beg permission from the doctor and explain to him that this could be good therapy for my son."

“You’re right, Dad, we’ll do that so bring her along and I’ll plead to the doctor that she needs to see her Daddy. I must go now, Dad, as I need to be with my darling in case he wakes up,” Carol concluded as the line clicked and Carol ended the call.

Chapter 34
The Count and Countess

Cal appeared and came over to our table. On seeing Daniella looking so distraught, she went round to the other side of the table and held the girl closely to her. It was obvious that she was upset with something but I left Daniella to tell Cal herself.

"Cal, Mommy said that Daddy is in a coma but I have to be brave and pray that he comes out of it," Daniella began as she looked into Cal's eyes. "However, I also know that he could die from his injuries. Granddad's taking me in the morning to visit him so I hope he stays alive until then."

This really affected Cal and I noticed tears in her eyes. She was overawed by Daniella's calmness and saddened by the girl's words. It was as though she had told her inner self to expect the worst and if her Daddy pulled through then that would be a miracle at the end of the day.

"Now, Daniella, and you too, Paul, I promised to tell you more about the Count and Countess," Cal said. "They've been coming here for well over five years now and the strange thing is that they just appear out of nowhere. I've mentioned this to my manager but he just tells me to have a few days off as I'm probably overworked. I know though that I'm fine but these people are mysterious to say the least as they never arrive in a car or call for a taxi. When they visit, they have the most expensive leather bound luggage trunks with brass fittings. The porter always moans because they are so heavy and God only knows what they carry inside them! Probably the contents alone cost a small fortune. The Count is old, as is his wife, and they wear the most beautiful gold, platinum, diamond and sapphire rings. They seemed to be part of a set with the Countess wearing a matching bracelet, necklace and earrings. They have to be worth millions but they're unafraid of having them stolen and have never used our security system or our overnight safe."

"How odd!" I remarked. "Who in their right mind would do such a thing? They gave Daniella a gift, a beautiful Cartier pen set; it's gold for sure and I've noticed it has sapphires and diamonds encrusted into the barrel. That's not all as they also bought her three expensive embroidered Lacrosse t-shirts. She loves them, don't you, darling," I added to Daniella as she grinned at Cal and told her that they were the best ever.

"It's really odd as I became concerned these people were not who they said they were, so I checked their passports and the addresses they gave as they never paid anything by credit card and always used cash. It was then that I came up with some spooky information. The address in Virginia was correct but according to the records, the house has remained empty since 1811! A letter I received made the situation even more mystifying as it was from a lawyer in New York who basically warned me to back off when he had learnt I was asking awkward questions about his clients. I did nothing after this and the Count and Countess continued to visit every year, saying absolutely nothing about my letter or anything really, as there was no way that I wished for the hotowners and the American lawyers to become entwined in a difficult lawsuit battle that might cost me my job at the end of the day."

"I love a good mystery," Daniella interrupted. "Perhaps, the Count and Countess are troubled spirits!"

"Don't Daniella as I'll be having nightmares," Cal said anxiously. "Anyway, I must go as I've stayed far too long and I've a great amount of work to finish."

On this last note, Cal went back downstairs to her office leaving us contemplating who this unusual couple was.

"My dear Daniella, this is turning into something incredible for one of my new novels," I remarked with a chuckle. "Should we mention anything to the Count and Countess when we eat with them later?"

"That's not a good idea, Granddad," she replied. "If they wish to say something to us, I'm sure they will. However, they don't scare me one bit and if they're wandering spirits maybe they can find a way to help Dad overcome his injuries."

I stared at my granddaughter, telling myself that she actually believed that these people had arrived for a purpose. Whatever she was thinking, the girl had a smile on her face.

"Granddad, I have no one to swim with so will you come into the outdoor pool with me? Please say yes as you did say you're a good swimmer," she pleaded.

I nodded and smiled at my granddaughter so she added, "Let's go and get changed then as I've never ever seen you in swimming trunks!"

We got to our feet and went to our suite where we changed into our swimming gear. This time the girl wore her new black bikini. I prayed that no one said anything to her as the two of us dressed in a t-shirt, shorts and flip-flops went out to the pool.

As we were walking along, I remarked, "Why the outdoor pool when we have our own facilities almost next door?"

"I know, Granddad, but I love the outdoor pool and the people staying in the suites are pretty old!" Daniella said as she grinned from ear to ear.

On our way to the pool, many people came over to the girl, stopped us, and said, "I hope your father gets better. And did you like your present?"

Of course, she thanked them individually, realising that she did not have to send cards after all. The swimming pool was not that full of people but there were some children of Daniella's age who smiled at her as I dragged over two sun beds. We got undressed and put our clothes and towels down. Daniella began showing off her trim little figure in her lovely black bikini.

"Oh, Granddad, you do look sexy in those new swimming shorts!" the little minx said. "I thought nowadays men of all ages wore trunks."

"Not me, Granddaughter," I said to the girl with the greatest of dignity as we got into the water. "Shorts are bad enough but I prefer ones down to my ankles!" I commented laughing my head off as I saw Daniella strike out towards the other end of the pool, turn on a sixpence and head back with the girl not even out of breath.

"That's impressive, darling!" I exclaimed to the girl. "Where did you learn to swim so well? Did Daddy teach you?"

"Very funny, Granddad," Daniella replied. "Anyway, come on as you've just been standing there doing nothing. Can you swim or are you fibbing to me?"

I swam breaststroke but she raced past me and waited for me to get to the other end.

"So you can swim after all," she said, teasing me. "How about the stroke I'm using? You'll get there much quicker." I could not argue the fact and floated on my back as the girl joined me and continued, "You're doing well, Granddad, and I love you so much. I have a good feeling about tonight and feel that Daddy's going to get better after we visit him."

I said nothing in reply to my granddaughter and just smiled to show her that I was listening. We stayed in the pool for a good two hours with hardly anyone coming to join us. Having welcomed us, the guests seemed to give us space on our own and that was good for both of us. Going over to our sun loungers, we lay down and were soon fast asleep.

When I awoke, I realised that it was one o'clock so I nudged Daniella to wake her up.

"Darling, are you hungry? It's well past lunch time," I remarked.

"I don't know, Granddad, as we ate breakfast fairly late but if you're hungry then I suppose I am too," the cheeky girl said sleepily to me.

Now dry, we went back to our suite where we had a quick shower and changed into something new and fresh. We put our other clothes away before heading down to the ground floor where lunch was being served. I looked at the time, and realised that it was a quarter to two and I wondered whether they would still serve us.

"How are you, Mr Riverton? And your father, Daniella?" one of the waitresses asked when they saw us.

Even the staff members knew our names since we had become celebrities for the wrong reason!

"He's not so good and lies in a coma," Daniella replied. "I know it's late but could Granddad and I have a nice chicken salad and perhaps a few French fries?"

"I'm so sorry, darling, and it was on the news that those nasty Americans have been charged with attempted murder," the waitress replied. "Two of them have admitted to the offence while the other two have been held as accomplices. The news reporter said that the men could expect sentences from twenty years to life. Anyway, enough chatter for now. Let me go and get you your meals. And do you want anything to drink?"

Daniella thought carefully and said in a grownup sort of way, "Alcohol is bad for you and should only be taken on special occasions so can Granddad and I each have an ice cold glass of Coca Cola?"

The waitress smiled at Daniella and grinned at me before leaving and going over to the bar to fetch our drinks. She came back, put them down and left for the kitchen. I wondered why she had not put down our order on her hand held computer but maybe lunch was at an end and she was just being helpful.

I could have downed a nice glass of cold lager but Daniella was in charge so I drank my coke quietly, just taking small sips to quench my thirst.

"Granddad, I'm sorry that I didn't get you a beer but I thought that it wouldn't harm you to drink what I was having!" the impish girl said.

Telling myself that the girl had read my mind, I gave her a grin and took a further sip of coke as the waitress appeared with our food. It looked scrumptious and appeared to be a good half a roasted chicken each with French fries in a separate dish. We tucked into our meal, enjoying the taste of the tender chicken, fresh lettuce, tomatoes, cucumber, Cheddar cheese and lovely baked potatoes.

We had soon polished our plates clean and laid our knives and forks down with satisfied sighs.

"I thought my little girl wasn't hungry," I remarked with a playful chuckle.

"I was wrong, Granddad, and enjoyed every single mouthful. The baked potatoes were out of this world and the chicken was heavenly," Daniella said cheerfully.

"I'm glad to see you eating so well, Daniella, as I know it's difficult for you as well as for me."

"I've already told you before, Granddad, that I have a good feeling that tomorrow Daddy will be reopening his eyes as he starts making a full recovery. Unfortunately, we'll have to go home first without him but Mommy will bring him back to us, I know she will."

I was desperate to say something to her but something stopped me as I felt my lips were glued together. It was as though she was being guided by someone or something and was able to see into the future. The thought horrified me but in some way, I believed everything the girl was saying.

The waitress came over and said to us, "At least you have good appetites! That's so nice to see. Now, how would you like some ice cream for dessert? It's got everything from fruit salad to five different flavours."

We told her that sounded great so she went away to fetch it. Five minutes later, she came over with the desserts, put them down in front of us and added, "Do you want some more coke?"

We nodded and the girl went over to the bar while we tucked into our ice cream. The flavours were an experience and consisted of vanilla, strawberry, orange, mango and banana. The taste was delightful and we said so to the waitress as she brought over the drinks.

"Amie, that's a nice name," Daniella said to the waitress who turned a shade pale and wondered how the girl knew her name.

She had only started work two days before and she almost ran from the table as I questioned Daniella.

"How did you know the waitress' name, darling?" I asked.

"I don't know, Granddad, but it suddenly came to me. I have no idea why!" my granddaughter replied.

This was becoming serious and we ate the rest of the ice cream in almost complete silence. After we had finished our cokes, we got to our feet and went to our suite to lie down before our heavy evening appointment with the Count and Countess. Daniella and I said nothing to each other until we awoke in our separate rooms. The girl went to have a shower, following which she dressed in an alluring low cut black dress, silk stockings and slinky high-heeled shoes.

"How come you're not ready yet, Granddad?" she asked. "It's almost seven and we're meant to be meeting them for dinner at eight. Do you have a suit with you?"

"Of course I do but why do I need to wear one?" I asked wondering how the girl was going to answer me.

"What do you think they are, Granddad? As you say, perhaps they're just a little eccentric but don't you think it's funny that the house has remained empty for so many years. I know what the lawyer in New York is hiding but I want to hear it from the Count and Countess' own mouths."

I now knew that Daniella could see into the future as well as into the past. I had no idea how that happened but the only possible explanation was that this gift came straight after the girl shook the Count and Countess' hand.

I went into my room to change into my new suit, putting on a crisp white Levi short-sleeved shirt and lightweight trousers. I decided not to wear a tie and kept the top two buttons of my shirt undone since it was hot even with the air conditioning on. I then wore a pair of cotton ankle socks and my smart black casual shoes. I went out of my room and found Daniella brushing her long blond hair in the mirror.

"You look beautiful, Granddad," she remarked as she looked up at me. "Anyway, shall we make a move as the Count appreciates punctuality?"

I nodded and grabbed hold of my jacket and put it on. Daniella led the way; it was as though she knew exactly where she was going.

As we entered the restaurant, the girl went over to a waitress and said all grown up, "We have a dinner invitation from the Count and Countess."

The waitress knew this was very unusual as they normally dined on their own so she asked us politely, "Can you two please wait here? I'll go and tell them."

The waitress thought that this was some kind of a wind up but she recognised Daniella as the daughter of the man who was seriously ill in hospital.

"Sir, you have guests for dinner," the waitress announced to the Count.

"Yes, yes, my dear," he replied. "Please bring Daniella and Paul over. We're waiting for them."

The waitress went away and came over to us looking extremely confused.

"The Count and his wife are expecting you. Can you come with me?" she said.

She led us over to their table that was in an alcove and was lit by candles rather than that excessive overhead lighting and looked so romantic.

After the girl left, the Count turned to Daniella and said.

"You look exquisite, my dear, and you're very smart, Paul," the Count said.

I noticed that he was wearing a Victorian style tailor-made suit, probably silk, as did the Countess who was wearing a long black dress that was not revealing at all unlike that of my granddaughter.

"Please sit down and join us as I'm forgetting my manners," the Count said as we sat down.

"Come next to me, my dear," the Countess said as she patted the seat next to her.

Daniella went straight over, kissed the Countess on the cheek and sat down by her. I found myself sitting opposite the Count who smiled at us both.

"My wife adores your granddaughter," the Count said. "It's so long ago that she enjoyed the company of a young child like Daniella who's beautiful and so well-mannered. We had eight children who unfortunately passed on many years ago. We'll explain all about our past life in our suite after the meal. Now, my dear Paul, I thought that we might enjoy some roasted venison that the hotel brought in especially for us. I've selected a bottle of quality Champagne as the taste is exquisite to go with it and a nice starter of fresh crab to begin our meal. Of course, the girl will only be drinking a single glass as we don't want her to become drunk, do we?"

In many ways, I liked the Count as he was pleasant and spoke excellent English even though he had an American accent. He also told the occasional jokes, which I had never heard before and wondered what era they came from. However, I remained silent on that matter when he suddenly said something extremely curious.

"I hear you're a writer, my dear chap, and your present book is all about your granddaughter. Is that right, Paul, as it really sounds so exciting with the animals that speak and the humans living with each other?"

I stared at the Count who gathered that his statement had made a direct hit on me. I had no idea how the man knew about the book. As the waitress came over and took the Count's order, I saw her curtsy before she left and thought it extremely odd in this day and age but told myself that this was a five-star hotel after all so perhaps they did this kind of thing in front of guests.

Meanwhile, the Countess had been grilling the young girl. "I'm very pleased you got my message, my dear, and I promise you that when you visit your father tomorrow he'll open his eyes and recognise you immediately. Do you understand why my husband and I chose you out of hundreds of millions of people to take over our heritage and mission that we're on? Our home will become yours, my darling, as we're old and need to move on but I don't wish to scare you at the moment. This is something we can discuss further in our suite after dinner. By the way, I hope you like roasted venison."

Chapter 35
A Sorceress is born

Daniella stared into the Countess' green eyes that were visibly bright and I was really curious to know what the girl was thinking.

"Countess, I feel different than before as I seem to be floating on a cloud. Somehow, I've known since yesterday that when I take hold of my Daddy's hand he'll reopen his eyes and begin to grow stronger. You and your husband did this for me, didn't you?" the girl asked.

The Countess smiled before saying further to the girl, "You didn't answer whether or not you like the roasted venison, dear."

"Sorry, Countess, I forgot about that question but I don't know as I've never tasted it before. Is it something like beef?"

"No, no, my dear," the Countess replied with a gentle smile. "It has a taste far richer than beef and I'm sure you'll enjoy eating it as well as the surprise we have waiting for you in our suite!"

"Is it something to eat, Countess?" Daniella asked.

"That would be telling, my dear," the Countess replied.

She was saved having to explain to the girl that two waitresses came in with our starters and some fruit juice to begin our meal. As the waitress poured the juice into the Count's glass, he tasted it as he would with wine and smiled at the young girl who then filled our glasses and curtsied before she left. I told myself that this was the Count and Countess after all and probably the management insisted on having two waitresses attending to them.

The crab cocktail was similar to prawn and enjoyed freshly made salad with a cocktail sauce but had instead pieces of tasty crabmeat. Thankfully, we were not given the claws to eat from so we found it extremely delicious and soon emptied our dishes. The fruit juice was welcomingly chilled. I thought it would be orange or pineapple but it was in fact mango. The moment the girl saw us finished she came over and removed the dishes. Several minutes later, the other girl appeared wheeling over a trolley with several lidded containers on it and a large platter filled with delicious looking roasted venison. Placing hot China plates down and telling us to be careful not to burn ourselves, the girl served out portions of four or five large slices of venison for everyone. Then, moving to the centre of the table, and opening the lidded containers, she spooned out onto our plates, roasted potatoes, vegetables, and several varieties of fresh greens and some tasty gravy on top.

The Count smiled, took a ten- dollar note from his wallet and handed it over to the girl who smiled and left us to enjoy our food. We began to eat but I noticed the Count's hesitance; it was as though he was waiting for something else.

When the other girl came over with the open bottle of Champagne, he said sarcastically. "I wondered where that had got to, young girl. I don't like having a meal without something to drink. I won't bother tasting it as the food will go cold so just fill up everyone's glasses and leave us to enjoy our meal."

It was obvious that the Count was truly annoyed, as he did not reward the girl like the first one.

"I'm sorry, Paul and Daniella but I don't accept sloppiness," he said. "Now, enough said, let's continue eating and I hope you enjoy the Champagne. One last thing before we begin, I want to offer a toast to the most beautiful young girl in the world who is extremely special and will soon discover who she really is."

We all sipped the Champagne and I glanced quickly at Daniella to see if she screwed her nose up as Champagne does have an acquired taste but she just smiled as if to tell everyone that she found it quite enjoyable.

We ate in complete silence, as we had done with the starters, and I wondered if perhaps in aristocratic company it was not polite to speak during a meal. The food was excellent but I said nothing until we had all cleaned our plates completely.

It was Daniella who opened the conversation. "That was so delicious," she said. "I never thought I could finish everything on my plate as I've been so worried about Daddy until I met you lovely people. Isn't that right, Granddad?"

"Yes, my dear, I've noticed a sudden spring to your step and I agree we have the Count and the Countess to thank for this," I replied.

"Well, well, well," the count spluttered since he was not used to receiving praise. "You embarrass us, Paul, and you too, my dear Daniella!" He then changed the subject. "Did you know that there was a Princess Daniella in the twelfth century who fell into a magical kingdom? She became happy and married her sweetheart, Prince Leonardo, while he became King and she his queen. I can't quite remember the name of the kingdom; it's on the tip of my tongue but I must be getting old!" he continued with a chuckle as he turned to his wife. "Would you like a dessert after that lovely meal or do you think it's time, Patricia?"

"I think it's getting late, my dear, as it is almost eleven o'clock, and what follows will take us several hours to accomplish and we're old now and need the rest," the Countess replied as both she and her husband got to their feet.

"Will you and your Grandfather follow us, my dear?" she said as Daniella and I got up from the table.

The elderly couple marched away sprightly for their age. In fact, I found it difficult to keep up with them but my granddaughter was close on their heels. I lagged a few metres behind, and on seeing me, the Count slowed his pace so I could eventually catch up with the party. He did not take the lift down as I thought he would but opened a door that led to several flights of stairs. The couple seemed to glide up them while I struggled behind with Daniella finally coming and giving her old grandfather a hand. I had no idea the hotel was so large and never knew there were further floors above the restaurant. I had always believed that there were only three floors in the hotel as the lift only went to the third floor and stopped. Once on the fifth floor, the Count walked along a hallway and came to a stout wooden door, which he unlocked with a key that he withdrew from his pocket. After he walked in, he began lighting up several candles.

"Come into our humble abode," he announced. "They keep it here especially for us." he added before going over to several hanging oil lamps that he lit with a lighter and made the room burst into bright light.

While Daniella bounced into the room, I entered extremely cautiously as the door slammed shut on its own. No one had touched it, I was sure of that, and I was getting concerned who these people were.

"Sit down, my dears," the Countess said. "Now, Daniella, we're in our room that lies hidden. In reality, we're not in Thailand at all but in our home in Virginia. Don't be surprised Paul but from time to time we come to this hotel and always take a suite or room depending whether or not they are full on the third floor. Now, while I go and prepare something, my husband will take over, won't you, darling?" she concluded sweetly as the Count smiled at his wife who toddled away at lightning speed.

I said nothing as the Count carried on with his story. "Daniella's aware who we are as my wife has visited her on several occasions although she doesn't realise it. Cal surprisingly knew more about us than anyone before but doesn't have the gift that Daniella has from birth. We've visited every country in the world looking for that perfect someone but never found them, that is, until now. When we learnt about your father, Daniella, and met you ourselves, we knew that you were the chosen one who will eventually take our place in society."

I chipped in at this point and said to the Count, "Are you and your wife mad? How can Daniella take over from you? Unless, as Cal told me, you're already dead! But why all this secrecy?"

"You're right, Paul," the Count said. "Our family has been dead for hundreds of years. My wife learnt about Daniella's gift and after hearing about her father lying seriously ill in hospital, we knew we had to step in now rather than when she gets older. This is one huge stride for a young girl to take so let me carry on where I left off. Please don't interrupt this time, Paul. Daniella received powers to see into the future and past from my wife. Of course, she's still young and has to learn how to control her abilities but these are just part of what she's to become."

I stared at the Count but this time remained silent as he continued to speak. "My wife's about to return!"

Out of nowhere, the Countess suddenly materialised in front of us. She stared at me but it was as though Daniella was expecting such things even though she said nothing.

Mysteriously, the Countess carried on from exactly the same point where her husband had just left off. "My husband courted me when I was just eighteen. We lived in a small hamlet called Oberalp outside Andermatt with hardly any visitors. We both came from royal blood lines and lived in alternative castles, but unknown to us, our parents weren't what we thought they were, and our daily lessons suddenly turned from English, Mathematics, History and others to spells, potions and sorcery. What we're trying to tell you is that the Count and I are practising sorcerers who were born in the fourteenth century. Unable to marry until our parents died, we found out the worst ever truth. They had passed over their powers of eternal life and of being able to see into the future and past. When our parents died, we married and were happy for several hundreds of years, until the nineteenth century, when jealousy set in and we were hunted like wild animals by the local villagers and were forced to move to America. "

The Count took over from his wife, saying, "Did you know your ancestors were of royal blood, Paul? And I believe that with your gift, Daniella, you must be a Princess!"

My granddaughter, as well as I, were shocked by such news and wondered which century they were living in.

The Count carried on telling us, "Patricia has just mixed you a potion that I want you both to take. If you don't wish to keep eternal life, Paul, then you have the possibility of transferring this over to Daniella's future husband. However, you must be certain he's one hundred percent and more trustworthy and that you don't pass over your power until he shows you that he's devoted to his future wife. Do you both understand? This is vastly important to remember. Are you willing to drink this, Paul? We have the most amazing gifts to give you afterwards!"

I stared at Daniella but her expression told me nothing. I glanced at the Countess who just returned a smile and put the two goblets down onto the table. Opening her leather bag, she took a bottle from it, removed the cap, poured the contents into the silver goblets filling them to the brim and left them there. I stared finally at the Count whose eyes were willing me to drink the potion. I took the goblet in my hands, as did Daniella, and we drank it in one sweep together. It was a strange kind of taste, like a mixture of orange, lime and strawberry but it had an element of iron added to it and unknown to us this was witch's blood. Once we had drunk the potion, the Count stared longingly into his wife's eyes as if to say that they're finally released and can at last die in peace.

"Now, my children, we've passed onto you all our knowledge and magical spells and all that you need in life. Just close your eyes and it will happen, whether it's someone who's dead and needs to be brought to life, or if you need a million dollars. Whatever you wish for will come to you," the Count explained.

Stunned by this statement, Daniella said quietly, "Do you mean Daddy will reopen his eyes and that Grandma can live again? But I don't want her to be ill and close her eyes forever!" Daniella saying such things shocked me but of course, to see Rebecca alive would be fantastic.

The Count answered us both as though he had been reading our minds. "All you need is a catalyst that will turn on your power," he said as the Countess reached into her bag and handed Daniella four more gifts wrapped in sparkling purple paper.

Daniella unwrapped the smallest one first and found a ring just like the one the Count was wearing. Daniella handed me the second package, which I opened and found a ring that I put on my middle finger; it fitted perfectly. Daniella opened her third gift and found another ring; it was of the most beautiful platinum gold, set with emeralds, blue sapphires and diamonds, which the girl put on her engagement finger. She thought at first it was the same as the one the Countess wore, yet on closer examination, realised it was very similar but set with additional emeralds. On opening the other gifts, the girl was stunned as she found a matching bracelet and a corresponding necklace and earrings.

"Come on, my darling," the Countess said with a smile. "We must carry on with the ceremony as otherwise it will be far too late and it's almost half past midnight!" I thought to myself what a strange way of saying the time, as she continued, "Let me help you put them on. As you can see, I wear mine all the while as they're so elegant to look at."

Daniella put out her right arm and the Countess placed the bracelet around the girl's wrist and fastened the secure clip tightly, doing the same with the necklace and earrings. She then stepped back as the Count took over from there.

"You look stunning, my dear!" he exclaimed. "As a sorceress, you'll be admired throughout the world. If you wish to travel into the future, as well as into the past, just close your eyes, think of the year and destination, and you'll be whisked away like magic and materialise wherever you think of going to. And you, Paul, if you want Rebecca at your side to guide you and your granddaughter, then so be it. All you have to do is think of her as she was before she became ill and she'll come back looking somewhat younger than you. However, she'll never be in pain again."

"Is that really possible?" Daniella asked optimistically. "I'd love to have Granny back as I've missed her so much."

"My child," the Count said to the girl. "I won't be doing anything as when you've completed the ceremony, you can do anything you want to. If that is to bring Granny back to you, then so be it. But remember before you wish for such a thing make sure that it's the right decision and that your Granddad wants the same as you do as you have to live in perfect harmony for the rest of eternity. Therefore, let's take it step by step and allow your father to reopen his eyes tomorrow!"

The Countess then spoke jointly with her husband. "Now, both of you kneel before us."

Kneeling before the two royals, Daniella and I wondered what exactly they were about to do.

"On this day, Daniella Riverton, you are appointed as Master Sorceress while Paul Riverton, her grandfather, is to become her Guardian," the Count intoned. "They are granted herewith the power of sight, mind and hearing drawn from the four elements of Earth, Wind, Water and Fire, and will from this day forth be granted eternal life and the ability to travel through time between the future and the past."

In these last few words, colourful sparks flew from the Count's fingers, hitting the wall and bursting into flames. We looked on in astonishment since he had not recited any spell, although we had been given a goblet of potion to drink. The only noticeable change to either of us was the colour of Daniella's eyes that had changed from sparkling blue to emerald green. Whether or not anyone would notice the difference was something we had to find out for ourselves.

The Countess took the girl's hand and said to her, "Do you feel full of energy, my dear? We've passed over our strength and magic to you. Whenever you need to use them all you have to do is concentrate. Now, before you go we need you to sign some official paperwork. Please read through it but this must be signed before you leave."

I picked up the reams of papers that the Count had taken out from an envelope. They were from a lawyer in New York, suitably named Riverton & Sons Inc. I showed the name of the lawyer to Daniella and we looked at each other and thought this was a joke.

On seeing our hesitation, the Count cried out, "No, my children, there's no coincidence. When we learnt of Daniella and discovered her surname, we realised that this girl was the chosen one to take our rightful place. Now, let me explain about these papers. You, Daniella, will automatically inherit our total wealth," he added as he turned to page three where it listed all the assets that the Count and Countess owned including a mansion house in Virginia with five thousand acres of pastureland and fifteen oil wells in Texas. In addition, there were goldmines, diamond mines in South Africa and South America and so many more listed assets belonging to the couple. I did not need to read anything further as it was obvious that the Count and Countess were handing Daniella over the complete ownership of everything they possessed.

The Count handed Daniella his pen, identical to the one they had bought the girl. She did not hesitate and I did not wish to stop her as she initialled each copy in turn before coming to the last one where the girl signed her signature in full, together with her date of birth, current address and that day's date at the side.

The Count and Countess took the copies and did exactly the same, inserting their initials and signing the last copy and putting their address in Virginia and dates of birth.

"We must leave now as our job is complete," the Countess said. "We have to return these papers to the lawyer who'll attend to the changeover of ownership. He'll put everything to you in writing as the new owner, Daniella. Don't worry about your father as you now know exactly what to do, my dear. For the next one hundred years, we'll be keeping watch over you. From there on, you and your grandfather, and grandmother too, if you wish to bring her back, will remain on your own and live on for all eternity!"

I gave the Countess and Count a grim smile as I had not realised how much our lives were about to change.

As they began to fade away from our eyes, they said one last thing. "Hurry up and get down to the third floor as these two floors will disappear in the next ten minutes."

Daniella and I gathered our belongings, including a copy of the signed documents, and hurried back to our suite, where we said goodnight to each other and disappeared into our separate bedrooms until the morning.

The following morning, I woke up to the sun dazzling through the cracks in the blinds. A knock at the door told me someone was waiting to come in. At first, I thought it was Daniella so I went to open the door. However, it was Cal who walked in.

After shutting the door behind her, she sat down in a chair and said, "I need to speak to you, Paul," she began as I looked at my watch and saw that it was still half past six. "The Count and Countess have left with their luggage. Their room is empty and all their clothes have gone and they've also put a thousand dollar note on the side to cover the cost of the meal and to share with the rest of the staff. None of the night staff saw them but after asking around I heard that you and Daniella had dinner with them yesterday evening."

"That's right, we did. Is there a problem with that Cal?" I asked inquisitively.

"Of course not, Paul," the girl said backtracking in case I had become offended by her question. "I was wondering whether or not they told you they might be leaving last night or early this morning, as Monica the waitress, who served you, said that the Count and Countess didn't leave until midnight. Tell me, Paul, did they leave you or Daniella any presents?"

"Look, Cal, all they said to me was that their work was complete and that they'd be moving on. However, they didn't say when or where they were going. They gave me this as a parting gift," I said as I showed the girl my sparkling ring. "And they gave Daniella a similar ring to this one, a bracelet, a necklace and earrings. I agree they're probably worth millions but it's up to them if they wish to give them away and we weren't going to refuse such gifts as they might have become annoyed with us."

"If you put it like that, Paul, maybe I'm chasing my tail and worrying about nothing. Anyway, I'll be going now," Cal said as she left me sitting there thinking.

Chapter 36
Happy Times Ahead

Another knock on the door told me I had another visitor. I went to open it and this time I was met by Daniella's smiling face. She was dressed in one of her new t-shirts, a pair of designer jeans and trainers. After she walked in, she settled into a comfortable chair next to the window.

"Granddad, it's seven and you need to get ready," she began. "While I sit here looking out at the beautiful view, you can take a shower and get dressed and then we'll go down for breakfast. After eating, we'll go straight to the hospital and awaken Daddy from his sleep and make Mommy happy again."

I stared at my granddaughter, grinned, grabbed some clothing and marched into the bathroom. After taking my shower, I dried myself, dressed and returned to my room.

The girl jumped up and said, "Are we ready for breakfast?"

I smiled at my granddaughter who took hold of my hand as she led me into the breakfast room where we found our reserved table. We served ourselves from a lovely selection of fried food and grabbed a hot milk coffee, added some sugar and took it to our table where we sat down and began to eat.

The breakfast was delicious as always. Several people came over and said good morning and we returned the greeting and resumed enjoying everything on our plates and drinking our coffee. We said nothing to each other during our meal and I wondered if the Count and Countess's politeness had rubbed off on the young girl. However, when my granddaughter saw me finishing my breakfast, she opened the conversation.

"Did you know that it's five to nine, Granddad?" she remarked while showing me her watch. "We only have one hour before we leave to see Daddy."

I prayed that Carol had gained permission from the doctor as with the power the girl now had, she could make things extremely awkward for everyone.

"I know what you're thinking, Granddad," the girl said to me. I had forgotten that she could read people's minds and see into the future or the past. "Don't worry, I'm not going to get annoyed if the doctor refuses me to see Daddy but maybe I can get him to change his mind for us!" Daniella added before laughing heartily.

With the glances the girl received from the guests, it was obvious that they had thought she had been told some good news about her father. If only they knew the truth, none of them would have believed a single word.

We left the table and went up to our room where we took a nice refreshing wash and cleaned our teeth before heading out of the hotel to a waiting taxi. After we got in, I told the driver the name of the hospital and the address and he smiled before driving off.

Before we arrived, Daniella said mischievously, "Granddad, do you remember the lovely air hostess? This is our third day and we didn't ring her. When we get back from visiting Daddy, can we invite her over so that she can show us around Chiang Mai?"

"That sounds like a really good idea," I replied. "Remind me when we get back and I'll give you my mobile phone to use."

"I don't need your mobile, Granddad, as I wished for a new one with all the latest technology and it turned up in my hand just as the Countess said it would!" she said as she withdrew from her pocket a smart new phone.

"So your magic does work!" I spluttered. "I thought you'd try it out on your Dad this morning but I suppose you wanted to see for yourself!"

"Is it that obvious, Granddad? By the way, we've arrived and it's ten minutes before ten," the girl said as I paid the driver.

"I hope your son's better," the driver said. "The hotel manager explained everything to me. By the way, did you realise that all you have to do is hand in the receipt," he continued as he wrote it out and gave it to me. "The hotel will cover the taxi fare."

I took out five pounds, smiled and handed it to the driver as Daniella and I got out and entered the hospital. I asked the receptionist the way to the trauma ward and we were directed to a lift and then along a corridor to a door. I rang the bell and waited for someone to answer.

A nurse opened the door and greeted us with a "Good morning, are you Miss Daniella and Mr Paul Riverton?" We grinned since it was obvious that we were expected. "The doctor has agreed you can remain here for a few hours but I doubt if you'll get any response from your father, my dear, as he has had a serious injury and his brain is in limbo. Your mother has been on constant watch over him in case he opens his eyes. I feel so sad for her and for you too, my darlings," she added to Daniella and me. "Anyway, enough chit chat; let me take you over to your mother."

I thought to myself what a pleasant nurse to have welcomed us like she did and her words went along well as we followed her over to a bed where my son was lying so still and Carol holding one of his hands hoping that he would respond.

As Daniella strolled over confidently to her mother, Carol turned to her daughter and then to me, and said, "Thanks for coming Dad, and for bringing Daniella."

I smiled at my daughter-in-law, wondering what my granddaughter was planning in her mind.

"Mom, do you believe in miracles?" the girl piped up. "I had a dream last night where I took hold of Dad's hand and he opened his eyes and stared into mine."

"Darling, that was just a dream!" Carol said. "If that happened, I'd be one lucky woman. Anyhow, please take hold of your father's other hand."

Daniella took hold of her father's hand, leant over, kissed him on the cheek and then concentrated hard.

"Reopen your eyes, Daddy, and start the long journey to get better for Mommy, Granddad and me. We need you so badly," Daniella pleaded.

I knew exactly what was about to take place. Carol hid her face in her hands since she did not want to see her daughter disappointed because she knew that miracles very seldom happened. Richard reopened his good eye, as the other one had stitches, and stared at his daughter and tried to speak. However, with so many tubes coming in and out of his mouth he found it impossible to even raise a smile. Daniella prodded her mother to show her that her Daddy had come back and Carol lifted her head and realised that her husband had come out of his coma.

"Darling, how did you bring your Daddy out of his coma?" she wailed. "I love you so much Richard! Let me go and tell the nurse."

Carol rushed away as she could not believe that her husband had literally come back from the dead. She almost bumped into a nurse who thought that the poor man was dying or something but on seeing Carol smiling, the nurse followed the woman over to the bed.

"Let me go and find a doctor. This is truly a miracle!" the nurse exclaimed as she ran out of the ward and into the corridor.

Meanwhile, I took hold of my son's hand and said to him, "Welcome back, Son, I thought you were a goner."

Richard tried to smile but his face was too badly beaten up to do so. At that moment, the nurse reappeared with another doctor who stared at Richard, checked him over to make sure that all his faculties were working and began to remove the tubes from his mouth and nose all the while making sure Richard's heartbeat and blood pressure were fine.

"I cannot believe this!" the doctor exclaimed. "When we were told that his granddaughter was coming to visit, we thought this was not a good idea as we believed that Richard was dying but miracles do happen, it seems! Now that he's awake, we can carry out some vital tests on Mr Riverton so if you don't mind, would you all like to leave?"

Carol stared at the doctor before saying, "I was given permission to stay with my husband but if you feel it's better that I go back to the hotel with my daughter and father-in-law, then so be it and I'll come back in the morning."

"If you don't mind Mrs Riverton as we can check over your husband and get him hopefully back onto his feet," the doctor requested politely.

Carol leant over and kissed her husband while Daniella smiled. My son stared at her with his one good eye since he knew why he had been given this second chance. We then made a hasty exit and went outside into the fresh morning breeze. It made a lovely change from the constant heat that we had endured since our first day. We took a taxi to the hotel, hardly saying a word to each other in the car since Carol was in complete shock and could not believe that her daughter had brought her husband back from the dead.

Getting out of the taxi, I paid the fare. Carol and Daniella had already gone inside and were greeted by several guests with even the manager joining them.

As I walked over, the manager was about to ask a question. "It's good to see you, my dear," he said. "I'm so sorry about your husband. Is he still in a coma?"

"No, no, no," Carol cried out. "He's just opened his eyes and I've left him to be examined by the doctors as they believe this to be some kind of miracle even though I always thought miracles were only found in one's imagination."

The manager smiled, held his hands together, raised them to the sky and said, "We all need a miracle in our life." At this, he left us and returned soon afterwards with our pass cards. "There's a surprise for you on the third floor. Your daughter and father-in-law already know all about it."

We grinned and got into the lift and went up to the third floor. We entered the third suite and when we walked in Carol turned to us and said, "This must be the wrong room as we didn't order a suite, did we?"

Daniella turned to her mother and said, "The owners of the hotel felt so bad about Dad's injury that they immediately upgraded us into a suite and have said that until Dad goes home we can remain in here. There's also a gym and swimming pool just down the hallway. Unfortunately, Granddad and I have chosen our rooms and you're left with the last one but they're all similar with queen-sized beds and every gadget you could dream of."

Carol went to her room to check it out and opened the wardrobe and drawers.

"Where are Dad's clothes and mine?" she asked.

I stared at Carol and replied, "They probably still have to move them across as you've only just returned and we didn't give them notice that you were coming. Anyway, what do you think of the place? It even has its own kitchen and dining area if we wish to order a meal, bring one in, or even cook."

My daughter-in-law grinned at me, as well as at her daughter, before saying, "This suite is lovely and Richard will think it's superb when he comes back but I'm not sure how long his wound will take to heal. I imagine you'll have to go back to England on your own. Will you mind doing that?" Carol said, giving us both a look of anxiety.

"That's okay, Mommy, we don't mind, do we, Granddad?" the girl said.

"Of course not," I replied to my granddaughter with a boyish kind of grin. Carol noticed but said nothing so I continued, "I imagine your mother would like to relax in a nice Jacuzzi! Wait until you see the size of that, Carol! You could fit the whole family in while you unwind in the water! Daniella and I will find Cal and she'll arrange everything and have your belongings brought over to you."

"A Jacuzzi sounds perfect so you and Daniella toddle off and then you can tell me everything that's been happening around here," Carol said as Daniella and I left her to relax while we went to find Cal.

We found Cal working in her office. She stared at us but immediately realised what we wanted so she apologised and said, "Of course, your mother will want all her clothes and your father's too as I hear that he's turned the corner and come out of his coma. Congratulations, my friends, as that's what I feel we've become," Cal added as she rang the porter and the housemaid to arrange to transfer everything from Mr and Mrs Riverton's room into the suite.

"Thanks, Cal," Daniella said enthusiastically. "We're just going out into the lovely garden for a while so perhaps we'll see you later."

Cal smiled as we walked towards the garden. Once we had stepped outside, we saw beautiful butterflies fluttering around and some sort of dragonfly. I did not realise these were native to Thailand but Daniella had brought me out here for a specific reason.

"Granddad, what do we tell Mom? Do we tell her the truth or would she have us locked away for insanity?" the girl asked worriedly.

I had wondered about that too and replied in a fashion, saying, "Darling, I think we're walking on eggs here and doubt whether your mother's going to believe this. Perhaps, we should bend the truth and tell her that a mysterious couple turned up and told us that Richard would reopen his eyes when his daughter took hold of his hand. We could add that they were psychic or something and that they gave us many expensive gifts to remember them by. You definitely have to tell her about the jewellery as otherwise she'll think the worst and that's the last thing we want her to do."

Daniella grinned at me. "You're right, Granddad, so let's stick to that story as if I told my mother that I was the Queen of sorcery; she'd never believe a word and will have me locked away as well as having you certified. Anyway, Dad knows what happened to him as I could see it from his one good eye. I know we'll have to tell him the truth when he's better."

I stared at my granddaughter and said, "Why didn't you heal all your Dad's wounds and let him come home with us rather than being kept in hospital for weeks or months?"

"I know that's how you feel but it wasn't the rightful thing for me to do as the doctors would have thought I was some sort of evil witch! We want to remain here on Earth with the least possible problems even though it was my father and your son. Whether it takes weeks or months for Dad to recover, we don't know so we must not tamper with the future any further. We must help the people who are about to die, having the worst possible sickness or living on the street in poverty. I now understand exactly what the Count and Countess would expect of us and Granddad you must trust me on this."

"Granddaughter," I responded to the girl. "Whatever the Count and the Countess did to you, they have turned you into a very special human being, giving us eternal life and the possibility of travelling into the future or the past. There's no one who deserves this more than you, my darling. I questioned their motives at first but now I can walk with my head held high as I follow you into our next quest."

Daniella smiled at me, before saying one last thing, "Granddad, you still haven't told me if you want Granny back? I don't know about you but perhaps we should leave her wherever she is, lying so peacefully under that old oak tree. If we ever need to call on her, we know where to find her."

Milton Keynes UK
Ingram Content Group UK Ltd.
UKHW010856140324
439440UK00014B/513